Praise for

NOT THE TRIP WE PLANNED

"Chickie and Maddy feel like old friends, and I'll take a trip with them—planned or unplanned—anytime, no questions asked."

—Molly Macrae, award-winning author of the cozy mystery Highland Bookshop series, the Haunted Shell Shop series, and *Crewel and Unusual*

"Two long-time friends become unlikely detectives in *Not the Trip We Planned*, a fun romp that will tempt readers to rethink any lingering stereotypes about the capabilities of older women to rescue themselves and others. When an old friend's husband dies under very sketchy circumstances, elderly sleuths Maddy and Chickie change their vacation plans and fly to Chicago, determined to do their best. But the investigation reveals more than what happened to Lena's husband. Maddy and Chickie also discover—and come to terms with—their own secrets and past mistakes as they attempt to solve someone else's tragedy."

—Mary Carroll Moore, bestselling author of *Last Bets* and *A Woman's Guide to Search & Rescue*

"What happens when two real life old friends write a novel about two fictional old friends who are helping a third cope with the mysterious and shocking death of her husband? You get a delightful book that is an ode to friendship, a paean to Chicago, and a hard but compassionate look at the challenges of aging. I reveled in the company of Maddy, a retired social worker, and Chickie, a writer and blogger, as they squabble their way to unraveling a tangle of deadly secrets."

—Ellen Kirschman, PhD, police and public safety psychologist and award-winning author of the Dot Meyerhoff Mystery Series

"*Not The Trip We Planned* is an insightful, witty read filled with just the sort of characters that make books come alive. Chickie and Maddy's surprise-filled journey illuminates the power of friendship, the joys and challenges of growing older, and the uncanny ability of women to suss out the truth—and help one another to face it."

—Rachel Stone, author of *The Blue Iris*

"*Not the Trip We Planned* by Linda N. Edelstein and Carol G. Kerr is a witty, heartfelt, and fast-paced journey through grief, friendship, and the surprising twists life can take. When Chickie Altman and Maddy Wells abruptly change their long-awaited getaway to support their old friend Lena, they find themselves tangled in a mystery surrounding the sudden, shocking death of Lena's husband, Edward. As they crisscross Chicagoland's iconic haunts, the duo uncovers secrets, wrestles with truths about Edward's life, and navigates their own complex emotions.

Edelstein and Kerr deftly balance humor and pathos, feeding us just the right clues at the right time while exploring the deep, unflinching bonds of lifelong friendship. This book flies by, driven by the sharp dialogue and the authentic connections that form when we truly let someone see us for who we are. *Not the Trip We Planned* is as much about the mysteries of family, friendship, and self-discovery as it is about unraveling the circumstances of Edward's death—a perfect blend of page-turning intrigue and emotional resonance."

—Christina Shaver, screenwriter of *Cecily and Lydia at the Waypoint* and *Everything Fun You Could Possibly Do in Aledo*

"*Not The Trip We Planned* is a captivating meditation on the nature of time, memory, and friendship. Through the characters of lifelong friends Chickie and Maddy, coauthors Edelstein and Kerr toggle brilliantly between past and present. Suffusing each sentence are the universal longings we all share: the need to feel relevant, to feel loved, to come to peace about the passage of time. The friends revisit a city that formed them in their youth, where, over the course of the story, they take the melancholy of years past and mold it into a present and future that is not encumbered, but enriched, by lived experience. Place and time are characters alongside Chickie and Maddy as we join them in their passionate quest to find the truth behind the suspicious death of a friend's husband. *Not The Trip We Planned* is a much-needed reminder that passion and relevance have nothing to do with age, but rather our internal selves and the choices we make. Come for the plot twists, stay for the musings on life and time. *Not The Trip We Planned* is a meditation on the passage of time and the nature of friendship cleverly wrapped in an engaging mystery."

—Alfredo Botello, screenwriter and author of *Spin Cycle* and *180 Days*

"Meet two vibrant, tenacious women 'of a certain age.' These good friends are thrust into an unplanned good-Samaritan adventure. The authors skillfully weave in the backstories, so we gradually get to know our heroes quite well. Written with warmth and sprinkled with humor, the pacing of the tale is engaging, the plot twists add just the right spark of surprise, and our heroes are so gritty, witty, and distinct that we want to read more."

—Deborah Shouse, author of *An Old Woman Walks Into a Bar*

"I was hooked from the start. Few authors are able to create two such delightful and complex characters as Chickie and Maddie. I feel as if I know them both and the close friendship they share. It's hard to put this unique adventure in any one category. This book made me both smile and think while reading even a single page. I loved the character development as much as the sleuthing. This is the kind of book I save to read in the evenings when I want to have fun while being taken on an unexpected adventure. You will fall in love with Chickie and Maddy. I did."

—Don Kuhl, founder of The Change Companies, author of *Changing with Aging: Little Stories, Big Lessons*

"In this captivating mystery, the authors weave together sharp humor, profound lessons on aging and friendship, and an inspiring reminder that it's never too late to change and thrive."

—Janice M. Prochaska, PhD, coauthor of *Changing to Thrive* and cofounder of Pro-Change Behavior Systems, Inc.

Not the Trip We Planned
by Linda N. Edelstein & Carol G. Kerr

© Copyright 2025 Linda N. Edelstein & Carol G. Kerr

979-8-88824-608-5

All rights reserved. No part of this publication may be reproduced, stored in a retrieval system, or transmitted in any form or by any means—electronic, mechanical, photocopy, recording, or any other—except for brief quotations in printed reviews, without the prior written permission of the author.

This is a work of fiction. All the characters in this book are fictitious, and any resemblance to actual persons, living or dead, is purely coincidental. The names, incidents, dialogue, and opinions expressed are products of the author's imagination and are not to be construed as real.

Designed by Suzanne Bradshaw.

Published by

3705 Shore Drive
Virginia Beach, VA 23455
800-435-4811
www.koehlerbooks.com

Not the Trip We Planned

A Novel

Linda N. Edelstein
& Carol G. Kerr

VIRGINIA BEACH
CAPE CHARLES

Chapter One

"Of course Edward dropped dead today. Inconsiderate old bastard," Chickie Altman grumbled as she hefted her suitcase onto the baggage scale. "I should have pretended I never got the text. Then I wouldn't be here spending money I don't have for a plane ticket I don't want." At sixty-eight, having lost a precious inch and a half to normal shrinkage, she stood on her toes and slapped her ticket down on the airline counter. The United Airlines agent at Washington Reagan International Airport, long immune to stories of personal misfortune, produced a compulsory smile and reached for the boarding pass.

Chickie mistook the smile for agreement, or at least interest, and explained, "People leave this world in the same way they lived in it. Well-behaved people go without a fuss and selfish people inconvenience everyone else." She pursed her red lips. "You see, Edward married Lena—a dramatic sort of friend—millennia ago when she was gorgeous, and he had what we used to call 'potential.' Lena is one of those friends we all made in our twenties and then spent the following decades wondering 'What was I thinking?' For the record, she is still gorgeous, and Edward became a very upscale plastic surgeon. Anyway, Edward realized his potential and then some, but his immersion into self-absorption was complete and permanent. It's always all about them. For example, as of this morning, Edward's dead, Lena's hysterical, and Maddy and I have been summoned back to Chicago."

"Did you expect him to check your calendar before dying? I'm sure a federal holiday would have been more convenient for your schedule."

At the sound of the familiar voice, Chickie spun around. "Thank God, you made it." She grabbed Maddy Wells in a crushing hug. "I was worried you were stuck in airplane mode and wouldn't get my message. We are booked on the next flight to Chicago, and it's leaving in an hour. You have to check in." She swung back to the agent waiting impatiently behind the counter. "She's here," Chickie announced unnecessarily and pulled Maddy closer, displaying her to the airline employee. Passengers behind them hissed. Maddy winced.

The reservations agent assessed the new arrival: a tall, Midwestern Emma Thompson in a well-worn travel vest, loose gray slacks, scarf, and light-blue eyes behind horn-rimmed glasses. Since second grade, and that was some time ago, Maddy had been the girl everyone wanted as their best friend—popular enough, kind enough, and thoroughly competent.

Even now she remained calm, absorbing the fact that two hours earlier, while she was in the air flying from Minneapolis to DC, Chickie had begrudgingly responded to Lena's urgent message, upended their previous plans for a long weekend getaway, and booked them both on a flight to Chicago. So, instead of the trip Maddy needed—museums, restaurants, and white wine with her old friend—she was scrambling to make the best of this new situation.

She briskly produced identification and answered the agent's routine questions. Satisfied, the woman pressed a long series of keys and located the reservation.

This was the first time in more than a year that the friends had seen each other in person. Emails, phone calls, Zoom and tele-friendship machinery didn't work well for their generation, people who needed to be in the same room, preferably with abundant food and leisurely hours for conversation. Chickie openly studied Maddy's appearance and was reassured by her friend's general sameness. That drab vest had been around forever, and her hardy look hadn't changed, but the brightly colored cane was new. It unsettled Chickie, although they had joked about it in phone calls. She shook off her unease and listened to Maddy effortlessly charm the agent who offered complimentary upgrades, but even that perk failed to soften her irritation at this unexpected, unwanted change of plans. Instead of the longed-for reunion à deux, the old friends were hustling into a melodrama à trois.

After Maddy mouthed "Thank you" to the travelers still in line, the two women hurried toward the TSA checkpoint, weaving around panicked latecomers and straying toddlers.

Clutching her boarding pass, Maddy said, "Remember when you could go to a real office and talk to a real person? One time, with my ticket, they presented me with a free plastic rain bonnet that had the agency logo on it."

"I never got a rain bonnet." Chickie rummaged through her backpack for a photo ID as they entered the long security line. She would not have agreed to fly off to Chicago if Maddy hadn't been involved. Maddy would never turn away from helping their old friend. Maddy invariably did the right thing, and it was unquestionably right to respond to Lena's desperate call for help. But Chickie had always been ambivalent about Lena and had never warmed to Edward. And most of all, she dreaded going back to the Midwest. She was tired. She had served her time as a wife—twice—and a mother—twice—and a PTO chair for three long years—a tenure worse than being a wife. She hated Chicago and had successfully avoided the place for more than forty years. If Edward had to ruin their reunion, why couldn't he have dropped dead in St. Tropez?

Unfortunately, if she'd allowed Maddy to go alone, she wasn't sure she could have forgiven herself. It wouldn't be the same as sending her friend on the *Titanic*, but it wasn't the *QE2* either. It made Chickie even angrier to know that she would sulk, grumble, and kvetch, but she would board that plane to the Windy City where, years earlier, the trajectory of her life had changed forever.

As the line lurched forward, with passengers wiggling out of light jackets and emptying pockets while talking on their cellphones, the teenage girl behind Chickie rammed a suitcase into her ankles, giving her something new to gripe about. Maddy stepped around them both and sped up. She placed her bag and cane on one conveyor belt and moved along. In the other line, Chickie removed her jewelry and sweater and dropped them into a yellow plastic bin, dumped her backpack in another, and marched through the x-ray booth, convinced she was now closer than ever to some dreadful diagnosis.

Chickie had just reclaimed her sweater and was readjusting a bulky necklace when a TSA agent called out, "Whose backpack is this?"

She waved her free hand at him.

"Can we examine it?"

She nodded, mentally correcting his grammar; *it's may we examine it*. But it was in her interest to appear good-natured, so she walked over and smiled mechanically as the gloved man unzipped and pawed through her belongings. She hoped her edibles remained inconspicuous, camouflaged in her bag of gummy butterflies.

Nearby, Maddy rested on a bench. Having collected her efficiently organized shoulder bag, she smiled watching Chickie reassemble her brightly colored self. With silver hair, clever eyes, and an overabundance of jewelry, her friend was a living protest against the invisibility of aging. The crankiness was window dressing that Maddy rarely took seriously. In fact, Chickie was the antidote to these past sad months since Maddy's husband Frank had died. For more than a year, Maddy had been stuck in the same routine with the same people. Every day was like the day before. After Frank's death, she had wanted life to remain exactly the same. And it had. Now she felt sentenced to one of those tony federal prisons: lots of comforts, but still a cell. Recent retirement made the feeling of uselessness more acute. Maddy stopped and cautiously looked around, as if the other passengers knew she was silently complaining. The only thing worse than being stuck was complaining about being stuck, and she refused to be that person.

She was determined to put a complicated year behind her. She was a widow now. By definition, that meant she was alive, and if anyone could help her feel like living was still a good idea, it was Chickie.

Her friend marched over with her backpack, pleased that her edibles had gone undetected.

Childish, she knew, but getting away with things was still very satisfying. Chickie's mood had improved, and deep dimples appeared on either side of her mouth. She nodded to Maddy's cane.

"Will you have any trouble walking to the gate? It's always the farthest one."

Maddy shrugged off her concern. "Walking is good for me. And I have my stick. I admit, I may use it to qualify for early boarding." Maddy shot a side-eye toward her friend, well aware of Chickie's irritation with her Scout-like allegiance to doing things right.

But Chickie was not paying much attention to the confession. Her gaze was fixed on the departure board. "Damn, we're delayed. God doesn't want us to go to Chicago. She/her wants us to grab a cab back to my house, examine your neat vacation spreadsheet, and decide which new restaurants and museum exhibits to visit."

"Edward died this morning and Lena needs us," Maddy reminded her sternly as they walked past the food kiosks and toward the distant gate.

Chickie looked over at her, frowning. "Exactly how did Edward die? That bit of information was missing from Lena's hysterical texts."

Chapter Two

Early Fall had produced another bright afternoon, and sunlight warmed the departure lounge. The women found two seats facing the large windows and settled down to wait.

Chickie searched for the day's Wordle, and Maddy pulled out her phone to call Lena. After an earnest fifteen-minute conversation, in which she made mostly supportive noises, Maddy went silent and stared at the planes as they rolled in and away, guided by men in neon vests and headphones who signaled instructions to the pilots seated far above them.

"Well?" Chickie asked.

Maddy shrugged.

"What did Lena tell you? She seemed to do all the talking. How *did* Edward die?"

"I don't know."

"What do you mean? One of the first things people say is how someone died. No one leaves it out. It's like announcing whether a newborn baby is a girl or boy. Or isn't that done any longer?"

Maddy was reluctant to encourage Chickie's chronic irritation with Lena. "She's probably in shock. You know Lena."

"I do know Lena, and . . ."

Sooner or later, Chickie would be face to face with the speculations Lena had shared with Maddy in the phone call. "She did imply it was tragic, sudden, dramatic—"

"Lena considered it tragic when miniskirts fell out of fashion."

"Seriously Chick, she was young then . . . and she had great legs to display," but Maddy's face registered concern. "I did ask—more than once—and each time Lena cried harder."

"Did she tell you anything at all?"

Maddy sighed with resignation. "Lena claims Edward was murdered."

Chickie half jumped from her seat and spit out, "Murdered? Plastic surgeons do not get murdered. Sued, yes. Murdered, no. Drunk driving, maybe. An outraged patient whose breast enhancement job was uneven; that's a lawsuit. Even butt implant slippage only gets you bad reviews, not a bullet."

Maddy glanced around. Several people stared at them, preferring Chickie's outburst to their news feeds or kitten videos. She lowered her voice and spoke deliberately. "Be patient. It's good practice for you. We will know more once we arrive in Chicago. Edward's death just happened this morning. Whatever the cause, Lena needs our help."

She turned away, choosing to watch the slowly changing departure board rather than her friend's sour expression. The flight delay grew, and information was offered stingily, just like the airline's tiny bags of pretzels.

Although it was sunny where they sat in DC, thunderstorms were reportedly roaming the Midwest. Maddy worried about the increasing delays and couldn't shake the fear that Chickie would bolt, and she would wind up traveling alone. She sat stiffly, keenly aware of her sweeping feelings of disappointment. Her longed-for reunion had disintegrated, vanished, and something unpleasant had taken its place. Next to her, Chickie continually refreshed her phone and muttered her key words as she typed: "Murder in Chicago, Edward Jordan, MD." Getting nowhere, she switched to: "Dead plastic surgeon, murder on Chicago's Magnificent Mile, and death by narcissism." Eventually her imagination wore thin, and she was forced to report, "Nothing in the news feeds."

By midafternoon, the women were buckled into an upgraded row with several inches of extra legroom that the agent had promised Maddy. Chickie reluctantly volunteered to take the middle seat next to a yoga-ready young woman on the aisle.

The well-intentioned millennial fussed over Chickie. "Can I help you with your jacket? That's a marvelous necklace—so cool. Just let me know if you want me to let you out, you know. My grandmother is just about my favorite person in the world; she's in Chicago. That's who I'm visiting. I wonder if you know her."

Maddy was amused to hear Chickie struggle to be polite. There was a time when her responses would have been something other than, "Thank you, that's very kind. Yes, yes. I haven't been back in forty years, so I probably don't know your grandmother."

But squeezed into the narrow middle seat, Chickie's graciousness was being challenged by the young woman's attention. Even with a clandestine nibble on her edible butterfly, it took restraint to avoid tormenting her young seatmate with rambling memories of pantyhose, typewriters, and just for good measure, her protests during the Vietnam War. Instead, she reached into her backpack for reading glasses and her laptop, but the chipper seatmate was determined to give conversation another try, "So what's taking you to Chicago?"

Without missing a beat and worn out from exercising self-control, even though the plane had not yet left the tarmac, Chickie said calmly, "Sudden death," and opened her laptop.

Maddy groaned.

The "I'm so sorry" was just a mumble, but Chickie heard her seatmate's sincerity, and it increased her irritation.

Maddy leaned across her and said pleasantly, "We met in Chicago when we were about your age."

Pushing Maddy's elbow off the seat rest between them, Chickie added, "Maddy literally picked me up off the floor and we have remained great friends all these years." She patted Maddy's knee.

Their seatmate giggled.

Chickie knew that young people loved a romanticized version of aging, which she was willing to allow—up to a point. "Just this morning, another friend from those years let us know that her husband had died unexpectedly and asked for our help."

"Oh, that is so kind of you," the young woman began. "I hope it goes well." She was less interested in the end result of aging.

"Our friend believes her husband was murdered," Chickie added with a dimpled smile.

The young woman averted her eyes and hastily put on her noise-canceling headphones.

Mission accomplished, thought Chickie as she began to compose her blog post, hoping this self-imposed writing exercise would defrost her writer's block.

The flippant description of their first meeting had prompted a powerful memory for Maddy.

༄

IT HAD BEEN an appropriately dreary Chicago day in early fall when she'd accompanied her husband Frank to a memorial service for Danny, a medical student who had died a few weeks earlier. The service was relentlessly sad; no one could find a way to convincingly say that his twenty-six years had been nearly enough. Speakers choked on their recollections. When Maddy ducked into the washroom afterward, she found Chickie, the student's young widow, curled up next to the sink, sobbing uncontrollably. Her long black hair fell over her face and her slight body was smothered in a short black skirt, sweater, and dark stockings.

Chickie had escaped to the bathroom for face repairs, but her high heel had caught in the floor drain and broken off, a symbol of the endless parade of uncontrollable events her life had become. She sobbed and swore as she imagined limping back into the pitying crowd of family and mourners. Tentatively, Maddy stood near the door, tempted to excuse herself and back out, but . . . she fumbled in her purse and said, "I have superglue in my bag. We could fix your shoe."

They took a long look at each other.

Chickie's wet eyes blinked in confusion. "Do you always take superglue to memorials?" It momentarily shattered the gloom. Helpless, cathartic laughter took over for them both. Without saying much more, they repaired the shoe, and their faces, and wandered back into the sad afternoon.

Several mornings later, they met again on the shoreline path along Lake Michigan. Maddy was sprawled on her favorite bench staring at the color and vastness of the water. It reminded her of the sky back home and helped her to unwind after finishing a double shift in the ER.

Chickie pushed her son, Sam, in a stroller along the path and recognized her. "My Fairy Gluemother; I didn't even thank you." Maddy rose from the bench to coo over Sam and joined their walk. The women and toddler strolled from Oak Street Beach to North Avenue and back, a couple of miles. Chickie explained that she had been allowed bereavement leave from her copy-editing job, but it would run out fast and she had to return to work. Saying that, she looked longingly at Sam. There was no family around to help; she and Danny had moved from New Jersey so he could go to medical school.

Maddy, too, had come from elsewhere. For her, college and social work school at the University of Chicago had been her refuge from the overwhelming sadness of her family in Montana after her brother John's combat death in Vietnam. Then, she accepted a job offer at the Northwestern Hospital ER and met her future husband Frank when they wrestled an LSD-tripping hippie, wearing a pink wig and nothing else, into restraints.

Hunched against the morning wind, Chickie asked, "Do you have kids?"

Maybe because Chickie was a stranger, a newly bereaved stranger, Maddy spilled the entire story of her recent miscarriage. "We really want kids, but we're having trouble," she said, surprised at her willingness to admit her secret to a stranger. But after all, when you have reglued someone's shoe on the bathroom floor at her young husband's funeral, you've already rewritten the rules for socially appropriate behavior.

∽

AT THAT MOMENT, a voice interrupted Maddy's reminiscences. "In the event of decompression, an oxygen mask will automatically drop from the compartment above. To start the flow of oxygen, pull the mask toward you . . ." When the flight attendant reached the part about securing your own mask first before assisting others, Maddy gently elbowed Chickie and offered, "If you need help, I'll adjust your oxygen mask."

"Thanks. Knowing you, I'd find it superglued to my face."

So Chickie was also remembering that other October day.

Just then, the plane accelerated down the runway and lifted off. The cabin quieted and dropped into that odd silence when everyone secretly wonders, *we will keep going up, right?*

Before they leveled off, Maddy began to unpack her supply of snacks.

"What did you bring along to eat?" Chickie asked, nudging Maddy's arm.

Maddy reached into one of the many zippered compartments in her large gray bag and handed her friend a tiny package of M&Ms. "It started when the kids were small. I never went anywhere without food and colored pencils."

"Please don't tell me that you also have diapers in that bag."

"I hate to think how close we are to carrying them again," Maddy replied.

That silenced both women until Chickie said, "You're the professional feelings person; what should we expect from Lena? I never have any idea what she wants from us, especially me."

"I can tell you that, more than anything else, she wants Edward back. Since that's impossible, she'll need comfort, not to be alone, someone to run ordinary errands, and someone to help her make decisions. We can do all that."

"Damn, this flight could turn out to be the best two hours of our reunion week," Chickie moaned.

At that, Maddy waved down the flight attendant and ordered two glasses of champagne. Chickie shot her a disapproving frown.

"Hey," Maddy protested, "I came to DC for relaxation and now I'm on a plane to Chicago for anything but! Yes, we will be helpful to Lena, but this week was originally planned as a vacation, remember, and I'm not the pilot, and it is"—she looked at her watch—"three p.m."

"For a Goody-Two-shoes, you drink early," said Chickie dryly. "I'll bet you harbor a dark side under that good scout exterior—"

"Now you're the social worker?"

"—And you compensate by being extra capital-G Good, which is exactly what got us into this."

"You were the person who booked the tickets."

"Because momentarily, I wanted to be Good like you. Now, I'm not so sure. I quit Girl Scouts after two weeks because they made us bathe dolls. It made no sense; neither does Lena's delusion about Edward being murdered."

Maddy pointed to the exit sign. "If you've changed your mind, there's the door." The champagne arrived, and she held on to both glasses, sipping deliberately from one. "When we were sitting in the lounge, you swore that you could handle returning to Chicago."

The edible butterfly was taking effect. Chickie didn't argue but returned to typing on her laptop and waited. After a while, she said, "The turbulence at thirty thousand feet is nothing compared to what we are going to find in Chicago."

Maddy did not look up but slid a glass across the tray table.

Chapter Three

Maddy stepped off the escalator at O'Hare Airport and steadied herself with her cane. "I wish we could go to a hotel, but Lena was adamant that we stay with her, at least until her brothers fly in."

Lena had texted them just before takeoff:

I will not be home when you arrive, but
you will be met at baggage claim and the
concierge will let you into my apt.

The friends approached the large area of creaking carousels. Chickie crowded with the other passengers until her bag slid down. She dragged it away as Maddy stood nearby with her carry-on, searching the faces of people standing at the perimeter. Almost immediately, a broad-shouldered man raised a paper with "Maddy and Chickie" scrawled on it. She grabbed Chickie's arm and when they approached, he smiled, brown eyes lighting up a pleasant, vaguely familiar face. "Welcome. I'm Raph Sodano, one of Edward's office partners. I'm going to drive you to Lena's," he said, putting out a hand to each of them in turn. "Don't I recognize you from one or another of Lena and Edward's events?"

As the three of them headed to the parking lot, Raph and Maddy sorted through years of extravagant Jordan parties and fundraisers, trying to locate each other in time. Finally, as Raph unlocked his car and stowed their bags in his trunk, both decided they had met at an anniversary party held at the Union Club in Chicago. Feeling comfortable, Maddy jumped into the front seat.

When everyone was settled, Raph backed the car out, but before they reached the airport's *Exit to Chicago* sign, Chickie leaned forward from the back. "Just how did Edward die?"

"I confess," Raph said, "I insisted on picking you up because I wanted a chance to talk to you. Lena has always referred to you two as her best friends, and I'm worried about her. I called right after I heard about Edward's death and of course, she was in shock. This is bound to be terribly hard on her. When I spoke to her, the police were just leaving her apartment and our third partner, Brian, was going with them to identify Edward's body. She's alone now, I think. It's essential that you are with her when the coroner's office sends investigators, probably tomorrow. That's our chance to learn more."

He merged into the stream of traffic and followed the signs to I-94 S. Rush hour was well underway.

"Why police? Why coroner's investigators? Wasn't it a heart attack or a car accident or something? Just exactly how did he die?" Chickie persisted.

"Oh, you don't know . . . Didn't Lena say?" He hesitated.

Maddy twisted in her seat and shot Chickie a glance that said *let me handle this*. She asked, "Raph, please. Lena has not been coherent in our calls. We need to know what happened if we're going to help."

Raph inhaled deeply and, without taking his eyes off the road, said, "Sorry. I assumed you heard. At about ten this morning, Edward was killed by a Chicago Metra train."

Neither woman had imagined anything close.

Maddy launched a barrage of questions. "Did he fall from the train platform? Where was he? Did he have a vertigo attack? Was anyone else hurt?" Her mind was crowded with dire scenarios; she struggled to make sense of the shocking information.

Chickie said nothing.

Raph pulled into the slower lane and tried to answer. "All I know is that it happened at a suburban train station miles from his home or office. I'm not familiar with the area. I don't know why he was there. I don't think anyone else was hurt. I will talk to Brian later; he had time with the police."

Maddy interrupted. "On the phone, Lena talked about murder and plots against Edward."

Raph's head snapped around to gape at her. The car swerved briefly before he pulled back into his lane, breathing heavily. "What! She didn't say that to me. I assumed some sort of tragic accident; he tripped and fell—that happens around here. Why would Lena come up with murder? Who would want to kill Edward?"

Chickie was glad that no one could see the skepticism on her face. "Well, you know him better than we do. Would anyone murder him?"

Raph stuttered, "That idea is absurd. I . . . I never considered murder. Did the police suggest that to her? I was worried about Lena before, but now more so. Lena is unprepared; not that anyone could be."

Maddy heard muttering coming from the back seat. It sounded like, "Down the rabbit hole. Some things never change."

Some things never change. That's for sure, thought Maddy.

She and Chickie had already become close friends when Lena, a Chicago City Ballet apprentice, moved into Northwestern's graduate student housing to live with her brother, a medical student. Freed from her overprotected life in Memphis, she'd reveled in the city and the world of dance—until she tore an ankle ligament and found herself on medical leave in the middle of a hot Chicago summer.

In the same sweltering brick building, two floors below, Maddy was on total bedrest in the final trimester of pregnancy with twins, reeling between utter boredom and a numbing fear that the babies would not survive. Her husband Frank, a frantically busy psychiatry resident at Northwestern, had literally stumbled over Lena in the basement laundry room as she clumped around in a walking cast dropping clothes and spilling detergent. He'd brought her home to Maddy as a gift.

Chickie, on the other hand, was living a few blocks away, entirely absorbed by the responsibilities of being a single mother and sole wage earner in Chicago, a city that would never feel like home. Other than her small son, Sam, any living creature who exhibited needs would have overwhelmed her.

Maybe that hadn't changed either, Maddy thought.

Not knowing what else to say, Raph concentrated on navigating the fast-moving traffic and pointing out new buildings, unaware that Maddy didn't hear a word. Until today, her time in Chicago had been joyous. It was where she'd checked off those boxes of conventional 1970s womanhood: college, career, marriage, and children. A dozen years ago, her twin sons had moved here to establish careers. For her family, it had always been the place of beginnings.

Silent in the back seat, Chickie peered out the window as the extraordinary skyline came into view. The city was almost unrecognizable as the place she had last seen as a twenty-eight-year-old in flight. She'd never intended to return. Her breath caught as waves of memories struck her. There were so few good ones. And now, to add to Chicago's deadly legacy, Edward had been killed by a train.

The light had begun to fade when the car reached Lena's posh Gold Coast neighborhood. The women exited the car, thanked Raph, exchanged phone numbers with him, promised to be in touch, and apprehensively entered the slim glass and steel building. Two years earlier, Lena and Edward had moved here from their beautiful vintage home several streets away, and neither Maddy nor Chickie had seen the new condo. Inside, the lush greenery of bamboo trees against creamy lobby walls more than made up for the severe exterior. Jakob, the promised concierge, ushered them into the elevator and up to the Jordans' penthouse, a spacious apartment that occupied the entire twelfth floor. He opened the door with the key Lena had provided and handed it to Maddy before expressing his condolences and hurrying back downstairs.

They parked their luggage in the marble foyer and wandered into the expansive living room, where an easterly wall of windows framed a mesmerizing view. The slowly darkening blue sky drew them over to gaze at the roofs of other buildings and beyond to the endless slate of Lake Michigan, half a mile east. The horizon line was sharp and, in the dark water below, a few tiny boats headed toward shore, having bravely squeezed in another outing before they would be hauled out of the water and stored during the long winter.

Chickie admitted, "I always forget how beautiful Chicago is."

Maddy was in complete agreement. "And this is quite a place," she said and turned away. Chickie stroked the velvet couch as she followed her friend out of the living room. On the right, a set of French doors opened to reveal a warm, heavily paneled library with floor to ceiling bookcases and a gas fireplace. "Nothing says money like a library stolen from *Downton Abbey*," Chickie observed, looking at cognac leather couches, an antique desk, deep club chairs, and assorted end tables.

Maddy walked over to a sturdy hassock in front of one of the chairs. "A stuffed armadillo! What a strange addition to this elegant room. You'd think anyone in the skin business would avoid that sort of thing." She shrugged off her multipocketed travel vest and saddled the poor creature with it, then bent to scratch the armadillo's ears.

Neither could resist wandering about the apartment, bright with mirrors and long views of the city skyscrapers through the south facing windows. Eventually, they found the luxurious master bedroom suite, with its home gym and another fireplace. The king-sized bed was perfectly made, but the rest was chaos. A closet door was flung open, and a trail of women's clothing blanketed the floor and hung from chairs. "It looks as desperate as Macy's on Christmas Eve," Maddy said, tripping over a pile of shoes and falling against Chickie. They steadied each other.

"Oh," Chickie whispered, her attention captured by a large, framed photo that lay on the duvet. There they were, in the "before" photograph; the handsome couple who could have been featured in a life insurance ad. It was a retouched moment, she thought, but Lena and Edward, arms around each other, laughing, had been real and the sight of them, the realization of what had been lost, tugged at her. "How old was Edward?" she asked.

"While he'd never want you to know it, Edward is . . . was at least my age, seventy-two or three."

"I never imagined he was that much older than Lena, but I hadn't thought about it. So, she was about twenty-one when they met," Chickie said, doing the math.

"Twelve years difference, I think," Maddy replied. "Edward saw her at a ballet showcase and made sure he was introduced. He was entranced. Remember what a talented, beautiful young woman she was. . . ."

"And how ambitious he was," Chickie added. "What I remember is Edward trying to humble brag about being invited into a new surgery practice. He thought he was much ado about something. And . . . he was on the lookout for a wife. It was time to round out his accomplishments," she finished.

"You are being uncharitable—more than usual. Lena, well, she loved and admired everything about him."

Chickie suddenly found the opulent room stifling. The loss was uncomfortably real. "This photo, the romance, and Edward finally ending up . . . well, it's a bit much for me. I'm going to figure out where the guest rooms are, and if I find armadillos—or anything else that used to breathe—I'm off to the Palmer House."

It was easy for each woman to settle into their neighboring guest suites, connected by a shared bath. Lena's guest rooms were nothing like the spare rooms in either Maddy's or Chickie's homes, where all the leftover furniture from past remodeling efforts was stored alongside detritus from adult children who had coaxed their mothers, "Please keep it for me. I might need it, but I don't have space now." There was no more taxidermied wildlife. Even though they had only made plans to come to Chicago hours before, the rooms were thoughtfully furnished with piles of magazines and inviting quilts and pillows that perfectly matched the nondescript blue and white paintings.

Shortly, Maddy discovered Chickie back in the library browsing the titles. "Between your blog and your half-finished novel, you'll have a book on those shelves soon."

Chickie hated to be reminded of her lack of progress on the manuscript, but before she could answer, the front door slammed, and the two women exchanged apprehensive looks. They listened to footsteps on the marble floor in the foyer.

"I'm back, I'm home—and you *both* are here at last!"

Chapter Four

Maddy and Chickie hurried toward Lena's voice and met her in the living room. As Lena reached out, her large cashmere shawl slid toward the floor revealing her thin body. The sleeveless black jumpsuit emphasized her vulnerability, and the two women instinctively moved toward her. She sank into their arms; her thick auburn hair fell across her lovely face, now ashen and tense.

The older women guided her carefully to the couch, where she dropped into the velvet sofa, kicked her shoes onto the sensuous white art deco carpet, and pulled her feet up under her. Clutching a velvet throw pillow, she curled into a tight ball.

"I'll make tea," Chickie offered. It was her general solution to problems that occurred before dark. She headed for the kitchen, but Maddy called after her, "Skip the tea and find something stronger to drink." Chickie reversed direction and hurried to the living room wall where rows of bottles were arrayed behind the elaborate art deco bar.

On the couch, Maddy murmured soothing words to Lena and got little response. Her eyes were half closed. Underneath, dark shadows were obvious even though Lena's heart-shaped face was artfully made up. She was utterly spent.

"How are you? Where have you been?" Maddy coaxed softly. Suddenly Lena snapped alive angrily. "What difference does it make?" She rose halfway, then not knowing what to do next, flopped back on the cushions and began to cry.

Chickie was uncertain—maybe sherry? The characters in her British TV shows regularly sipped sherry. She filled two small glasses, brought them to her friends and stood helplessly before them. Lena sobbed. The tears had started on an angry note, but within seconds she cried as if her heart was broken. Probably it was.

Finally, she began to talk, and the words tumbled out. Many were incoherent, but the other women were unwilling to interrupt, even to clarify. Lena hiccupped, sipped sherry, cried, and talked. An hour later they convinced her to take a nap. With the new widow tucked into her home office because she would not sleep in the bedroom she shared with Edward, Maddy and Chickie moved to the kitchen. They nibbled cheese and crackers, and Chickie attempted to put the events into some order based on all they'd recently heard.

"Let me see if I've got this straight: Lena said Edward slept in one of the guest rooms last night because he felt the beginning of a cold, and he left earlier than usual this morning before Lena rose. She assumed he was headed into a normal workday, but when she called his office around nine to discuss their dinner plans, the receptionist informed her that Edward had cleared his calendar. He left a voicemail saying he was headed north to a breakfast meeting in Wilmette. Lena hadn't known about this change of schedule. She tried his cellphone. No response. She texted him. Nothing; only silence. It was so unlike him not to respond quickly; she began to worry."

Maddy shook her head. "Lena must have gotten panicky."

"Yes, especially because it wasn't until shortly after eleven that she received a text from Brian Haskell . . . have we met him? Anyway, Brian texted: *Where are you?* She texted back: *Home.* He called immediately. The Wilmette Police were at the scene of Edward's death and had just phoned to report they'd found business cards in Edward's wallet."

Chickie stopped speaking long enough to imagine the scene and shuddered with horror. "Edward had been struck and killed instantly by a Metra train. Brian relayed the brutal facts to Lena on the phone and assured her that he was on his way. He instructed her to sit tight, avoid the news, and not answer calls."

Lena had given them a jumbled version of events. Hearing the details now in an orderly way shocked Maddy even more. She tried to banish the images from her mind. "No wonder Lena is a mess. The shock and hearing the news so starkly. A train. He was killed by a train. I'm not surprised that she sat in her living room paralyzed by shock and disbelief. It seems that the only thing she did was text us while she waited for Brian. I have a vague recollection of him; but it sounds like he was sweet and patient and waited with her until the cops came for the formal death notification an hour or so later. I didn't even think about the fact that they would have asked her to go identify Edward's body. How awful."

Both women cringed at the thought.

Chickie said, "Luckily, Brian offered to go with the police so she wouldn't have to. That must have been around the time Raph received a text from Brian and called her, based on what he said in the car. Okay, so then Lena poured herself a drink and got her brother Aaron on the phone to tell him about Edward's death and ask what to do next. She had no recollection of what he suggested other than to advise her to call a local friend. He assured her that he and their older brother Mitchell would arrive as soon as possible. Lena's only other clear memory was reading my text that we would both come, and she does remember your call later in the afternoon to tell her our arrival time. Did I leave anything out?"

Maddy thought for a moment. "Well, at some point Brian phoned to tell her that he took care of the identification. I can understand why none of it seemed real to Lena. It still doesn't."

"And then she kept her appointment for a massage? I find that a wee bit strange."

Maddy shrugged and rolled her eyes. "She always has a massage on Thursdays and habit is powerful. She was on automatic pilot. I know that feeling; I've been there."

"I'm more confused than I was before—" Chickie began before the sound of Maddy's phone stopped her. Maddy mouthed, "It's Raph" and listened.

Twenty minutes later, Lena woke up and joined them. She refused food but wanted a Manhattan, so she moved to the living room, where she expertly mixed ingredients. Chickie trailed behind her while Maddy took the opportunity to tidy the kitchen, knowing she should resist, but wanting to straighten up before the housekeeper reappeared in the morning.

Lena smiled after her. "I love Maddy, but she's too good." She grabbed Chickie's hand and pulled her closer. "You're not. You need to help me! Somebody killed Edward. I feel it."

Chickie stiffened. Everything about Lena's comment was distressing. She had learned from her own repeated clashes with loss that there was no point in providing grief instructions. Reality eventually wins out over feelings. Lena wasn't there yet; it was way too soon. "I will help you figure things out," she promised, "but we have to be realistic." She detached Lena's well-manicured fingers and called to Maddy, encouraging her to join them.

Through the large windows, the city lights pierced the black sky and surrounded the apartment. The intimate scene was made surreal by Lena, who stalked the room and insisted over and over again, "Edward has standing in the community; there are people who envy him, who sue him. Maybe one of them is deranged; you know that happens. When he got the Darnell Award last month, you should have seen the envious looks—even from friends. Someone pushed him in front of that train!"

"Accidents happen," Chickie said. She tried to explain that the medical examiner and police would investigate. "We have to trust them."

"They don't care. It's simpler for them to believe Edward had an accident, but Edward is a careful, careful man who doesn't have accidents," Lena shouted at her, smacking the arm of a chair for punctuation.

"Maybe there was a problem Edward didn't tell you about," Chickie said tentatively. "Vertigo, low blood pressure . . ."

"I would have known! I would have known. We didn't keep secrets from each other."

Disgusted, Chickie blurted out, "Everyone who has a life worth living has secrets. No one reaches seventy-whatever without hiding something."

"Stop saying that. We didn't keep secrets from each other."

Chickie lowered her voice. "We received some more information while you were napping. Raph called and told us that Edward did not fall from a train platform, but he was on foot at the pedestrian crossing in Wilmette. It's an unlikely spot to murder someone."

"How would you know? You haven't been within a thousand miles of Wilmette in years."

Chickie started to respond but Maddy stepped in. "Chick, you made your point; no need to be harsh." She was only able to bring the conversation to a close after she promised that they would visit Edward's office the next day, look through drawers and papers, and search for anything that might explain his death.

Chickie's Blog:

Old Dogs, New Tricks
(A Writer's Reflections on Growing Old
and Growing Up)

Course Correction

Sorry for the lateness, dear readers, but it has been a hell of a day. It's left me thinking about being thrown off course. You imagine that marriage or a baby or the unexpected death of a loved one will change your life, and it does. We expect to be knocked over from these obviously huge events. But a simple encounter, a book, or another unremarkable event might also be the thing that takes you off your planned path and onto a different one entirely. You can't usually predict what person or event will change your life. No bell rings, no light turns green, no text chirps on any of your devices.

Between the time I started writing this post and now, all sorts of unpleasant events have taken place. Undoubtedly those will appear on another day's blog—after I've had time to think. But today I am left with the idea of course correction. A year ago, my life had a major course correction. It wasn't the first time my life had veered off track, so maybe I should have been smarter, but there were no warning bells; well, none that I heeded. Maddy, my longtime friend who happens to be in the next room as I finish this, called; her husband had died after a brief illness, and I flew West to try to help. It was what you might expect: a lot of sitting around interrupted by periods of anxious activity and stretches of immobility broken by necessary decisions. I talked some, listened more, answered phone calls, and washed dishes. Friends came and told stories; Maddy replied with stories of her own and cried a bit. I made the beds. I met some of their friends I hadn't known before. I watched their sons wander the house, both inconsolable. No surprise, their lives had changed.

But here's the ordinary event that set me on a different path. I overheard a conversation between Maddy and her neighbor. They were laughing about their husbands' lack of skills with the barbecue, a male stronghold in their neighborhood. They talked with such fondness about raw hamburgers and burned fingers, about men grilling in the rain, about women praising inedible creations. I felt something shift inside me, like a door closing. I swear I heard it click shut.

When I went home several days later, I told my husband either he had to leave, or I would. Divorce or no divorce. It didn't matter who walked out. I was already on one side of the door, and he was on the other. The kids were launched. There was no way back. I knew I was done. It wasn't good enough that he didn't cheat or beat me. That bar is too low. I don't want some random mourner at my funeral saying, "Shitty marriage, but it sure lasted a lot of years; let's hear it for length of service."

For a long time, I told myself that my marriage was good enough. But something changed in me when I listened to women who had strong, not merely adequate marriages. Good enough wasn't good enough anymore. Frank's death made it painfully clear. Life is short. Time runs out. My decision wasn't easy to explain to anyone, but I was past explanations—one big benefit of aging.

Life can change when a new idea enters your mind and settles in like it had always lived there. Knowledge that had been barely visible to me became boldly visible; whatever had been below the surface now stared me in the face. And then, the only possible answer was to take a completely new direction. I don't know why, but I have an awful feeling that, for dramatically different reasons, I'm in a similar situation.

Chapter Five

Maddy was disoriented when she woke up, until she realized she was in Lena's guest room. She heard running water in the adjoining bathroom and knocked lightly. "Good morning," she called softly.

"I'm looking in the mirror for chin hairs; you can come in," Chickie answered. "It's amazing how good lighting makes these silver hairs glow."

She was wrapped in an oversized terry cloth bathrobe monogrammed *GUEST*, studying her face. Satisfied, she dropped her tweezers into a travel bag and said, "All done. Next, I moisturize my face. Then I put artificial tears in my eyes and rinse my sinuses. These days, moisture comes in large jars and expensive tubes."

Maddy leaned against the door, watching her friend's routine. She was reminded that she, too, had routines, pills, and exercises that grew exponentially year by year. Yoga had been a welcome addition to her life; unlike the plastic *S M T W T F S* pill organizer she'd received as a birthday present from a well-meaning friend. Two years ago, she'd added those light blue Parkinson's tablets and a twice-a-week Rock Steady Boxing class. She'd been dubious, but now enjoyed the exercise and camaraderie almost as much as she adored her purple boxing gloves. One surprise of aging, even without illness, was the time required for basic maintenance. Not getting ahead; simply not falling behind. She yawned, "I need coffee."

"I need more than coffee if we are really going to scavenge Edward's office looking for muddy footprints or other clues to an imaginary murder," Chickie growled.

"Will it improve your mood if I remind you that coming to Chicago means we will see my boys. I've been texting them. Needless to say, they are surprised that you and I are here."

Chickie got on famously with the almost middle-aged "boys," Rex and Gus, who lived and worked in Chicago. *How responsible they are*, she thought enviously, *an architect and a newspaper journalist with real paychecks, possibly with retirement plans and health insurance with low deductibles.* Chickie sighed and packed her tubes and jars away, knowing it was her turn to report on her own progeny. "It's a good thing Sam's wife works for Goldman Sachs because he is steadfast about freelance photography and on a shoot in Yellowstone. My son walks to the beat of his own drum. If I hadn't been there pushing and panting, I'd wonder if I really was the mother of both my children. You know that after Steph's last break up, she moved to Paris. I doubt her Phi Beta Kappa key opens many doors in the half-star hotel where she works."

Maddy put an arm around her old friend's shoulder and the two of them followed delicious smells into the grand, white kitchen where the housekeeper was squeezing fresh oranges and setting out coffee.

They climbed onto counter stools and gratefully accepted fragrant coffee served in delicate porcelain cups.

Chickie said, "I'll bet there isn't a mug from the National Zoo with a photo of Quing Bao, the panda, or one that says, 'I heart DC,' or a giveaway from anyone's chiropractor."

"This coffee is perfect," Maddy purred to the housekeeper. She wondered if there was an environmental placebo effect: beautiful surroundings create the belief in great coffee.

The housekeeper thanked Maddy, gestured to a platter of gorgeous out-of-season fruit, and excused herself to begin to clean and prepare the guest rooms for Lena's brothers, leaving the women to marvel at the appliances. The centerpiece of the room was a spectacular La Cornue range that almost overshadowed the Sub-Zero fridge and other wonderful gadgets.

Watching two perfectly cut bagels toast to a golden crisp, she told Maddy, "These gadgets are amazing. There's not a GE or Maytag in sight. Less than twenty-four hours, and I now covet a life of privilege."

"Wow, that was fast." Maddy removed both hot bagels before Chickie could drop them, slathered one with butter, and sat back down at the marble counter, close to the exotic fruit. She added French fig jam and considered the blackberries and papaya. Taking both was excessive, so she contented herself with a handful of dark berries.

"Be honest, Maddy. Wouldn't you enjoy one of these beauties?" Chickie waved from the refrigerator to the stove.

Maddy muttered through her mouthful of bagel, "I could never hide a La Cornue stove from my self-righteous friends. I recently felt daring enough to buy an expensive pair of comfortable shoes. But then I lied about the price."

"That's the answer. If you got the La Corneau range, you could order an Amana decal."

"That's undercover privilege," Maddy quipped, smiling at her own cleverness. "No, I'd feel guilty and then I'd invite everyone over to share . . ."

"You can't share privilege," Chickie said with mock disgust. "That makes it not-privilege. Privilege is having; it needs to be exclusive. Personally, I'm ready for senior privilege; that's not the same as youthful entitlement." She sipped her coffee.

"Speaking of privilege . . ." Maddy said, then glanced toward the doorway.

Chickie looked at her watch. "Last night Lena said she was going to take a sleeping pill, but the coroner's investigators will be here soon. You need to wake her up and get her pulled together."

"Me? Because I'm the social worker?" Maddy eyed Chickie suspiciously. "I'll bet that an accomplished journalist can also do the job. Why not go in there and sing, 'Here Comes the Sun' . . . forget it, your singing will frighten her."

"You know you're better at motivating reluctant humans. If you rouse Lena, I'll see that you are awarded with a Wake-up Cranky Camper merit badge. It's like a battlefield commission."

At nine, the concierge called to announce visitors. Maddy greeted two somber investigators. Patrick Reilly introduced himself and his younger associate, Lotte Drumski. Maddy led them through the apartment and into the dining room where they met Lena and arranged themselves around one end of the olive wood and chrome table. Maddy turned up the lights in the chandelier, then seated herself on one side of Lena and nodded to Chickie to sit on the other side of their friend.

Patrick Reilly refused an offer for coffee and began the interview by reciting a series of platitudes quickly followed by business. "We have to ask you a series of questions to further our investigation of Dr. Jordan's death."

Lena winced.

"Had the doctor had any recent health problems?"

"Only mild arthritis and high cholesterol."

"Had he recently seen any physicians?"

Lena answered "No" to this question and a dozen more.

Watching Lena become increasingly frustrated, Maddy asked, "Wasn't it simply a horrible accident?"

Reilly paused and answered earnestly, "It's our task to understand what happened; right now, we don't know. We have to consider every possibility." He continued with Lena, "Do you know why he was in Wilmette? Does he have friends there?"

"Edward has friends everywhere. But if he was visiting, he would have told me."

"Why might he have gone near the railroad tracks? Was there a business reversal? Was there any evidence that he was depressed?"

At that, Lena stared angrily, not answering. Maddy reached over and took her hand.

When further questions probed into current stressors and personal relationships, Lena erupted. "Why do you ask these questions? I'm not stupid! You are implying... Well, he wouldn't. Why are you here? Someone killed my husband and you're doing nothing. Nothing! Shouldn't you try to find out who pushed Edward! Someone did; Edward would *never*... I don't know why, but someone killed him. Go do your job."

Lena stood up and stomped her foot dramatically, then strode out of the room. Maddy followed her, and Chickie was left staring at the coroner's team.

"We'll go now, but we might need to contact Mrs. Jordan again."

Chickie wasn't put off that easily. She put her hand up. "Just a moment. Edward died at a train crossing in the morning in good weather, in a busy suburb. Surely, there were people around doing whatever people do on Thursday mornings. But, listening to your questions, I didn't hear anything about possible foul play, and you only made a vague nod to accidental death."

Drumski looked to Reilly, who answered, "Our legal task with every incident is to determine whether a death was from natural causes, homicide, suicide, accident, or cannot be determined. We know it is difficult for all those affected."

"Yes, yes, yes." It was as annoying as listening to the recorded message on her insurance company's phone system, right before they redirected her to the Russian Space Station. "I understand your restrictions in talking with us, but you are the investigators. Does the evidence take you in any particular direction?"

"We will be available to answer questions when the investigation is complete. We don't have answers yet."

"I'm not asking if you have answers. What have you learned? It was a train crossing. Were there witnesses?" Chickie persisted.

"Yes."

"And they say...?"

Reilly pressed his lips together. "We are in the process of doing our job. Until we have a cause of death, we can't certify it."

Chickie tried a few more futile questions. Frustrated, she collected a business card from each of the investigators and walked them out. Seesawing between her journalistic curiosity and repulsion at knowing any more about Edward's death, she closed the heavy walnut door and stared dumbly at it, wondering what to do next.

Laughter from the kitchen gave her hope that it might be safe to return to her friends. Lena sat at the marble island. In a swift change of mood, she was giggling and explaining to Maddy that the investigators didn't matter. "They aren't allowed to say anything."

Maddy hovered nearby and handed her a perfect, warm bagel, which the other woman flung into the sink. "I'm not hungry, but I am full of energy," she said, bending to do a supple ballet move using the counter as a barre.

Maddy shot a swift, worried look at Chickie, who grabbed a rosy peach from the bowl and turned away to examine the indoor herb garden.

"I didn't take a sleeping pill," Lena said, half apologetically, half boasting. "So, I had a lot of time to think about our conversation last night. I realize I was overwrought, and you two were right . . . You two are always right," she added less charitably.

"We're always right? I want it in writing," Chickie answered, sniffing the basil.

"You know I take you both seriously, even when Chickie is mean to me. Last night you said that we would have to wait a while for the coroner's results. I understand that."

Both women sighed audibly and relaxed. Thank God, no more murder plots. Edward's death was bad enough. Maddy felt like a proud teacher whose struggling student has finally mastered a difficult concept. She began to shower Lena with compliments but was quickly silenced by the widow's next statements.

"I am going to schedule Edward's memorial service immediately. It will take time to find his killer and while that's going on, the gossip and news coverage will increase. The service needs to happen before his murder becomes common knowledge. People talk; I hate it."

Chickie tried to interrupt, waving her half-eaten peach in Lena's face. "Wait . . ."

But Lena excitedly jumped off the stool and placed her hands on Chickie's shoulders. "It's a good plan. Today, while you and Maddy search Edward's office, I'll arrange everything for the service. That will give you the time you need to talk to people and gather information. You're a hotshot journalist."

Chickie turned to Maddy for help. "Did Woodward . . . no, I guess I'm Bernstein . . . start this way?"

Maddy stood speechless. Her mind raced, trying valiantly to unscramble the news she was hearing. In a sea of bad ideas, which was the worst? The original task of searching the office? Edward being murdered? A quickie memorial service? No need to choose; they had to deal with all the above—three terrible ideas. She began delicately, "Lena, I know you're determined, and you need some sort of outlet—"

Lena smiled broadly and tightly hugged Maddy. "I knew you would understand. I'll get started, and I already called Edward's receptionist to tell her you will be at the office this morning and have my permission to remove any items that aren't considered confidential medical records. After you drop your bags at the hotel, you need to search his office carefully. The evidence to prove he was murdered could be there!" She darted away looking almost happy.

"I think we've been dismissed to collect Edward's mouthwash," Chickie informed her friend.

Maddy started to protest Chickie's sarcasm but stopped. Chickie was right—this time.

Resigned to their assigned tasks and eager to avoid the incoming family, they packed. When Lena called to them from another room, "My brothers and their wives just landed in Chicago and are on their way from the airport," Maddy promised to call later, and the two friends quickly rolled their bags to the elevator.

Chapter Six

In the cab, enroute to the Palmer House Hotel, where hastily made reservations awaited them, Chickie snapped at Maddy. "You promised me, 'We can take care of the ordinary little errands like casseroles, cleaning bathrooms, and which Armani suit Edward wears on his final outing.' None of this is ordinary!"

Maddy shrugged; in her professional life, chaos had been ordinary.

Chickie continued. "We are enabling her cockamamie conspiracy notion. Two old lady sleuths; it's a Netflix series that quarantined patients would have binged on during the pandemic. I don't know how you let her talk us into searching Edward's office."

"Not searching; we will bring home his personal possessions."

"Renaming it doesn't make it less wacky."

"Are you finished?"

Chickie nodded reluctantly.

"Trust me, you will be more effective rummaging through Edward's office than if you stayed at Lena's to bake your first funerary casserole or organize Edward's thirty cashmere sweaters by color."

Chickie settled down. "I don't know if I love that you know me, or I hate it."

"You love it."

"And I hate that you know that."

The Palmer House was located two miles south of Lena's apartment, but a world away in style. Lena had been horrified that her friends chose to stay at the old Chicago landmark. She wanted to see them ensconced at the Peninsula Hotel—"Such a good spa."

But Maddy had insisted, "The Palmer House has always been my favorite Chicago hotel. Did you know Bertha Palmer instructed her chef to create a chocolate dessert bigger than a cookie but smaller than a cake that could be carried to the World Columbian Exposition, and that was how brownies were invented! Imagine that! My Aunt Lulu took me there for lunch when I was twelve."

The cab approached the landmark Palmer House Hotel, constructed in 1871 as a wedding gift from Potter Palmer to his new wife, Bertha. After being open for a short thirteen days, it burned to the ground during the Great Chicago Fire. Whether due to a cow, weather, or human error, the destruction did not foreshadow trouble for the Palmers. They had a long marriage, an enduring role in society, and a successfully rebuilt hotel. The women entered the Palmer House; it still retained the feel of another, gentler era. They walked up carpeted stairs to the lobby and were welcomed by classic columns, an ornately painted ceiling, and travelers who relaxed on chairs and couches; no one was in a hurry, no one was hunting for a murderer.

They rolled their bags to rooms that were dated, especially when compared to last night's Gold Coast accommodations. Chickie opened her door and turned on the lights. She looked around. "This is vintage Tante Lulu." She dropped her backpack and suitcase on the floor, her sweater on the bed, and followed Maddy into the adjoining room. She sat on the bed as Maddy opened her weekender, shook out several pairs of seemingly identical black and gray slacks, and hung them in the tiny closet.

"Is mania a bereavement thing or, as I've always suspected, Lena has a disorder called Endlessly Craves Attention, chronic?"

"It's not mania or attention seeking. You always think of Lena as a pampered poodle. She is privileged, of course, but she was neglected in other ways. Her brothers were more interesting to their parents. As a daughter, Lena was only expected to be beautiful and marry well."

Even when Chickie's eyes glazed over, Maddy continued. "That's a narrow life for a woman as talented as Lena, but it's what she did. She gave up ballet to become a wife, but she's amazingly disciplined, and, as you well know, she has been very successful. Don't discount her work on boards, raising funds for the cancer center at the hospital."

"How do you mental health professionals explain the breakneck memorial service?"

"The expeditious Gold Coast memorial service gives her urgent work to do." Maddy emptied the rest of her suitcase, placed her book on the nightstand, plugged in her phone cord, and carried a plastic case into the bathroom.

Chickie opened the bedside table to look for a Gideon Bible. She felt strangely disappointed when that relic of childhood travel was absent. "I feel so much older than Lena, like I've lived several lives while she is perpetually young. Especially with us, she devolves into a dramatic teenager who resents being seen as a dramatic teenager."

Reentering the room, Maddy acknowledged, "You have experience with a daughter; I don't."

"My daughter lives in Paris with a Frenchman who presents a clear and present danger. I do not want Steph living in another country, especially one that is beautiful . . . and where they eat tripe. If my mother wasn't dead, she'd drop dead," Chickie whined. "What if my daughter never comes home?"

Maddy studied Chickie from across the room. "That's Steph's decision to make. We all made choices; we all made mistakes. And look at Lena. Years ago, like us, she could have gone in any number of directions. But after she met Edward, one direction eclipsed all the others. Nobody gets to walk every path at once. She made a choice."

"More accurately, she was chosen."

"Okay." Maddy returned to the closet to get her vest and a dark gray scarf.

"Do you think that accounts for Lena being Dorian Gray and me being the portrait? She stays young forever, and I wrinkle for both of us?"

"Sure, aging is optional," Maddy said dismissively, pressing buttons on her phone. She found the most direct route to Edward's office. "Let's get this over with." Chickie went to her room, glanced disinterestedly at her suitcase, grabbed her backpack and a sweater, and they set off for Michigan Avenue.

※

"THIS ELEVATOR MUST be on a bungee cord." Maddy held on to the door frame as they stepped onto the luxurious carpet on the seventeenth floor. The building directory faced them. Drs. Haskell, Jordan, and Sodano Enhancement Surgery Center, Suite 1700. An arrow pointed to the right. Maddy led the way. "It looks like they have half the floor."

Edward's Michigan Avenue office in the heart of Chicago's Magnificent Mile argued convincingly that beauty could be constructed, given the right amount of money and talent. There were promises wherever they looked. The elegantly paneled hallway led to a glass double-entry door. On the left, a gold logo swirled into a perfect feminine profile. "She needs a sagging chin; I have a sharpie in my bag," Chickie said.

"Reality doesn't live here," Maddy whispered. "This entire space says that they can transform a humble empty structure—in this case walls and floor—into beauty. The implication is that they can also do it for us."

"My humble structure is already a work of art."

"Be sure to mention that to Edward's partners and see what kind of cooperation we get."

Below the logo, the partners were listed in gold script:
Brian Haskell MD, LLC
Edward Jordan, MD, LLC
Rafael Sodano MD, LLC

Preparing them for the morning's mission, Lena had explained that Brian and Edward had met at Northwestern Medical School, and when Brian's family was ready to fund a Michigan Avenue practice, he'd invited Edward, then Raph, to join him.

Lena was proud of the clever partnership. Brian was the business guru; Edward had amazing technical skills coupled with a persuasive ability to sell procedures; and Raph was the quiet workhorse who was happy to take the more serious reconstructive and occasional hard luck cases that came their way. They had been a winning team. The combination benefited them all—good business, goodwill, and invitations to join the right boards across Chicago.

Chickie pushed the door open, leaving her handprint on the glass. The young receptionist had intense black hair and magazine-like makeup, making her look older than her probable late twenties. She looked up, interested. Ever since she had accepted the job at HJ&S Enhancement Surgery Center, she'd thought of herself as a beauty profiler, and her job provided daily opportunities to practice those skills. These two aging women seemed to be likely candidates for eye and neck lifts, but as they neared the counter, she revised her guess to complete lifts. Yes, complete lifts would enhance their attractive vitality.

Then her interest faded. If their clothing and jewelry were predictors of what they were willing to pay for beauty enhancement, these women might only be in the market for a couple of eyebrow waxes from the salon downstairs. "Do you have an appointment? We don't have time for walk-ins." The well made-up eyes brushed over Maddy's cane with pity and a touch of contempt.

Maddy felt it all but straightened up and glared at the receptionist, who was probably an undiscovered Kardashian sister—Krystal perhaps. She was tempted to bring her cane down with a bang on the polished marble counter. Instead, she clarified the purpose of their visit. "Mrs. Jordan told you we were coming. We are old friends of Dr. Jordan and his wife, and we are trying to help her with these immediate tasks in such a sad and challenging time." The platitudes tumbled out.

Krystal stood stiffly behind the counter, unresponsive, so Maddy ditched the banalities and tapped her stick on the floor. "Let's not waste your time or ours. We'll take Dr. Jordan's personal items and get back to Lena."

Chickie watched with admiration. Maddy could be annoyingly accommodating at times, but she knew how to take command when required.

Krystal moved quickly around the marble counter, but before she could lead them into the private area of the suite, Maddy paused. Receptionists have an eye on everything. She stopped the young woman, softened her voice, and gestured to the sleek portrait of Edward on the wall. "It must be hard for you to see photos of Dr. Jordan alive and handsome. I imagine he was a good man to work for and it was such a sudden loss."

At this, Krystal seemed sincerely sad and shaken. "It doesn't seem real," she said tearfully.

Maddy encouraged the receptionist to reminisce.

"He was the best boss, and his patients . . . well, those women's lives were totally changed, uh . . . utterly transformed . . ."

At the second superlative, Chickie wandered into the waiting area and collected a copy of each available pamphlet, seized by the idea of a feature article on cosmetic surgery. *Writers are thieves*, she thought, not for the first time. The inside cover of one glossy pamphlet featured a photo of Edward and his two partners. They all looked so clean and presentable, quite the sort of doctor you'd want refashioning your skin. She began to read the booklet's first page.

> *Every face is a work of art. Depending on your needs, one of our revitalization procedures could help you achieve a more youthful and rested appearance.*
>
> REJUVENATE YOU *"The Mini—The Mini lift attends to your lower face, targeting sagging skin and jawlines. This procedure is for younger patients looking for a lifted, smoother lower facial line.*

REJUVENATE YOU "The Uplift"—*The Uplift is a mid-lift and focuses on correcting sagging that occurs below the eye and above the jaw. This procedure eliminates drooping cheeks. It can also be incorporated with other facial procedures. We say midlife, mid-lift.*

It went on to describe additional procedures, much like side dishes on a restaurant menu, but instead of mac and cheese or green beans with toasted almonds, Chickie was urged to consider an ultrasound to lift and tone sagging, loose skin; liposuction or freezing to remove fat; and collagen injections to give her skin bounce. She involuntarily pushed her cheeks higher and felt them drop. Her body hurt from merely contemplating all the plumping, freezing, and sucking. She tucked a selection of reading material into her backpack and looked up to see Maddy pass through an open door behind the receptionist. She hurried after them along a long hallway, where murmurs sounded from behind closed doors.

Krystal opened a door near the end of the hall and allowed them in but remained at her post. "I was told that you were coming to remove personal papers only. The doctors said that the file cabinets are locked because those are confidential medical files that belong to the practice. Dr. Haskell and Dr. Sodano will contact Dr. Jordan's patients and see to the business end of things."

Maddy responded with appropriate reassurances, but the receptionist didn't leave until they all heard the soft sound of the suite's front door opening, promising her a new profiling challenge.

Chickie toured the office, surprised that it was an ordinary box with a single window looking into the offices of the building next door. The room was businesslike. The row of expected file cabinets lined up against one wall and a couple of patient chairs faced a sleek black desk. The only personal touch was an oil painting of a lone dark figure plowing a field, and that seemed grim. This room was modest, unlike Edward's domestic taste for shine.

The one touch that continued to shout achievement was the photo wall—the one that patients had to face as they walked out. Edward posing with a former Chicago mayor, a man who certainly never had his face refreshed; Edward with a couple of politicians since indicted for various crimes; and Edward with beautifully dressed women at what seemed to be charity lunches. There were many pictures of Edward looking elegant, dressed in evening wear at important events with important people, most of whom Chickie did not recognize. But this was Illinois; she suspected they were still serving time.

Maddy had moved immediately to the desk and was sitting in Edward's chair, her cane resting against the sleek dark surface. "While you were stealing pamphlets, I learned a few things from the receptionist. She told me that Edward never came into the office yesterday but left a message instructing her to cancel his morning appointments."

"That's about what she told Lena."

"Also, last Wednesday Edward snapped at her, something he had never done in the six years she has worked here. It was so unlike him."

"Did she know why he was in a lousy mood?"

Maddy shrugged and opened the top drawer. She removed a photo of a face marked up to show where it would be cut and fixed and handed it to Chickie, who dreamily chanted, "We, the doctors of Tabernacle of Beauty, in order to form a more perfect human, provide for our common bank accounts, promote the beautification of aging women, and secure the blessings of vacation homes for ourselves and our families . . ." her words drifted off when she noticed that Maddy had lifted a second photo from the top of the desk.

Chickie moved behind her to look at the dramatic photo of a young ballet dancer. Confused, it took Chickie a moment to recognize Lena performing at the Civic Opera House, years before Edward had met her.

"The only picture on his desk and it's from decades ago?" Maddy whispered. With difficulty, she pulled her attention away from the photo and turned to the desk drawers, carefully going through the contents of each one, finding little that was personal and nothing that was useful for understanding recent events. No farewell note, no cryptic messages, no threatening letters, nothing. Maddy continued to open drawers. Of course, there was no written calendar or datebook full of suggestive information. And no blank pad that could reveal indented writing to provide a clue. She felt let down.

The receptionist returned with a banker's box for them to use in packing up Edward's possessions. Maddy absently said, "Thank you, Krystal," without noticing the bewilderment on the receptionist's face. She slipped the framed photo into the box, along with the engraved *Edward Jordan, MD* nameplate, and the embossed leather desk set. From the drawers she added a few other personal possessions that probably meant little to Edward and would mean less to Lena. He had an extra shirt, deodorant, a comb, and lotion. This seemed particularly sterile, but it was all that was left. Had the receptionist or his partners gone through his desk yesterday? Would they admit it?

Chickie stood watching and, as if she read Maddy's thoughts, she called the receptionist back. "There is almost nothing very personal here. Edward's office looks unlived in. Has anyone else been in to clean, to . . . help out?"

"Oh, no."

"Edward kept a remarkably minimalist office. Was that typical?"

"Not usually. This is particularly neat because last week the doctor threw out tons of stuff."

"When last week?"

"I don't know. It had to be early in the week because that stack of mail," she said pointing to a pile on the file cabinet, "arrived midweek and the office was already very clean when I brought it to Dr. Jordan."

Maddy asked gently, "Didn't the extreme cleanup seem strange?"

"Well . . ." She hesitated. "You know, he had cut back on his schedule to have more time for sailing. 'Gliding into retirement,' he called it."

Maddy knew no such thing but nodded in agreement.

Suspecting she had said too much, the receptionist suggested, "Maybe you should talk to the other doctors . . ." and stopped mid-sentence as the door was pushed further open.

"Do I hear my name being spoken in vain? Vain being the operative word in these offices." Chuckling, Dr. Brian Haskell walked through the door. Only his joke was well worn; the rest of him was shiny new. He looked like he'd stepped from the glossy photograph in the waiting room, a human experiment in photoshop. His skin was smooth and lightly tanned; there were no age spots lurking near his ears or on his forehead. For a man in his early seventies, he was missing all the emblems of age; no jowls or sagging skin and instead, he had some lovely lines around his brown eyes—not too few, not too many, just right. Chickie was intensely curious about Brian's appearance and most captivated by his hair. Was it his, or someone else's? It was full and gloriously silver. Chickie wondered if she could sell a magazine article that correlated physical appearance with career choice. Brian radiated confidence and unquestionably looked the part of a successful cosmetic surgeon, necessary, she guessed, if people were allowing him to permanently rearrange their faces.

The result of Chickie's mental walkabout was that Maddy was left to deal with the more immediate demand for social engagement with Dr. Haskell.

"We've met," Maddy remembered, smiling at Brian. "It was at Lena's last big birthday party. This is a very different visit. Chickie and I flew in to help, and Lena asked us to pick up Edward's personal items. There isn't much here. I understand that he was cutting back at work . . ." She paused, hoping that her vagueness would encourage the doctor to fill in the missing information.

Brian talked freely. "Edward had begun to say he hoped to sail into retirement."

Geez, Maddy thought, *the phrase was mediocre when delivered by Krystal.* It sounded worse with repeated use. But Brian had moved on, aware that Chickie was staring at him, at his hair. He walked toward her with an outstretched, well-manicured hand. "We've met?"

She took his hand. "Years ago."

Brian frowned, trying to place the meeting.

Chickie helped. "Back when you were opening your first office down the street."

"That was a long time ago. But people tell me I'm memorable."

Chickie smiled warmly. "Yes. I was in my mid-twenties, recently widowed, and you suggested that I come in for a nose job since I was, as you explained to me, 'back on the market.'"

With no change of expression, Brian tilted his head and moved to see her profile. "Yes, you should have taken me up on it." He lifted her ringless left hand. "Well, it's never too late."

He looked again. "But those dimples are first rate; you've had good work. And now ladies, I will let you get on with your unfortunate task. I had to rearrange my day yesterday, and I have to go back to work. I've been working on a letter to send to patients and, just now, I had to break the news to my brother Charles, another old friend of Edward's. You seem to have things under control. Ask at the desk if you require anything more."

Chickie shut the door behind him, and without turning around growled, "Do not comment."

Grinning broadly, Maddy moved on to gather the papers and magazines from Edward's file cabinets and desktop. She stacked them and sat down again, flipping through a few trade journals, many advertisements, and a few letters. Moving *The American Journal of Cosmetic Surgery* out of her way, a hand-addressed envelope slid from its pages. The ragged edge showed it had already been opened.

"Your almost ex-husband is a lawyer. Is reading Edward's mail a federal crime?"

Chickie had no idea about the legalities; she was interested in expediency. "Only if you steal it directly from his mailbox. But you've been authorized by his widow, so at worst, it's rude."

That sounded reasonable, so Maddy slipped the papers from the envelope and started to look at the first page. "Dear Dr. Jordan, This letter may be a surprise, but I hope you will—"

There was a knock on the door. Maddy quickly slid the pages and envelope into the box and concealed them under the magazines. She arranged the shirt and desk set on top as the door opened.

Both women looked up as Dr. Raph Sodano, the third partner, entered the room. He looked delighted to see them again, and Maddy smiled brightly from her seat behind Edward's desk. He said, "I didn't think I'd see you so soon. How is Lena holding up?"

"Not great," Maddy answered honestly. "She still believes Edward was murdered."

He shook his head.

Maddy hurried to say, "It's probably shock and denial. There is little reason to think anyone would want to kill him . . . right?" She studied his face.

He blinked. "No reason I know . . . After all, he's a doctor."

The women exchanged brief glances and let that non sequitur go by.

Maddy asked, "Do you mind if I ask you more about Edward?"

Raph looked cautious but nodded.

"How was he last week? Different? Ill? Troubled?"

His dark eyes grew serious but not argumentative. "This isn't because Lena thinks he was murdered, is it? What are you suggesting?"

Chickie tried to answer him without answering him. "When you told us he was on foot at a pedestrian crossing, it made us wonder if he had problems. Dizziness, heart trouble, health or . . . maybe even personal issues. He might have confided in you—as another doctor and a friend. It would devastate Lena to think Edward hid problems from her. They were remarkably close."

"I see," he said thoughtfully. "I would have felt the same if my late wife had kept her illness secret."

Maddy jumped in. "Exactly. No one wants to be shut out by the person they love. Did you know about any illnesses or problems? How did Edward seem to you recently?"

He leaned against the wall and frowned at the somber painting above Edward's desk, contemplating her question. "It's strange. You are aware that we've known each other for years, but now that you ask me, I realize we were never close. I worked alongside him steadily, admired his work, and got along amiably, but it was all professional. He was very private. Last week, he did seem withdrawn, preoccupied, enough so that I asked if he was okay. He assured me he was fine." Raph's gaze dropped to Maddy. "You're looking for an explanation other than Lena's conclusion of murder, but be careful, the remaining possibilities might be worse."

As he spoke, Chickie grabbed a few random photos of Edward off the wall and arranged them in the banker's box, now almost full.

Maddy's eyes followed Chickie as she closed and lifted the box from the desk.

Raph reached for it. "I'll take it."

Before Maddy could refuse, Chickie handed it over and asked, "Is there a way we could messenger the box to the Palmer House? We checked in this morning. They'll hold it for us."

Maddy complied. The letter could wait for an hour or two. "We planned to walk around Streeterville and visit our old haunts. It's been ages since we were here together and we're curious to see the changes."

"Then that box will be in your way," he said. "Glad to help. I'll take care of it now while you finish up. How long will you be in Chicago?"

"Several more days, at least," Maddy said.

As soon as Raph left, Chickie looked around before she picked up her backpack. "Let's go. We have completed Lena's bidding. There's no note from Edward saying, 'In case I fall in front of a train, check Brian's alibi,' as much as that would delight me."

Maddy was still thinking about the letter. The intriguing opening line made her want to follow the box and read the rest as soon as possible, but she agreed to leave, not wanting to call attention to the hidden envelope until she and Chickie were alone. "There's nothing personal left, and I guess we are not going to be refreshed, remade, or rejuvenated today, unless you . . ." She suggestively patted her nose with her index finger.

Chickie walked out, purposefully ignoring Maddy, who followed and called to her, "Let's take advantage of the washroom before heading out. At our age, we don't want to miss an opportunity."

Raph was at the reception desk when they reentered the waiting room. "Your package will be delivered to the hotel," he reassured them, starting toward the private offices. Then he returned. "I have a call I must take. But if there is anything Felice or I can do for Lena—anything—please let me know. There is always so much to do at a time like this. I have your phone numbers; we can stay in touch while the two of you are here. Give Lena my love and condolences. I'll call later."

"Who is Felice?" asked Maddy.

"I am," said Krystal through gritted teeth.

Chapter Seven

"Now that I know I can freeze or liposuction my fat away, let's get some food," Chickie said as they exited the office building onto Michigan Avenue.

"Good idea. When I've been in town to see the boys, I stayed in their Ravenswood neighborhood and never revisited our old stomping grounds. Let's find a place in Streeterville and criticize all the changes made since we left. That's what old people are supposed to do."

They walked east along Ohio Street toward Lake Michigan, quickly noticing the dramatic changes that had occurred over the years. Their moods became pensive. They wandered into the ever-expanding Northwestern University Hospital complex, a greystone village of its own.

Time had marched on. Not only had time marched on, time's boots had thoroughly trampled most of the familiar sights from the days when they had claimed this area as their own.

Chickie paused at the metal plaque attached to the wall of Prentice Women's Hospital. "I gave birth to Sam here when the building was new and state-of-the-art, but this says it was torn down in 2013, and this is the new-brand-new Prentice." They walked on and she reluctantly admitted, "I also became a very young widow in one of these buildings. Since coming to Chicago, I've been stalked by ghosts. Not just Danny—I expected him to still be here, waiting."

Maddy turned sharply. Chickie rarely talked about her first husband.

"That's the way it works with me, "Chickie explained. "When I leave people in a certain place, they wait for me. Unfortunately, this trip has invited others to dance around in my brain."

Maddy knew exactly what her friend would never acknowledge, so she finished Chickie's thought, "And of course, you wonder if they think about you. Unlike the overconfident Dr. Haskell, you are memorable, and you can be sure that your children will always remember you."

Chickie snickered. "Sure, but that's called haunting."

"Good point. It depends on how we're remembered, I guess."

"I hate to admit how much it would please me to have a place in someone else's cherished memories."

"Maybe that's why you like writing so much. We exist at least as long as we're remembered by someone," Maddy said, thinking of Frank and her brother John.

They went into Beatrix Streeterville and were seated at a table near the windows, where they looked out to their past. Chickie remained uncharacteristically quiet as the server brought water, menus, and ideas for lunch. As soon as he left, Maddy said, "I know those years were happier for me than for you. You went through *so* much. I was settling into marriage and parenthood at the same time your life was completely upended by Danny's death, single parenthood, and then a new job."

"Usually, that time of my life seems long ago and far, far away, but not today. Even though everything, including you and me, looks so different, the past is right here." She glanced around the crowded restaurant, as if some old friend from forty years ago was about to wander in and join them. Instead, two women in lab coats, probably doctors from the nearby hospital, walked by and were seated at the next table.

Noticing, Maddy said, "Remember when it was taken for granted that our careers would always be less important than those of our husbands? It feels like almost nothing remains from my wifely time in the early eighties."

"My resentment about wifely expectations remained for a long time," Chickie said. "I married and moved here with Danny right out of college so he could go to medical school. I had studied writing, but I became a copyeditor because it was a steady paycheck, however small.

Danny and I both concentrated on him. I can't blame him for being ambitious, but why didn't I pay more attention to my own life, the part that was mine, that didn't belong to the marital *we*?"

"You eventually did, and you succeeded. You write articles; you even write books."

"Ah, my barely researched, unwritten book, just waiting for my attention. Let's be honest," she said, as if Chickie could be anything else, "it took Danny's death. I didn't choose to change; I didn't choose to grow. Reality dictated it. I had to raise Sam alone; family was more than a thousand miles away. I didn't remarry for nine years. When people describe growing up, they make it sound like an organized process—or at least comprehensible. I look back at my coming of age and what I see is a worried young woman scrambling around the floor chasing mercury from a broken thermometer. It was a hard way to become an adult." Chickie shuddered at the memory. "We used to talk endlessly about self-actualization . . . after decades I've barely gotten to *self*." She waved to the waiter, signaling the end of that particular reminiscence.

Maddy suggested her carb cure. "French fries?"

"With a grilled cheese sandwich . . . and a pickle."

"You got it." Maddy ordered, well aware of her own struggles to find a voice. Ever since she could remember, she'd wrestled with long-standing tendencies to "always play nice," "don't compete," and most crippling of all, "never appear to be selfish." It had stopped her from having more than one adventure and embarrassed her more than she was willing to admit, even to Chickie. She, too, was eager to change the topic. "When I was going through the newer mail in Edward's office, I found an opened letter that looked personal."

"Let's see it."

"I reflexively shoved it into the box when the door opened, thinking the obnoxious doctor was back, so it's on its way to the Palmer House. I only read the first line before we were interrupted. It said something like 'Dear Dr. Jordan, This letter may come as a surprise, but I hope you will read it to the end.'"

"That doesn't sound like much, but we can take a look at it when we get back to the hotel."

"It could be blackmail," Maddy speculated. "Maybe Lena isn't as delusional as you think."

"It could be Publisher's Clearing House or a Nigerian prince who is stranded in Madagascar and needs a loan to feed starving ring-tailed lemurs."

"But Lena believes so strongly that he was killed. Maybe she has some intuition."

Chickie looked alarmed. "Done in by a Botox rep? I think you've been watching too much TV. Or is this your form of empathy, supporting Lena's wish to find a criminal. I can believe there were plenty of people who didn't like Edward, but come on . . . murder? To be accurate, White, arrogant, upper-middle-class doctors don't get murdered very often."

Maddy was piqued by Chickie's glib response, but before she could organize her thoughts, Chickie continued. "Maybe Edward was a real person under that perfect plastic exterior, and I would bet my next mortgage payment that he had secrets—probably lots of them—and they make it more likely that his death was due to a brain aneurysm, stroke or, I'm going to say it, suicide. It particularly irks me that I'm supposed to go along with Lena's flight from reality. Maybe she should write the novel, and I'll join a Board for Bored Adults. Why not be more honest, especially with us?" Satisfied, Chickie turned back to her sandwich and missed the change in Maddy's demeanor.

Matty stopped eating. Her blue eyes, usually soothing, narrowed into angry slits. She'd had enough of Chickie's easy responses. Why had she bothered to retire? At least, as a hospital social worker, she was paid to deal with difficult people. "You seem to be saying that friends deserve honesty. Am I correct?"

"Of course." Chickie glanced up, startled by Maddy's frosty look. "Why are you staring at me like I dropped a bag of puppies into the Potomac?"

"Because you are the last person allowed to criticize secrecy. You haven't earned the right to preach honesty or full disclosure!" Maddy had been quietly seething for months and planned to confront Chickie in an organized, polite manner during their reunion, but this sudden flight to Chicago had ruined her intention to gently explain her hurt and anger. Resentment was bubbling inside her and she was unable to remember all the carefully constructed words. She barked across the table, "Secrets? You left your husband a year ago, but you only told me last month! And you *had* to tell me because I announced my visit. I'm not sure when you would have let me in on your secret otherwise. You left me in the dark for almost a year! How could you do that to me?"

Chickie tensed; her heart banged in her chest. "I was waiting for the right time." she tried, tugging at the neck of her sweater.

"The right time came and went months ago."

Seeing Maddy's hurt expression, Chickie realized she was in serious trouble and that every phone conversation omitting the news of her separation from Michael had compounded her mistake. Her bravado vanished. "I didn't tell you about Michael because I didn't want to add to your grief. After Frank's death, you had so much to worry about: you, the boys, your Parkinson's. And then it got harder and harder to tell. And the longer it went on, the easier it became to avoid talking about the separation."

"Do you realize I read it in your blog six months ago? Is that where I need to go to learn about your life?" Maddy said.

"I knew you would read it. Doesn't that count as sharing?"

"No, that counts as avoidance or secrecy or running away—take your pick." Maddy shot her friend an accusing look.

"You had so much to deal with, and anyway, my dissolving marriage wasn't about you. I didn't want to rehash its pitiful expiration."

"I'm not sure I believe you. Since I told you about my condition, you've decided I'm fragile; that's why, isn't it?"

Chickie blinked, confused. "Fragile? No, you're my Rock Steady boxer." She shook her head repeatedly. "Don't take this the wrong way, but you were the inspiration for my divorce."

"Me?" Maddy fiercely bit into her sandwich. A glop of melted cheese fell out the other side and landed on her gray slacks. Without looking, she popped it back into her mouth and choked out, "What do you mean I was an inspiration?"

"For you, losing your husband was tragic, but I used to daydream about losing mine. And you have to agree that divorce is better than murder." It had seemed so reasonable to Chickie.

Not to Maddy. "Isn't the separation," she couldn't quite say *divorce*, "a huge loss? All the years together with Michael, the loyalty, kids, the life you built—"

Chickie cut her off. "That wasn't my life. The loyalty, the shared intimacies; you're describing your life with Frank. Not Michael and me. We were falling apart quietly for years. The only time I miss him is when I need a bowl from the top shelf in the kitchen. So, I bought a step stool."

The meal continued in silence until Maddy, relieved that she had voiced her hurt and now wanting to lower the tension, said decisively, "We need to know what the coroner found. That's where the definitive answer will be."

"I agree, but that could take some time; the coroner may have real murders to deal with."

"You're the journalist. Do you know anyone in the coroner's world?"

Chickie was eager to make amends but had little to offer. "This is Chicago. I live in DC, remember?"

"We both lived here. And we had a lot of friends in the medical community. Maybe someone from the old days is still well placed."

Maddy bent to her phone, found the website of the coroner's office, and began looking up the staff. "Why is this name familiar? Avril Clairwell?"

Chickie stared at her without responding.

"Wasn't Av Clairwell a classmate of Danny's? That's not a name I would forget. Sounds like a film star, not a pathologist. I remember her after Danny died; she was around a lot. I think you and she once stopped by with some soup when I was on bedrest." Maddy frowned. "If I remember her, you must."

Chickie leaned back in her chair, rubbing her lips with the back of her hand. Coming back to Chicago was probably a mistake. Definitely a mistake. She said nothing.

Maddy looked at her impatiently.

Chickie pulled out her credit card. "I'll get this," she said abruptly and signaled the waiter. As she paid the check, Maddy's phone pinged a text. She grinned at her son's name, other thoughts momentarily forgotten. "Oh, Rex is downtown and can meet us. Let's go." She happily gathered her sweater and cane.

Chickie didn't move. "Not me. I don't think so."

Maddy was stung by Chickie's response. "But I want you to see him, and him to see you. It's been a year. I don't know what his schedule is, and I know he won't want to miss you."

"Some time before we leave Chicago. I promise. Maybe dinner. I . . . I . . . but not right now!" Chickie sounded definite.

"I don't get this! What's the matter?"

"Look. You do feelings for a living. I do feelings when I have no other option. This slog down memory lane is hard, worse than I expected. I was naive about coming here and this city is getting to me. Go ahead and see Rex. I will meet you back at the hotel and wait to hear from you before I have dinner."

On a subdued note, Maddy left. She certainly didn't want to drag Chickie along unwillingly; that was becoming an irksome habit. Seeing Rex alone would have its own pleasures.

Chickie watched her go before she pulled out her phone, scanned her contacts list for a long while, took a deep breath, and began to press the keys.

Chapter Eight

Chickie's anxiety skyrocketed as she argued with herself whether this visit was a good idea. Had she been driving, she would have made a U-turn right over the highway divider on DuSable Lakeshore Drive, but the Lyft continued to head north. Twenty minutes later, she reached the Rogers Park neighborhood of Chicago—culturally diverse, populated by residents affiliated with Loyola and Northwestern, and home to unique shops, restaurants, entertainment, and street gangs. When Chickie had lived in Chicago, the Rogers Park neighborhood was described as up-and-coming, as if it were mere moments away from a housing renaissance.

Well, it had finally up and came, thought Chickie as the driver turned off Sheridan Road onto Morse Avenue and pulled up in front of a large Painted Lady home. The ornate Victorian multicolor houses are well known in San Francisco, but Chicago has its own Ladies, many on the northeast side of the city and in the suburbs. This particular home was a beauty, with unusually soft grays and yellows that complemented the white trim.

Chickie took a deep breath, pushed the iron gate, and started along the flagstone path. Before she had stepped a foot onto the porch, the door flew open and a tall woman about her own age, hands on hips, stood grinning down at her. Avril still had the quintessential Midwestern look—open faced and healthy. Chickie relaxed and moved toward Avril Clairwell's open arms.

After the house tour, after she made friends with a frisky black lab named Madame Curie, after she picked up and put down a half dozen photographs, and after she chose ginger from Av's ridiculously large selection of teas, Chickie followed her into the garden, now faded but still set with comfortable chairs and a heater to assist the thin October sunshine.

"It's been a long time," Av said.

Best to get the obvious out of the way as quickly as possible, Chickie realized. "And we know which one of us made it so long," she responded, biting her lower lip.

"I guess you've been busy," Avril said and sat patiently.

"Decades of busy? My friend Maddy would call it *avoidance*."

"Maddy! How is she?"

Chickie provided a summary of Maddy's life. She would have happily gone on longer, but after she said, "She and Frank had a good marriage," Avril quietly inserted, "It does happen."

"Has it happened to you?" Chickie asked, recalling a photo in the living room.

Av nodded.

"I like knowing that."

"I suspect you are here for a reason other than working on Step 9," Av said.

Chickie flushed. "The one vice I don't have . . . yet . . . is drinking. Isn't Step 9 the AA grand tour where you go from person to person and make amends?"

Avril didn't help out this time.

Chickie continued. "I thought I came to ask for your help because I need medical information from the coroner's office, but you're right. I want to apologize."

Avril only raised her eyebrows.

"I've wanted to apologize for forty years. Av, I'm sorry I disappeared on you." It came out as a whisper. "I've regretted it from the minute I bolted. It was shabby, and every Yom Kippur I atone and atone and atone. I've tried to be a more courageous person since then, and sometimes I think I've made progress. I've certainly had enough opportunities recently."

"What took you so long?"

"I don't know . . . fear, probably."

"You just vanished from Chicago. Up and gone. It was cowardly, a word I would not have associated with you before then. You left me angry . . . no, hurt. The anger took a while. Even twenty years ago, I would have thrown you out of my home, but one advantage of getting older seems to be that the past has settled back where it belongs instead of endlessly creeping up when I least expect it. I marvel at how many experiences take forever to collect cobwebs and become history." She noticed Chickie begin to relax and banged her teacup on the arm of the wooden chair. "I may sound civilized, but I still want an answer. Why did you leave so suddenly with no explanation?"

Chickie was ashamed. She couldn't look at Avril and maintain any sort of voice, so she found some low branches on the maple tree and spoke to them. "I wanted to get away from here. And I wanted to be a writer—not that being a copyeditor was bad, but I wanted the chance to start over in DC."

"Well, I wanted to be treated like I mattered."

Chickie could not respond. She got to her feet, "I'll leave."

"No, no, no. Sit down. You don't get to throw an apology at me and run."

Chickie sat and waited.

Finally, Avril spoke. "We were never going to have a future; that wasn't who we were. I knew it. But I believed we were truly friends."

"We were. Of course, we were!" Chickie protested, waving her hands.

"I had breast cancer in my forties."

Chickie's hand flew to her mouth.

"I'm fine," Avril said. "But the strange thing was, as I vomited my way through chemo and losing my hair, I wanted to call and tell you. Even though we hadn't spoken in decades, I wanted to hear you make hair jokes and help me feel normal. And, by leaving the way you did, you took that comfort away from me."

"I'm sorry. I can't make up for those years. I wish I could." Chickie stopped speaking. Every fiber of her being wanted to make excuses, to justify her departure, to say that she also had a hard time, but why add new weaselly behavior to long standing cowardice? Through her watery eyes, Chickie saw Avril's face soften and risked, "I'll work on bald jokes in case you relapse." For one bright moment, all the intervening years with their separate lives vanished, and two smart, young women grinned freely at each other.

Eventually, talk turned to Edward's death and Chickie tentatively asked for Avril's help.

"You worked with the coroner's office as a pathologist for years before you retired. Your name is still on the website. Could you find out what the story is about Edward's death?"

"Of course, I can try. I do some pro bono consulting and help out when there is a mass casualty. So, I still know the people over there pretty well."

An hour later, the two women stood again at Av's front door, having made loose plans to stay in touch. Avril said, "You know, you're not off the hook, but you have made a dent in Step 9, and I want you to meet Chrissie. The two of you will get on famously and ignore me."

"Never again."

As the two women embraced, Av whispered, "I loved you so much."

"I loved you too, but I wasn't . . ." It went unsaid. The old differences were part of the past.

Chickie walked east to Sheridan Road; she had no idea why she was happy. She had hurt an old friend, and she had relived memories of fear and cowardice, but she felt light. Unable to decide what to do next, she walked south toward the Chicago Loop. She couldn't get her mind organized, so she kept going, knowing that she was miles from her hotel. She replayed the conversation with Avril, berated herself, composed better apologies, then berated herself some more.

She reached Granville Avenue, cold and tired, more than three miles south of Avril's home, before she understood that her friend had forgiven her.

She continued to walk. At Wilson Avenue, Chickie caught her reflection in a store window and looked at the old woman who was finally learning that healing happens in strange places and at odd times. That thought calmed her, but the sunlight was fading into dark, and she was exhausted. She walked a few more blocks before she caught a cab back to the Palmer House.

⁂

WHILE CHICKIE HAD been heading anxiously toward Rogers Park, Maddy walked through Streeterville, savoring Chicago, particularly this neighborhood where she had lived and worked. The high-rises and medical buildings shadowed the blocks at this hour but didn't dim her fond memories of pushing a double stroller on these streets.

She spotted Rex. He sat in the window of the West Egg Café and stared down into a coffee cup. Maddy tapped the window with her cane, and he looked up with a solemn expression that reminded her of Frank. She hurried inside and hugged her firstborn. Rex was the older son by three minutes and, since infancy, the more serious, introverted twin. Outwardly though, with the same blue eyes and thick blond hair as his brother, they looked enough alike to cause confusion for new acquaintances.

After Rex ordered his late lunch, Maddy brought him up to date on her visit so far.

"It's hard to believe Edward was killed by a train," he said. "What a gruesome way to die."

He shuddered and took a slug of coffee. "What does Lena think happened?"

"She's alarmingly interested in the idea of foul play. Maybe she knows something that we don't but the more likely idea—that Edward committed suicide or had an accident—seems intolerable to her."

"You've said she can be dramatic," he remembered.

"As Chickie reminds me regularly, but enough about that. I do want to grab a few happy minutes with you before you have to go."

Maddy had a list of questions that were never answered on the phone or in emails. Now, her son sat across from her; she could fish for current news about his work as an architect, his veterinarian partner, and other basics of maternal curiosity. As she leaned across the table to begin, the server put down Rex's sandwich and her iced latte. Maddy sat back and paused politely.

Rex picked up his sandwich but held it midway to his mouth. "Mom, before we discuss anything else, like my relationship and whether I have a good winter coat, can we talk about your health? I know you don't want to, but Gus and I need to know. With this 'condition' as you insist on calling it, should you be living alone now?"

Maddy groaned, displeased by the conversational detour. "Lots of people live alone.

There are fourteen million of us," she quoted from some online source, pleased that she had memorized that number. Her sons needed reminders that she wasn't alone. "Of course, I'm aging. That happens every day of my life! And Parkinson's is real, but I am *not* suddenly fragile." Her voice rose.

"Mom," Rex hushed her, "I know, I know, you've told me." He cursed his brother for foisting this conversation on him and tried a strategy his mother had taught him when he was a dating teenager. "It's not you, it's me. I hate the idea of you being alone up there. Gus worries, too. It's not enough to rely on the Apple watch we bought you. The family tracking system is good but—"

"What!"

"The tracking system only gives us your location. What if you fall and hit your head while you are proving how tough you are? No one will be around."

Maddy could feel herself getting defensive. She vaguely

remembered Gus mentioning a family tracking thing, but . . . They could follow her and see where she was every minute? Not that she had anything to hide, but no—no spying on her. "I don't require supervision. Look, I'm probably in the best physical shape I've ever been in. My doctor prescribed Rock Steady Boxing . . . and I'm good at it!" Then, seeing her son's strained expression, she added, "I *know* this is hard for you boys . . . men. And with your father gone, I expect you feel responsible. I wish I could spare you." She looked out the window to collect herself.

Rex signaled to the server who was wandering past with a coffee pot and watched intently as his cup was filled before plunging ahead. "Well, Dad is gone, and we don't have confidence that your new boxing skills and your purple gloves are enough to keep you safe. Gus and I think you should move to Chicago."

Maddy continued to gaze out the window at the street. "I don't recall asking you or your brother for advice on my health or living arrangements. I am still very capable of taking care of myself."

Rex studied the remains of his turkey sandwich as if there were answers written on the lettuce scraps. The restaurant suddenly seemed to be absurdly quiet.

Maddy finally turned from the window and studied her watch with distaste. "Look, I know you're suggesting a move because you love me. But I want—I *need*—you to refrain from advice on this topic. And tell your brother that it is not healthy for worry to dominate your life or mine."

"Please stop sounding like you're presenting a paper at some social work conference. Dad was always more reasonable. We . . ." Then Rex noticed his mother's face and stopped. He had gone too far, and she was fidgeting with her cane, trying hard to mask her fury. She looked like she was ready to charge out of the restaurant. He reached for her hand. "Mom, we worry about you. And you've always said you loved Chicago."

She left his hand on hers but did not return the gesture. "I do not need your help now, and I'm not alone in Minneapolis. I have a strong community of people my age; friends who are going through life changes like mine. It's home." She sat straight and looked around. "Where's the waitress? I'll let you get to your next appointment."

Chapter Nine

After a short, very quiet ride, Rex cautiously suggested that Maddy might like the Lurie Garden in Millennium Park. "You'll find it calming." But the native prairie flowers, butterflies and fine examples of urban horticulture did nothing to lift her mood. Why did Rex have to ruin lunch? The twins outnumbered her, now that Frank was gone. Another mark of aloneness.

Sighing, she reluctantly admired the sculpted fifteen-foot-high hedge, a landscape feature designed to evoke Carl Sandburg's description of Chicago as the city of big shoulders. It did nothing to inspire her. Her own shoulders sagged, and she settled on a nearby bench to ruminate on bossy offspring until, tired and stiff, she walked to the hotel, where she gratefully stretched out on the floral bedspread and closed her eyes.

When Maddy awoke, her room had darkened. She turned on the lights and checked her phone; no message from Chickie. She listened at the connecting door. Silence, so she plugged in the coffee maker on the desk and brewed a cup of dark roast. She took a few sips, then forced herself to perform stretching exercises to loosen her muscles and clear her mind.

The room telephone rang. The front desk had a carton for her.

The box from Edward's office! Of course. She had forgotten, distracted by her anger with the twins.

Maddy tore into the box as soon as it was delivered, determined to make up for lost time. The letter was still there, right where she had stuffed it under the magazines. She read it several times and was staring into space when her phone pinged.

The text from Chickie read:

I'm back. Come next door when you can.

Maddy had been so absorbed by the letter and its implications, she hadn't heard Chickie return. She opened the door. Chickie was sprawled on the bed, leaning against the wooden headboard. Her bare feet were propped up on pillows. Two small bottles of whiskey from the help-yourself bar were empty on the nightstand. She swirled one finger in circles in her water glass, moving the dark liquid in a spiral. Maddy, who was well aware of her friend's minimalist alcohol habits, wondered why Chickie was suddenly going for this personal best. She stood at the foot of the bed and looked down at her. "When did you get back?"

"A little bit ago."

Long enough to visit the mini bar, Maddy thought. *It's unlike Chickie, but who cares.* She had big news to share. "I have something to show you." Maddy tried to hand her the letter.

Chickie didn't stretch forward to take it. "Don't you want to know where I went?"

Two whiskeys too many, Maddy thought, dropping her hand. "Where did you go?"

"To ask Avril Clairwell for help."

This was a surprise. "So, you did remember her?"

"I did," Chickie said.

"That was a long visit. You were gone for hours."

"That's nothing compared to being gone forty years. There was a lot of catching up to do," Chickie said glibly. "And so much sharing, just like you and me this afternoon. Then I walked to Irving Park before I caught a cab."

"You needed to exercise?" Maddy asked, already knowing the answer.

"I needed to think."

"And . . .?"

Chickie looked up and grinned, displaying both dimples. "Do those open-ended questions usually work?"

"Yes, especially when I'm questioning a nondrinker who downed a double whiskey and is longing to tell me what happened."

As usual, Maddy was right about this talking thing. *What a day. Apologies, confession, forgiveness. It's practically Biblical,* Chickie thought hazily. She took a deep breath. "Avril and I were very close during my last months in Chicago. She's marvelous, but it was a crazy, strange time for me, and I wasn't in the same place as she was. Then I got the writing job in DC and left . . . bolted, I guess."

Maddy moved Chickie's feet and dropped down on the bed. "She always seemed wonderful. Was she hurt by your inelegant departure?"

"Yes. She told me I was a coward." *Confession on top of confession. My soul will be spotless,* Chickie thought. "I may have repaired a tiny bit of that today. I hope so."

"Good."

"And she will help us. She'll make some calls to people at the coroner's office."

"That's useful, but . . . but would you have seen her if we didn't need help?"

"I hope I would have. I've outgrown so much: Michael, my clothes, dark hair, why not cowardice?"

Maddy was intensely curious about Chickie's relationship—was it a relationship?—with Avril but forced herself to respond simply. "Good."

"And your time with Rex?" Chickie asked.

"I'll tell you about Rex later, but right now you have to read this." Maddy was unwilling to wait any longer and tossed Chickie the letter.

The journalist donned her reading glasses, grabbed the envelope, and slid out three typed pages.

GenomicsX,
22-24 Beaumont Street
Oxford OX1 2LW, United Kingdom.

Dear Dr. Jordan:

This letter may come as a surprise, but I hope you will read it through to the end. If you were in Hawaii in 1971, I may be your son.

My mother, Mai, learned she was pregnant after a US Navy doctor she dated in Hawaii had to return to service. She and her mother, Vietnamese refugees who had escaped to Hawaii, chose to raise me on their own. We lived a safe and comfortable life. They worked on the campus of Punahou school and lived in the community of staff members there. As you will see from the attached CV, I was able to get a good education and am now living in Oxford, England, where I work in the field of genetics.

DNA sequencing brought me the information that you could be my father. Because of my field of work, I definitely understand that information like this can be unwelcome and certainly should be questioned and confirmed. I am simply sharing what I learned with the hope that you might be curious enough to meet me.

I am not interested in making any claims or demands; I am simply curious because I have observed fathers and sons together throughout my growing up and have never had an image of who my own father might have been or might be today.

I will be in Chicago for an international genetics conference from October 6–11. If you would be willing to meet for a drink or a meal, I would welcome the opportunity to know a little about you and your life.

> If you are not interested in any future contact, I would understand, but I hope we can meet at least once. You could decide if you want to learn any more about me or any connection we might have.
>
> I would be grateful to at least know, yes or no, if you would like to meet. You can reach me at wedwards@genomicsX.net.
>
> Most sincerely,
Winston Edwards

Chickie read, sat up straighter, and reread the letter carefully. The pleasant fuzzy feeling from the alcohol couldn't compete with this shocking news. Next, she scrutinized the enclosed curriculum vitae. "Oh." Her mouth actually formed an *O*. "He writes an impressive letter. Could he really be a child from the years Edward was in the Navy? I know that he served in Vietnam; did he go to Hawaii?"

Maddy shrugged.

"Winston Edwards, that's an ironic name. And he studies genetics."

"Freud would say that he was unconsciously drawn to the field to solve his own past. More to the point, the envelope had been opened when I found it, but we don't know when it was opened or why it was shoved into that journal."

Chickie looked at the postmark on the envelope. "We can assume Edward read it in the last ten days. And"—she double-checked the calendar on her watch—"the conference is going on right now."

Maddy stood with her hands on her hips. "What a shock. It sounds like Edward never knew anything about Winston. Do you think he told Lena about the letter?"

"No, she would have told us. We have to show it to her, but her brothers are staying at the apartment, and we can't drop it on her while they roam the halls."

Both women envisioned that scene. Oh no.

"Okay then," Chickie said, "first things first. Who is this Winston character and how do we approach Lena?"

"For this discussion, you cannot be the only one with a drink," Maddy said authoritatively.

Chickie pointed to the small refrigerator. "Help yourself."

"Better yet, let's go somewhere with food."

"I can't walk anymore today," Chickie moaned.

"This is a hotel," Maddy reminded her. "There's no shortage of bars or restaurants. I'm surprised that your education still has serious gaps. I could get a luggage cart and wheel you down if you can't walk to the elevator."

Chickie swung her bare feet off the bed and squinted unhappily at her shoes. The incredulity of Edward having an accomplished son had to get in line behind her reunion with Avril. She was careening toward numbness. "My imagination never included a Winston. We have no idea if this letter is the only communication between them. For all we know—which is nothing—Winston is the reason Edward canceled his appointments on Thursday. Maybe they met."

Maddy looked miserable. "Poor Lena. Give me a quick minute to wash my face and we can descend to the bar on the lower level. It's secluded and we'll be able to talk." She returned quickly, zipping her vest and continued the conversation without a pause. "Once he read the letter, do you think Edward would have told anybody about having a child? Do you know anything about his time in 'Nam or an R&R in Hawaii?"

"I have no idea." Chickie rose and felt dizzy, reeling from alcohol on top of having allowed so much emotion to dominate her recent days. No wonder she avoided feelings. You have to be tough to indulge in sensitivity.

Maddy barreled on. "For that matter, how did Edward's DNA get into a database?"

"Maybe a family ancestry thing. I've heard endless anecdotes about revelations no one expected."

Maddy picked up the letter and folded it into her pocket. "I dread talking to Lena. If this is legitimate, she has a stepson."

Chickie pulled on socks, grabbed her laptop, and slipped it into its case. "It won't be hard to learn more about Winston Edwards."

On the lower level of the hotel, the women found a quiet corner in Potter's Bar where they could converse without being overheard. Seclusion was useful until they wanted service. Maddy finally succeeded in staring down a young server who indifferently took their orders for food and drink; hamburger and beer for Maddy, generic pasta and tea for Chickie, who proposed a toast with Earl Grey decaf. "To life! Endlessly surprising. No wonder it kills us."

Instead of chastising her friend, Maddy excitedly joined in. "This letter changes everything. And it complicates the question of what happened to Edward."

"Fraud or not, we have to share this letter with Lena, and that won't be easy. Any suggestions?" Chickie said.

"I know you prefer more avoidant paths, but the straightforward truth is simple. We say we found a letter in the office and it's important that she read it. She's a mess right now, but at the core she's more solid than she looks. At all costs, let's keep her family out of it. That's more drama than even Lena can handle."

Chickie sighed. "Before we do or say anything, we have to learn more about this genetics whiz kid." She pulled out her laptop and logged into the Palmer House Wi-Fi. After scanning various sites for several minutes, she hadn't found a photo. "There is a real man named Winston Edwards on the GenomicsX website. And he has a history—school, publications, that sort of thing, like the CV. Maybe it's the same person, but that doesn't mean he's Edward's son. And there is a genetics conference in Chicago going on right now. I'll check that next."

Maddy didn't share Chickie's skepticism. "Why would anyone pretend? There's nothing much to be gained."

Chickie's mouth twisted. "Were you truly a social worker? Even in Minnesota, there must be a few people who aren't nice. Who gets thrown into prisons? The neighbor who neglected to sort his recycling?"

Maddy may have rolled her eyes but, in their secluded corner of the bar, it was too dark to tell. Their food arrived and Chickie closed the laptop.

Maddy swallowed a bite of hamburger and mused, "We don't know anything about the family's circumstances or culture. If his mother and grandmother were Vietnamese immigrants in Hawaii working at a school, perhaps they considered it discreet to ignore Winston's paternity. Maybe they searched and failed. Maybe they didn't want to know what happened to Edward."

Chickie shrugged. "The letter implies that Winston planned to wait to hear from him, but we don't know if Edward responded."

"Or if they met. Check your computer again. Maybe you can find out more about the conference and whether Winston is in attendance." Maddy paused. "We don't know if he's aware that Edward died."

"If Winston pushed him in front of the train, he's probably got a very clear idea about Edward's well-being."

"Chick! Why can't you give him the benefit of the doubt. He may have just lost his father."

Chickie chose not to respond.

As their dishes were cleared, Maddy said, "We need to make some decisions, most importantly, when do we tell Lena. What do you think?"

Before Chickie could offer an opinion, Maddy answered her own question. "I wish we could wait, but we aren't going to stay here forever and what if he decides to contact Lena? What if he turns up at the apartment? But first, we must find out the day of the memorial service. If it's soon, we wait."

"Do you want my opinion on anything else?"

"What if Winston shows up at the memorial? If he is in town and curious, he could read the announcement of the service and appear. I can't picture, given Edward's social standing and Lena's style, that it will be closed to everyone except family." Maddy continued to create increasingly dreadful scenarios. "Technically Winston may *be* family. What if . . ."

While Maddy busily outlined future problems, Chickie grabbed her laptop and began to search again. In a few moments, she turned the screen toward her friend and showed her a clear headshot. "He is real. The right age, and he has a very familiar look around the mouth."

Chickie's Blog:
Old Dogs, New Tricks
(A Writer's Reflections on Growing Old
and Growing Up)

Relationships, Value and Eternity

Well, readers of my own multitudinous years, I am still in Chicago, and I learned something big today. Please indulge me; I will get to it in three sentences, but I must lay some groundwork.

Groundwork: I was born into a family that believed in forever as the minimal amount of time we devoted to relationships. There was no such thing as short, brief, time-limited, or God forbid, temporary relationships. All connections had to be eternal.

Those were my three sentences: now, on to my epiphany. Today I realized that relationships can be important, and meaningful, and still end. This has come as a shock, but it makes me feel better about the ending of my marriage.

More importantly, I reconnected with an old love today; someone I cowardly ditched years ago. Let's be clear; it wasn't bravery or morality that made me reach out. I needed a favor for a friend. In my defense, I have always wanted to reconnect, and I have been ashamed of my behavior, but . . .

You can probably imagine my anxiety and dread about getting together. Double it and add nausea. Anyway, it is good to know that some people are far more gracious than I am; my old love is one of them. I was received with kindness.

This relationship had been brief. It never had a future. Nonetheless, it was loving and healing when I desperately needed both. I have been reassured that I had also been kind and loving (hopefully), until I was spineless and gone (unfortunately).

Here's the blog post message. Relationships can end; they can die a natural death like a plant or, hopefully, each of us. Relationships are not less valuable if they don't go on forever. Yet again, (when will I learn?), it's in the ordinary daily acts that our lives are built. Moment by moment. Now, wish me luck. I have to remember this insight all week.

Chapter Ten

Saturday was cloudy with an on-and-off drizzle—mostly on. Chicago was having a mood.

Chickie's old habit of protesting Midwestern weather kicked in and she rummaged through her bag to pull out her brightest sweater, a rich burgundy wool. It was a notable exception to the colorless day designated for planning Edward's memorial service. Outside the Palmer House, she held the borrowed hotel umbrella high while Maddy studied a map of the Loop and made decisions. Maddy liked to know where she was going.

"We'll walk. Lena's apartment is only a mile or so. I brought the letter from Winston Edwards, but we only give it to her if she is alone and if the situation feels right."

"It will never feel right," murmured Chickie but her friend had already turned east, away from the hotel. In a very few minutes, Maddy lifted her cane to point out Cloud Gate, the centerpiece of Millennium Park. "I saw this yesterday when I explored the Lurie Garden. Compelling, isn't it?" Chickie stared up at the enormous shining steel sculpture known locally as The Bean. Because of its curved kidney shape, the seamless steel reflected the clouds, the neighboring skyscrapers in round distorted forms, and the tourists with colorful umbrellas juggling their cameras to take pictures underneath the massive sculpture.

Chickie suggested that they take a selfie together, but Maddy was intent on directions and destinations, and not in much of a touristy mood. "Not now. We need to see that Lena gets the memorial service she wants," Maddy said, picking up speed.

Chickie kept pace. "Okay. When do you think she'll have it?" she asked, bowing to Maddy's broader and more recent expertise in death decorum.

"Usually, it's held any time up to a year after the funeral. But some people choose to have the service at the time of burial or cremation. It worries me. Edward's body hasn't been released to bury, but Lena sounded like she's in a hurry. She may opt for a memorial as soon as next week."

"This could turn into a long visit."

Maddy's face took on her toughest look: side glance, full frown plus pursed lips.

"Relax, Maddy. It was a statement of fact, not a prelude to throwing in the towel," she said, although that thought had crossed her mind each day as she covertly checked the plane fares back to DC. "Save your displeasure for Lena's family. From everything she's ever said about them, her brothers are tough, and their wives were mentored by Imelda Marcos."

"Politics or shoes?"

"I believe it was a general course of study; a sort of finishing school in entitlement."

Despite her flippant remarks, Chickie did share Maddy's concern about Lena, especially now that the family had arrived. Lena seemed to yo-yo between eggshell fragile and truck tire sturdy. Neither Chickie nor Maddy could predict which mood the family would elicit.

Maddy habitually spoke to the bright side. "Remember, Lena served on not-for-profit boards for the last twenty years. In equivalent paycheck years, that's a century. She's not likely to be a complete pushover. And it's a promising sign that she asked Raph to do the eulogy. That choice shows good judgment. Lena believes he will be professional, kind, and all that's required."

"He's the one I'd choose to unwrinkle my face," Chickie said, squeezing the soft pouch under her chin. "I'll do the obit and whatever else Lena needs; research, phone calls, dealing with nosy friends, even arm wrestling her brothers. Spare me, please, from anything related to food service."

Maddy agreed very quickly. As much as she loved her old friend, Chickie's lack of talent in the kitchen was only surpassed by her horrible singing voice. "No one will argue with you," Maddy assured her, stopping on the sidewalk for a moment to watch two girls in bright South Indian *lehengas* and a dog chase each other around the Millennium Fountain in Wrigley Square.

"Every time I woke up last night, I thought about Winston and the possibility that Edward had a son he never knew. It makes me more curious about Edward now than when he was alive, which seems like a terrible thing to say, but it's true. We hardly knew him."

Suddenly, arms grabbed Maddy's shoulders from behind. She spun around, walking stick raised, ready to whack an assailant.

"Hey! Go easy, Mom," Rex yelped, jumping back. He held his hands up in surrender. "I went to the hotel, but you just left. I shouted, but the two of you were speeding along, obviously solving the world's problems, and you didn't hear me." Rex's Bulls cap and sweatsuit were damp from chasing after them in the light rain. He wiped his face on his sleeve before ducking under the umbrella to wrap an arm around Chickie. They hadn't seen each other since his father died. She was delighted but in the next moment, she saw Maddy stiffen when her son bent to kiss her cheek.

Uh-oh, Chickie thought, *their coffee tête-à-tête must have gone sideways yesterday.* Maddy hadn't said anything, but mother and son both looked uncomfortable. Even children with steady jobs and insurance can provoke their mothers, she guessed. "I need to run across to the drugstore. I'm expecting a headache," Chickie extemporized. "Can you two amuse yourselves for a few minutes?"

Maddy would have let Chickie scurry away so she could deal with her son privately, but Rex held Chickie tightly. "No, Aunt Chick, I'm here to eat crow. You can join in."

"Crow isn't kosher."

Maddy still hadn't said anything.

Rex grinned invitingly at Chickie. "Mom is angry because Gus and I want her to move to Chicago."

Maddy faced him. "Mom is angry because her two sons are treating her as if she cannot plan her own life."

Rex couldn't help it. He winked at Chickie and said, "When Mom talks in the third person, you know she's definitely angry." Then, more seriously, he bent toward his mother, cajoling. "If you lived in Chicago, you would be closer to us; like Sam is with Chickie."

Maddy did not relent. "Mom is angry because you put a tracking thingamabob on my watch—which will disappear as soon as I figure out how to defuse it."

"It's an app, Mom, not a bomb."

Even without a social work degree, Chickie knew enough to stand back, but she silently rooted for Rex because he rarely challenged his mother without his twin as backup. From repeatedly being told off by her own children, she knew that shake-ups kept mothers humble and always on their toes. In Maddy's vernacular, this would be a growing experience.

A young couple squeezed past on the sidewalk, forcing the three of them to sidle into the courtyard, where Roman columns created a half circle around the simple fountain. The light rain had stopped and Chickie sat down on the concrete ledge. She watched Maddy with undisguised fascination.

The twins' innocent invitation was an assault on Maddy's decreased control over her life. She had seen her husband's health fail, she had no illusions about where Parkinson's eventually goes, and she routinely learned of some friend's sudden life-limiting illness. But fear of the future was not a confession Maddy was prepared to make to her son. Instead, she said curtly, "I know you boys are well-intended, but you cannot treat me like I've become feeble. I haven't been tucked away at home being a professional widow for the last year." She paused and watched water cascade into the pool for a long moment. "Well, what I mean is, widowhood and Parkinson's do not define who I am and what I decide for the future," she lied. "But I am certain that we have not reached the time when you choose where I should live!"

Rex listened half-heartedly; he knew his mom. "Look, I came to apologize, not to fight with you. I didn't mean to sound obnoxious or imply that you needed our help. When you said you were coming to Chicago, we decided it was the perfect time to tell you that we'd enjoy having you here permanently—there's nothing wrong with that. Imagine, you would be able to personally examine our winter coats and, if you were exceptionally well-behaved, we might tell you about our relationships."

Chickie's restraint vanished. "You're not getting a better offer than that. If I didn't hate Chicago, I'd move here and check on their winter coats. Do you boys also move heavy objects?"

"I'm brains, I'll help you with your phone. Gus is brawn."

Maddy shook her head. Rex may have inherited his father's seriousness, but he also had Frank's charm. "Message received, but I'm still in the driver's seat. Don't push for change because it would make you and your brother more comfortable having me here."

"Go ahead, continue to think of us as four-year-olds strapped into car seats in the way back. I've done more than my half. Now, it's up to Gus if he wants to make a case for Chicago—or send a moving van to the Twin Cities." He kissed them both and grabbed Maddy, who finally relaxed and settled into a tight hug before turning back toward the street. "Gotta go."

"Want to process your feelings?" Chickie called to Maddy's back as the taller woman marched out to Michigan Avenue and waved her cane at a passing cab.

Chapter Eleven

When Chickie and Maddy arrived at Lena's apartment, her brother Mitchell jerked the door open. He was impeccably dressed in slacks and a blazer, and resembled his sister, fair and fine-featured. But the attractiveness was spoiled by his scowl and the impatient tapping of a rolled-up Wall Street Journal against his thigh.

They followed him to the dining room, where Lena chatted amiably with her assembled family. Long ago, they had met Mitchell's wife, Barbie, the second runner-up in a past Miss Memphis contest; Aaron, Lena's favorite brother; and his equally attractive but untitled wife Nancy. They were all seated at the table. Empty coffee cups had been pushed aside so that the sisters-in-law could take notes on Lena's linen stationery.

The friends paused in the doorway. Mitchell marched past them into the dining room and stood at the head of the table, all the better to glower down at his younger sister, determined to finish the discussion that Lena's friends had interrupted. "What are you thinking? It's ridiculous to plan a memorial service before the burial." He snapped the *WSJ* against the polished tabletop.

"Absolutely. It isn't done," echoed his wife, Barbie.

"There's always a first time, "Aaron answered for his sister. He was a darker version of his siblings, the brilliant middle child. In their family, Aaron had been the person most reliably on Lena's side since they were children, and he was the brother she'd lived with when she first arrived in Chicago. Aaron had been around through her injury and the end of her dance career; he had promoted his baby sister's romance with Edward, and before he moved away to take a fellowship, he had helped Lena reinvent herself after leaving the ballet corps.

"Why does Lena have to rush into a memorial service?" Barbie shook her head in shocked disbelief as if Lena had proposed lighting a funeral pyre on the roof deck.

The siblings and spouses continued to squabble. Bored, Lena turned her attention to her friends, who remained in the doorway. "Hi, want something to eat?" she asked placidly.

Chickie and Maddy shook their heads.

Lena pointed to empty seats.

Both fought the urge to flee the building, but loyalty to Lena demanded that Maddy remain, and loyalty to Maddy meant Chickie would tolerate this crowd. They pulled out chairs and sat down. Maddy removed her gray scarf and vest with a bit of show, hoping to disrupt the quarreling, but the friends' presence did nothing to inhibit the brothers and their wives. The decibel level remained high as each person exercised his or her inalienable right to proffer opinions.

Nancy, more worried about attendance than whether a shotgun service was appropriate, wailed, "So fast! There's no time for people to rearrange their meetings or schedules. Who will come?"

Maddy shot Chickie a horrified look that said "Winston!" and Chickie quickly looked away, afraid she would laugh.

"People will be notified by phone and email. It will be selective," Lena purred.

Barbie glared at her husband. "How can you let your sister do this!"

He glared back and restated his opposition. "It's too soon. You should listen to us." Maddy was reminded of her family's rescue cats, one adopted for each twin, and her scarred attempts to squeeze them into the cat carrier for trips to the vet, but strangely, Lena seemed to thrive in the midst of her sharp-clawed family. Her mood was spirited, and she continued to describe her plans as if everyone thought it was a marvelous idea to have Edward's service the next day.

The next day! This was the first time the friends realized how quickly Lena intended to move. Chickie snuck a peek at Maddy, who worried aloud that everything had happened very fast, but Lena shook her head firmly. She leaned close to Maddy and said urgently, "Do not side with my brothers. Nothing is going to change Edward's death. I know how this unfolds—people will talk. He would hate it. I hate it. I want to get the public rituals done before the town gossips take over."

Maddy wondered what type of gossip Lena hoped to avoid. Murder? Or did she realize that an accident or suicide was more likely? What had she told her family? And Lena still didn't know about Edward's possible son. Preoccupied, Maddy missed Lena's next couple of comments, but turned back in when Lena touched her arm. "Don't mind my family. I've been contending with this crowd since I could talk."

"Is this how deceased people are treated in Chicago?" Barbie demanded.

Chickie wanted to answer, "Well, we usually prop the body up on a bench at the closest bus stop, unless the weather is inclement. But Edward never took public transportation, so we probably have to develop Plan B." However, she was in Lena's home and, difficult as it was becoming, she was determined to remain a team player.

Unfortunately, some individuals on the team were less successful at playing well with others. Barbie persisted, "What are people going to say?" as if that was a genuine question.

Maddy was well acquainted with the predictable banalities and limited inventory of comments for deaths and funerals, and she shared some of their concerns, but even so, it was time to end this empty conversation. She smiled brightly and declared, "We're going to make it a lovely service; don't doubt it!" She stood, wheeled around, and left the dining room. Lena followed, gesturing to Chickie. "You can help me look at the menu."

Appalled, Chickie whispered, "I'm not great with menus," as she was marched to the kitchen.

"Everyone knows that," Lena said calmly. "Your beat was never the Women's Page. You have your assignment for today, Edward's obituary. And tomorrow I'm counting on you for day-of emergencies or gentle bullying."

Chickie wasn't sure that was much of a compliment but knew she had been excused from hand holding and food decisions, so she willingly settled down with the other two at the kitchen island. She peeled an orange as Lena read the food list to Maddy, who murmured appreciatively until a high-pitched voice from the doorway interrupted.

"You can't be serious."

The three women looked up, startled. Barbie, with the stature of the wife of the eldest son, stood, one hand on her hip and a frown plastered on her face. "I've listened to your food list. What are you thinking? Don't you realize that there is nothing gluten-free, very little nondairy, and if I am correct, which I suspect I am, the pastry will have nuts." Barbie's eyes searched the ceiling in an appeal to whatever greater power resides in lighting systems.

Help didn't come.

Chickie sized up Barbie, then looked at the Sub-Zero. *She might fit if we took out a gallon of skim milk.*

Lena also studied her sister-in-law, listening to every word. Her eyes stayed focused. She tilted her head and nodded every ten seconds or so. When Barbie took a breath, she cooed, "Darling, what would I do without you? So much to consider."

Barbie nodded with satisfaction. Clearly her supervision had been successful.

Then the house phone rang. Lena's gaze remained on her sister-in-law, "Please help me. I think it will be Dr. Sodano. He's here to talk about the eulogy. Go and charm him while Maddy and I finish up."

As soon as Barbie was out of the room, Lena folded the untouched list. "I have to scan this to the Union Club. They need it by one o'clock. Maddy, would you go and rescue Raph? He's not cut out for this crowd. They eat sweet-tempered doctors for breakfast—and then purge. Chickie and I will meet you in the study."

"What about the changes?" Maddy asked.

"What changes? This list is perfect."

"The nuts and gluten and kelp and seeds and worms—whatever she said."

"Don't be silly."

On principle, Chickie encouraged Lena. "Maybe it works in Barbie's Dream Kitchen, but not in yours." Lena glowed at this rare praise from Chickie.

Maddy saluted them and hurried out to rescue Raph. He was being handed around the living room like a tray of hors d'oeuvres, and Maddy stood helplessly for several minutes until Lena entered, grabbed her and Raph each by the hand, and smiled at her brothers. "Stand down. I'll yell if I need you," she said and quickly steered them into the library and closed the door.

Chickie was seated on the couch, where Maddy joined her. Raph looked around and smiled when he saw the armadillo footstool. "I remember when Edward brought that back from a convention in Texas. He loved it. I wouldn't have dared bring it into my home." Raph stepped around the armadillo and took a seat.

Lena remained standing. Her face was pale and strained, and they could now see that her confident veneer had been worn paper thin by wrangling her family. She kicked off her shoes and roamed the room, visibly agitated. She alternately made fists and stretched her fingers; she picked up books and papers and, without looking at them, piled them up on the desk. When a few pages fell on the floor, Lena looked as if she would burst into tears. Maddy jumped up and straightened the pile. She took Lena's hand and stood next to her without saying a word.

Lena leaned into her and repeated, "I don't know if I can do this, I don't know . . ."

From the armchair, Raph deftly moved to engage her, asking gentle questions. "I need to prepare the eulogy." He spoke with quiet confidence that seemed to calm the widow. "I can easily talk about Edward's career accomplishments and some of your joint philanthropy. I know about his not-for-profit boards and the like, but he never talked much about his past, and I don't know where he was born or much about his early life. Could we start there?"

"That's a problem. Edward had few memories from his childhood, and I don't think he would want me to share any of them. If I tell you, will you help me figure out what to say tomorrow?"

All three nodded, now apprehensive.

"It was a horribly sad story, and he was fiercely private. We have very few pictures of his family."

"He was born in Madison, Wisconsin, where his parents taught at the university. You see why he's so smart," she smiled. "But they were both killed in a car accident when Edward was seven. An icy road, his mother at the wheel. No one else was involved—only a horribly big tree.

"After their deaths, he spent the school year with his mother's parents in suburban Chicago. They were old school; very stern, not the best guardians for a sensitive boy. I never met them but, from all accounts, they sounded grim. The grandparents fought over him, the only grandchild on either side, but his mother's family had the money, home, and means to offer a prestigious education. The summers were entirely different. He stayed with his paternal grandfather on the family farm in Wisconsin."

She got a little teary and began to play with the pens on her desk, clicking them open and closed. She told them about his childhood love of painting, "I think it was an escape from his grandparents, probably like kids' video games today. He discarded paints once science took over his life."

Raph asked, "How did he discover science?"

"That was the sunny part of Edward's life. During the summers, he was close friends with a neighbor, Dirk, whose dad was the local doctor. Those two were very important to Edward; the dad took them hunting and the boys were sworn blood brothers."

She stepped over to the bookshelves and pulled out a cracked leather photo album. She removed a photo and walked from Maddy to Chickie to Raph showing them the snapshot of two ten-year-old boys in shorts and muddy T-shirts. They each held a frog for the camera. Chickie was jotting down notes for the obit, and out of habit, she took out her phone and photographed the old snapshot and the names and date neatly written on the back. She studied Edward, slim and dark next to his sturdy, freckled friend. Both boys grinned proudly. Lena patted the photo gently.

"His good grades got him into a new fast-track MD program the government was rolling out at Northwestern to address a national doctor shortage."

Raph spoke up, "I do remember him once talking about that. Medicine was a sure thing, he said. People would always need good health care; it was a safe choice. And science has a beautiful orderliness."

Lena added, "He opted for a Berry plan fellowship so he wouldn't be drafted and could enter the Navy for his medical internship. Dirk was already a Navy medic."

Raph and Chickie scribbled notes.

"At first, he was on a hospital ship, then in Da Nang. On days off, he and Dirk worked together in a clinic the Navy operated in a nearby village. Seeing children with cleft lips and palates got to him. He knew they could be helped so he began to use his free time to repair both children and adults. It put him on the sure path to surgery. He liked to fix things.

"But then, Dirk was killed on a run to pick up battlefield casualties. Edward flew home with Dirk's body and was sent on R&R to Hawaii before he completed his tour of duty. Everything about that time broke Edward's heart."

Raph muttered, "That war wrecked the nation and a generation of us in so many different ways."

"Took my brother too," Maddy said quietly.

Lena looked up in solemn surprise. "I'd forgotten that."

Raph added, "You're not alone. The entire nation tried to forget Vietnam."

Lena walked up behind Raph's chair and kissed him on the cheek.

He reached for her hand. "Thanks Lena. I can fill in from there. I met Edward after his discharge when we were both in surgical residencies. That work is good for numbing emotions, but at a cost," Raph sighed.

Lena sank down into a chair. She looked small and deflated.

Raph hurried to ask a few final questions. "I'll talk mostly about Edward's life as an adult."

"Yes. Keep it simple and show them what a good man he was." Lena started to tear up again. "That's what I want; I want them to leave thinking how fine he was, not about what happened to him!"

"His life, not his death." Raph calmly rose from the chair and knelt close to Maddy to ask if she was planning to stay with Lena. He smiled at her assurance and squeezed her hand.

"I'll be here." Maddy said, feeling a surge of sadness. She had known Edward for decades and never questioned the smooth, confident persona he displayed to the world, even to friends. She should have known better. Despite forty years of working with suffering humans she had sensed nothing of his tragic losses.

At the door Raph said, "I'll work up a first draft and send you a version this evening, Lena. Will that work?"

"Yes," Lena said, "that sounds perfect. Thank you. My sisters-in-law are taking me out for lunch and shopping before we look at the room I've chosen at the Union Club." She looked at her friends. "Please come with us. I can't be alone with the two of them; they outnumber me and will have me dressed up like a Barbie doll widow. Pun intended. Nancy was pretty well-behaved earlier, but wave designer clothing in front of her and . . ." Her voice was light, but Maddy heard the earnest appeal and agreed to join them.

Chickie also responded with sincerity. "Lena, I promise to get the obituary written and sent to the papers in time for this evening's print and online editions. I can do it, but I need to get started now. I'll call you with something soon, and we'll meet the deadline."

"You usually like shopping," Lena said, pretending to pout. Teasing Chickie lifted her mood.

Chickie was more than willing to cooperate if it meant that she would be left alone for the next several hours to write and have time to pursue her own private agenda. "Usually, malls are my happy place but, in this case, Maddy can psychoanalyze my preference to stay behind and write an obituary rather than share a dressing room with your sisters-in-law."

Chapter Twelve

The apartment emptied out before noon. Raph had to return to his office to clean up overdue paperwork and offered to drop Chickie at the Harold Washington Library. Maddy, Lena, Barbie, and Nancy waited for a cab to drive them to their lunch reservation at RL on the Magnificent Mile. Lena's brothers hung back until everyone had gone, then took a cab to GolfLab, a company that promised new technology that could analyze their golf swings and develop a plan to upgrade existing clubs or build new ones. Everyone was doing what they did best.

RL, the upscale Ralph Lauren restaurant Oprah favored, was the manifestation of an imagined good life. Photos and prints of polo ponies and yachts decorated the glossy navy walls. Guests were further soothed by the clubby feel, attentive servers, pure white linen, fresh flowers, and cautious music.

Nancy insisted on changing tables because there was a draft, and Barbie tormented the server with questions about ingredients. But once the salad with bony anchovies was repaired, and the correct brand of fizzy water was located, lunch at RL Chicago proceeded without further disruption. Although the sisters-in-law had seemed intent on revamping the staff and the menu, they were equally steadfast in avoiding any reference to Edward. Instead, they were deferential to Lena with the same patronizing attitude to "little sis" that Lena's two brothers always promoted. Lena played along. She kept up her end of the charade, showed no emotion, and only left the table once to take a call from Chickie. After what seemed like years to Maddy, it was time for their appointment with the personal shopper at Saks.

As the others left the restaurant, Maddy hung back and removed a twenty-dollar bill from her wallet. She hid it under her plate hoping it might cover some of the beleaguered server's next therapy session. Then she hurried along, morbidly curious to see what an appointment booked for family "memorial wear" would entail. She had never permitted herself to use a personal shopper and her only point of reference was *Say Yes to The Dress*. Should she expect a somber Randy to carry in endless selections in black?

To avoid entrapment, she'd proactively planned an escape route. As they entered Saks, she said quietly to Lena, "You know, I am not sure I have stamina for the whole afternoon. I might need a nap. Would it be all right with you if I slipped out in about an hour and skipped the Union Club?" She held up her walking stick in case Lena needed a reminder that she had a qualifying affliction. She knew Chickie would be proud.

Lena agreed immediately.

When they arrived on the designer floor at Saks and, as instructed, asked for Heather, they were ushered to a spacious suite with comfortable chairs, neutral colors, and soft lighting. Heather appeared, solemnly introduced herself as their style consultant, and expressed her condolences. She offered everyone cucumber water, tea, or coffee. Barbie asked for Pellegrino with a twist.

Having been cued up by Nancy, a rack of subdued style options was wheeled in for their initial consideration. All the dresses were black or navy.

"Equally acceptable," Heather assured them, but Nancy was having none of it.

"No navy for the widow," she said, crushing the blue dresses toward one end of the rack. Heather didn't blink, but Maddy flinched and had to refrain from rushing over to smooth out the wrinkles. Their style consultant removed the first black dress from the rack and Lena began to undress. She seemed brightened by the idea of choosing an outfit that Heather described as, "soothing but stylish for a new role and a difficult day."

Lena slipped the sheath on and smoothed it over her hips. She faced the mirror, then looked questioningly at the others.

Nancy said, "It works; serious but not depressing."

Barbie sipped her water and pretended to whisper. "It's a little sexy. Be careful. That partner of Edward's has had a crush on you for years. You don't want to give him the wrong idea."

Lena simply shook her head dismissively, but Maddy, who had been examining the seams and hems of dresses, forced her voice into neutral. "Oh, which partner is that?" The other three brushed aside the question in favor of an animated discussion of hem lengths. Maddy was reluctant to ask again. Could it be Raph? No, Brian was the one who rushed to be with Lena. But he was married. Raph? He had certainly been concerned about Lena, driving out to the airport to pick them up. Suddenly her right side stiffened, a sure sign she was tired and stressed. She leaned against the wall and said nothing.

Nancy contemplated the rack of dresses for a long moment before addressing Heather, "Do you have any black pants suits, something in an ankle length pant?"

Heather departed.

As Lena tried on a second dress with Maddy's help, Nancy sidled closer and closer to one of the banished navy dresses, finally holding it against her and swinging left and right in front of the other mirror.

"You ought to try it," Lena said, unleashing the shopping fervor that had been simmering in both Nancy and Barbie. She whispered to Maddy, "Withdrawal. They probably haven't been in a dressing room in several days. Their main activity is shopping four days a week and returning stuff on day five. You don't want to get in their way."

Maddy had to admit that she was learning a great deal about Lena, and it was well past time to update her views. Lena had preserved a lithe and light-hearted appearance, perhaps surgically enhanced, but today Maddy saw depth and solidity. She found the whole process fascinating, except for this recent suggestion that one of Edward's partners had a crush on Lena.

When Heather brought in the second round of dresses and pants suits, Maddy seized the opportunity to excuse herself and slip away. She breathed more easily once she reached the escalator, and on the first floor, she paused at a display of charming silk and cashmere scarves. Maddy stared. She had just spent several hours with three women who had no problem requesting a different restaurant table, fizzy water, or ankle-length pants. They didn't seem to worry about being selfish. Maddy stroked a soft lilac and gold scarf and thought about this predicament.

Fifteen minutes later, back on Michigan Avenue, she wore the splendid scarf and clutched a Saks shopping bag that held the old gray one. She ordered a Lyft. It was a short ride back to the hotel and she relaxed in the car, selecting the best moments of funeral shopping to present to Chickie.

The Palmer House was calm and quiet. "Not the trip we planned, but the trip we're on," Maddy muttered as she slid the room card into the lock, heard the pleasant click, and opened the door to blissful silence.

EARLIER, AFTER RAPH and Chickie escaped from the Gold Coast Memorial Planning Session, he drove Chickie to the Harold Washington Library on South State Street. She had seen photographs of the fortress-like building, but it was her first visit, the library having been built long after she left the city. For Chickie's entire literate life, large public libraries were a sanctuary. She sought them out when she traveled, whether for work or pleasure. Chickie settled herself in the public reading room and looked around, content. She belonged among all the readers and words, enjoying the good lighting and a common hush that offsets loneliness. She intended to explore the building, particularly the Collections Department and the Winter Garden, but not until she wrote and submitted Edward's obituary.

That task was routine, completed within an hour. She called Lena, who was then eating lunch at RL. She approved the obituary. "A couple of paragraphs; I guess that's enough for everybody but me. Thank you." Then, very Lena-like, she switched moods and cryptically whispered, "Ask Maddy to tell you about the anchovies; got to go," and hung up.

Anchovies? Chickie was sure that even Scout Maddy's empathy was being strained by the sisters-in-law. Certain that she had the easier task, Chickie submitted the obit in time for the online and print editions. Then she turned her attention to her private agenda, determined to quench her curiosity. There was more to learn more about Edward, a man they had found perfectly dull until this week. Because of her position at Reuters, and their corporate subscriptions to news archives, Chickie had broad access to public records. She started with Edward's reputation on doctor review sites and found some effusive online comments by sycophantic patients. These were countered by others that mentioned he "could have been warmer," and one or two other vague complaints. Reading between the lines, Chickie surmised that several former patients did not turn out as beautiful as they had hoped. Plastic surgery had failed to solve all their problems. She jotted a note to herself to find out if the surgery practice used reputation fixers to bury grievances.

Next, she checked the state licensing board, which had received some ordinary complaints, none worth a murder. Then, she logged onto the Cook County Clerk's office. The electronic docket search revealed a couple of civil cases, but they were several years old and had all been settled. Chickie wondered what the Tabernacle of Beauty paid for malpractice insurance; it would feed a family for a long while, she guessed. Again, there was nothing to indicate that Edward had done anything that would drive someone to murder him.

She knew Maddy was intrigued by the existence of Winston. Could a secret son be possible? Winston's online company bio mentioned he was born in Hawaii. That fit. Earlier in the day, when she'd given Raph information for the eulogy, Lena said that Edward had accompanied Dirk's body home and been assigned R & R leave in Hawaii. That was the only trip Chickie knew about, although there may have been additional ones. It was a place to start and had to have happened in the weeks after Dirk's death. She pulled up a photo on her phone—the reverse side of the one of two boys and their frogs. It was carefully titled Edward and Dirk Mattingly. She ran Dirk's full name through a search in the online Mineral Springs newspaper archives and, of course, found the announcement of the death of a local serviceman, the doctor's son. It was long on tragedy and short on facts, so she used the name and date to scan Navy records to confirm the details. Just as Lena said, Dirk had died on a failed combat rescue flight. The quotes from his young wife and father were heartbreaking.

Chickie took photos and kept reading. If Edward subsequently went to Hawaii, he would have been there in February or March of 1971. She could double-check that possible conception with Winston's birthdate. It was on the curriculum vitae he'd included with the letter, no doubt intended to impress Edward and prove that he was not a crackpot—at least not an unaccomplished crackpot. Out of habit, she took photos of the documents. Then, she moved on to confirm the early life of the mysterious Winston. This was an easy search, since he was with a well-recognized genetics research firm in Oxford and had gotten there through the predictable academic pathway that required publications and presentations to all the right people in all the right places. The titles of the academic papers were incomprehensible and probably irrelevant, but the search engine also produced links to international conferences, including the one currently in Chicago, and there she could see a photo and brief biography. It was the same photo they had seen last night.

She followed him all the way back to his early school days and made some guesses based on the brief information in Winston's letter to Edward. She was able to confirm that there had been a Winston Edwards at Punahou. He'd been a cross-country runner there and genetics major at Johns Hopkins. After his AB and a masters in genetics, he went on to Oxford for a PhD. A photo from Oxford matched the picture of the man presently attending the Chicago genetics conference. *Okay, so he is real. That didn't make him Edward's son.* And she reminded herself of what Lena would say—just because he looks pleasant doesn't rule him out as a killer.

She made more notes. Finally, she accessed the genetics conference schedule and carefully went through the list of speakers on the day of Edward's death. Sure enough, Winston Edwards spoke about Watson-Crick and cytosine in the morning and sat on a panel afterward. Hmm, sorry she missed that talk. If everyone fell asleep listening to him, he could have snuck out and murdered the man he believed to be his father. But schedules change, so she'd have to check. If he didn't work out and Lena still needed a murderer, maybe they could pin it on Barbie.

Chickie's Blog:
Old Dogs, New Tricks
(A Writer's Reflections on Growing Old
and Growing Up)

Family Bonds

As I've written previously, I'm visiting Chicago, where I lived for six life-altering years. The trip continues to be an eye-opener. Readers, if you are ever searching for a writing topic, dive into your past. I'm finding that my trip down memory lane is practically drowning me, never a strong swimmer, in reflections. Today, watching a friend manage her well-meaning but incredibly conventional sibs, I've been thinking about the bonds of family.

I moved away from home when I graduated from college and never went back. Many of our generation did the same thing. Although my family has remained very important to me, the group certainly contains a few I would not choose as friends. We don't have much in common. We think and live very differently. I've never appreciated the cliché "blood is thicker than water." My friendships are not anemic, and a couple of my blood relationships are practically hemophiliac.

I do believe these bonds have a lot to do with the past. We create these deep ties, however conflicted, early and they are not easily broken. I asked my friend Maddy, who is a social worker. She said family solidarity is a fantasy but deeply, deeply held, almost primitive. We feel disloyal if family ties disintegrate. We feel disloyal if we cut the ties—even if it is the only way to preserve our sanity or safety. We preserve the myth of family even when reality dictates otherwise. Here's a story Maddy told me: her friend had an awful, abusive mother and when she died, Maddy said (in her ever-empathic way), "I'm sure you are relieved." Her friend was stunned, momentarily angry, but very quickly realized the truth—yes, she was relieved to have an awful relationship finally end.

Chapter Thirteen

Maddy and Chickie arrived at the polished brass doors of the Union Club to double-check arrangements for Edward's memorial service and pitch in, if needed. Hannah, the director of catering was summoned, and she reassured them that the staff had almost finished readying the Heritage room and had carried out all the instructions in record time. Everything would be ready for the noon service. When Hannah learned they had not previously visited, she invited Chickie and Maddy to explore and have coffee before they went upstairs to survey final preparations.

The women immediately ducked into the ladies' lounge. When they had lived in Chicago as young women, the cost of the Union Club was far out of range for them and their friends. The feeling of intimidation had not quite vanished. Neither admitted that the elegant private club made them self-conscious, but both stood in front of the large mirror, brushed off their black slacks and straightened their tops. Maddy wore a gray turtleneck sweater with her new, soft scarf. In her opinion, although she would never have mentioned it, the small aqua penguins on Chickie's black blouse were questionable. The dark blazer covered most of the birds, but still. Each woman applied lipstick. Chickie added a swish of blush and offered it to Maddy, who declined.

The club's designer had gone for an expensively modest look with dark wood paneling, heavy trim, and floor-to-ceiling bookcases crammed with leather-bound classics on the top shelves and inviting beach reads below. They admired the overstuffed sofas and well-worn seating.

"Like the British drawing rooms in your PBS shows," Maddy whispered. She was right. If the family spaniel bounded in carrying a limp pheasant in his jaws, neither woman would have blinked.

"I read that private club licenses have been revoked because their fireplaces were too small to roast an elk," Chickie explained as she eyed the massive stone structure. "My first apartment was smaller."

Behind her, a young server grinned approvingly and asked them to make the first decision of the day: which type of coffee or tea to enjoy while they waited. Some minutes later, from the depths of a soft leather club chair, Chickie admitted, "I like this place." Her latte was perfect. She wanted to take her shoes off and settle in forever.

"And I thought you didn't believe in private clubs," Maddy reminded her from the nearby couch.

"I try not to be narrow-minded."

Maddy murmured distractedly. Her attention was fastened on the tea service that had been delivered to the low table in front of her. Next to the teapot, there was a matching floral cup and saucer, a scone and tiny bowls with jam and clotted cream.

"As I age," Chickie continued, "I've come to increasingly appreciate comfort. I recently gave Sam my sleeping bag and all my camping equipment. I consider it another step toward self-actualization."

"The new you is ready for radical acceptance of ease and luxury?"

"I think the trending term is 'embrace.'"

"Ah, you are embracing luxury and comfort on your journey. It's always a journey, I think, especially when we slog along toward self-actualization." Maddy nibbled the scone.

"Yes, it's all about psychological health; I knew you would understand."

Reluctantly, they finished their beverages and Hannah returned to escort them up the wide mahogany staircase to the second-floor room Lena had chosen for the service. The Heritage Room was an oval, simple and beautifully proportioned. The walls were decorated with panels of pale-yellow wallpaper interrupted by four sets of matching double doors, each trimmed with ornate white molding. The patterned blue and green carpet reminded Chickie of her tour of the White House when she first moved to DC.

"Let me know if you need anything. My office is on this floor," Hannah said and left. The two women toured the room quietly. Approximately forty chairs were arranged in rows in a U shape with the innermost row marked "reserved." A microphone stood on a small podium with two dozen bottles of water on the hidden shelf. No Union Club speaker would ever suffer from dehydration.

Two tastefully lavish floral displays had been placed at the rear of the room, but Lena had nixed video and photographic displays. "If they don't know what he looked like, they shouldn't be in the room," she said tartly, so Maddy and Chickie left the pictures they had collected from Edward's office in the box at the hotel.

A bar and buffet table were set up against the east wall. All the linens were starched and white. When the friends entered, two Union Club staff members, also starched and white, set out napkins, arranged food, and carried carafes of coffee, tea, and wine. It wouldn't be a large crowd; they expected between thirty and forty guests.

Lena knew that the speed of the memorial service made it impossible for many friends to attend, and that was fine with her. A few might be miffed, but their reactions were irrelevant. Given that Edward had no extended family, and he and Lena did not have children, there were surprisingly few people to please when it came to making arrangements. So, Lena pleased herself and that meant all public rituals would be small and speedy. Her grief was private and belonged to her alone. And the rest of her inner circle silently agreed that since the papers had already reported Edward died in front of a train, speculation was inevitable. Fewer guests, less conjecture.

"It's beautiful," Maddy said. "Perhaps you could stage my service here."

"Not your style. Your service is going to be at Lumberjack Jack's Saloon on I-35 outside Minneapolis, while the regulars play pool,"

Chickie declared. "And it will be a cash bar."

Maddy was planning her retort when they heard sounds of distress coming from the adjacent room. They looked at each other and approached the door. Weeping. They pushed open the door to enter a simple kitchen area. The young woman who had been in the Heritage Room folding napkins was wringing a dish towel into an impossibly tight coil. She stared down at four sumptuous trays of small sandwiches. The friends followed her gaze to the splendid little treats. There were no crusts on the bread and herbs and flowers decorated each sandwich. The platters looked perfect, but the woman's whimpers drew their attention back to her.

Chickie nudged Maddy as if to say, "Go, do your thing," so Maddy approached the woman. She didn't have to ask any questions. Seeing a sympathetic face, the server threw her hands up and uttered tearfully, "It's not my fault!"

"What happened?" Maddy asked. "Everything looks lovely."

"The sandwiches! Mrs. Jordan's sister-in-law just called, and Hannah referred her to me because I'm in charge. My first time being in charge!" she wailed.

"Everything looks lovely," Maddy repeated.

"No!" she pointed to her cell phone. "That woman asked about vegan choices for guests, and when I said I didn't know, she shouted at me. But I'm doing exactly what Mrs. Jordan asked for!"

Both women frowned. "Don't worry," Maddy said. "We can guess who called."

Chickie walked around the table to inspect the sandwiches. Her latte-induced good mood had dimmed, and she blamed Barbie. She shooed the young woman away saying, "You go ahead and finish your work. We will fix this situation, I promise."

Maddy knew exactly what Chickie had in mind. She unwound her scarf and pushed up the sleeves of her sweater, then hesitated. "Are you sure?"

"Yes, I vote to get involved and keep the peace. We do not want to hear from Barbie during the service, and Lena will have so much going on that we could substitute White Castle sliders and she'd never know."

The young woman had left the room, gratefully busying herself with drinks, so she didn't hear Maddy say, "Vegan, here we come."

They got to work on one plate, removing meat and anything else that Maddy said was an animal product. They ate the evidence and rearranged the sandwiches. When they finished, Maddy found a note pad with the Club logo, ripped off a sheet, carefully printed 'VEGAN' and placed it on one of the trays. Like a pair of Cheshire cats, they shared conspiratorial smiles and departed the back room.

With time to spare, and no longer grumpy or hungry, they settled in the last row of chairs. Maddy texted with her sons. All communication for the last two days had carefully steered clear of topics related to moving to Chicago, health, or aging. They were presently reduced to weather and updates about Lena.

Chickie removed her shoes and dug her feet into the soft carpet as she rechecked Lena's to-do list. Done, done, done. As she had gotten into the habit of doing several times every day, Chickie looked for a message from her daughter Steph announcing that she was returning home. It wasn't there. By 11:30, with Chickie's shoes on and Maddy's cane parked in the coat closet, they dragged the two large floral displays closer to the back row of chairs and stationed themselves at the open doorway.

Shortly before noon, guests began to wander in, guided by a discreet sign downstairs and the courteous staff. Maddy and Chickie were kept busy answering—or not answering—questions.

When a few bold invitees ventured, "I'm uncertain; how did it happen?" or "No one has said exactly what caused Edward's death," they responded with a prepared answer, "Details are still vague," and directed guests to the memorial book on a nearby stand.

Maddy and Chickie recognized a few people. Brian, Edward's partner, arrived with a refreshed blond who was probably his wife and pushed a very, very elderly woman in a wheelchair.

"Who's that?" Chickie mouthed to Maddy.

"I assume it's Brian's mother in the chair. Lena says they adore her; she lives with Brian and his wife. "

"In the house?"

"Of course, in the house. Where else?"

"I don't believe it. I'll bet he wheels her out of the storage locker for public appearances."

"Really Chick, obnoxious men can still love their mothers."

Chickie had stopped paying attention. Her eyes were on a handsome pair of twins who had reached the top of the stairs. She left her post to join them. "Rex, Gus. Is showing up part of the campaign to lure your mom to Chicago?"

Gus reddened but Rex answered resolutely. "I'm as stubborn as she is." Gus elbowed his brother. "Seriously, Lena has always been great to us, and we wanted to pay our respects, even though we have to go back to work right after the service. Mom knew we would be here." They moved toward Maddy as Felice, the Tabernacle of Beauty receptionist entered, glanced appreciatively at the Wells twins, avoided both women, and took a seat on the far side of the room.

The guests were on time. All attendees were well dressed, somber, and most were of a certain age—Medicare qualified. They greeted each other quietly, introduced others, and made small talk until Lena entered, a brother on each elbow. She wore her new black outfit in a way that made several women envy bereavement: a simple, exquisitely cut black sheath, bare legs in stiletto heels and ropes of pearls. Her hair swung around her pale but composed face and she looked almost sexy. Almost. Lena said hello to everyone, whispered to Raph, and exchanged kisses with most before sitting in the front row. She looked around, then sent her sister-in-law Nancy to find Maddy, Chickie, and the twins, and move them right behind her. Nancy looked lovely in the navy dress from Saks.

The Union Club staff closed the heavy doors.

Maddy opened her handbag to check her supply of tissues.

Chickie leaned across Gus. "Got any M&Ms?"

She handed Chickie a tissue and a look. "Do you think Winston might show up?"

"He's worked very hard to get this far. Who knows?"

Maddy sat very still, curious, imagining possibilities. Would Winston make an appearance? What might happen? She was relieved when the service began.

Lena had decided not to speak. When the room had settled into silence, her oldest brother, Mitchell, welcomed everyone on behalf of the family. A pianist from the Chicago symphony played "Pathetique."

Lena's brother Aaron read Ithaka by C. P. Cavafy. If it was good enough for Jackie Kennedy Onassis, it was good enough for Edward.

Maddy felt strangely unmoved. It was all too neat, too proper she thought, until Raph came to the podium and gazed warmly at the crowd. He recalled his own invitation to join the practice years before, his steady admiration for Edward's skill as a surgeon, and the collective shock at the sudden loss.

He put on his reading glasses and began confidently, "Wordsworth, and later the Beach Boys, remind us that 'the child is father to the man.' Our early days shape the people we will become. This was certainly true for Edward, who was orphaned at age seven and lived with his grandparents until college."

Raph skipped details about Edward's youth, just as Lena had requested, and moved into stories about the man's strong intellect and motivation to practice reconstructive surgery.

"Young Edward, never Ed or Eddy, chose medicine and pursued it with dedication. He opted into a federal program that funded him to go to medical school, serve two years as a Navy doctor, and then return to a selected residency.

"Dr. Edward Jordan came of age during the war in Vietnam. It was a very different time. Today, young people visit Southeast Asia to enjoy the food and beauty, but our generation went as soldiers. From boot camp, Edward was assigned directly to the USS *Repose*, a

Navy hospital ship, where he had a steep and immediate immersion in addressing and repairing the wounds of war. At first, he loved the intensity of the work—twelve operating rooms receiving soldiers helicoptered in from the field, and he was able to practice the incredible range of repairs needed to save lives and limbs. But Edward eventually found the ship confining and transferred to the Naval Support Activity Station Hospital in Da Nang—the largest casualty receiving hospital in Vietnam. His best friend Dirk was a medical corpsman and the two were reunited in Da Nang and volunteered together at a community clinic.

"But then Edward suffered another shattering loss. Dirk was killed on a mission to pick up battlefield casualties. Though Edward rarely talked about that loss or any of the devastation he witnessed in that country, he returned home knowing he would dedicate himself to practicing reconstructive surgery."

Raph paused, took a sip of water, and found Maddy smiling at him. He ad-libbed, "Edward suffered sudden losses. He needed and wanted security and stability. It helps to explain his choices."

The room was silent. He gazed around at the assembled group. "Now we are back to Chicago, where you all have come to know him. Brian, our fellow partner, was a year ahead in the residency and, with an eye for talent, recruited Edward for private practice. His skill in repair and reconstructive surgery was evident, and the shared practice was a path to security.

"In 1982, Edward met the lovely Lena and together they created a full life in this city, but Edward also never gave up volunteering to do surgery for cleft lips and palates at Chicago Children's and has since endowed a parent education program and a children's art room that carries his name." Raph repeated a couple of humorous stories that flattered Edward, and the guests murmured appreciatively.

"To close, allow me to say that the great losses Edward faced in his life played a significant role in the man he became. He was always striving to create and protect a secure and predictable world for those he loved. He will be missed, not only by those of us in this room, but also by many he served with his talents and his generosity."

Raph looked over the edge of his reading glasses and said, "At this time, the family invites any of you who might like to speak a few brief words in Edward's honor to come to the podium." The executive director of Youth Dance spoke about Edward's generous donations and a resident from Northwestern Medical School remembered Edward's mentorship. The vice commodore from the Chicago Yacht club solemnly announced that the board had established a youth sailing scholarship in Edward's name and belabored an anecdote about sailing in rough weather.

During the final elegant encomiums, Chickie wondered what her own eulogy and laudatory speeches would sound like. She was clever, rough around the edges, a lousy wife . . . it would depend on who spoke. She'd have to discuss the guest list and potential speakers with her children, maybe leave a rough draft of laudatory remarks and preferred adjectives. Sam and Steph would certainly love that conversation. She hoped that one of her mourners would be honest enough to describe how messy life is, how carefully made plans are shattered, and, on some days, how much work it takes to get from morning to evening. Her own life certainly had been untidy and now, in spite of the airbrushed speeches, it was clear Edward's life also had dark patches. Maybe looking backward, when life is all done, decisions look less disordered, and some sort of pattern emerges. *Something else I can write about*, she realized.

Brought back to the present by guests stirring in their seats, Chickie took a final look around the room to study the mourners. *Bingo*, she thought and said to Maddy, "Back row on the left."

Maddy nodded and slowly swiveled in her chair. A solemn, dark-haired man with Asian features sat quietly in the shadow of one of the large floral arrangements.

Chapter Fourteen

After the service concluded, the twins ducked out, and the rest of the guests moved quietly toward the food or toward Lena. Maddy stared at Winston, or at least the man they imagined was Winston.

Chickie said, "He looks like the photo from the company website. I'm going to check him out before he decides to take off," and she was gone before Maddy could decide whether it was the right direction to take. She stood slowly, uncertain of whether to follow. One of her legs was stiff, so she walked cautiously and was midway across the room when Raph stopped her. He held his reading glasses and a couple of pages of notes.

"You did a great job!" she said enthusiastically, patting his sleeve.

He waved the papers. "I should have consulted you; I could have used a social worker's perspective on what to say and what to omit."

Maddy colored slightly. "I would love to help. Next time, call. Although I don't wish you to have a lot of upcoming memorial services. You were the perfect person to tell Edward's story, and you captured exactly how Lena wants him to be remembered."

Raph beamed, "Perhaps . . ." but at that moment, his partner Brian interrupted their conversation. Maddy slipped away. She had noticed a familiar Chicago face, much older now, seated alone in the middle of a row of empty chairs. Dr. Gerald Stanton was a med school professor who had mentored both Edward and her husband Frank. He had sent a gracious note after Frank's death.

"Dr. Stanton?" She placed her hand on his shoulder and leaned over his chair. He had begun to gather up his jacket and a silk scarf, ready to leave, but paused. Maddy reintroduced herself and his face brightened. She eased into the nearest chair, and they happily indulged in a series of "remember when" that proved long-term memory is indeed an enduring mental process.

Maddy found the recollections sweet, not maudlin. "The work and family problems that kept me awake many nights, feel like old friends today. I'm losing sleep over other worries now."

Dr. Stanton agreed. "Time is my enemy in so many ways, but as a friend, it softens memories. The years have rendered old worries harmless, and the events, stressful at the time, have faded like the ugly wallpaper in my mother's hallway. I now know how those problems turned out. The kids graduated or not, the biopsy was malignant or benign, the relationship endured or ended. Good or bad; it's done. One fascinating aspect of being an old man is that the important questions of my youth have been answered." He paused self-consciously. "Sorry. Since I turned eighty, I indulge myself by reflecting on the past more than most people appreciate. Enough rambling. This has been terrible news. How is Lena?"

"She's stronger than she appears."

"Good." He lowered his voice to say, "I don't want to be intrusive, but I'm confused about the cause of Edward's death. Accident or suicide?"

Maddy hedged, not knowing quite how to answer. "One always wonders in a situation like this. The results will be in today or tomorrow."

"I apologize if I'm putting you in an awkward position."

"You're not, and I suspect you are asking for a reason. What makes you think of suicide?"

Dr. Stanton stammered and turned his hands palms up, as if he was uncertain whether to continue.

"Please."

"I know Eddy—but I never knew he didn't like being called Eddy—wasn't well. We talked several times during the year and had cocktails together two weeks ago. He was worried."

The surprise must have shown on Maddy's face. "What was wrong?"

"It's not my place..." Dr. Stanton was increasingly uncomfortable. "I should go. I'm afraid I burdened you with information that Lena may not know. I will talk to her if you wish, or you can inform her that her husband consulted me, and she can always call me." He stood up and excused himself.

Maddy remained playing with her scarf, troubled. Another grim secret, she thought, feeling the weight of more confidential information. *Do I radiate 'professional secret keeper, professional secret keeper, come right this way?* She looked uneasily around the room for Chickie and spied her still talking animatedly with the dark-haired man. He must be Winston.

The night before, fueled by the Palmer House's famous Bertha's brownies, they had agreed to wait until Lena's family left town before springing Winston's letter on her. It would have to happen soon. They concluded that they were on safe, or at least excusable, grounds to delay the news because it would turn her world upside down again. Now, it looked like the letter writer was seated in the chair next to Chickie. His existence—son or fraud—could send Lena's world flying off its axis.

Chickie better find out if Winston seems trustworthy before they tell Lena. Perhaps Chickie needed help; she was heavy-handed at the best of times. What if she came on too strong and scared him away? Maddy's anxiety skyrocketed. She rose with effort and approached the row of chairs where the stranger was seated next to her friend, leaning in, looking engaged. As she came close, Chickie gestured to her, "Maddy, come meet Winston. He's visiting from London to attend a neuroscience convention. His mother knew Edward a long time ago, and when he saw the death notice in the *Tribune*, he came to pay respects on her behalf. Isn't that lovely?" Chickie asked as if she hadn't spent a good part of the previous day trolling him online. "I was explaining that we have known Edward for a long, long time."

Chickie was uncharacteristically chatty, confiding useless facts about Lena and how she had come into their lives before meeting Edward, and dangling other details to ensure his continued curiosity.

Maddy confined herself to studying Winston's reactions. After years of doing clinical intakes, Maddy assessed the man in chart-writing terms: Medium-height, dark-haired male, brown eyes, olive skin, probably mixed ethnicity, a few gray hairs, appears to be mid-forties, good hygiene, well nourished. Athletic build, dressed in dark business suit, Oxford blue shirt and maroon tie. Alert but subdued.

Whatever frustration or loss he might be experiencing, it was not visible. And he seemed comfortable in a sea of strangers. Maddy was beginning to relax when Chickie's sweet chattering took its usual direct turn. "So, this friendship must go back a long way. How did your mother know Edward?"

Winston shifted his gaze momentarily and answered simply, "Edward was in the Navy on R & R in Hawaii. My mother and her family were born in Vietnam, but she and my grandmother fled to Hawaii when she was in her late teens. She met Edward there."

"Have you ever met him?"

"No, they knew each other before I was born, during the war. I happened to be here in Chicago and saw the notice of the memorial service. The service wasn't marked as private."

The more Chickie questioned his story, the more defensive, and the less genuine Winston sounded.

"Does your mother know you're here?" Chickie pressed.

"My mother died six years ago, but I happened to see the obituary, and it made me think of her and want to come. The notice didn't say 'private service.' I'm not a funeral crasher."

"Do you always read obituaries when you travel?" Chickie asked, showing both dimples.

Winston's smile froze. He was obviously relieved when Raph approached bearing two glasses of wine for the women. Winston started to rise, but Maddy laid a gentle hand on his sleeve and said, "Please stay for a few more minutes. You take this glass. I am going to get some lemon bars for all of us. I need to stretch my legs. Winston, this is Raph," she said. "I'll be back."

Winston spoke up immediately to say what a good job Raph had done. "You told his story with such detail and warmth. I was very grateful."

"Grateful? How did you know Edward?" Raph asked, confused.

Winston flushed and rose from his seat. He stepped backward, stumbling and pushed the wine glass into Raph's hand. "Excuse me for a moment; I see an opportunity to speak to Lena." He walked away.

Raph turned to Chickie. "That was sudden. Did I interrupt something?" The two of them watched Winston walk toward the circle where Lena was greeting guests, but then he veered off directly toward the exit.

"Odd," Raph said. "He looks familiar. Do I know him?"

Before Chickie could come up with an evasive reply, Maddy appeared with a tower of sweets balanced on a plate and a glass of Chablis in her other hand. She flinched at the sight of the empty chair and swung her head around in time to glimpse Winston's back as he disappeared through the doors.

"He's gone. You let him leave," she said accusingly to Chickie.

Raph's gaze moved between them.

"Chickie, what did you do?" Maddy asked more sharply. "You let him escape! You interrogated him in your usual stubborn way and he ran. What were you thinking? We had planned it out carefully; can't you follow the simplest instructions?"

Stunned by her friend's accusatory tone, Chickie fired back. "In fact, I did exactly what we decided." She opened her hand and waved a business card in front of Maddy's face. "Mission accomplished," she said acidly, "and without your supervision! I'm amazed the boys want you to move here; you'll arrive with a suitcase full of helpful suggestions on how they ought to live their lives. Well, if you have no further instructions for me, I'm done for the day!"

She stood up, nodded to Raph with a forced smile and spoke to Maddy. "I'm going to mix and mingle as much as I ever manage and will see you later at the hotel. Don't rush back. I'm able to push the elevator buttons without assistance."

Maddy stared at Chickie's back as she walked away. Blushing, she sat down heavily and held the dessert plate out to Raph. "Chickie and I have both had a rough week. Please forget you saw that kerfuffle." She sagged back against the chair and swallowed a hearty gulp of the Chablis.

Raph studied the plate, accepted a lemon bar, and concentrated on chewing for a moment. "I assume that nervous man—Winston is it?—has some meaning to you and Chickie. Do you want to tell me about it?"

"I can't," Maddy said regretfully. She dearly wanted to explain to Raph and bring him in to help shoulder their load of secrets, but not yet.

"Edward's death and tending to Lena seem to have brought up more conflict than you expected," he said tactfully.

She was disturbed that Raph witnessed her sharpness with Chickie and was eager to shift the focus away from the outburst. "You mentioned the other day that your wife had died; was it recent?"

"No," Raph answered, going along with her obvious change of topic. "Five years ago. Leukemia." He eyed Maddy's empty glass. "Would you like another?"

"Hmm. No more alcohol. But I'd welcome a cup of coffee." As Raph headed toward the buffet table, Maddy absently ate a second lemon bar, uncomfortable about how she'd treated Chickie, but resentful, nonetheless. Since arriving in Chicago, she'd been trying so hard to keep everyone happy, or at least less miserable, and no one appreciated it. She studied the room and could see the pain in Lena's face, the worry in her brothers', and the curiosity that many guests tried unsuccessfully to conceal. A few people lingered in front of the drinks and talked in the strained, hushed voices reserved for grave occasions. It wasn't difficult to imagine their conversations—a story about Edward, expressions of concern for Lena. And Maddy could see from the postures and glances around the room that a number of guests were discreetly probing into the cause of Edward's death.

Poor Lena. With all her quirks, she was not a gossip and must hate this type of attention. Lena stood near the podium, her back straight. Brian, Felice, and a dozen or so others gathered around her, but not too close because her brothers had not left her side; that was good. She kissed and shook hands; she accepted condolences and shared memories, occasionally patting her eyes with tissues provided by Aaron. Before Felice left, Lena took her aside to whisper together and they shared a warm embrace.

Maddy suddenly felt deeply tired. When Raph returned with coffee, she shook her head. "I think I need to check on Lena, find a washroom, and then head out." She got up slowly, holding the back of the chair to steady herself. She saw him watching. "Parkinson's," she said, "but you probably guessed that."

Raph smiled. "My mother had it; didn't slow her down either."

Maddy took her time in the luxurious ladies' room and examined the different products laid out on the marble vanity. She folded a few tissues into her handbag. When she emerged, she confirmed Lena's plans to have dinner with her family and said goodbye.

Raph waited at the top of the stairs. "If it's okay, I'll walk you back to the Palmer House."

"You didn't drive?" Maddy asked.

"I took the Metra, but I need some air and exercise before I go home."

"That would be lovely."

The capricious Chicago weather had turned unseasonably warm, and it was pleasant to head east on Jackson toward the lake. In four days, the trees had gone from crimson splashes at the tops of the maples to full splendor. Reds and golds took over and green retreated. Maddy began to feel better. At the corner of Dearborn Street, she had an idea. "Let's go this way," she said pointing to the left, "and visit The Flamingo! I need something grand and playful on this day." She was glad to be outdoors, but more than that, she wanted to postpone her conversation with Chickie.

It was impossible to miss the five-story high Calder sculpture in the spacious plaza of the Federal Building.

"It's fifty tons of firehouse red steel," Raph said. "My wife Luisa convinced me to go on an architectural walk around the Loop and the docent told us. She explained that it was a flamingo and everybody on tour nodded as if that was obvious, but I still don't see a bird."

Maddy admired his honesty and pointed upward, "I think that's a wing. Frank used to laugh at this statue and say, 'Isn't it like the government to install a giant flamingo in a climate that would kill it!'" Maddy recalled again how much she liked this city. She fished in her bag for her phone and asked Raph to take a picture of her under The Flamingo.

As they walked on toward the hotel he asked, "How is it now, with Frank gone?"

"My life feels so different, even though much of it has stayed the same. This year is better. Getting past the first Christmas, the twins' birthday, Frank's birthday, our wedding date, the anniversary of his death; each of those was rough. Once all the firsts were done, something in me eased."

They reached the Palmer House. Raph said, "I worry about Lena. I don't think she knows much about being alone."

Maddy agreed. "Learning to rebuild your life doesn't come with instructions. You think you have it under control and then some little thing grabs you, like grocery shopping." She looked up at Raph for confirmation.

He recalled his own struggle with grief. "One evening, I came home from the store with Cherry Garcia, Luisa's favorite ice cream. It sat in the refrigerator for months. I couldn't eat it, and I couldn't throw it away."

Maddy winced in empathy. "I was furious with Frank when I had to put the tax materials together last year."

Raph tried not to laugh.

"Also, Lena's very busy now; it will hit her when everyone leaves."

They said goodbye and Maddy watched him walk toward the Metra station and felt happy. It must be the sunshine. While she waited in the lobby for the elevator, she reflected on her conversation with Raph and found herself wondering what Lena did know about being alone. But then again, what did she know?

She found Chickie's note slipped under her door.

Chapter Fifteen

In the eighth-floor exercise room of the Palmer House, Chickie sat on the recumbent bike and pedaled furiously. Her ever-patient yoga teacher always cautioned, "Where attention goes, energy flows." When she relived her anger at Maddy for that public scolding, she pedaled fast, but when she recalled how Maddy earnestly veganized and rearranged sandwiches, her mind relaxed and so did her speed. Ugh. Either way, she knew they were bound to have a discussion and "process" the exchange.

By the time Maddy entered the exercise room, Chickie's workout had come to an exhausted standstill.

"I'm glad you left a note, so I could find you. Let's talk," Maddy said, all smiles.

"What a fine idea!" Chickie answered, smiling even more broadly. "I was thinking about what a growth experience it will be to process the memorial service and your bad manners."

Maddy winced, but she sat down on a workout bench across from her friend and admitted, "I overreacted when I saw Winston leave. I thought we lost our chance to find out if he is Edward's son."

"You didn't trust me to question Winston, and you were rude about it. You do know people other than you have capabilities. Granted, you might be at the top of the Life Management Skills class, but the rest of us can make coffee, conduct interviews, and blunder from morning to evening." She began to pedal fiercely again.

"To be accurate, you cannot make coffee. Otherwise, you're

correct." Maddy had been distracted by her conversation with Dr. Stanton, she'd been in physical pain, and she was having a difficult time at the first memorial service she'd attended since losing her own husband. She hadn't meant to reprimand Chickie. She conceded, "You know that I have more trust in you than most people I know. You are indomitable!"

No one had ever called Chickie indomitable before, but she was not ready to relent. She was not going to make it that easy. She bent over her bike and pedaled faster.

"I'm sorry," Maddy said. "Look at me. I'm sorry. I was wrong."

Chickie was thrilled to stop pedaling. "Was that so hard?"

Maddy bristled. "You just went running off—"

"So that's it. I hustled while you needed more time to think. Maybe you spend too much time deliberating instead of acting. Today, when I made our plan happen, you were more than ready to believe I screwed it up, but I got Winston's card in the first two minutes of our chat."

Maddy was hurt. And surprised. Chickie was usually direct, but rarely sharp with her.

"Do you believe that?" she asked.

"Do I believe what?"

"That I think about things, but I don't do much."

Chickie saw that Maddy had taken her comment very seriously. Finesse was not her forte, but this mattered. "I believe you try to be Too Good and that slows you down. There is such a thing as Too Good, or there ought to be. Being Too Good keeps you focused on others; it gets in the way of being yourself. It makes you slower than you need to be. Maybe that's why you feel stuck in your life now, but hey, analysis is your field, not mine."

"Oh." The words stung Maddy, and she yearned to protest but the observation was uncomfortably accurate.

Chickie assumed they were finished with the conversation and clambered off the bike. She wiped her face and neck with a towel. "Let's go. We've processed enough, even for you."

Maddy wasn't done at all, but further conversation about being Too Good had to wait. "I need to tell you about my conversation with Dr. Stanton," she said. "And you must tell me about Winston."

Upstairs in her room, Chickie knelt in front of the small refrigerator and removed two small bottles. "I've never attacked an in-room bar the way I've ravaged this one." She unscrewed the red wine and handed a white to Maddy.

"We could go downstairs," Maddy offered reluctantly from the club chair.

"Not in my tush-hugging exercise pants. They're stuck to me and I'm too exhausted to pull them off," she grumbled and climbed onto her bed.

In the armchair, Maddy slouched down, kicked off her shoes, and lifted her bare feet to the bedspread, pouring her wine into a glass. "Take off your sneakers."

"They're cross trainers." Chickie sipped from the small bottle. "The hotel doesn't change the sheets every day, but they refill the fridge; it's a Christmas miracle."

"You don't celebrate Christmas."

"That makes it more of a miracle for me."

Maddy described Dr. Stanton's knowledge that Edward had a medical condition and had refused to disclose it. Maybe Lena knew; probably not. More secrets. The days were skidding from bad to worse to worser. Illness could depress anyone, but for a man like Edward, who wanted to control his world, any impairment was a powerful reminder that too many events were out of his hands. It didn't matter that Edward had passed the age when people retired. It was all about control.

You would know about control, Chickie thought, but she listened and then recounted her meeting with Winston. "He gave me his name, mentioned the conference, and told the story about his mother knowing Edward in the distant past. It was all well prepared, all planned. He didn't deviate. At first, I couldn't challenge him directly, Lena was standing twenty feet away, so I played up the close relationship, hinting that we held the keys to all the Jordan secrets. I made sure he wanted to know more."

"That's calculating."

"I wasn't doing therapy; I was fishing."

"I thought he seemed like a sincere person," Maddy said.

"You do see the glass half full." Then pointing at Maddy's glass she said, "At least until you swallow the contents."

"These are very small bottles," Maddy said. "I'll be right back. My fridge is stocked too." She returned with two reds and drank them both as they talked. Having little real information about Winston, speculation was all that was left to them. Finally, Maddy asked, "Do you believe Winston is Edward's son?"

"Could be. The age is right. It's a strange claim to make if it's false. He's got a reputation to protect. Geneticist screws up and accuses dead doctor of being his long-lost father. That's not exactly the headline that will fast track him to tenure or a corporate vice presidency. Or whatever he's after."

Still smarting from Chickie's, "You're Too Good and that slows you down" comment, Maddy decisively seized Chickie's phone. "We need to talk to him again. Hand me Winston's business card."

Chickie complied and Maddy texted Winston:

> This is Chickie Altman. We met at Edward's memorial service today. If you want to continue the conversation and learn more about Edward, or if you want to contact Lena, perhaps we can help you. Please join my friend Maddy and me at seven tonight at The Gage on Michigan Avenue.

He responded immediately:

I'll be there.

Chapter Sixteen

At exactly seven, Winston entered the noisy restaurant, recognized the women from the memorial service, and slid into the leather booth next to Maddy. She pushed a basket of breadsticks toward him and was readying herself to tiptoe toward their topic when Chickie zeroed in.

"I'm pleased that you were willing to meet; it's been a long day. This is awkward for all of us, so I am going to tell you that on Friday, as a favor to Lena, we went to Edward's office to sort out his papers and bring home any personal items. We found an opened letter, and we read it."

Maddy reached across the table and put her hand on her friend's arm to slow her down, but Chickie shook it off. "We think you wrote that letter. You do know what we're talking about, right?"

Having recently experienced the sharp version of Chickie at the memorial service, Winston was somewhat prepared. However, he was shocked that they'd seen his letter to Edward and hung on to the phrase, "opened letter." Edward must have read it; somebody read it.

Just then, a waitress stopped by, and he ordered a gin and tonic before cautiously asking, "Was the letter out there, on his desk? You said it was opened; had he read it?"

"First things first. Did you write the letter?" Chickie asked again; she waited for confirmation.

Maddy looked across and saw that Chickie was holding her breath. Neither woman had much patience to play a cat and mouse game with this man, but they waited.

The gin and tonic arrived and Winston took his time, sipping from the tumbler. He sighed. This elderly pair was his best chance to meet Lena. He had seen Edward's widow glancing at them, keeping them in sight. She trusts them. He answered, "It is mine. You said it was opened; does that mean Edward read it?"

Neither woman responded.

"I never heard anything. I am glad to know it was delivered; I wondered. And he never answered. Do you think he read it?"

"We have no idea. I found it with other papers on his desk," Maddy said. "Are you sure you never met with Edward? Maybe he agreed to coffee?"

Winston shook his head. "What did Lena say about the letter?"

Again, neither woman responded.

He looked back and forth between them. "You haven't told Lena? Or shown it to her? Are you protecting her? From me?"

Maddy was moved by the emotion in his voice. "Lena is overwhelmed. We decided it was wise to sort things out first."

Chickie remained skeptical, "We need to know more about you before we dump information like this on Lena."

"I get it. You're both very protective of her. Everybody is. I noticed that at the service."

"You do realize," Chickie interrupted, "it goes way beyond Lena. When other people learn about you, they will wonder about you and the timing of your arrival. They will question your involvement in Edward's death."

"Involvement? I assumed he fell." Winston looked baffled, then alarmed. "It was an accident, wasn't it?"

"Nothing has been determined."

"Oh my god," he whispered. "Do you think there's some connection between my letter and Edward's death?"

Both women started to speak.

Maddy stopped. "Sorry," she said, "Go ahead."

Chickie asked, "What connection could there be?"

He looked at her quizzically. "I'm not stupid. I have assumed Edward never read my letter, but if it was opened and he had, then it probably surprised him; maybe it upset him or angered him. I don't imagine it was welcome, certainly not immediately. What if Edward read it and was distracted; he didn't pay attention and stumbled onto the train tracks. I know he was killed by a train."

There was a long silence. The three of them understood that stumbling was only one possibility. The others were far worse. Finally, Chickie eliminated the nastiest option. "We think you were speaking at the genetics conference when he died, but schedules change."

Winston grabbed at the opportunity to clear himself. "What time was Edward killed?"

"At 9:06 am. The train had just left one station and was eight minutes away from the next."

"Thursday?"

"Yes."

Winston's relief was immediate. He blinked and pushed the hair away from his forehead. "Oh my God. My talk was at nine o'clock. and I stayed on the dais until eleven at least. You must believe that."

Maddy nodded, also relieved.

The implications of this conversation finally reached the scientist. He sat up straight and stared directly at Chickie. "You suspected me? You already checked my schedule; you thought I pushed him! You suspected me?"

"Of course," Maddy said earnestly. "She had to rule you out."

Winston looked at the two of them with new respect, as if he hadn't quite seen them before. They were nothing like his own mother. He tried to adjust.

"There will still be questions and gossip, so brace yourself," Maddy warned.

Winston looked down and seemed to notice how tightly he clenched his glass. He opened his hands and stretched his fingers.

"Thank you for telling me that the letter was opened. I've run so many different scenarios of how Edward might respond."

"Were you planning to contact him while you were in Chicago?" Maddy asked.

"I hoped to hear from him once he read the letter. I wanted him to respond, and I might have tried again before I left Chicago. I don't know. But he died the day after I got here. I was this close." He gritted his teeth as he held his thumb and forefinger up, almost touching. "I couldn't stop wondering if . . ." His voice trailed off.

The women remained quiet.

"My letter was only for him, and now it's public property. It was supposed to be private. Who else will read it?" He dragged a hand through his hair. "How pathetic. Man tracks down his father, who is so happy that he falls under a train. I learned more about my father at the memorial service today than my mother ever told me." He brightened momentarily. "Thank God she isn't alive to hear about this."

Maddy was moved to console him, but Chickie warned her off with a look.

"How did you decide Edward was your father?" she asked.

"I'm a scientist. I study genetics." He scoffed, "A therapist could do wonders with me. Man without a father makes a career in genetic research. I'm a cliché."

Maddy saw that Winston was beginning to feel very sorry for himself; a direction that would be useless. She interrupted his downward spiral. "Tell us how you figured it out," she coaxed. "It couldn't have been easy."

"It's not terribly complicated these days. Millions of people have DNA samples in private and international databases. I have easy access. Edward's sample was there, in one of those Find Your Ancestor archives. I hypothesized he could be my father based on my genetics compared to his, plus the limited research I could do about timelines. You know, my birth, his service in Vietnam, that sort of thing. I found news photos of him; I imagined I saw a resemblance. Don't you think so?"

Both women nodded. Especially around the mouth, Winston did look like Edward.

"It's easily confirmed with better DNA testing but, from what I found, the probability is astoundingly good. If we had a DNA sample, we could test that hypothesis. And look . . . I do get that this could be all wrong and a dead end. But now, even proving he wasn't my father would be a relief! All these years, it's the not knowing that confounds me. I want answers." He brushed back the dark hair from his forehead again."

"You are not alone in wanting answers. So do we," Maddy said soothingly.

"What happens next?" He sighed heavily and looked up, clenching his fists, and rubbing them against his knees under the table.

Chickie answered, "Well, we have to tell Lena about the letter and that can't wait any longer. We don't believe she knows anything about you, but . . ." she shrugged.

"After you talk to Lena, do you think she'll want to meet me?" Again, he looked hopeful and Maddy realized that the link to someone, anyone, who knew Edward mattered deeply to him. But Lena was a wild card. Losing her husband and discovering his son several days later; that would be a lot for anyone. Lena had never desired children and now she had a middle-aged stepson.

Neither woman could provide hope.

Winston's curiosity reasserted itself. He asked, "What do you know about how he died? Everything public is so vague."

"We don't know," Maddy said.

Chickie wondered about the change in his demeanor. "You seem very calm about all of this."

"I'm a scientist. When I was a kid, I wasn't calm. I was fiercely curious. I didn't have a dad. I studied how fathers and sons behaved in restaurants or at school, simmering with so much envy I thought I would explode. I badgered my mother and grandmother with questions; I sneaked into drawers and looked for clues. There had to be a dad for me to be in the world, but I got the same story over and over. He was an American Navy man, they'd say. 'He left because he had to go back to war. You are handsome like him. No more questions.'

"Vietnamese children, even Vietnamese American children are expected to be obedient. They hinted that he had died in combat. I liked that version. I imagined he was a noble hero who never knew he had a son.

"Later, as a teenager, I did my own research but didn't get very far except that I learned a lot more about the Vietnam War. The 'noble hero' took a beating. At that point, my curiosity shut down. I'd met lots of kids who had lousy relationships with their fathers and who told me I was lucky to be fatherless. At the time, I decided I liked that conclusion. Anyway, I had a direction, science. Please, don't make me out to be some unloved boy. I wasn't. My Ba and Mai were strict and stern but loving parents. That was my mother with me in the photo I sent. And there were men on the faculty of the boarding school where we lived who were fatherly in ways that helped.

"I chose genetics because I had a great undergraduate course in it; that's what I thought at the time. Later, studying in the UK, I got drawn into the corporate world of new developments and have been there ever since." It was a relief for Winston to speak about his fatherlessness. He had been silenced his entire life.

"Are you married?" Maddy asked.

Winston blushed. His calm seemed shaken by the ordinary question.

"No," he answered sharply, then stopped. His color increased.

The women wanted to look at each other but knew better. They kept their eyes on him.

"No, I'm not married. A couple of months ago, I read some new articles about the state of genetics research and started searching again. I did a test, not expecting much, but then I checked back and there was a convincing potential match in Illinois. I admit, I wouldn't have come to this conference otherwise. I have friends on the planning committee and, when I said I would come, they invited me to speak on the opening day, right after the keynote. It all came together at the last minute."

"The conference was a legitimate excuse," Chickie amended.

"I guess, but my Ba would have said it was intended, so I wrote the letter; the one you read."

It was an oddly intimate moment. They all sat quietly until Maddy could not resist saying, "It was a lovely letter, and you can take comfort that he read it," succumbing again to her lifelong urge to smooth the sharp edges of sadness. She continued, "We can't know what Edward felt, but it means something that he kept the letter."

Chickie had another explanation that she did not share. Maybe Edward kept it to show to a lawyer or the police if he was contacted again. "We'll never know," was the best she could offer.

They looked at each other quietly for a long moment.

"Not knowing isn't new to me," Winston sighed. "What are you going to do?"

The two friends looked at each other and back at him. "We'll make a plan to tell Lena, and we'll call you in the morning," Chickie said.

Maddy added, "You've come this far. Don't quit now."

He left, and Maddy immediately whispered, "You heard him, didn't you? He said he sent a photo with the letter, but we didn't find it. Either Edward kept it, threw it away, or someone else read the letter and kept the photo."

"Now you are starting to sound like Lena."

The two friends remained at the restaurant, deciding how to handle the coming day.

Chickie quickly concluded that Maddy would be the best one to break the news of Winston's existence. "All those social worker skills; you don't want them to atrophy," she argued as she ordered Maddy another glass of red wine. "I'll bet people have heard all kinds of bad news from your unlipsticked mouth. How often have you told someone they will be hospitalized involuntarily, or that their spouse died in the ER, or that their child suffers from schizophrenia? Me, I deliver my insights on paper or computer screens. I don't see the faces of my readers. Anyway, Lena trusts you more. She tolerates my prickliness and loves my support, but you are the one to tell our brand-new widow that she might have an unacknowledged stepson."

"Admit it—you're afraid."

Chickie eagerly threw both hands into the air, almost toppling Maddy's wine glass. "I admit, I confess, I don't want to be there. It requires your delicate touch."

Maddy didn't argue. Maybe it was that second glass of wine, or imagining Chickie saying, "Twenty questions Lena, and here's a clue—he's bigger than a breadbox," but she agreed to announce Winston's existence.

The timing was fixed when she received a text from the unsuspecting widow: *my family is leaving in the morning and are insisting I join them. My life is here. I told them you were coming over in the am to keep me company* followed by a string of tiny, unintelligible emojis.

"Ha!" Chickie said joyfully. "I already made plans for tomorrow morning. I'm hoping my meeting with Alma Alberti will answer some questions."

Chickie's Blog:
Old Dogs, New Tricks
(A Writer's Reflections on Growing Old and Growing Up)

I'll Show You Mine

Well intrepid readers, it has been quite a day. Based on my recent activities, this evening's topic is "what to say and what not to say." I attended a memorial service for a not particularly close friend. In the days leading up to the service, I learned more about him than I had previously known. Some details were flattering, most were less than wonderful. Then, this morning, I listened to a eulogy transform, select, slant, emphasize (you get it) the facts to create a lovely picture, highly skewed toward sainthood. I don't mind; this was a memorial service, not a British tabloid, but it caused me to think . . . If there are a dozen flowers in the vase, six red and six yellow, and I pick out the six red blooms, I have an all-red bouquet. If I pick out the six yellow ones, I have a different look. If I mix and match . . .

Anyway, my point, before the metaphor wilts, is that all those combinations tell us something, but none of them tell us everything about the flowers in the vase. Each bouquet is valid—as far as it goes. None of them go all the way. six red flowers are true—until we add more.

Then, the six red flowers become an incomplete, even misleading version of reality.

The accurate picture of flowers in a vase is the combination, just like my not particularly close friend was a combo of admirable and less admirable qualities.

It left me thinking about what we highlight and what we hide when we engage with others and how incomplete a picture we present.

Chapter Seventeen

Maddy lay still in the dark hotel room. Filled with dread and uncertainty, she stared into the shadows. What had they been drawn into? How would Lena react to Winston? This was a terrible time to announce his existence, but there was never going to be a right time.

It was still dark when she turned on the hot shower, a gift for stiff muscles that the young could not fully appreciate. Finally, room service opened, and while she waited for her comforting pot of coffee, she diligently performed her exercises rehearsing different versions of, "I have some surprising news I need to share with you . . ." with each change of position. Every scenario ended with the same image, being strapped into a rollercoaster seat with an old friend she didn't know that well anymore. And people feel very differently about roller coasters. Lena's behavior in the last several days made it clear that she was no longer the malleable young woman they had originally befriended. But no imaginable range of experience could prepare anyone to lose their husband and discover a stepson in one week.

Maddy was relieved to hear Chickie moving around in the adjoining room and knocked.

"I have a carafe of coffee to share. It's still hot."

The journalist came in, hair wrapped in a towel. Otherwise, she was ready to go, dressed in slim navy slacks and a coral sweater, no jewelry. "I've already heard from Winston; he must still be on UK time. He wants to confirm that one of us would call if Lena is willing to meet him. I reassured him that it was still the plan. He's due to return to London in forty-eight hours but will change the reservation if Lena agrees to see him. He wants this meeting very badly." Chickie dropped the damp towel on the floor and poured coffee. She cradled the cup in her hands and inhaled happily. "Coffee used to be so cheap, I could afford it. I learned to drink it in college before I even knew you."

Maddy picked up the towel and draped it over a chair. "Was there ever a time we didn't know each other?"

Chickie made herself comfortable on Maddy's bed, spilling only a few drops on the blanket. "In the shower, for the hundredth time, I tried to imagine why Lena seems so sure Edward's death was murder, not an accident or suicide. I understand her reluctance to accept suicide. No one wants to think someone they love would do that, right?"

"Intentionally abandon them, yes. It's too awful to accept."

"But accidents happen. Murder seems so theatrical. And we would have had some hints by now; the police would be around. It's been five days," Chickie said, but stopped when she realized Maddy was no longer listening.

Maddy stood at the open closet door with her back to her friend. "What should I wear?"

"How about your scout uniform?"

Maddy didn't turn around. She was trying hard to decide on an outfit suitable for delivering unwelcome news.

Chickie joined her and examined the few hangers. Maddy's travel wardrobe was shades of gray and black. "It all looks bad-news appropriate."

Maddy frowned. She would never want an orange sweater like Chickie's, but her practical wardrobe could use more color. Maybe, for the winter, navy would be nice. She pulled out the lighter gray slacks and a soft linen shirt.

Chickie looked puzzled. "It must be a talent you learned from birthing twins. Only you could tell one pair of loose gray slacks from the neighboring loose gray slacks."

Maddy continued to deliberate. Somehow wearing the same scarf she'd worn to the memorial service felt wrong. She reached for a gold and gray striped one, took out her travel vest and held her sartorial choices up for Chickie's inspection.

"Bold."

Maddy dressed in the bathroom and returned looking apprehensive. "I'm hungry. I should have ordered Bertha's Brownies from room service. I can't deliver shocking news without nourishment."

"And Lena's house is devoid of food?" Chickie marveled at Maddy's ability to turn on, and mostly turn off emotions and focus on food. Good thing, or as a social worker, her friend would have starved to death. But she knew what Maddy was facing and felt guilty. "If you want company, I'll postpone my meeting with Alma."

They both knew she would, but they also knew that Maddy would never ask. It was a well-practiced dance—minor guilt reduction on Chickie's part and another step toward Very Good Person for Maddy. "Keep your meeting. Isn't Alma the famous Washington gossip?" she asked, trying to remember if she had met this woman.

"That is understating her considerable talent. When she lived in DC, she knew everything about everybody. Her husband was a lobbyist, and we all believe she taught him all he knew. When he retired a couple of years ago, they moved to a house in Wilmette to be near their grandkids."

"Wilmette? The town where Edward had his accident."

"Or his on-purpose. If there's any gossip to be had about Edward, Alma is our girl."

Chapter Eighteen

At ten o'clock Maddy slowly clambered out of the Lyft, conscientiously holding her cane. She missed the days when she gracefully leaped from cars, bikes, and other moving conveyances.

Jakob, the concierge, called the elevator. "A reporter from one of the papers showed up this morning, but Mrs. Jordan's brother made short work of him. I'm glad you're here in case he decides to come back. The family headed out a little while ago and she's alone up there," he said. "I can't believe that Dr. Jordan is gone, just like that." He snapped his fingers.

"We are all shocked," Maddy said entering the elevator. "Please keep your eyes open for anyone who might cause trouble for Lena. No one plans for sudden loss, but we find ways to get through it." Jakob smiled and nodded as the doors closed. Maddy was uncomfortably aware of how trite she sounded. *Maybe I could develop a Bromides and Banalities line with Hallmark? Or maybe paper greeting cards give away my age.*

When the elevator opened on the penthouse level, Lena stood waiting at the apartment door wearing loose jeans and a long, embroidered pink velvet tunic, no shoes. "I needed the family to be gone," Lena called, "but I don't want to be alone." She hugged Maddy and dragged her inside.

The apartment was full of evidence of grief and goodwill. A pile of opened and unopened cards lay on the foyer table. Maddy was delighted to see the nonvirtual, paper sentiments. In the kitchen, the housekeeper pulled dead flowers from vases and rearranged the remaining blossoms into new displays. There were trays of beautifully prepared foods and baskets of sweets. Her eyes lit up at the sight of a mushroom quiche.

The housekeeper handed Maddy a plate and she enthusiastically picked through a wicker basket stuffed with pears, cheeses, sausage, several varieties of crackers, a couple of gorgeous raspberry galettes, and boxes of different varieties of nuts.

"If nuts cure grief, I'll be joyful by the end of the week," Lena said, as she reached for macadamias and dropped several next to the galette already on her plate.

Maddy helped herself to the remaining raspberry pastry, a pear, and added a generous slice of quiche, the longed-for Bertha's brownies relegated to history. They poured coffee and carried trays to the library.

Lena sank into a club chair and balanced the plate on her lap, barely nibbling the galette. In a nearby chair, Maddy deliberated, breathed, forked the quiche into her mouth, and breathed some more. If Chickie had this job, Lena would have learned about Winston before one bright berry had touched her lips, but Maddy was looking for the right time, as long as the right time presented itself in the next half hour. Any longer and she would have an anxiety attack.

Lena poked at the food on her plate, lost in reveries, bare feet crossed on the armadillo's back. "My handsome Edward loved this ugly creature because," she said, dropping her voice in order to imitate her husband, "they're tough. Tough on the outside, tender at the core, like me." She smiled at the memory. "Apparently you can get armadillos made into baskets or purses. I think that's horrible, but Edward found this fellow amusing. And useful as a footrest."

Maddy wasn't sure that a mammal footrest was much of an improvement over a basket or purse, but one look at her friend's face and the thought died unspoken.

Lena's lovely face showed a week of grief—her features drawn, without her usual vitality. "I'm not sure what to do with myself now,

Maddy," she moaned and put her plate down. "I can't sit here and do nothing, and I have tons of energy, but it doesn't go anywhere. It feels like I'm running in the fog. I can't make up my mind, even about simple things. Our lawyer wants to talk to me, and our financial adviser has left messages. I know all about our money and our estate plan, but they treat me like an idiot, and they all sound alike. There must be a webinar on *How to Approach the Grieving Widow*. Did they do it to you? Did they lower their voices with practiced sincerity, and blather, 'We have to move on. Edward would want it.' They always say 'we'—my investment adviser and the old queen. Well, I don't want to move on; I don't see anything in the real world for me. I look out and see . . . nothing, nothing . . ." she trailed off.

Maddy took a deep breath and said, "Look, when Frank died, someone told me, 'Accept that you are in an altered state.' And you really are; you can't be your regular self or even your old self. This is new and you need time to take it all in. One hour at a time." And this next hour was guaranteed to prove that accepting unwanted reality takes time.

Lena nodded, appearing to like her friend's advice, so Maddy decided to dive in. She thought about Chickie's text: *As you delicately reminded me, keeping secrets from a friend, even with good intentions, is a betrayal.*

Maddy placed her fork carefully on her plate. "Look, on top of everything that's happened in the past few days, I have more surprising news I want to share, need to share." Lena's quota for surprising news had already been reached and breached. She didn't look very interested, calmly lifting her coffee cup to sip.

"I actually think it's good news," Maddy said. "Yes, potentially good news."

"You're getting remarried!" Lena tried to summon enthusiasm.

"No, no," Maddy hurried on. "Remember when you sent us to Edward's office to collect his belongings?"

Lena nodded, slipping back into her fog of disinterest. "Yeah, a lot of black pens, I'm sure. You said you'd boxed up everything personal."

Maddy shakily put her plate down, rose and leaned against the bookcase. Standing helped; she felt stronger. "Yes, and in the box, we found a letter tucked into one of Edward's medical journals." She stumbled over her words and Lena watched with new curiosity.

"What? What did you find?"

"It certainly wasn't intended for us to read, but it had already been opened, and it wasn't clear if the letter was business or personal."

"What did you find!" Lena demanded.

"You need to read this." Maddy took the folded envelope from her vest pocket and handed it to Lena who grabbed it with a trembling hand, then darted around the room searching for one of the many pairs of reading glasses she had scattered throughout the apartment.

Maddy watched tensely as the younger woman sat down and read Winston's letter, both pages, then read the first page again. A parade of emotions played swiftly across the pale face before Lena grew completely still. All emotion vanished except in her eyes. In those blue eyes, Maddy saw reality clash violently with denial. Lena's long marital history was at war with this latest possibility. The struggle continued for minutes, until Lena's confusion seemed to subside.

She sprang up. Her hand smacked the empty coffee cup on the side table, and it flew across the room, breaking against the marble fireplace. She strode toward Maddy glaring, her face scarlet, shouting, "Why didn't you tell me immediately!" She waved the letter at Maddy. "Why didn't you tell me? Why didn't *he* tell me?"

Maddy leaned back into the bookshelves but said nothing, didn't touch her friend, and willed herself to stay calm.

"This has to be a scam," Lena said in a lower voice, fighting for control. She pushed past Maddy to circle the room, muttering savagely. Abruptly, she stopped, crumpled up the letter and tossed it to the floor. She kicked it with her bare foot before turning back to Maddy.

"How dare you," she said accusingly, "holding onto this letter and then bullshitting me that you have good news. Next, you'll give me your psychobabble that Edward's death is an opportunity; a door closes, a window opens, clouds have silver linings . . . and . . . and . . . !" She stormed out of the room in the direction of the kitchen.

Maddy found the crumpled letter and stuffed it back into her pocket. She grabbed a wastebasket and knelt at the fireplace, carefully picking up pieces of Lena's shattered cup. She was still searching for shards when Lena strode back into the room cradling Grey Goose vodka and a carafe of orange juice. "Are you playing Cinderella?" she spat out.

Maddy moved the wastebasket to the wall, rose, and spoke in a low, tight voice. "I love you, Lena. But don't confuse the messenger with the message."

Lena just managed to set the bottle and juice down on her desk before she burst into tears. With her back to Maddy, she wiped her face on the velvet caftan and attempted to mix a drink. Her hands shook as she dumped inches of vodka, followed by a splash of juice, into a crystal glass.

Maddy went to put her arms around her, but Lena shook her off roughly. "What gave you the right to withhold this? Don't you think I've been kept in the dark enough for one week, you nosy old broad."

Maddy bit her cheek to hold back a nervous laugh. She picked up her plate, still loaded with quiche and nuts and moved to the couch, composing herself, trying hard not to be defensive.

"Once we read the letter, we couldn't drop it on you. Announcing it before the service would have been cruel, and your family would have jumped in and interfered."

Lena heard the argument, but Maddy's logic didn't matter. Clutching her cocktail, she roamed the room. Maddy took a deep breath and continued. "Chickie and I never intended to hide Winston, but we decided to first investigate whether there was any validity to his claim. It seems to have substance."

Lena suddenly stopped and stomped her bare foot. "Ouch!" she yelped, catching a sliver of the broken cup in her heel. She hobbled out of the room shouting, "Don't you dare move, you."

Maddy grabbed her phone and texted Chickie:

> I told her, and I hate you, and we are no longer friends.

Good girl was the response, followed by an emoji of hands in a scout salute.

Lena took a while to return, a Band-Aid on her foot, not calmer but more determined. "I know you. You think he *is* Edward's son, or you would never show me this letter. What if *he* killed Edward!" She was excited by the prospect of a real suspect. "He's a verifiable person, right? You already figured that out for me. Do the police know about him?"

"You can share this news with them," Maddy said in her calmest social worker voice. "But we learned more once we nosed in. When Edward died, Winston was giving a speech at a big convention; it's now online. Chickie sorted that out pretty quickly. It doesn't mean he couldn't have arranged a hit, I suppose," she added, feeling foolishly complicit. She quickly reversed course and continued. "I have to tell you that he is an unlikely killer. He's a genetic scientist with a good career. And here's the other thing. This man, who allegedly," she emphasized that last word, "is your stepson, showed up at the service yesterday. We met him."

Lena gasped. "What was he doing there! How could he!" she stammered.

"He came to pay his respects," Maddy explained.

Lena found it hard to catch her breath. Finally, she croaked, "How, how did he know about the service?"

"The memorial service was announced in the *Tribune*, and he also had a Google alert, whatever that is, on Edward's name."

"Where was he? I don't remember seeing him. Although a pink flamingo could have been sitting behind me and I'm not sure I would have noticed."

"But Nancy would have commented on the inappropriateness of

all those pink feathers . . ." Maddy said before stopping herself.

Lena gave her a genuine smile, so Maddy seized the advantage, "We'd already found internet photos of him before the service, so Chickie and I kept our eyes out for him. He must have come in late because we only noticed him at the end. Chickie briefly spoke to him. That's how things unfolded."

"But . . . but . . ." Lena stood up waving her arms, breathing heavily.

"Wait, please." Maddy stayed seated and pleaded with her friend. "Let me finish. Remember, Winston is in his mid-forties; he happened before Edward knew you. We talked to him again last night and have ended up believing he is an honest person who genuinely, earnestly, wanted to meet Edward and get to know him."

"So you say," Lena challenged. "You're easy; ever a tender-hearted social worker. Has he won Chickie over? Cynical Chickie is a better test."

"She's more than halfway there. Winston's grieving. Edward's death is a loss to him too; he hoped to meet a father he never knew."

"Don't compare our losses!" Lena sputtered, goodwill gone. She stood over Maddy and frowned down on her, hands on hips. "Well, well, you certainly became his fan, Aunt Maddy," she drawled. "His loss! The hell with his loss."

She reached over and grabbed the remaining nuts from Maddy's plate and washed them down with a gulp of her screwdriver. She returned to the desk for a refill. Maddy followed and threw a few ice cubes into the glass before Lena could lift it. In return, she received a look she hadn't earned since the twins were teenagers.

Uncomfortable, Maddy returned to the couch fighting the bodily sensation of again being in that roller coaster car crawling, crawling up to the top of the hill, teetering, and careening down. She still had more to say and spoke steadily. "And he would like to meet you if you are in any way interested. He respects your privacy and understands you are already in shock and might never want to meet him. He is braced for that. But you are one person who knows and loves Edward, someone he's longed to meet." She closed her eyes and waited.

Lena stalked over to the window with her new drink, her back to the room. Her shoulders rose and fell. Minutes passed. Maddy excused herself. In the bathroom, she splashed cool water on her neck and wrists and peeled the damp linen shirt away from her chest. She took her time returning to the library.

Lena had rounded the corner, and her attention was now fixed on her late husband. "How is it possible that we never knew about this? I don't want a stepson!" She sat down again and blew her nose. She rose and paced the room. She kicked the armadillo. But curiosity won. She could not help herself from asking, "What is he like? How does he look? Does he resemble Edward? I mean, he is half Vietnamese if this letter has any truth to it, right? I bet it is all made up. And he probably wants money or thinks he can use me. How can he prove this?"

Maddy's eyes lingered on the orange juice and vodka on the sideboard, but she restrained herself and reached for her empty coffee mug. "Come with me while I get some more hot coffee," she said, "and I'll tell you as much as I know. But these are important questions you could—and should—ask Winston in person." Maddy took another deep breath. "Today, if you want." She walked out of the room ahead of Lena, hoping she would follow, and had filled her cup before Lena padded barefoot down the hall.

Lena stood in the middle of the kitchen, confounded. "I don't know what to do, I just don't." She was worn out and that worked in Maddy's favor.

Leaning against the counter Maddy said steadily, "Okay. You don't have to like him or believe him or ever see him again, but I don't think you will feel right if you back away." Maddy was pleased with her directness.

Lena looked surprised, almost angry, then her face steadied. Wiping her mouth with a linen table napkin, she asked, "Okay. What do I wear?"

Chapter Nineteen

As soon as Maddy anxiously left the hotel to announce Winston's existence, Chickie suffered a short-lived bout of guilt, quickly replaced by deep relief. She selected her favorite Mexican silver necklace, the one that always set off metal detectors, added matching earrings that Maddy would consider excessive, and walked the short distance to the Chicago Athletic Association Hotel.

"Do you remember this place?" Alma asked in lieu of a greeting.

Chickie looked around. The dramatic changes made to places she had once known reminded her forcefully, again, of the years that had passed since she left Chicago. This building was no exception. She had always loved the elaborate Venetian Gothic-style building originally designed to impress the World Exposition visitors in 1893. After that, as a private club, it had been a respite from the surrounding city, but by the time Chickie lived in Chicago, the club was mildly shabby and very masculine, with several dining rooms, a downstairs gym, and low lighting that effectively hid worn furniture and obvious signs of a tired, uncared-for building. She and her first husband Danny enjoyed dates here, coaxing the single drinks they could afford into an evening's entertainment. Now, the hotel looked to be one of the most successful renovations she'd ever visited.

Alma gave her a quick tour of the first floor, leading her through the playful game room where guests were already enjoying bocce ball, billiards, shuffleboard, and chess, into the Cherry Circle restaurant, a throwback to Chicago backroom power lunches from the first Mayor

Daly's years. They returned to the heavily paneled bar area that faced the lake and found two slouchy chairs near a window overlooking Millennium Park and ordered coffee.

Alma said, "I've got lunch upstairs later with a women-in-politics group, but tell me all about home," meaning DC.

After Chickie surrendered whatever meager bits of DC gossip she had to offer in order to make the information trade less lopsided, they got down to it.

"I'm here because a friend died suddenly. His wife and I go back many years, and she asked for help. Frankly, I wonder if you know anything about his death?"

"Do I know him?"

"Dr. Edward Jordan."

Alma's eyes opened wide. "The plastic surgeon in the Wilmette train accident? He was a friend of yours?"

"Yes, what do you know about him?"

"I know he died. There have been other suicides at that crossing. He wouldn't be first."

"Why are you assuming suicide? It hasn't been determined."

Alma shrugged. "Daylight, good weather, a well-marked pedestrian crossing; it makes sense. But you're friends with his wife. Ask her. Wives know everything, even when they think they don't."

Chickie had no problem criticizing Lena but resented Alma's smug tone regarding her friend. "Let's momentarily look beyond your dubious assumptions. What have you heard?"

"Nothing about suicide."

Chickie impatiently called out Alma's style of doling out crumbs of information and reminded the other woman of past favors. Taken aback, Alma admitted, "I did hear your doctor friend might be named in an investigation. And a medical man caught in questionable practices is catnip to the press. Unfortunately for the family, when the legit press tires of him, the internet will continue as long as there are readers, and that seems to be forever."

"What type of investigation? Exactly what did he do? I can't believe Edward would be involved with anything medically shady," Chickie pressed, her heart sinking.

"Nothing medical. From what I hear, the brouhaha is about China and the doctor's art imports. The provenance is dubious, and people are talking."

Chickie was stunned. Art imports from China? "Edward Jordan. We are talking about the same Edward Jordan? A Chicago plastic surgeon."

"The very same. You know doctors have outsized egos," she tossed out glibly. "I heard he imported art from China and there seems to be a problem. The North Shore is like a small town, people talk. It's all secondhand, maybe third, but you asked."

Second or thirdhand meant the story had spread. Chickie replaced her coffee cup on the nearby table so Alma would not see her trembling hand. She tried to sound casual. "Maybe it was a mistake, or he was duped."

"Maybe, but maybe not. Look, I've got to make some calls before my brunch meeting. I hope you wanted that heads up. It's better to prepare your friend if she doesn't already know. You have my number and email."

"Sure, thanks," Chickie said for lack of anything else. *Not precisely the news I want to bring Lena,* she thought. *I'd rather give Putin a pedicure.*

She wandered back to the game room and found a seat where she could pretend to watch a vicious game of shuffleboard between a father and son while she reviewed Alma's news. It baffled her. It wasn't reasonable that all these surprises about Edward happened in the same week. Life isn't a TV drama, where revelations are required every five minutes to keep the viewers awake.

Then she realized they hadn't occurred together, not at all. His illness had been progressing for years, but he hadn't told anyone. And for some reason, Winston had begun searching for his father again after years of disinterest and only then found Edward's DNA in the data bank, and Edward's attempt to become an art investor wasn't brand new either and may have resulted from the declining physical condition that Dr. Stanton hinted about, a condition that would force a cutback in work.

The secrets were exposed all at once when Edward died—because he died. Had he lived, the events would have remained his to disclose, or not, as he chose. Chickie's anger flared. He'd had choices. He could have been more honest about his health and told Lena. And why the hell was he investing in art! That was foolish, no, it was arrogant. Even his surprise son—hadn't he ever heard of birth control? Mistakes piled on mistakes. One thing for sure, she didn't want to hear Maddy explain his depression, helplessness, or whatever compassionate formulation she would construct to explain his latest screwup. Chickie didn't want anyone to interrupt her anger, not yet.

Just as the shuffleboard game ended in good-natured laughter, Maddy's text came through: *You have until twelve thirty to locate Winston. Lena will meet him. Warning: she still wants a murderer, but I am doing my best to discredit that idea.*

⁀ව⁀

MADDY SANK BACK into the club chair and rested her feet on the armadillo. Surely, the animal deserved better than spending an eternity in a city high rise under an old lady's tense feet. I'll bet its friends didn't have surprise step-dillos to deal with. She closed her eyes and replayed the last hour that felt like a week.

Once Lena decided she wanted to meet Winston, there had been an avalanche of questions. Maddy walked Lena through more biographic basics on Winston, why he was not looking for money, and how he had traced the genetic path to Edward. She had been convincing; she dearly hoped she was correct.

When they got to the genetic tracing, Lena let out a small shriek. "Edward never would have agreed to it if he'd been sober, but a couple of years ago, we were at my brother's New Year's Party in Memphis and that is always out of control in a Southern sort of way. Mitchell, or more likely Nancy, had decided on ancestry DNA reports as a gift for our mother who was building a family tree. After several signature cocktails, my brother went to each family member saying, 'Open wide.' He swabbed Edward's cheek and handed him another drink. Mother lost interest in the project when she realized there weren't going to be any Mayflower ancestors. This was a couple of years ago and I never heard anything about results. Could that be the sample Winston found? Wouldn't alcohol kill everything? Maybe the swabs got mixed up."

Maddy agreed that questions needed to be answered but reminded Lena that it wasn't uncommon to locate people through popular ancestry testing sites. "Remember, Winston is in the genetics field, so I expect he knew how to double-check the validity of any apparent match. You certainly could, and should, ask him how he decided this was possible."

"If he's such a genetics genius, he would know how to fake results," Lena added petulantly.

"Why? What would his motive be? If he's a fraud, it would wreck his career," Maddy added.

Chapter Twenty

Chickie found a well-lit corner of the Chicago Athletic Club Hotel's foyer, leaned against the marble wall, and squinted at Maddy's text message.

The meeting was on. Whether it was a good idea or not, the encounter between Winston and Lena was probably necessary, so she called Winston to say that Lena would see him at twelve thirty. When the geneticist learned Chickie was only a couple of blocks away, he tentatively asked if she would join him at the Art Institute until it was time to appear at Lena's home. She agreed, feeling sorry for the nervous scientist. *Who's the Girl Scout now?*

Arriving at the Balcony Café on the second level of the Modern Wing, Chickie spotted Winston seated at the counter playing with a croissant and studying a gallery guide. She climbed on the stool next to him and glanced over at the map. It was open to the layout of the famous Clarence Buckingham Collection.

He slid the paper across to her. "Visiting the Art Institute was on my list of things to do in case I never heard from Edward."

"Yeah, I go to libraries in every new city." She was useless at small talk. It didn't help that Winston's anxiety practically glowed from his face and tense body. He poked at the remnants of his croissant and admitted, "This is worse than waiting to hear whether I got the job or the big grant."

"You could never be truly prepared to meet Edward or Lena, could you?"

He shrugged and reached for another piece of croissant, but the pastry had been reduced to crumbs. He dusted his hands on his jeans. "I assumed I'd never find him, but I never completely gave up searching. Still, you can't hang on to hope forever—it hijacks your life. Now, it's all shifted to Lena and I'm as close as I'll ever be."

Chickie murmured agreement; hope was overrated.

"The weirdest part is that Edward was alive when I wrote the letter, but he was dead within a day of my arrival. What are the statistics on that?" He started to arrange the crumbs into small piles.

Chickie wanted to take the plate away from him, but he was obviously having a tough time. She tried to listen, but Alma's jarring news distracted her. Could Edward be implicated in some sort of art scam? If it was true, the scam meant more complications, more pain for Lena, more secrets revealed, and more negative publicity. Before dropping wild speculations about art fraud on her friend, Chickie had to gather facts, fast.

Completely unaware that his companion was involved in her own troubled world, Winston talked on. He imagined aloud what Lena might say or do. "I don't expect her to see me as a relative, at least not right away. But what if she thinks of me as an interloper? A threat. God, what a mess. But at the same time, I'd feel like such a coward if I snuck out of town. And there's always the unlikely chance she might welcome Edward's son." Temporarily, he ran out of whatifs at the same moment Chickie was hatching a plan of her own, so she was unprepared when he looked up and asked, "What do you think? Where do you think I stand? Am I an interloper?"

She answered without thinking. "Sure, I can't imagine where you'll fit in. And the timing is terrible. If Edward receives more publicity in the next few days, your sudden appearance might be noticed and if it is, there will be questions." She pulled out her phone; she had to find the phone number of a *Tribune* reporter who owed her a favor. She didn't notice Winston's shocked reaction to her unfiltered response.

He stared wide-eyed. "What questions? Who would know about me besides the three of you?"

Chickie answered while she tapped at the phone and searched her contacts. "If reporters dig into Edward's life, there's a chance they'll discover you. It's not his death that will keep the story alive; it's the potential scandal."

Knowing nothing about the art scam or the real possibility of increased press coverage, Winston's mind raced in another direction. "Are you suggesting that my existence, the appearance of an unknown son, is such a scandal that reporters will care? Or do you believe that my letter led to Edward falling in front of a train, or worse yet, jumping? Is my existence that shameful?" This was his nightmare. Winston threw his napkin on the table and marched out.

Chickie sat and stared after him, momentarily confused. *I'm thousands of miles away from my own children, which barely keeps me safe from offending them, and yet I find an opportunity to trample on the sensibilities of a stranger.* She groaned, slid off the stool, and went after Winston. Her intention had been to warn him that he could become a notorious side note to any story about Edward, his paintings, or his death.

Winston hadn't gone far. He was downstairs in front of a large glass case, gazing at a bronze Shiva draped with a snake armband. The magnificent Buckingham Collection, with work from China, India, and Vietnam, drew thousands of visitors each year. Chickie walked up behind him and said, "I'm sorry; I was distracted by other problems. Nothing to do with you." She turned away. "Let's get some fresh air. We have time to go into the garden before meeting Lena." Winston looked from the snake to the writer and clearly preferred the snake, but Chickie was his ticket to Lena, so he reluctantly followed her out.

In the North Garden, they stood in the grass to gaze at Calder's Flying Dragon. "It was his final dragon," Chickie said.

Winston studied the sculpture, then shook his head with disdain. "It's not a dragon, it's a dragonfly."

Ever the scientist. "Come on," Chickie said. "I'll show you a garden in Millennium Park that Maddy and I discovered the other day, and it's on the way to Lena's." They crossed the busy street to the Lurie Garden and climbed a few steps. She waved her arm toward the east. "The last time I was in Chicago, this space was a concrete canyon, well below street level, filled with railroad tracks and remnants of boxcars that had carried cattle into the stockyards."

Winston interrupted her. "I know you're trying to be nice to me in your own strange way, but I'd rather know the truth. Does Lena see me as responsible for Edward's death?"

"No, Maddy already dealt with Lena's suspicions. She explained you were at a convention so you couldn't have killed him. I think that's settled."

"What?" Winston shouted and stared down at her. "So when Lena learned about me, she decided I'm a killer! She imagined I would cause his death! She said so?"

I must remember to carry my edible butterflies, Chickie thought. *This is why writing works for me; simply press delete and the words are gone; first drafts are always garbage.* She moved closer for a second try, gently touching Winston's arm the way she'd seen Maddy do. Then she summoned up her most confident mother tone, hoping it masked her own escalating distress.

"Listen to me. I know Lena. She is in the middle of strong, confusing emotions. Stop thinking about yourself for a moment and try to understand her. Lena's husband—her best friend, her protector—died. She is scrambling desperately for answers. The situation is already bad and will become worse for a long time before her life improves." Just as she feared since receiving Lena's desperate text the week before, Chickie's own memories had broken through. "Every widow aches for a story that allows her to believe her husband loved her and . . . and that he didn't willingly or carelessly abandon her. Can't you understand? She wants to be able to keep loving Edward."

IT WAS A quiet taxi ride north. As they entered the Jordans' penthouse, Winston lagged behind Chickie, walking carefully with his hands in his pockets. He studied every bit of furniture, art, and photographs. It was his first, and maybe his only time visiting Edward's home.

Maddy led them to the empty dining room, where they talked inconsequentially, tension rising with every reference to the weather, art, and traffic until Chickie burst out with, "Well, where is she?"

"I'm here," Lena answered quietly from the doorway behind Chickie. They all looked up. Her hair was tied back, and her face looked free of makeup, which was unlikely. Lena wore loose navy silk slacks, an exquisitely cut cream shirt that looked like it was made for her, and probably was, and silver strappy sandals with surprisingly high heels. Chickie was impressed, what woman wears heels in her own home?

Winston, who had been seated next to Chickie, stood up but didn't walk toward her, even though she was only several feet away. "I am grateful you are willing to meet me. I expect I am an unwelcome surprise." He didn't extend a hand; simply waited with an expression that was somehow both grave and friendly.

Lena examined Winston from head to toe, looking hard for signs of Edward in this stranger. Maybe. He was shorter than Edward and broader across the shoulders. Obviously biracial, but they shared dark wavy hair and a thin mouth that naturally curved upward.

Lena remained in the doorway, oblivious to anyone but the man who might be Edward's son. Finally, she sighed, looked down at her shoes and said, "Why didn't I know about you? What, or when, did Edward know?" The pain was evident in her face when she looked up at Winston, who had remained standing.

Chickie desperately wanted to leave. Listening to pain, even pain that had its roots in decades past, is real and new when the results of those old actions stand right in front of you.

"He didn't know," Winston said evenly. "By the time my mother realized she was pregnant, Edward was gone from Hawaii, back to finish his tour of duty. And my grandmother, my *Ba*, forbade my mother from looking for him. She was a formidable woman. My mother, Mai, might have tried secretly to learn where he went or if he survived the war, but I was never told, and frankly, I don't think she ever learned a thing. They pretended he was dead. To them, he was. They wanted me to believe it too. But to me, he wasn't dead . . ."

"Dead" landed in the room harshly. Lena drew a breath.

Winston looked away, blushing. "I'm sorry; that was wrong-footed." He hurried on. "But that describes Edward's presence in my family. He didn't exist; I had somehow arrived magically. I was a happy gift for them, they claimed. We never talked about my creation or my loss. They both had bad experiences with men, especially my grandfather, back in Vietnam. He was very abusive, and they'd fled the country with help from a priest in the school where they worked. They probably would have preferred me to be a girl, but . . ." He shrugged. "They came around in time and kept me." He offered them this obviously rehearsed, light rendition of his story and the women cooperated with forced smiles.

Lena asked, "Did you contact Edward before this letter?"

"No. If Edward knew about me before I wrote the letter, it wasn't from me."

"Please sit down," she said.

Both Maddy and Chickie felt weak from relief.

Lena took a chair across the table from Winston, next to Maddy. When the social worker reached over to put an arm around Lena, she smelled alcohol and suddenly all feelings of relief vanished. She shifted away into her seat.

Lena leaned forward, put her elbows on the table and rested her chin on her clasped hands. "Is your last name really Edwards?"

"Yes. I had always assumed that my mother chose a generic

American name to help us blend in. It's all legal. I never realized the significance until recently. Winston is from my mother's original last name, Nguyen, which is pronounced sort of like "win" in English."

Lena smiled. "Do you want to make a claim on Edward's estate?" Three of the four people in the dining room gasped.

Maddy jumped up. "I'm going to bring us some food."

"Good idea. I'll help." Chickie followed and it took only seconds for the two of them to disappear.

Still seated, Winston answered calmly. "At least you haven't called me a murderer. I'll take that as a step in the right direction."

Lena's eyes opened wide.

It was Winston's turn to smile. This was his one chance to make a connection to his father's wife; he was not going to pass it up. "I will sign any paper you put in front of me that says I have no claim on Edward." He paused. "Or you. And I will do it today. We can draft it here and now with Maddy and Chickie as witnesses."

Lena remained quiet.

He continued, "I have the advantage. I've had years to imagine finding my father. I've had thousands of conversations with him, with you, and with the siblings I don't seem to have. I am brand new to you. The idea of you is not new to me, not any version of you. I have an excellent imagination."

Lena tried to speak and couldn't. She covered her eyes, then said, "You sound like your father," and she burst into tears.

Winston's excellent imagination had not covered this reaction. He rose and urgently followed the sounds of voices that came from the kitchen where Chickie and Maddy huddled at the expansive marble island. The housekeeper had left a plate of sandwiches on a sleek metal tray. Napkins and silverware were ready. Iced tea was poured into four crystal glasses. Chickie was whispering and Maddy leaned close, holding one hand over her eyes.

The only word Winston heard clearly was, "art." Who was Art? A relative? He had no right to ask. "Are you okay?"

Their heads jerked up guiltily. Both reached for the food, almost toppling the glasses.

Winston gently lifted the large tray. "Let me carry this. Lena is crying and I came to get help."

"Maddy, you take a few minutes to think about Alma's news, and I will serve lunch and calm Lena," Chickie said, hoping against hope that Maddy would insist on taking over and she could run out into traffic.

"Good idea." Maddy said. "I'll be there in a few."

Chickie followed as Winston carried the unwanted tray of food into the dining room where the three of them looked at it dully. He placed it on the far side of the table, removing only the glasses. Soon Maddy entered and slid into place beside Lena. No one made a move for the sandwiches.

"I do have more questions," Lena said sweetly, no hint of tears or menace in evidence.

"So do I," smiled Winston, wishing the glass in front of him held his grandmother's Mekong whiskey instead of iced tea.

Sensing the intimacy of the moment and the questions to come, Maddy said, "We'll give you some time to talk. Call if either of you needs us," and headed out of the room again. Chickie followed, knowing Winston wanted to ask questions about other relatives, Edward's medical history, and sure that Lena wanted to know about his mother and how she'd met Edward.

Twenty minutes later, when the two friends tentatively returned to the dining room, the stale sandwiches remained untouched, and the atmosphere was something like a Star Trek episode where the Klingons and humans craft an uneasy peace because that's the only way forward. It wasn't the zombie apocalypse, but it certainly wasn't a Christmas rom-com. The best Lena could say was, "I don't think you're the murderer but perhaps you are a fraud."

"Give me a chance."

She stared at him. In spite of her harsh words, it was clear that she kept searching his face for signs of Edward. "Okay, I know you believe, want to believe, you found your father . . . but can you prove it is my Edward? This man!" She reached into her pocket, pulled out a small photograph, and flung it toward Winston. When it fluttered to the floor, he bent to pick up the candid shot of Edward in tennis whites, laughing as a large standard poodle jumped for his racket. Winston looked at it for a long time, his head down so no one was able to read his expression.

"Would you have a DNA test?" Lena asked.

Winston nodded without looking up, then said firmly, "Yes. Of course." He was still riveted by the photo in his hands. "We can do a standard paternity test here in Chicago with a hair root, or a toothbrush," he added, the scientist reasserting himself.

"Could his hairbrush work?"

"It might," Winston replied. "And if not, we can get a very high level of proof if you ask the coroner's office for a blood sample. Because the death is being investigated, they will have one."

Lena paled and looked pained by the thought but also oddly determined. "God, I don't want to talk to those people ever again."

"I can do that for you," Chickie volunteered. "My friend has already offered to help by getting the coroner's results for us. She's still connected and if I remember Chicago, that counts for a lot. She'd know how to work out a DNA test."

Lena looked relieved. She turned to Winston, "Okay?"

He looked at her solemnly and nodded. "It would mean a lot if you believed me. Once you're convinced, I would love to know more about Edward, to see pictures like this one, maybe be allowed to learn about him." His voice was rough with emotion. "I always knew there was a real person somewhere out there, but not in my world. In Vietnamese there is the same word— *nhớ ai đó*—for 'missing someone' and 'remembering someone.' I missed him, but I never had a memory. If you are ever willing to share memories, tell stories, then I would have someone to remember."

Chapter Twenty-One

Chickie walked Winston to the door, agreed to set up the DNA test, and promised to keep him in the loop. She was back in the library in time to witness the latest installment of chaos. Lena waved her arms, swinging her phone and gesturing dramatically at Maddy. "Oh God, I forgot. It's a good thing Cheryl texted me. I'm supposed to be there! I supervise the afternoon shift," she gasped.

"Where?" Maddy asked, confused. "No one expects you to be anywhere right now."

Lena turned from Maddy to Chickie and back again, displaying her chirping phone.

"I *do* want to be there," Lena said, bursting with new energy. "It's Doughnut Day at the zoo!"

Is this what it's like to work in an emergency room, Chickie wondered? How did Maddy do it for all those years? She caught Maddy's eye and found her own concern mirrored there.

"You know!" Lena practically shouted. "My Doughnut Day." As one, Maddy and Chickie slowly shook their heads.

"I've told you about it. You've both donated in the past," Lena said, looking at them quite sanely. She lowered her voice. "I know it sounds crazy, but it really *is* Doughnut Day at the zoo. A dozen local doughnut makers are giving away samples to our ticket holders, and we already presold a thousand tickets."

Neither Maddy nor Chickie understood what she was talking about, each baffled in her own way. Maddy worried about Lena's emotional well-being, and Chickie could not imagine how to break the news about Edward's questionable business sideline. Why didn't the damn man stick to refashioning faces?

Lena took their silence as a positive sign. "This fundraiser was originally my idea, my baby. It's the fifth year. The hospital cancer research center raises money on ticket sales, and we rely on goodwill from doughnut makers and our volunteers. I have to be at the zoo."

Maddy was appalled. "No one thought that you deserved a few days off for mourning?"

"This is a group text, a reminder to a dozen women. It doesn't matter. I am *not* going to miss it. It's normal and right now, it's the only small bit of my life that's in my control. If you want to be helpful, come with me. We can talk about Winston and eat doughnuts at the same time! This will be good for me! Let's go." Lena scurried down the hallway to change clothes.

"Is this what you call mania?" Chickie asked, not bothering to whisper.

"Maybe it will be good for her. She's showing initiative."

The writer rested her head against the wall, eyes closed, wishing she knew how to pray.

Maddy tried to cheer her up. "What do you suppose socialites in mourning wear for Doughnut Day at the zoo?"

There was a low moan in response.

Maddy shrugged, "Pull yourself together, Chick. You have to tell Lena that the authorities are looking into Edward's art importing hobby."

"You make it sound normal, Maddy. It isn't! They are questioning whether Edward was deceiving people; I believe the word you are having trouble pronouncing is *fraud*."

"You are the woman who specializes in words. Just find a time to tell her. I performed the morning wake-up and I announced Winston's existence, no small feat. Now, you are in charge of revealing the latest secret. We're a team and my friend, you are up to bat." Enjoying

Chickie's misery more than a friend ought to, she grabbed her purse and added, "I *love* the zoo. I haven't been there in years. I'm sure I have some sunscreen with me."

Chickie watched Maddy rummage in her bag. She probably still carried tampons; she hadn't been there in years either. Quite cheerfully, Maddy found a tube of 55 SPF and handed it to Chickie. Of course, Maddy *loved* the zoo. She probably earned her first merit badge teaching a chimp to say please and thank you. She rose, wearily thinking that her experience of friendship was like parenthood: no one told her how to do it, she often failed spectacularly, and still, she hung in endlessly. How tribal.

"Lena?" Chickie called. "Do you have a sun hat I could borrow?" She was not about to spend money on a logo cap, visualizing one adorned with an emblem of a baboon in heat.

A Lyft dropped the women at the north entrance of the zoo on Stockton Street. To the delight of Chickie and Maddy, the outside looked remarkably the same. The Lincoln Park Zoo had been the place where, weather permitting, the young mothers walked their children for long hours. It was free, it was outdoors, and there was little that the kids could destroy.

As they crossed the lawn, Lena looked at Maddy's walking stick as if she had never seen it before, hesitated, then asked, "You are okay with walking, right? If you need a wheelchair—"

"Nope," Maddy cut in sharply. "I'll use this stick to get to the front of the doughnut lines," and marched ahead of the others through the gates and toward the penguins.

"The doughnut stands are all set up in the central section of the zoo," Lena told Chickie. "Walk south toward the African apes and the Waterfowl Lagoon. I'll find you when I'm finished working. Here are tickets for sampling doughnuts." She shoved a list of locations and a sheaf of tickets into Chickie's hand, looked around for Maddy, and when she couldn't see her, gave a second set to her friend. "I guess Maddy is eager to see the animals," Lena said and waved as she hurried away in her skinny jeans, luxurious shawl, and low-heeled leather boots.

"I'm sure that's it," Chickie mumbled as she picked up speed to locate Maddy.

She found her at the giraffe enclosure admiring Etana, a magnificent creature who had to be fourteen feet tall. The beast strolled, seemingly interested in her small world, as if she had not seen this bit of scenery a thousand times before. Chickie was torn between the thrill of viewing Etana and deep anger at enclosures. No giraffe volunteers to spend winters in Chicago.

As if Maddy read her mind, she frowned at Chickie and said, "Do not attempt to break in and free that animal. She's an old lady and you cannot ride her back to DC."

Not bothering to ask how Maddy knew what she was thinking, Chickie handed her a list with the names and locations of the dozen temporary doughnut stands. "Lena has darted off to validate and appreciate the many volunteers who are going to turn fat and sugar into money for the hospital's cancer research program."

"Maybe the cardiac unit would be a better recipient."

"Or diabetes," answered Chickie.

They headed into the central area of the zoo. It was a good-natured crowd, made more so by the escalating sugar-highs as visitors sampled yeast doughnuts, cake doughnuts, doughnut holes, crullers, and excellent jelly doughnuts, all washed down with specialty coffees. Forty minutes later, after viewing the kangaroos, snakes, and elephants, they reached the front of Donut Delite, their seventh stop, and accepted miniature chocolate cake doughnuts.

Maddy looked around to be sure Lena was nowhere in sight; then impatiently guided Chickie into the shade, where they swallowed the doughnut remnants and wiped their mouths. "We will catch up with Lena soon. Take that opportunity to inform her that Edward may be involved in a breaking art scam. It's bound to appear in the papers, or she'll get a call. We have to warn her. It may turn out that he is a victim. Maybe he was a buyer but had nothing to do with deceitful sales."

"It didn't sound that innocent. Alma said it was a problem of provenance, about the honest history of the artwork."

"For a smart man, that's awfully stupid."

Chapter Twenty-Two

Eventually Maddy and Chickie wandered back to Penguin Cove, where the charming African creatures put on a fine display playing on the rocks and in the water. Chickie read aloud from the sign, "Strategically designed rock formations and nesting areas facilitate species specific behaviors, such as burrowing and nesting. African penguins must burrow to breach behind-the-scenes nesting boxes."

"After all those doughnuts, I need a nesting box," Maddy said, as close to a complaint as Chickie had ever heard from her.

The other zoo visitors were as entertaining as the inmates. There were flocks of parents valiantly trying to prevent their children from assaulting the endangered species. The friends felt compassion for the women who failed at the task, tempted to help one young mother who had three children but only two hands. "Motherhood is so humbling," Maddy said.

"Only if you take it seriously," Chickie said, glancing at her phone.

"Anything wrong?"

"Not any new wrong. It's my daughter. Every time I get an email from Steph, I hope she will tell me that she broke up with her *amoureux* and plans to return to the US. Instead, she is letting me know they are going to Amsterdam for the weekend to celebrate their six-month anniversary."

"Look on the bright side. Maybe they need to celebrate six months because they know they will not reach one year."

"Thank you. This time, I appreciate your optimism. What gift do I send for this special anniversary? One ticket, one way from Paris to DC?"

Maddy grinned. *At least Chickie's kids let her live wherever she wants.*

Lena found them sitting in the bleachers around the penguin pool. She had spread good cheer, thanked volunteers, solved a few unspecified doughnut problems, weighed in on whether the chocolate cake doughnut was the one to choose if you could only have one, assured more than one volunteer that the calories weren't terribly high, nibbled proffered samples, and arrived back to join her friends just as Maddy began to seriously wilt. In contrast, Lena was feeling upbeat after the most normal hour she'd had in a week, and, for the first time, she announced she was hungry.

Chickie pounced. "Great, let's go back to your apartment."

"No need. We can walk down to Park Place Café, sit on the terrace, and talk about this Winston thing." She led them to the restaurant, which was blissfully cool and had a mellow afternoon crowd. They took a table on the edge of the brick patio. Lena went inside to order while Chickie and Maddy again searched their phones for any mention of Edward and the art scam, relieved to find nothing.

"Tell her while she's in the middle of a doughnut overdose. That's when I'd want to find out," Maddy suggested.

Chickie promised to introduce the art scam as delicately as possible. Maddy grimaced.

Lena returned carrying a tray laden with cold drinks for the three of them and a plate of tacos for herself. She threw herself into lunch. Aware that Maddy was watching her closely, Chickie waited until Lena finished one, then chose her words carefully. "In the spirit of honesty, I want to tell you something. Let me preface it by saying, we all make mistakes; we jump into situations . . . whether it's ego or foolishness."

Lena looked up from her plate and nodded seriously.

"We forgive the people we love, and we eventually forgive ourselves," Chickie babbled.

"I know where you're going Chick."

"You do?"

"Yes, and I understand. It happens. You think you know more than you do, so you take a crazy chance."

"Exactly, and you mess up . . . badly, and it's hard to face the consequences, but people you love are hurt."

"But they heal," Lena insisted.

"Exactly!" Chickie raised her hands skyward.

"You worry too much," Lena said. "Steph and Sam will be fine."

"Huh?" Chickie's hands fell to the table.

Maddy told me you left Michael," Lena said offhandedly.

Chickie blinked repeatedly.

"What took you so long?" Lena asked sincerely.

Chickie was derailed. The news about Edward fled from her consciousness as Lena continued. "It's always been clear what Michael saw in you, but what did you ever see in him? You gave it a good try, I'm sure. But you have always been an unconventional woman trying exceedingly hard to live a conventional life. You were bound to break away."

Finally, Chickie choked out, "Why didn't you ever tell me?"

It was Lena's turn to look surprised. "You never asked."

EXITING THE ZOO, they bumped into the last shift of Doughnut Day volunteers, one of whom rushed up to hug Lena. "So good to see you out and about. You've got to move on!"

Lena called after her, "Thanks for all your hard work!" Out of the other woman's hearing, she grabbed Maddy's arm and hissed, "I hate when people tell me to move on. And I'm equally angry with the supersomber ones who want me in black forever. The first group hopes I'll ignore my grief like nothing happened, and the second group would be thrilled if I locked myself in the condo because they're afraid I'll steal their husbands!" She shuddered as her voice rose. "I'd prefer the lowland gorillas."

The three women walked on the gravel path. Maddy tried to speak but Lena shook her head and cut her off. "Most of all . . . most of all, I'm angry at Edward for leaving me alone in this world. He's gone and I'm left to deal with the gossip and the casual cruelty. I could kill him!"

Chickie moved to Lena's side and forced the widow to look at her. "Sudden widowhood does that. I vividly remember how raging I was after Danny died. And being so young, I expressed it poorly—and often. People don't like that." She laughed remembering herself.

"What did you *do* with all that anger?" Lena asked. "People expect me to be sad; they tolerate certain feelings, but they don't like anger."

"Yes!" Maddy stopped abruptly and whacked her cane into the dirt path. "Being well-behaved can be hazardous to your health. Your anger will fuel the energy you need to fight your way through grief. Don't let anyone tell you otherwise!"

Chapter Twenty-Three

In the cab, Maddy invited Lena to join them at the Palmer House. There would be time to talk and unwind. "Chickie has two beds in her room," she offered before they dropped her on Astor Street, but the new widow waved them off with a determined smile. "I'm fine now. Doughnut Day lifted my mood. Call me in the morning."

The car continued south, and the two older women were unusually quiet, knowing they had failed to tell Lena about the art scam, but both were thrilled to head back to the hotel with nothing more on the schedule.

Maddy planned to suggest room service.

Chickie hoped Maddy would suggest room service.

At the Palmer House, they hurried upstairs. Maddy was joyfully switching into sweatpants and her favorite, only, pair of purple socks when her phone pinged with an incoming text.

Reluctantly, she knocked on Chickie's door and was welcomed in. Chickie sat in bed wearing pajama pants and an RBG T-shirt, tapping on the laptop that rested on her thighs. She didn't look up. "I want to finish my blog post. Then, I will take a long bath. Afterward, I will be accommodating and eat whatever nostalgic food you choose. Velveeta sandwiches?" Chickie looked so comfortable.

Oh well. "We just got a text from Lena." Maddy dropped her phone on the bedspread, with the text lit up. Chickie stopped typing and glanced over at the screen. Lena had written: *You were right. I'm not ready to be here alone tonight. I'm changing clothes and will call you from the car. I have a plan.*

Chickie's shoulders slumped. "Why can't Lena sob and scream, or shop, or have a mani-pedi? Why does she have to stay so busy? Maybe I should change tonight's blog post to *10 Popular Ways to Grieve That Don't Exhaust Your Friends.*"

Maddy shrugged. "It's better this way. She'll be with us for one more peaceful night, and we'll break the news first thing in the morning."

Chickie closed her laptop.

They looked at each other for a long moment, weary, each of them wanting to be a good friend, but suspecting virtue might be out of reach. Finally, Maddy dropped into the armchair and asked very evenly, "What do you think Lena's plan for the evening is?"

"God, maybe it's karaoke," Chickie answered, digging deep into her bag of dreaded activities.

"Never," Maddy assured her, "but what about a charity benefit with droning speakers?"

"And equal amounts of small talk," Chickie shivered. "I know . . . I know what the plan is. Lena is bringing over her high school yearbook and she's going to page through it, photo by photo of all the popular girls and tell us what each one is doing now, a thousand years since graduation."

Maddy rose from the chair. "Move over."

Chickie shimmied to the far side of the bed. "This evening may test your resolve about being a good person."

Then the friends lay down to await their fate. It didn't take long.

Maddy's phone rang, and they were pleasantly surprised to hear they would not have to go out again. In the cab, with music playing loudly on the radio, Lena announced, "Massages. Just what we all need. I've booked us into the Hilton Palmer House Spa. They're open until nine p.m. and it's all on me. See you in a few." She hung up.

Relief washed over them. Finally, an activity that would not raise either their cortisol or glucose levels. Lying on a table being gently pummeled to the sounds of whales talking to each other would be delightful.

Within half an hour of her arrival, phones were tucked away, and Lena had them all wrapped up in ridiculously fluffy robes and paper slippers while they sipped cucumber water at the spa.

Lena handed each woman a list of spa services. "I need a Thai massage."

"I'm being practical—I'll have the shorter massage and the longer antiaging facial," Chickie said.

Maddy read the offerings and announced, "I have decided to get stoned." She tried to keep a straight face but failed.

"It's about time," Chickie said; she'd gobbled an edible butterfly as soon as Lena called.

"See, here it is!" Maddy pointed to the printed sheet. "Hot Stone Massage. I've always been curious about that. And that Chicago Fire and Ice one is definitely out—we had enough icy sidewalks and hot summers when we lived here years ago."

The women were ushered into different darkened rooms with piped-in music designed to make them feel beautiful and mildly high. The effect was soothing and wiped away the last traces of the day.

Lena's plan had been a good one, and it wasn't over. When the three friends were eventually reunited in what Maddy called the spa departure lounge, Lena announced that food had been ordered to Chickie's room. They drifted upstairs in a collective hazy mood and found the sensible salads and hydrating beverages, collectively determined to share stories that had nothing to do with death.

Lena brought up the meeting with Winston. "It went as well as possible, I guess. Never in a million years would I have imagined that Edward had a son. His life was so organized, so controlled."

Since she was talking frankly about him, Chickie ventured a question she had long wondered about. "I'm curious, did Edward ever want to have children?"

"I think you, of all people, already know the answer," Lena sighed.

Maddy looked puzzled but before she could ask, Lena continued. "We rarely talked about children. My family pressured me to breed but I never felt sure, and I hated being pushed by my mother. Edward always said that the world was already crowded; something could happen to us; or something could go wrong with the child. Being a doctor, he was inordinately worried about inherited disorders. We postponed and procrastinated and then it was too late."

Chickie said brightly, "And now you have Winston."

Lena gasped, then looked shocked, and finally began to laugh. "He's toilet trained, school is paid for, he's talented, and behaves beautifully in social situations. What more could I want?"

Apparently, the spa had been good for everyone. Maddy had begun to long for sleep when Lena surprised them. "Did you keep secrets from your husbands?"

Ugh, Maddy thought, *Lena got her second wind.* Maybe slumber was not happening yet.

She waited, hoping Chickie would shut her down. She didn't, so Maddy attempted to derail the subject. "Secrets happen. For many reasons—some good, some not-so-good. It's normal."

Maddy did not want to explore this, especially not late in the day.

"I know now that Edward never knew about Winston's birth, but it makes me wonder if there were other secrets," Lena confided.

Chickie began to panic. This direction was dangerous. There were health and business secrets to be disclosed, but tonight was the wrong time. She quickly redirected the conversation. "Edward liked control, not for bad reasons. He wanted you to have security. That's why money mattered. It was security. I'll bet that's why he didn't want children—too unpredictable."

Maddy suddenly remembered the earlier conversation. "Lena, what did you mean when you said to Chickie, 'you of all people know the answer'?"

Lena looked at Chickie, who kept her head down, industriously chewing a cucumber, so she brought her gaze back to Maddy. "Years ago, when Edward and I were first married, I got pregnant. He had made it very clear that he never wanted children, so I didn't tell him. I called Chickie, flew out to DC for a few days, and had an abortion. So yes, I had my one big secret."

Maddy longed to ask, "Why didn't you call me?" but she knew the answer. Lena confirmed it.

"You know I love you madly, and we were always closer, but Chickie's not the type to ask questions or burden me with sympathy. That was what I needed."

Lena's explanation made sense, but Maddy felt stung and excluded even though the secret was decades old. She turned on Chickie, failing to keep an edge out of her voice. "Well, did you keep secrets from your husbands? You had *two* chances."

Chickie's heart pounded. A secret-sharing session was a stupid end to a very long day. They were not sixteen years old. Nor was this a sixties-era encounter group.

Maddy continued to look sternly at Chickie. "Your turn."

This wasn't like Maddy. She was rarely aggressive. Chickie tried to tread the middle ground, answering truthfully but lightly. "I didn't have time to keep secrets from Danny. It was over so fast."

"What about husband number two? There was time," Maddy persisted.

"Yes, I had many secrets, most of them harmless; some of them were none of his business." Chickie tried again to lighten the conversation and asked teasingly, "And you Maddy, are you going to confess that you used margarine instead of butter in a pie crust?"

Lena laughed but the second after Chickie spoke, she knew her effort at humor had backfired.

Maddy sat back and took a long deep breath. "I know I appear stoic and annoyingly cheerful. And sometimes I deserve your jokes, but I haven't lived in a tower."

Lena moved closer to Maddy. "I didn't mean to start a tell-all session. It's just that Edward's death has left me with so many questions. At least in the moments when I can think, that is. I'm sorry if I blundered." She squeezed Maddy's hand.

Maddy gently removed her hand on the pretext of reaching for water. Without preamble, she told them in a flat voice, "When we were in New Mexico with the Air Force, I was assaulted by Frank's senior officer. Then he whispered in my ear, "One word about this to *anyone* and Frank is not getting transferred to Walter Reed. And he will be stationed overseas. Without you and the brats." The next day he called at a time he knew Frank would be out and repeated that threat. I believed him."

Lena asked solemnly, "What did you do?"

"I shut up; I never told Frank. I never told anyone. Ever." She looked drained. "When #MeToo exploded, the flood of those women's stories hit me hard. There were so many, and they felt so familiar. It forced me to remember being a young woman in the sixties and seventies—without the flowers, love beads, or Joan Baez. Men took their power for granted and so did we. We put up with sexism silently, and it was everywhere, not just in the military. Subtle or crude, it was at school, on dates, in jobs, in expectations and ambitions, everywhere. Not getting caught in it would have been as likely as running through rain without getting wet." Maddy's voice shook.

Before Lena or Chickie could say a word, Maddy stood and left the room.

Chickie's Blog:
Old Dogs, New Tricks
(A Writer's Reflections on Growing Old and Growing Up)

Secrets

I've been forced to think about secrets lately. I

don't want to focus on the secret keeper—but on the person kept in the dark, the person who was deceived, the person who was shut out.

Here's an example: a woman has a child after a brief relationship and never tells the biological father. Let's skip her reasons (this is a blog, not a book); they are probably legitimate. What about the father? He had no choice because he had no knowledge. He has less power.

Or here's another: A husband spends much of the family savings on a pet project, and because he oversees the money, his wife remains ignorant of the change in their financial security. She cannot choose whether to get a job, be supportive, or go after him with a machete. My point is that the secret keeper has an awful power, probably intensely stressful, but a power that comes from having knowledge that affects others without their participation.

Deception gives power to the deceiver and takes it away from the deceived. It is irrelevant if it is "for your own good" or "I'll take care of it," "I didn't want you to worry," "I didn't want to look bad." Being kept in the dark robs us of the ability to choose, and that matters.

Chapter Twenty-Four

Lena swung the bathroom door open and shouted at the shower curtain. "I got . . . I got a call, I don't, I don't believe it," she stammered.

Chickie peeked around the plastic curtain. Lena stood in the middle of the small room, trembling in her red silk pajamas, and waving a cellphone in the air. It wasn't difficult to guess the nature of the call, but she asked anyway. "What happened?"

Lena sputtered incoherently until Chickie understood that a friend called to warn her that the morning edition of the *Chicago Tribune* had run a story alleging Edward's involvement in an art fraud. Her message delivered, Lena raced out of the bathroom to find Maddy. Chickie turned off the water and toweled quickly, all the while cursing Edward's judgment, "friends" eager to share bad news, the *Tribune*, and readers of everything other than the dictionary and her blog. She pulled on pants and a sweater and hurried downstairs to pick up copies of the *Chicago Tribune* and *Sun-Times* before joining Lena next door in Maddy's room.

Instead of her hoped-for brunch at Beatrix Restaurant, Maddy called room service for coffee and pancakes. In spite of decades of evidence to the contrary, Maddy retained an unshakable confidence in basic carbohydrates during a crisis. While the three women waited for food no one wanted, they all grabbed reading glasses and combed the news. Lena sat close to Maddy on the queen bed, each reading articles on their phone screens.

Across the room, Chickie spread the newspapers out on the desk and quickly scanned the pages.

"The story in the *Trib* doesn't appear until page three and they haven't leaped to wild conclusions. Their headline is 'Art Scam Revealed' but Edward's name is buried in paragraph eight. That's good."

"But the *Sun-Times* has him on page one!" Lena shrieked back and read aloud, "Dead Gold Coast Surgeon Named in Art Scam." Her voice went up an octave as she recited the entire piece. It suggested that Edward peddled fake Chinese art in Chicago. The writer speculated on whether he was a criminal or a dupe. Fraudulent or foolish? The story ended with, "*A reliable source told the Sun-Times that the roots of this deception lay in a trip to China taken by Charles Haskell, a Lake Forest businessman. We have been unable to reach Mr. Haskell for comment.*"

Lena put her face in her hands and burst into tears. "Charles? Edward wouldn't have anything to do with Charles! No one has anything to do with Charles." When she looked up, there were only blank expressions staring back. "Charles is Brian's brother," she explained. "I can't imagine him selling art unless there's a market for Britney Spears on velvet. As far as anyone knows, he's never had a real job. Charles is the guy who's always looking for the next 'big,'—which always means questionable—deal." She tossed her phone across the bed.

Determined to figure out Edward's involvement, Chickie attempted to question Lena. "Try to put aside allegations of a scam for a moment, and tell us everything you know about Edward selling art."

Lena shouted back, "Edward's involvement in art was entirely straightforward. He bought some paintings, that's all. And there is no scam! Art has mattered to him since he was a child! Last year he became intrigued with Chinese art from the years of the Cultural Revolution." She gained confidence as she explained.

So, she does know something, Chickie thought and felt her anger rise. "Really, I have trouble imagining Edward swooning over those cartoony posters of determined peasants smiling broadly at their mistreatment."

Lena jumped up, outraged. "Not those red posters! You've been to our home; haven't you seen the paintings in our library? And in the guest rooms? I think there's also one in Edward's office. They're beautiful oils made by underground artists in the sixties and seventies. That's what Edward collected."

Chickie and Maddy vaguely remembered a grim oil painting in Edward's office, notable only because it was at odds with the glitzy photos.

"Edward never mentioned Charles's name to me. We've known that man forever and he has always been trouble. I can't imagine how someone as kind as Brian could be cursed with such a sleazy younger brother."

Chickie started to say something about brothers of a feather, but Maddy cut her off.

"Lena, let me see if I understand. Edward began to collect Chinese art about a year ago. He purchased paintings by artists who had worked in secret during the Cultural Revolution."

Lena nodded.

"Somehow, these pieces became available in recent years, and Edward had access to them."

Another nod.

"And you never heard him refer to Charles in connection with these purchases."

"Right."

"And, he only bought paintings, never sold them. Right?"

Lena's hesitation did not go unnoticed. "If Edward sold any art, Charles had to be behind it. No one seems to understand that Edward is the victim here! This must be connected to Edward's murder."

Lena's explanation was fuzzy, but her friends were loath to challenge it. Maddy glanced at Chickie, who mouthed an obscenity, so she quickly returned to Lena only to be interrupted by a knock on the door. Maddy opened it for the room service waitress, who wheeled in their breakfast order. She fumbled for a tip.

Swiveling from the desk, Chickie reluctantly admitted to Lena that an old friend mentioned Edward's name in connection with art deals the day before. "I've been trying to track down her rumor since then."

"You knew about this yesterday?" Lena squealed. She lunged across the room and loomed over Chickie. "How could you not tell me, warn me! I thought you were my friend. You should have told me so we could keep these lies out of the news!"

"There's no such thing as keeping lies out of the news," Chickie snapped back.

Maddy stepped over to Lena and laid a firm hand on her shoulder, gently pulling her back. She spoke in her rarely used, but never forgotten, crisis-unit voice, "Look at me." She waited until Lena met her eyes.

"We *are* your friends. What Chickie heard yesterday were unsubstantiated rumors with no timeline and no available facts. She's been investigating and we planned to tell you this morning. We are as shocked as you are by this news."

Lena shook Maddy off and began to flap her arms in frustration. "My God, every day there's a new secret. First Winston, now this. What else? What else haven't you told me?"

"That's it," Chickie said quickly. "You know everything we know."

Maddy added, "Now we need to figure out what happened and find a way to deal with it."

For the next half hour Chickie pressed phone numbers, talked to anyone who might have information, asked for details or other sources, and left urgent voicemails. She called in favors and knew enough people with access to legitimate information that she expected a response, especially since the story had already been published in two major Chicago newspapers.

Behind her, Maddy sipped coffee, and Lena stalked the room like the caged tiger they had seen at the zoo. Maddy offered her the plate of pancakes, but Lena turned her back on the food.

At that moment, Maddy's phone dinged with a text. She saw the sender's name and the message: *Can you call me?* She looked at Chickie and said, "I'll take this in your room."

Winston answered instantly. "Did you see the story about Edward? Did you know? Is it true? The Google alert on Edward's name lit up with references to an art scam. What's happening?" Winston stopped and blew out a long breath.

Maddy sat down heavily on Chickie's bed. Winston sounded more anxious about this story than he had been about meeting his Chicago family. No time for any hypothesis, no experimental trials, Maddy thought, no scientific method could prepare him for this shock.

"Maddy?"

She hadn't realized he was waiting for her answer. "We know. So does Lena. She's here at the hotel with us, furiously protective of Edward and astonished at the allegations against him. But we don't have real facts yet, although I expect Chickie will remedy that as soon as possible."

"I'm scheduled to meet Chickie at ten thirty to go for the DNA test. Do you think she'll cancel?"

"I'll see that she keeps the appointment. The paternity test is important no matter what else happens. There's nothing you can do about the latest wave of bad news."

He groaned. "I finally found my father, but he's dead. And now he may be a criminal!" he spat out with more bad temper than Maddy had previously heard.

"This will be hard, but stay in the moment. Sometimes good people do bad things—knowingly or unknowingly. Edward could be a criminal and a victim and your father. You're a scientist. Save your conclusions until you know more. And expect to meet Chickie as planned."

Her right leg was stiff, her body ached, and she felt the effects of intense days and little sleep. On top of that, she was uncomfortably aware that she had developed real affection for Winston.

Chickie would certainly question the wisdom of attaching to this stranger. But then, she always preached skepticism, healthy or otherwise. How had they stayed friends for all these years?

Chapter Twenty-Five

"That was Winston confirming his appointment with Avril," Maddy said when she returned to her friends. Chickie gratefully used the opportunity to excuse herself to dress.

Muttering, Lena moved to the foot of the bed and turned on the television, scanning stations with the remote. The volume remained very low and Maddy was grateful to have time to think. They couldn't stay much longer in Chicago, and she felt physically depleted, but being here with Chickie, scrambling around being useful, had energized her in ways she hadn't felt in years.

The last few days stood in glaring contrast to the past thirteen months where she had drifted along, sometimes vague about which day it was. It hadn't mattered. She hadn't needed to change her routines, so she didn't. And the future, well, what does a seventy-two-year-old woman work toward?

Of course, she had gone through the motions, said all the right things, joined her friends for lunch and paid her bills on time, mostly. She had even taken up boxing as prescribed for her Parkinson's, but she had not looked ahead. She'd managed her grief and her life. Lena would go through all this in her own way. She'll drift, or race, or slog through mourning like she's in a dark and muddy tunnel, and this week is simply the beginning. Grief will not be rushed.

Fifteen minutes later, Chickie popped in wearing a violet blouse under a well-cut blazer and simple gold jewelry. Maddy thought the journalist looked like herself, but an elegant version, all ready to join

Winston at Avril's office.

As soon as she left, Lena declared, "I'm going back to Chickie's room to shower, return a few calls that I can't ignore, and then we can get out of here. I promise I'll eat a big lunch. You'll stay close?" The last question held a plea.

"Of course," Maddy answered with resignation. She longed for time alone. She no longer needed television in the background, frequent phone calls, or endless books on tape. Grief does change, but it takes time. She looked at the new widow standing in the doorway.

Lena looked longingly at her friend. "You know Maddy, as gutted as I am, and as crazy as I feel, I do recognize that you're right beside me. Thank you."

Maddy's heart melted, and she launched into her morning exercises with enthusiasm. Then, having been Good, having stretched, and having ingested pancakes for three, she deliberated on whether her gray or black slacks were best suited for what looked like a cooler day. Gray, she decided and added the new lilac scarf.

Lena's ability to linger in bathrooms was legendary, so Maddy poured another cup of coffee, straightened the bedspread, and settled against the headboard, grateful to escape into her mystery novel.

Several chapters later, about the time she felt certain she knew who had murdered the small town knit shop owner, her phone buzzed. Gus's photo appeared on the screen. Maddy tried to rise above the irksome memory of him devising the plan to move her to Chicago so they could look after her, but this was the wrong time to revisit that particular disagreement. She took a deep breath. "Gus, good to hear your voice."

"Mom, the article in the *Trib*—no way I saw that coming."

Maddy reassured him that journalists were supposed to report the news, not predict it, but Gus also had another concern.

"Chickie left a message telling me to work my contacts and see what I can find out about Edward's business dealings. You want me to do that, right? I know how protective you are of Lena; what if I find bad news?"

"Gus, you're a sportswriter, not an investigative journalist, but if you can bring any clarity to this mess, we would all greatly appreciate it. We have to deal with reality, whatever it is."

"I thought that's what you would say, just checking. FYI, Mom, Rex didn't mean to aggravate you. Moving to Chicago was just an idea. It would be nice to have you closer."

"Let's take this up later; I have to go."

When the phone buzzed again, she assumed Gus was calling back, but it was Raph.

"Hello?" she answered eagerly, but before she could say another word, Raph told her that he had read the *Tribune* article. "We've already gotten a dozen calls from colleagues and friends and even the reporter who wrote the *Tribune* piece. Brian is frantic about how a sudden death and now alleged fraud by a partner will damage the reputation of the practice. I don't want to worry you, but after Brian read the article, he summoned a PR consultant from a firm he employs, and he called Lena. I overheard him on the phone; he wants everyone on the same page, which means he wants his story to be Lena's story. I believe he wants her to come to the office so that the consultant can coach her."

Raph's tone was grave. "I'm worried about how Brian will lean on Lena. Edward was one of my business partners for years, and we owe his wife a great deal of consideration. I'm not sure Brian sees it the same way; he knows how to apply pressure when his charm doesn't work. I think you need to protect her interests. Could you come to the office and be with her?"

"You don't trust Brian?"

"I know his 'strengths and weaknesses,' as they say in your profession."

"Okay, I'll talk to Lena."

"Wait!" he interrupted. "Brian left to pick her up some time ago so they're probably on the way back to the office now. I hesitated to involve you. I had to wrestle with my loyalties, so I may have wasted time."

Maddy thanked him and hurried across the room to double-check on Lena's whereabouts. As she was about to knock, she noticed a piece of hotel stationery had been slipped under the adjoining door. *Sorry. Quick change of plans. I have to meet with Brian about business and will be in touch about the rest of the day. Lena*

Maddy knocked on the door anyway, hoping to catch Lena before she left. No response. She knocked again. Lena had been planning to return some calls. Obviously, that was before Brian reached her. Maddy grabbed her phone from the bedside table and texted Lena:

> Where are you?

No problem, with Brian, back soon

> Here at the hotel?

No

> Edward's office?

Yes. Don't worry. I'll check in later

Maddy texted Chickie:

> Meet me at Edward's office NOW. Lena's gone off with Brian. Raph is worried. I don't like it.

Chapter Twenty-Six

At the time Maddy had been settling into her mystery novel, Chickie was standing in the street waiting for Winston to arrive. She waved at the familiar Chicago Yellow Cab and climbed in. "This company was around in my time."

They whizzed down Harrison Street toward the coroner's office and Winston listened uncomfortably to Chickie banter with the cabbie about the Chicago Cubs. He longed to interrupt. The story of Edward's alleged involvement in an art fraud disturbed him deeply, and he was impatient to ask Chickie about it.

Winston wasn't sure he liked Chickie, but he was surprised at how quickly he had come to trust her and Maddy. His pursuit had been a solitary one until this week. Now after all these years of longing, there was a good chance he had finally found his father. These women were determined, real people with reliable facts who were quickly replacing his old dreams and wishes. Even Lena might become his friend, or some other ill-defined relation. They had Edward in common and the mystery of how and why he died was important to each of them, for different reasons.

Seeing the rooms Edward had lived in, and the photo, had stirred him emotionally. He wanted Lena's memories, especially details of his father's likes and dislikes, but whenever these wishes threatened to emerge, he suppressed them. What was his place? With all his rehearsals, he was unprepared for this moment. He had waded into an alien ocean and his habits of thinking like a scientist were not reliable flotation devices.

He stayed silent while Chickie and the driver discussed the Cub's future prospects and gazed out the window at a stretch of the city he hadn't seen until now. West of the Loop, they passed the elaborate facade of the old Cook County Hospital. It startled him; the Beaux-Arts building would look more at home in London. The rest of the buildings in the area were remarkably ordinary, verging on ugly. Within blocks they pulled up at the bunker-like Cook County Medical Examiner's Office.

"Go Cubs," Chickie called as the driver pulled away, and they approached the entrance.

In the lobby she paused to text Avril, who was meeting them.

"Don't you live in DC? How do you have friends in places like this?" Winston asked as they walked along the quiet corridors.

"It's an old story. But consider yourself lucky or you would be standing in a long, slow line to get through the red tape here. Avril is a semiretired pathologist who still does contract and volunteer work for the coroner. She is also remarkably kind and offered to help us fast-track this process."

At that moment, a tall woman in a lab coat strode down the hall toward them and hugged Chickie warmly. Chickie returned the greeting with a double-dimple grin and introduced Winston. Avril knew all the details from an earlier phone call and didn't ask questions. She greeted Winston with a handshake and was not shy about studying his face.

"I appreciate your help," he said. "Chickie implied that I could grow a full beard before getting the results on my own."

She brushed away his thanks and winked at Chickie.

The three of them walked down a long corridor past glass-fronted offices that all looked alike. They turned left and Avril ushered them into an office and then to a lab in the back where they sat side by side in molded plastic chairs.

"I have the next-of-kin consent form signed by Lena," Chickie said, removing her backpack and pulling out a folded paper. "I also have a power of attorney for health care from her, so you are allowed to talk to me."

"Good. And you?" Avril asked Winston.

Winston nodded, handing her another consent form signed by Lena and him. "You do a blood draw and paternity test here to check for a match, right?"

Avril studied him again. "Yes," she said slowly. "I will compare your draw to the sample taken from Edward's body. I'm sure I can get some information expeditiously, but you do have the choice of going elsewhere. Are you certain you don't want to make this procedure more private? Not everyone wants to share paternity news with people they've just met."

"I appreciate the offer, but no," Winston said, shrugging. "I'm closer than I have ever been in my search, and I want to know as quickly as possible. I'm okay with you both knowing the results. Whatever the test result, I'm not going to ever meet Edward, and I'd rather get it over with. I'm ready to do it now, here."

When Avril left to get the supplies she needed, Winston continued to pour out his thoughts. "I think it matters to Lena to know too. I've been a bizarre, disturbing intrusion into her life; that's done. But wouldn't she like to know if I am Edward's son, and that I want to know about the good in him?"

Chickie looked frankly at Winston. "Yes, she wants to know. It's a good idea that you decided to stay in Chicago a while longer, and I do think Lena needs someone else who wants to believe in Edward." Whether he deserves it or not, she decided.

"You are certainly a surprise to her. If Edward was alive, I suspect she would have been shocked, angry, rejecting, disbelieving, all of it. But that world is gone; it's been upended and now you're an unexpected link to him. While this is a strange complication, you might also cushion the loss. If you are his child, I don't think she'll turn her back on you."

Still, as they waited, neither mentioned the news stories about

Edward's alleged scam, although Chickie anxiously pressed buttons on her phone, checked for returned calls or emails, and scoured the internet for follow-up stories.

Winston listened to her muttering, drank terrible vending machine coffee, and felt the tension; the stakes were high for all of them. He wondered whether he did have faith in Edward. Faith was hardly scientific. And now, with Edward dead and disgraced, did he want a match? Strangely, he did. He was invested in answering the lifelong question about his father.

Avril returned and led Winston through some paperwork and lab procedures. He asked a few technical questions that Chickie didn't follow, then rolled up his sleeve. Avril efficiently drew blood for the test and applied a band aid. "In my experience, those commercial genealogy tests on the market are accurate, but now you will know for sure."

Winston agreed.

"I will call you either way, match or no match," she said kindly.

Winston stood, grateful to have gotten this far but also unsettled by being so close to a definitive answer. He turned to Chickie, "If it's okay with you, I need to go for a long walk, but I'll get us a cab and drop you anywhere you want to go."

Chickie said, "Go ahead. I'll call you later. Right now, I'm hoping to stay here and visit with Avril.

The doctor's eyebrows rose.

"If you have time?" she asked Avril, who nodded and smiled.

Both women shook hands with Winston and reassured him they would be in touch.

When he left, Chickie asked tentatively, "Coffee or real food?"

"The only reason I came in this morning was to meet you and get the lab tests underway, so let's go to lunch. I have my car." As the two women walked to the parking lot, Avril said, "I expect the medical examiner's full report will be ready soon; I'm going to ask if I can deliver it—that will be easier on Lena."

Getting into Avril's Subaru and buckling her seatbelt, Chickie marveled that she was sitting in Avril's car after all these years, having a normal conversation and going to lunch. Maybe the world was flat! She was prepared to believe anything was possible. Chicago had redeemed herself.

"Interested in Italian?"

"That sounds perfect." She would have said yes to jellied moose nose because she wanted time to talk with Avril, but before they made it to Harrison Street, Maddy's text arrived. Chickie read:

Meet me at Edward's office NOW. Lena's gone off with Brian. Raph is worried. I don't like it.

Avril saw Chickie's dimpled grin crushed by distress and didn't wait for the explanation. "Change of plans? Got to run?" Irony rich in her voice, the pathologist couldn't help herself from asking, "Where can I drop you?"

Chapter Twenty-Seven

Realizing that Lena had left the hotel with Brian, Maddy rushed to find her shoes, grab a sweater, and head for the elevator. Halfway down the hall she stopped and limped back to get her cane.

The doorman flagged a taxi, and she settled into the backseat. The driver cut over to Michigan Avenue, turned north, and ten minutes later she exited the cab in front of Edward's office building. Only when she arrived on the seventeenth floor and wanted to text Chickie did she realize that she had left her phone on the bedside table at the Palmer House.

Aggravated and increasingly tense, she told herself, "I am not afraid of conflict, I am not afraid of conflict," and pushed open the glass doors to face the snippy receptionist they'd met earlier in the week. With a professional smile she said, "I'm here to see either Brian or Raph." *Yes, use first names. Good strategy, Maddy.*

"I remember you, Mrs. Wells," the receptionist said frostily. "I cannot disturb any of the doctors right now—their wishes, not mine. It may be a while."

Maddy's face settled into stern resolve. "I am here because Dr. Sodano asked me to come." She hefted her walking stick and said, "I will quietly accommodate myself over there while you notify Raph that I've arrived." She wheeled around and headed for the chair that had a view of both the entry door and the back corridor.

Recalling Raph's urgency about the meeting now in progress, her anxiety lurched skyward, and the questions began. *Where is Raph? How could I be so stupid to forget my phone?*

Downstairs, Chickie stomped into the building, embarrassed that she'd ditched Avril yet again. She paced the elevator, furious, ready to take it out on any available obstacle, animal, vegetable, or mineral. She shoved the Temple of Self-Care doors open and strode directly over to her friend, who perched on the edge of a stiff chair looking unusually grim.

"Well? Tell me what happened."

In a low voice, Maddy relayed the conversation with Raph and her inability to get into the meeting. "But I left my phone at the hotel so I couldn't update you."

"Not a problem!" Chickie nodded and returned to the polished receptionist, delighted to pinpoint an opponent. Maddy followed. "Nice to see you again, Felice. We are here to join our meeting with Dr. Haskell and Ms. Jordan."

Felice's tight smile showed perfect teeth. "I'm so sorry. That is a private meeting. I explained to Mrs. Wells—"

Chickie raised one finger to her pursed lips. "No, that's not the correct answer." Then she took Maddy's elbow, and they marched to the door of the inner sanctum. It was locked. Chickie knocked hard over and over. Felice belatedly moved toward her as Raph pulled open the door.

"Glad you're here," he said as they followed him down the hall, Felice trailing behind. "Lena is in the conference room with Brian and Sean Mulvaney, the PR consultant."

"What are they talking about?" Maddy asked.

"I wasn't invited, so I decided to gate crash with you two."

Raph opened the door to a small, luxurious conference room. A round cherry table and four gray leather chairs filled the space. Three seats were occupied. Nearest the door, the consultant, a slim man in his forties, sat poised over his opened laptop. On the far side of the table, Lena sat very close to Brian, or Brian sat very close to Lena, it was difficult to tell. It was easier to see that his suit jacket was draped around her shoulders to protect her from the chilly room. She looked relaxed and beautifully put together in a soft blue cashmere sweater and large pearl earrings. Seeing her friends, she broke into a big smile. Next to her, Brian recognized the new arrivals, and his face darkened.

The small conference room became uncomfortably intimate when Chickie, Maddy, and Raph crowded in, followed by Felice. In a tight voice, Brian said, "It's all right, Felice," and waved her away. He stood, squeezed himself around the table toward the two standing women, and confronted them. "What are you doing here?"

Before either woman could answer, Raph explained in a low calm tone, "First of all, these are Lena's friends—people she invited to Chicago for support. Second, if you have arranged this meeting to discuss the best ways to protect our shared practice, you forgot to include me."

"And third," Maddy added, "Chickie knows more about this art scam than anyone else in the room. We all belong here."

Chickie slipped behind Brian and dropped into the chair he had vacated, keeping it close to Lena. Raph guided Maddy to the remaining leather chair and left to find more seating. No one spoke. Brian leaned against the wall sulking, Mulvaney tapped on his laptop, and the women gazed at before-and-after photographs of body parts on the walls.

Raph returned with two elegantly designed folding chairs and placed one next to Maddy. Brian dragged the second one around the table to insert it at Lena's other side. He patted her hand and tried to rearrange his miffed expression. "You feel safe here, don't you, honey?"

Maddy exchanged tense glances with Chickie, but Lena gazed at Brian coyly and nodded. "Absolutely, especially since my friends are here." She teared up and Brian quickly handed her his handkerchief. She carefully dabbed at her eyes. "I want them to stay."

Brian leaned over and gave her a quick hug. "Whatever you say, Lena. But," he added sternly, first to Chickie, then to Maddy, "everything discussed here remains confidential. Got that? Both of you?"

They ignored him and shifted their gazes to the man who was tapping on his laptop. He stopped. "I'm Sean Mulvaney with O'Conner, Stein, and Mulvaney. OSM has handled public relations for the practice for years."

"And you are meeting with Lena because . . . ?" Chickie asked.

Before Mulvaney could respond, Brian said, "OSM has been very helpful getting us interviews, speeches, that sort of thing."

"Will Lena be making speeches?" Chickie asked innocently.

"My specialty in the firm is reputation repair, cleansing bad press," Sean said.

"He's the partner we need at the moment," Brian barked at her.

"I see. Sanitary services for professionals." Someone was going to pay for Chickie's missed lunch with Avril, and Brian was a worthy choice, more worthy than most.

Sean frowned but moved along bravely. "I'm new to this problem, so before we decide on a strategy to counteract the news reporting, I'd like to have someone fill me in on the events. If it's okay with everyone, Chickie could start since she purportedly has the most up-to-date information."

Brian shifted in his chair, watching control slip through his skilled fingers. Chickie nodded to him, relishing the moment. She began crisply, "Yesterday, I heard the first rumor about an alleged art scam from a personal source and started making calls, but I got nowhere. This morning, we all saw the coverage in the *Trib* and *Sun-Times*. I went to other contacts and I've been told that today's columns were only the beginning and there will be more coverage, stretched out as long as anyone reads it. We have to hope for another, more sensational story to move it off print and lower its position on the internet."

"We can do that," Sean offered.

"Let me put it in context," Chickie said. "Edward's death a week ago was a tragic loss for all of us, particularly Lena, but not a headline. The likelihood of an art scam created a story that will bring his death back for another look. Just a few moments ago I learned more."

She did not reveal that one contact was a retired DC police officer who owed her a big favor. The cop had friends in Chicago who were willing to share bits and pieces about Charles. The other source was a young online investigator from DC who knew a great deal about art fraud from her dad in the FBI and was able to explain, for a price, the general mechanism of art scams. As Avril was driving her to this wretched meeting, she'd been on the phone, frantically taking notes and reading emails. "What failed to appear in the papers is how it all began: two years ago, when Brian's younger brother Charles—"

Raph muttered "Charles!" Brian's younger brother had searched for sweet deals since his twenties. At parties, the women avoided him while a certain cadre of men reveled in hearing about his outrageous schemes. Raph said, "I remember when his investment opportunities included breeding white buffalo. That was before he pushed us to get behind hypoallergenic compression socks. If I remember correctly, Brian, you liked that one. Then last year, Charles came to us with questionable sugar-filled protein drinks he urged us to endorse."

An exploitation expert, thought Maddy and peeked at Chickie, who winked.

Chickie too, relished the stories of Charles's enterprising nature and jumped back in to explain the background of this particular fiasco. "As I was saying, two years ago, Charles was in the city of Shenzhen. That's in the Guangdong Province in China where there are thousands of factories and manufacturing plants. He was looking for business opportunities.

"I ought to explain that Shenzhen is noted for reproductions. It's very common in China for art students to learn their craft by copying famous works, and they are masterful at it. It's a valued skill. Until recently, innovation was frowned upon, and copying remains a huge business."

Sitting shoulder to shoulder around the table added to the intensity of Chickie's story. She went on, "A small group of students picked up Charles at Dafen Oil Painting Village, ostensibly thrilled to be able to practice their English. They flattered him. It didn't take long before they shared their story with Charles, namely that they were art students studying with a famous artist who had painted in secret during the Cultural Revolution. Underground work, very hush hush. Even now, the artwork was politically dangerous to show."

Raph whispered to Maddy, "Risk, profit, secrecy—he couldn't pass it up." Maddy bit her lip to keep from laughing. This time, she didn't dare look at Chickie.

Brian slammed his fist on the table, "Pay attention! We must get this under control!"

Chickie looked at her email from the retired police officer and picked up the story. "The students finally offered to take Charles to an underground exhibit of their work. This probably struck Charles as very adventurous; opportunity calling. After all, he was a savvy American, and they were young people in China." She glanced at Brian. "They stuck with him, got a cab, and brought him to a narrow, out-of-the-way warehouse crowded in among larger manufacturing buildings. Of course, everything was written in Chinese. The sign probably translated into, 'Gullible Americans, Right This Way.' They brought him into a dingy room. Paintings hung on the walls and a few pieces of sculpture were mounted on pedestals. This was their own art—paintings of horses and figurative sculpture. Then they brought out homemade alcohol and tiny glasses and everyone drank."

"They didn't even have to roofie him," Lena said bitterly.

She may have rose-colored glasses on when it comes to Brian, but Lena is definitely not naive about Charles, Maddy realized.

"They didn't allow Charles to buy anything that night, heightening his interest. The next day, after the young people said they trusted their new American friend and were reassured that he was not a government spy, they showed him other work, more expensive landscapes, portraits, even some semiabstract paintings. They sold him two pieces made by their mysterious teacher." The whole room groaned softly.

Brian's face darkened, but Chickie added, "Charles should have suspected something. Dafen Oil Painting Village is world famous for reproductions. As of yesterday, they featured some lovely work by Georgia O'Keefe on one of the websites."

Maddy shot Chickie a look that warned her to tone it down.

Reluctantly she did. "Charles showed his acquisitions to his interpreter later in the week.

After the interpreter talked to Charles's host and they went round and round, the host explained the scam to him. At first Charles was embarrassed and then enraged, but it didn't take long before his wheels began to turn, and he realized he could do better. He could do unto others."

Brian lurched out of his seat, clearly pained, and left the room muttering about water. Raph conferred with Maddy; the others said and did nothing. When Brian returned, not meeting anyone's eyes, Chickie continued ruthlessly, "The next part of the story comes from some Chinese students in the US who want to be allowed to remain here. They said Charles hired several art students and tried the scam—"

"Please stop referring to Charles's business dealings as a scam," Brian said tartly.

"What do you prefer? Inaccurate advertising? Alternative facts? Maybe something simple, like fraud," Chickie responded, fully fed up with both Haskell brothers.

"Nevertheless, she persisted," Maddy said.

Mulvaney raised his hands in a supplicating gesture. "Let's finish up the story so we can form a plan."

"Charles hired several art students for this new business venture and brought his innovative sales methods to New York, where he invited a select group of doctors attending a conference to come down to Greenwich Village to view these posters and paintings in a small space on Greene Street. In this way, he bypassed galleries and anyone who might have real knowledge of art, another forward-thinking business practice. Edward was one of the doctors that night. Charles confided in them that the supply of paintings was limited because the painter was old and dying. The oils and posters had been smuggled out by students as a way to get money to their devoted teacher. Edward bought two paintings that day."

She looked at Lena's gloomy face and added, "He wasn't the only one; others also made purchases. One of those doctors said Charles was initially reluctant to sell to Edward because he was Brian's business partner, but—"

"See, Edward was a victim. I told you." Lena grew animated, leaning hopefully toward Chickie, who smiled sadly at her friend.

"It gets complicated," Chickie said. "It seems that Charles's initial hesitation vanished when he saw Edward's enthusiasm and encouraged him to find other buyers, insisting it would mean the world to the artists." She did not share her conclusion that Edward was a fool at best and complicit at worst. "Edward admired the art and accepted Charles's story that this was a good investment for a good cause."

"Where the hell is Charles now?" Raph asked Brian.

Chickie answered. "Cayman Islands since Saturday, supposedly making deals to repay money and avoid jail. That's why he's been chatty with the authorities. Others have different motivations for talking. The students and the other doctors who invested in his scheme or bought paintings all have something to say. I wouldn't believe any of them one hundred percent, but their stories do hang together."

"This is not the cautious, controlled Edward I know," moaned Lena, covering her face with her hands. Hidden, she missed the glances that ricocheted among Chickie, Maddy, and Raph, revealing compassion for her and shock at the folly of Edward's decisions.

Having lost all control of the meeting, Brian angrily jumped out of his chair, almost knocking it over, but there was no place to go. He stood behind Lena and rubbed her shoulders until she was ready to rejoin the meeting. Then he resumed his seat and whispered into her ear softly. She lifted her head and smiled at him gratefully, then said to the others, "We don't need the money. He bought a few pieces because he loved them. He always loved art; that's all."

Maddy said softly, "Edward may have gotten involved as a way to make money if he was looking toward retirement. His practice income would diminish. That could have been an incentive."

"Never!" Lena exploded. "Edward could have retired, and we would have been fine, not as fancy, but fine. I'm the one that manages most of our accounts. He loved the art! And I thought a return to art was a great idea; as a kid, Edward had painted. We threw a party about six months ago because he wanted to give more exposure to the artists who'd painted in secret during the Cultural Revolution. He was proud when our neighbor Arden bought one."

Chickie exclaimed, "So Arden is your neighbor! That name was mentioned, but I didn't know who he was. It explains a lot. Edward didn't realize that Arden's girlfriend is from a wealthy Hong Kong family, and she sent photos back to relatives and friends in China. I guess they had heard about this type of scam and told her. Of course, in turn, she told Arden, who talked to Edward—"

"Oh, I know when they talked," Lena interrupted. "About a month ago, Arden invited Edward up to his Wisconsin place to fish. Edward returned early. He was raging about Arden's arrogance. 'That know-it-all, blah blah, he is never coming into our home again.' Edward refused to explain why he was so angry at Arden."

Chickie struggled with how to best disclose the next bit. "After the party at your house, Edward arranged for Arden to buy two more paintings through Charles. Sometime after that purchase, Edward had his first doubts. I don't know how or why he began to suspect that the paintings were not from artists in hiding during the Cultural Revolution. My source says that he was actually hoping to get the paintings back from Arden when he went to Wisconsin."

"How could he keep all that from me!" Lena burst out. "I feel like a fool!"

Chickie did not add that the journalist who gave her much of this information also revealed that a Chicago reporter had called Edward last week, days before his death, hoping to get his comments for the piece. Edward knew he would be exposed as a fool or a fraud.

Mulvaney gathered himself together, adjusting his sports jacket and checking his elaborate watch. He signaled to the others that he wanted to speak. "It was good that you called me in, Brian. The reputation of this practice is obviously in danger. We can help. I will write up a proposal for you, but basically, I suggest a three-pronged approach.

"First, media. Online, we bury references to the scandal by producing copious content that will take its place. After all, content is king. Print media: we garner good press, for example, your newsletter announces that the practice partners are joining a mission to Africa or India to repair facial deformities. We can get you two interviewed for print. Maybe there's a new procedure that you have developed. We can discuss details later.

"Second, community relations: I suggest funding a scholarship or donating, and showing up, at a local clinic. Let's arrange for a couple of awards or citations.

"Third, meta-analysis: Charles is not the problem—"

"Not the problem? Haven't you been listening?" Raph stopped Mulvaney cold, his innate politeness gone. He was disgusted by Mulvaney's ridiculous three-point plan and infuriated by the suggestions for new procedures, bogus good works, and jaunts to other countries.

"Charles is not the problem for the practice," Sean insisted. "He is not relevant. Edward is the problem. It is imperative to distance the practice from him. I suggest we use some well-placed stories about his declining health and faulty judgment."

Brian had been nodding along with Mulvaney until he noticed Lena, wide-eyed with fury. "Enough; thank you, Mulvaney. Please put these ideas in writing as soon as possible. We appreciate your time." He swiveled to Lena and took her hands, "We will protect you."

Lena looked dubious. "I'm not hard of hearing. Your reputation protector plans on blaming Edward and maligning his reputation."

Brian gently shook her hands. "We are family. Edward was like a brother to me—"

"Isn't one brother hiding in the Cayman Islands enough family?" Maddy said through gritted teeth, but she could see that Lena still viewed Brian as a source of protection. She frowned at Chickie when Brian announced that he was taking Lena out for a very late lunch as a reward for holding up so bravely.

Chickie frowned back when Lena agreed.

"Let Brian worry about me for a couple of hours. You have been on duty nonstop for days and now you can have time off," Lena assured them.

Chickie knew enough not to say anything; assessing Lena's well-being was Maddy's specialty. She must have earned at least one badge in rescuing friends from aging predators. But all Maddy said was, "Gus will come to your place later with information he is gathering from the other *Trib* reporters, and we will be there."

Brian helped Lena up. Before following them out, Mulvaney slid his laptop into its OSM leather case and reached over to grab Chickie's hand. "I've read your *WaPo* work online; love it. If you ever need OSM, call me."

Chickie extracted her hand and gave him a look that left him scuttling out of the conference room. Raph, Maddy, and Chickie stared at each other.

"After all that 'reputational management,' I need a shower," Maddy muttered tensely. "But I'm equally interested in food before we have to see Brian again."

"My car is here," Raph offered. "How about a quick trip to Greektown for some saganaki and ouzo? It will give the illusion of escape, and we can easily get back to Lena's on time." Maddy smiled and he headed out the door, saying over his shoulder. "Meet me in front of the building in ten minutes."

Chickie's phone pinged with a text from Winston as they stood on Michigan Avenue.

Avril called to confirm the results were a match. Who/when/how is it best to share news with Lena? Maybe it's best if Avril delivers this information plus coroner's report tomorrow sometime. Call me? Maybe call Avril and let me know a plan for tomorrow?

Chapter Twenty-Eight

Brian took Lena's arm possessively and left the conference room, steering her toward the freight elevator. "We'll go right to the parking garage. I don't want any lurking journalists to bother you."

Lena stumbled getting into the cavernous service elevator and reached for him. "I appreciate you wanting to shield me." She enjoyed his concern even though he was likely to exaggerate the risks to enhance his own importance. "Brian," she looked up at him and asked, "Tell me the truth—you did know what Charles was up to, didn't you?"

He pressed the button for P2 and said nothing.

Lena took his silence as assent and continued with more energy. "I think he used Edward as a chump! And you're too smart to have been completely blind to it all." She finished with the lovely smile that had always worked wonders with Edward when she wanted to soften criticism.

He smiled back. "Brothers can't always control each other. You have brothers. Did they tell you about the mischief they got into?" He took off his wrinkled linen jacket and threw it casually over his shoulder.

"This is hardly mischief," she bristled.

"Charles may be my younger brother, but he doesn't tell me every business venture he gets involved in." He waved his hand dismissively and pushed the elevator button again even though they had almost reached the parking level.

"Well, now that you know, what are you going to do? Charles has been cheating people, apparently without any remorse! You can't defend him after what he did to your partner!" She backed away from him.

"Now, Lena, that's not fair. Edward made his own choices and had his own reasons. I could ask you the same question. Didn't you know what he was doing?"

Lena looked struck and when Brian reached across to touch her shoulder, she stiffened.

"Sweetheart, you and I are on the same team. We've been dealt a bad hand and I'm trying to make the only smart move left. Protect the practice because that is what pays all of our bills, yours included!" The elevator stopped. Exasperated, Brian shoved the door and squinted under the fluorescent lights of the parking garage. "I don't see anyone."

"I think I ought to go home."

"No, Lena. It isn't safe," Brian urged, guiding her to a large BMW sedan. He held the door, and she sank into the black leather seat. Despite her irritation, she was pleased he had insisted on taking her out. Brian was good at taking charge. Maddy and Chickie were her defenders, of course, but men took protection seriously. They had a different energy that she enjoyed. She missed Edward.

"Buckle up," he called as he whipped the car out of the garage. They made a quick trip up Michigan Avenue and stopped in front of Trapani, a local favorite. Brian jumped out, handed his car keys to the valet, and helped Lena out just as her phone buzzed with a text from Maddy. She read aloud:

We're dining at Greek Islands. Remember coming here in the '80s? We'll be at your place by five or five thirty unless you text otherwise.

Brian nodded indifferently.

The hostess recognized Brian immediately and led them to a

secluded banquette. She handed them large, elegant menus and asked if he wanted the usual.

"Yes, and for the lady . . . I think a sherry."

Lena liked sherry, but no one ever ordered for her, not even Edward. Was this protective? Or controlling? She was too weary to care and had only one goal for the meal—protect Edward's reputation.

"They have my favorite comfort food here," Lena said, skimming the familiar menu. "I haven't eaten today. I'll have the burrata, the cavatelli, and a glass of *vini rosati*."

Brian ordered, dismissively adding, "We're hungry."

As soon as he left, Brian said, "I consider it my job to provide comfort and protection for you." He patted her hand. "We will get through this together. Let's try, before the food comes, to have a common understanding so you are prepared if anyone asks questions. We want a family front, so to speak."

"My family doesn't include Charles." Their drinks arrived and she knocked back the sherry.

Brian's forehead wrinkled. "For right now, all of us are family—all of us. The only possible way to proceed is to insist that we know nothing about either man's hobby of collecting art. And if Edward or Charles resold pieces, those are private transactions among adults."

Lena said nothing. His callousness was distressing, but she didn't know how to change his mind. Glancing around at the dark walls and neutral decor, she noticed a few men at the bar and a large table of young women loudly celebrating something. They were all involved in their own lives.

Brian talked on. "Lena, I don't approve of Charles's scheme, but he's family and I am certain the best way to get this whole thing tamped down is to ride it out with good legal and PR advice. And we've got that. The interest will die down. So what if a few rich people overpaid for crappy art? They love to overpay; it makes them feel superior."

Lena looked at him dully. "And it doesn't matter that Edward is dead and that there are headlines suggesting he's a criminal!" Her voice had edged up. She waved to their server and asked for her wine to be brought immediately. "What is your story? The one that you want to be en famille."

Brian slid closer and said, "We protect Edward. And you. And the practice."

She raised her eyebrows doubtfully. "In that order?"

The waiter arrived with her wine and their first courses, providing a distraction.

Lena was content to dig her fork into the burrata and smear a slice across golden toast before she returned to her worries. "I don't understand why Edward was willing to get involved with Charles. No one in their right mind wants to do business with your brother. For all we know, he had something to do with Edward's death," she said carelessly.

Brian reacted immediately. "That's ridiculous, and I'm disappointed that you would ever think such a thing. As for their business dealings, what difference does it make now? Edward wanted in, and we'll never know why."

Lena teared up at the dismissive tone. He immediately softened his words. "I mean, oh sweetie, that came out all wrong," he protested, offering her his napkin.

"Don't *sweetie*, me. Don't patronize me!" she said. "Yes, 'we'll never know'—because he's dead! Dead! But I don't understand how he was drawn into this type of deal, and why he didn't tell me or why he worried about money. Oh god, there is so much I don't understand. These behaviors are all so unlike Edward!"

Brian snuck a look around the restaurant. No one was paying attention to them. He took the final swallow of his bourbon and said, "You can tell people that Edward believed he was making a good investment for himself and for a foundation that supports youth in Asian art. It makes sense. Edward was thinking ahead to retirement and wanted to give back."

Lena corrected him. "Edward already supported youth foundations, and he was not planning to retire."

"He was slowing down, but maybe he didn't want to admit it. Maybe he didn't want to worry you. Doesn't that sound like him?" Brian asked, eyes focused directly on Lena.

She slid along the leather banquette in order to look at him from farther away. "What do you mean, slowing down? He only talked about not wanting to crowd his surgery schedule. And maybe to travel more. We hoped to sail on the *QM2* to London later this year for a vacation. What do you mean *slowing down*?"

"Edward was billing less, and he wasn't involved in most of our marketing plans. He showed no interest in my proposed institute, New Generation Bodies. You know, people have different levels of energy as they age. Mine is the same as when I was thirty, but that's not true of all men." Brian shrugged nonchalantly and reached up to stroke his unnaturally firm jawline.

Lena's cavatelli with Sicilian meat sauce, Brian's old-fashioned steak pizzaiola and two more glasses of red arrived. Brian ate enthusiastically while Lena picked at the pasta; her head was beginning to throb.

Between bites, Brian gazed at her, and she ignored him. "Eat, you deserve a good meal." He wiped sauce from his mouth. "As we know, I'm the expert on women's looks. For someone who has been through an ordeal, it doesn't show on your lovely face."

Lena acted as though she hadn't heard the comments. This dinner wasn't going as she had hoped. Instead of Brian's handsome face, she wished that Maddy's kind one or Chickie's honest one smiled at her from across the table. The food lost its taste and talking like this only made her long for Edward more desperately than ever. A fresh wave of grief surged over her, and she could barely breathe. Dropping her fork, she rose unsteadily. "I'm done; I need to go home," she said and fled to the washroom.

When she returned with reddened eyes and repaired makeup, the table was cleared, and Brian was slipping the credit card receipt into his wallet. He looked worried.

Chapter Twenty-Nine

Lena was more composed after they walked around the block. She felt ready to make the short ride back to her apartment. The street was quiet; there were no strange cars or men with cameras. Her neighbors walked their dogs and music floated in the air, but Brian insisted on calling the doorman and they went around to the alley and up in the service elevator.

Walking down the quiet hallway on the penthouse level, Lena hunted in her bag for the apartment key, found it, and let them in. Brian took off his jacket and headed for the art deco bar in the living room to pour a stiff bourbon while Lena kicked off her shoes and asked, "What time is it? Maddy and the others will be here around five thirty."

He glanced at his watch. "There's plenty of time. I'll mix you a dry martini."

Lena refused and stood bleakly at the windows looking at the lake, unresponsive to Brian's attempts at conversation, so he retreated to the velvet sofa and sipped his drink. He considered leaving before the others arrived but wanted to hear whether Maddy's son had new information.

Brian had no idea why those two women made him uncomfortable. He dealt with women their age every day; they were his bread and butter. But these particular women were too smart and confident—it made them unfeminine, unattractive. But then, he didn't like his wife very much either, and she had been the perfect homemaker and mother. Brian frowned; these odd types of thoughts entered his mind more regularly in recent years, but fortunately they were still easy to dismiss—unlike his growing impatience.

He followed Lena as she drifted out of the living room and into the library. He'd only been in this room with Edward and rarely. It made him uneasy. "Ready for a drink?" He held up his almost empty glass, and Lena glanced his way but shook her head. "I'll be right back," he said and left to refresh his own. When he returned, Lena was looking around the room as if she was searching for something.

"What's up?" he asked. "What did you lose?"

She moaned softly as she sank down into one of the deep armchairs and put her feet on the armadillo. "I lost Edward. This place is so empty now." The tears started again.

Brian shifted on his feet. The meeting with Mulvaney had been a fiasco, he hadn't even finished his meal at Trapani before his efforts to get a coherent story failed, and now Lena, all loveliness in pearls and cashmere, was proving to be more stubborn than he had imagined. How had Edward once referred to her? "The iron foot in the satin pointe shoe?" Not so funny now.

He moved toward her chair and moved her feet so that he could awkwardly crouch on the armadillo. He took her hands. "Listen to me and everything is going to be all right." Then he dropped her hands, took both sides of her head, and guided her toward him. She smelled bourbon on his breath and resisted. He did not let go and pulled her face to his, kissing her roughly.

She tried to twist away, but he held her face firmly. "I've always wanted to do that, I admit," he laughed and let go. He sat back on the footstool and gazed smugly at her. "Politically incorrect, I know, I know." He smiled. "But I couldn't resist. You're very beautiful. When you're ready, we could be good with each other."

Lena bolted up, filled with disgust and fury, desperate to put distance between them. She had to wash her face before her friends arrived. She needed to get away. But as she stood, Brian grabbed her around the hips and jerked her toward his lap. Lena arched her back and pivoted hard toward the door. Her elbow caught him above the ear and Brian toppled backward over the armadillo and onto the Persian carpet. He reached out and seized her ankle. Instinctively she kicked out hard, caught him on the nose and raced out of the room without looking back.

There were sounds in the entry hall. "Lena, we're here."

Brian was struggling up from the floor, trying to stanch his bleeding nose with a pocket handkerchief when Maddy, Chickie, and Raph arrived at the library door. The armadillo was lying on its side, one glassy eye fixed on the ceiling.

"Oh, I thought it was stuffed," quipped Chickie, "but he's obviously been quite lively."

"Where's Lena?" asked Maddy sharply and without waiting for an answer, she hurried out of the room, calling her friend's name. Raph followed her.

Chickie stood with her hands in the pockets of her slacks. She stared at Brian and said nothing.

"I tripped over that goddamn animal and bashed my nose on the chair arm trying to catch myself," he said, not meeting Chickie's gaze.

"How novel—a bucking armadillo," she answered. "With that skill, I'm surprised their numbers are declining."

"Lena's crazy. I'm glad you're here," he added, grabbing a handful of tissues off the desk as he left the room, pushing past her. "When does Maddy's son, whatever his name is, get here?"

She ignored him and bent over to right the armadillo. "Nice work," she whispered, glad there were no blood stains on the carpet. Schmuck. They had arrived at the right time; Maddy would extract the entire story from Lena, not that it was difficult to figure out.

Exhausted, Chickie sat alone in the room finally noticing the unremarkable Chinese art on the walls.

The buzzer sounded and footsteps rushed past the library into the foyer. Maddy welcomed her son Gus with a hug. She looked at him expectantly and he patted her head fondly. "I've got more of this story—or at least the facts you're interested in." Then, as Chickie entered the room, he called over Maddy's shoulder to her, "Hey, there's my role model!"

They introduced him to Raph. Brian approached the group in the now crowded entry hall and stuck out his hand for an introduction. "Pleasure to meet you. Always useful to know an investigative reporter."

"I'm assigned to sports," Gus corrected, looking toward his mother, who wore a tight smile he recognized as anger. At least it wasn't directed toward him.

Brian gestured toward the living room. "There's more room for all of us in there," he said in a hearty voice, clearly recovered. "Well Gustav, let's hear what you have to say."

They followed. Gus looked hopefully at Chickie and Maddy for some direction, but at that moment Lena joined them, walking purposefully into the room gazing only at Gus, who leaned down to give her a hug. She looked up at him with a smile and said, "You look like your dad did at your age." Clearly exerting self-control, she avoided Brian.

Brian left the bar, where he added ice to his glass and dropped into one of the chairs. Raph made a point of standing close to Lena, who had positioned herself in front of the windows. It had gotten dark and lights from TV screens in nearby apartments gave a liveliness to the cityscape, festive compared to the apartment's dark mood. Maddy motioned Gus to the couch and joined him there. Chickie was unable to sit; she paced the room, walking back and forth behind Brian's chair.

Gus took out his notebook and launched into his story. "There is compelling evidence that the art Dr. Jordan sold was fake, meaning that it may have been painted by a Chinese artist, but it is not the work of any of the men and women who worked in secret during the Cultural Revolution. In fact, there isn't a tremendous amount of work from that period, but it has been cataloged and is shown from time to time, mostly in Asia. It's not clear when Dr. Jordan learned the paintings were fake. The broker, Charles . . ." he paused to look at the name in his notes.

"We know who was involved," Brain interrupted.

"Now we just refer to Charles as 'Scam Likely,'" Chickie offered.

Brian glared. "What we want to know is what media coverage to expect. We're trying to do damage control here, not build a legal case!"

Lena had been looking fixedly out at the lights and the lake, but she wheeled around and spoke in a tone no one in the room had ever heard.

"Damage control! Damage control?" she spit out each word. "You self-centered bastard."

Brian started to rise as if to soothe her, but she held her hands up and said, "Back off. I'm done with your self-serving effort to craft a sweet, simple, sad story out of this; to lay blame on Edward, who has no way to defend himself or explain these circumstances; and above all, to distance yourself from this mess. The news about Charles will be whatever the news is about Charles. You and your brother can concoct any story you want—you're both creative. Say the white buffalo did it; I don't care, but leave Edward out of it. If you talk about him, if you say one word about my husband, I can promise you that I will use every dime I have to make you sorry.

"The hell with your 'Let's be on the same page' bullshit. I'm already damaged and Edward is gone. Maybe he was a fool; maybe he got tricked. If he made a mistake, even if he knowingly committed art fraud, it is not going to change where we are right now. He's dead, I am grieving, and Brian, I want you out of here. Now."

There was complete silence marred only by Gus dropping his notebook. Behind Brian's chair, Chickie stopped pacing, stood with her arms folded, and grinned proudly.

Brian tried, "Now, Lena—"

"*Now*, Brian. OUT." She turned to Raph and said, with a dramatic shift in tone to sweetness, "Raph, would you walk Brian out, please. I wouldn't want him to lose his way and fall again. I appreciate you being here tonight, but I don't think there is anything left to discuss. I can fend off any media inquiries for the next few days and play the widow with well-choreographed drama if needed. With regard to Edward's poor decisions, I plan to consult my own attorneys, and they can also handle any issues related to the surgery business. They will be in touch."

Raph stepped into the tension in the room and said calmly, "Good idea. Let's go Brian." He moved between Lena and Brian and gestured toward the door.

Brian stood for a long moment, indecision evident, but he was smart enough to read the room. No friends here. He turned on his heel and walked toward the door. "I'll be in touch, Lena!" he said sternly as Raph opened the door to follow him out.

"Brian?" Lena called softly.

He turned hopefully.

"Brian, there's no more being in touch. I know enough about your personal life to keep Sean Mulvaney and his reputation defenders in business for years. It's in your interest to keep me happy. That's not a threat; simply common sense. Keep me happy and quiet."

The apartment door closed but Brian's curses were clearly audible as the men walked toward the elevator.

"He's got quite a vocabulary," Gus said to Chickie. "If I'd ever talked like that, I would have been grounded."

"Correctly so, and Lena has handed him a permanent time out."

"You've given me an idea." Lena strode toward the house phone. They heard her instruct the concierge, "Two gentlemen ought to be coming through the lobby. If the gentleman in the linen jacket tries to return tonight or ever, don't let him in. He's not welcome." She hung up the phone with a bang.

Maddy, Chickie, and Gus were standing in the living room when Lena returned. "I'm shaking," she said.

"Irrelevant. You were brilliant," Chickie said.

Maddy grabbed her in a tight hug. From the depths of her friend's embrace, Lena said, "I never got dessert."

Maddy held her at arm's length. "Finally, a problem I can fix. We know your fridge."

Sitting around the kitchen island, the four of them dug into custom sundaes. Maddy rhapsodized about the eternal appeal of hot fudge on vanilla, and Chickie didn't want to contradict her, so she simply waved a jar of Marshmallow Fluff in the air before scooping it over coffee ice cream. Gus dropped Reese's peanut butter chips over a mound of mixed flavors, marveling that a home with skinny adults and no children was so well stocked with dessert essentials.

Lena was triumphant. She gobbled ice cream, looked up to grin at her guests and spooned more cookies and cream into her mouth. Every time she said, "I did good," the others echoed with enthusiasm, "You did great!"

When the ice cream was gone, Gus said, "Lena, I do have some more information from the *Trib* investigation, but only if you want it."

"Will it ruin my mood?"

"I don't think so." Gus put his notebook on the counter in front of him. "The big picture is that art fraud is on the rise globally and can be very lucrative. And complicated legally."

"Wow, Charles finally stumbled onto a money-maker," Maddy said, putting her spoon down.

Gus continued. "Edward's purchases are not a problem, though likely not worth what he paid. But that is not a legal issue. The gray area is selling art, because the critical question is whether Edward intended to deceive anyone who bought from him. Did he know the paintings were fakes? That will be hard to prove.

"The story is likely to fade fast. Authorities need new information from Charles or other buyers to keep this newsworthy, and I don't think it's there. Edward's coincidental death won't hold attention unless there are rapid new disclosures."

Lena gazed thoughtfully at Gus. "He would never have knowingly hung fake art in our apartment. He was too proud. And protective of his home and me. I see now, in retrospect, that Arden must have accused him of knowingly selling garbage. Edward had no idea. He was frantic and wanted the whole mess under control. I'm not objective and I hate thinking he was a fool, but I'm certain he wasn't a criminal. That makes all the difference in this endless day."

She looked around at each of them, "I'm okay for now. And Chickie showed me a text from Avril. She is coming to deliver the coroner's findings in the morning. I will ask Winston to be here too. I may have another sleepless night, but I prefer to be sleepless on my own, here. I'm ready. Gus, can you give them a ride to the hotel?"

Chickie's Blog:
Old Dogs, New Tricks
(A Writer's Reflections on Growing Old and Growing Up)

Revisiting Friendship

Being back in Chicago after decades of avoidance, I'm confronted by the past. It has caused me to think about friends, so I am sharing a conversation I had this evening with my close friend Maddy. It had been an intense day, even for feeling types like she is. This is pretty much how it went, cleaned up and without the hums, likes, and pauses.

Me: Over the past decades, we've each met a lot of people. Why do we only desire to become friends with a few of them? You probably have more friends than I do, but still . . .What is it? And why do some friendships last a lifetime and other ones, with equally good people, dissolve?

Maddy: Yes, there are always relationships that end badly. That seems like the subject of endless TV shows. The ones that endure, those friendships are fascinating.

Like us. We're durable.

Me: We're made to last . . . We could have lost touch when I left Chicago. No harm done. But instead, we hung on.

Maddy: That sounds desperate.

Me: No. Actually, you bring out the best in me. I'm nicer with you. That's one reason why we're friends.

Maddy: You make me braver. Maybe I'll buy a bright blue blazer.

Me: Don't go crazy. Maybe start with a washed-out blue vest. But that's my point—growing, stretching, it's starting to sound like cosmetic surgery.

Maddy: That's because we are almost self-actualized.

Me: It's a good thing you're a shrink. You will be able to tell us when we are fully self-actualized.

Maddy: I hope we have enough cognitive capacity to enjoy it. It would be a pity if dementia beats actualization to the finish line.

At that point, Maddy raided the mini bar.

Chapter Thirty

Wednesday morning, Winston walked anxiously along the downtown streets near his hotel. It was barely light. None of the stores had opened for business yet, so it was him, a few joggers, and far too many homeless people still asleep in the cold doorways. Insomnia was becoming a habit. He had been unable to rest, thinking incessantly about his letter, trains, Edward, and Lena. Since the memorial service, since he met these Chicago people, the days had been difficult, and the nights were worse. And today was likely to be the most impossible day of all. Winston knew what was coming and dreaded Lena's reaction to the coroner's report because he was pretty sure that the finding would be suicide—the conclusion Lena feared and fiercely denied.

There were still hours before that meeting. *What if Lena doesn't accept the results? Will they show pictures of the scene? Photos never tell the whole story.* He was seized with the need to see where Edward had died. Winston began to run. He was almost at the entrance of his hotel when he slowed down, panting. It was crazy. *He'd indulged his obsession before and where did it get him? Edward was dead today and he would be dead tomorrow and every day after that. The search was over.* He was about to enter the hotel when he turned around for a last look at the line of cabs waiting at the curb.

A cabbie called to him, "Need a ride?"

That decided him. Winston climbed in and they sped north along a deserted DuSable Lakeshore Drive and parked at the small strip mall directly across from the Wilmette train crossing. The driver went into the nearby coffee shop, and Winston leaned against the front bumper of the cab staring wide-eyed at the red and white gate, high in the open position. He watched a few commuters and locals drive slowly across the tracks. This was where Edward died, but there was no sign of Thursday's tragedy. No tape, no markers, nothing to indicate a death had taken place a week earlier. It was back to normal; just another affluent suburb slowly coming awake.

Finally, he crossed the street, moving nearer to the tracks to study the scene, trying to imagine Lena's scenario of a murderous assault. It was difficult. The land was Midwestern flat in all directions with a few struggling trees and low shrubs growing alongside the tracks, but the visibility was wide open. From where he stood, the Chase bank and storefront rug shop on the far side of the tracks were easily visible.

He used his phone to take a series of shots. Facing him were six huge warning lights at the crosswalk. Matching lights also faced the other direction. In addition to the large red and white gate for vehicles, there was a small one for pedestrians. There was no place for a person to hide or to conceal even a small dog.

Winston was debating whether to get even closer when the harsh sounds of a horn blasted through the sedate suburban morning, freezing him where he stood. Bells clanged, the gates dropped, the large lights flashed. Within seconds, a train barreled through noisily from the north. Winston instinctively stepped back, his hair and sweatshirt blowing wildly as the train flew by to the next station. He glimpsed passengers reading newspapers, books or looking down, probably at their phones. A few peered out at him. In no time, the train had vanished on its daily route into the city. So, this is how it would have looked and sounded a week ago.

Shaken, he took a deep breath, stowed his phone, and hurried back to the parked cab. As he opened the door, he turned and looked again at the crossing. His suspicions had been right, those tracks were not the scene of an accident or a murder in broad daylight.

AVRIL WAS READY to deliver the coroner's report. She parked in a lot on North Avenue, intending to give herself a longish walk to Lena's building. Although she had delivered unwelcome news many times in her long career, these were Chickie's good friends and she wanted time to rehearse exactly what she would say, not say, and might say, if the opportunity presented itself. As she passed the Museum of Contemporary Art on East Chicago Avenue, she noticed Winston seated on one of the lower broad steps, his head turned down and away. The evening before, when Avril had phoned him to confirm Edward's paternity, Winston had freely asked questions. Now he was avoiding her. She had a good idea why. Avril walked toward him slowly. He rose, looking tired and uncomfortable, and stepped down to the sidewalk. "Want to walk to Lena's with me?" she asked conversationally.

He flushed, not moving.

"You're unsure about going." It wasn't a question. She sat down on the cold step, and he joined her.

"Maybe it's better if I skip this meeting," he tried.

"Better for whom?"

Winston looked out at the passersby and spoke so softly she could barely hear him say, "In addition to telling Lena that I am actually Edward's son, I expect you are going to tell us Edward committed suicide."

"That idea doesn't seem to surprise you."

His voice stayed slightly above a whisper. "I wanted to be able to agree with Lena that his death was an accident, or even murder, so I went to the train crossing very early this morning.

"Even if I hadn't seen how flat the area is, I don't need actuarial statistics to tell me that few people are accidentally hit by commuter trains and fewer die from being pushed in front of them."

"You've suspected Edward's death was suicide for a while then. Is that why you want to avoid the meeting? Or is there another reason?" Avril tried unsuccessfully to make eye contact with him.

Winston looked farther down the street for a few minutes before he admitted, "I wonder if my letter was the final straw. I don't want people thinking that he read the damn thing, was horrified to have an unknown, unwanted son, and jumped in front of a train rather than meet me. How do we know that my relentless desire to find a father didn't trigger Edward's wish to die? We can't prove otherwise." He swung back to look at Avril with wet eyes.

"Proof! You're a scientist, act like one," she said sternly. "Come on, can you really credit one letter announcing the existence of an accomplished adult son as a reason to die? I disagree with your horror story and believe the truth is far more human. Perhaps a tragedy with victims, but not a crime. I think you ought to come with me to Lena's house, but I can't force you." She stood and slowly brushed off her jacket and slacks, giving Winston a chance to join her. He reluctantly got to his feet.

They walked in silence for several blocks. It had become another glorious October day, cool, the trees resplendent in greens and golds, but Avril wasn't fooled. Chicago did that, delivering spectacular weather that raised everyone's hopes only to defeat weary residents with a quick downturn to low temperatures and brutal wind. The city was a tease.

"Chickie and Maddy seem to like you, and Chickie, for sure, is not easily won over."

"You never told me how you know Maddy and Chickie," Winston responded, kicking through a drift of leaves swirling toward them.

"Ah," she smiled, "I never knew Maddy well, but Chickie . . . I was here in a medical residency, and we met through her first husband, Danny. We became close friends after he died, but she was flailing and wanted to put Chicago behind her, so she moved on to DC and became a writer. We've been out of touch."

"She's prickly," Winston said tentatively.

"Yes, but a good soul and very funny. I missed her terribly when she left. Chickie is the person you want on your side when life treats you roughly; she's fierce and loyal. Well, usually she is."

"And now you have your friendship back."

Poor guy is desperate for a Hallmark ending for someone, anyone, Avril thought. "We'll see. Just because you found a person once lost to you doesn't mean you regain the years you lost." She picked up the pace and pointedly began to describe details of the classic greystone townhouses they passed.

When they arrived at Lena's building, the concierge looked Winston over very carefully. He had been warned by the nightman to make sure a certain gentleman was not admitted.

Satisfied, he called upstairs to announce them and when they arrived at the top floor, Chickie met them at the door to Lena's apartment. "Ready?" she asked and ushered the two of them into the living room, where Maddy eagerly rose from the velvet couch. Chickie introduced Avril.

Maddy greeted her warmly, referring to a couple of old encounters when they'd all lived in Chicago. Chickie interrupted, "I'm making coffee if you're up for it; their machine is a work of art. Lena's changing her clothes." She couldn't help looking at her watch as she strode back to the kitchen.

"Waiting patiently isn't Chickie's strong suit," Maddy said as Avril and Winston took seats across from her in matching chairs.

"Character is pretty consistent, isn't it?" Avril laughed, pulling several green folders from her case. She placed them on the small table between her chair and Winston's. He and Maddy stared, mesmerized by the carefully labeled cardboard files until Chickie returned and handed them coffee. Automatically, they sipped from the delicate Limoges cups and waited. Eventually, Avril put her coffee down and walked across the room to gaze out the window toward the lake, a clear blue morning. Chickie also rose and roamed the room with her phone out, scrolling and reading. Maddy tried to engage Winston with a few desultory comments, but he was lost in his own thoughts, and the closed green file folders dominated the mood of the room as the silence grew. Finally Lena walked in quietly wearing a dark linen trouser suit and ballet flats.

Winston searched Lena's tired face for clues as to her mood. She noticed and smiled halfheartedly at him before staring seriously at Avril when Maddy introduced the doctor. Lena moved to the couch close to Maddy.

Avril had been in this situation many times. She placed the thinner folder on her lap and smoothly took the lead. "Thanks, Lena, for letting us meet in your lovely home. And for giving your consent for the DNA test. I have two matters to cover, and then I will try to answer any questions you have.

"First, as you all suspected, Winston is Edward's biological son. I have numbers and formal results to give you, but the bottom line is confirmation of paternity." She paused. No one made a comment or asked a question, so she gazed back and forth between Lena and Winston.

The silence was complete. She opened the file and held up several sheets of paper stapled together. "This information can raise a lot of questions and more importantly, it can evoke strong emotions, all of which are worth acknowledging and can take time to sink in. But the DNA facts are conclusive.

"To be clear Lena, that DNA information belongs to you and Winston, and only you two hold the privilege of disclosure. Share it or not, it's up to you. It's not in the coroner's record or the investigation of Edward's death." She handed the papers to Winston and passed duplicates across to Lena.

Winston poured over the numbers while the widow looked at him with a mix of fascination and solemnity. "I'm no longer shocked, but I don't know what else to say."

Winston heard Lena's words but didn't raise his eyes from the numbers swimming on the page. *Damn,* he thought. *It's real. It's on paper, confirmed by this doctor, accepted as fact. Is this how the search ends, in some lavish Chicago living room with an exotic species of stepmother?* He had spent a lifetime trying to answer one question. Check. Now what? A chill gripped his body, and he peeked around, afraid that one of the women would notice. He clumsily stood, grasping the paper with a shaking hand. "Thank you for including me," he told Lena. "I am grateful, but I should probably go now and give you some privacy to talk privately."

He tried to keep his voice steady. "I will be in Chicago until tomorrow night. If you want anything, please ask." Gesturing toward Chickie and Maddy he added, "They know how to reach me and, just in case, here's my information." He woodenly placed a business card on the coffee table in front of Lena. She reached for it and stared at the name and phone number, but didn't say a word, so before anyone else could speak, a thoroughly rattled Winston left the room.

Maddy quickly touched Lena's arm. "Do you want him to go?"

Chapter Thirty-One

"Maybe you want Winston to hear the rest of what Dr. Clairwell has to say."

Maddy's suggestion startled Lena. "Do I?" Confused, she redirected her question to Chickie who nodded. Lena leaped up and hurried into the foyer after Winston. The others heard a lengthy, muffled conversation.

"You have a terrible job," Chickie said to Avril who shrugged in response to the Chickie-style compliment.

In a few minutes, Lena returned with Winston trailing behind her. Her confusion was momentarily replaced with confidence as she said, "Since Winston is Edward's son, he has the right to hear the coroner's report." Then, uncertainty returned, and she looked to Avril for reassurance. The doctor agreed and waited until stepmother and stepson were seated before she opened the second, thicker folder and removed a sheaf of pages. "The coroner authorized me to tell you that his investigation is complete, and Edward's body will be released today. His personal effects will also be released." She placed a single sheet of paper on the coffee table. "I have written down all the details of that process, and I know Maddy and Chickie will help with related tasks."

"We'll take care of everything," Maddy offered immediately.

Lena didn't hear a word. "And . . . ," she whispered.

"The finding for cause of death is suicide."

Winston's deep intake of breath was audible. Otherwise, the silence was huge and heavy, filling every corner of the room until Lena moaned and dropped her head, shaking it slightly from side to side. "I don't believe it," she said in a shaky voice. "It doesn't make any sense. He wouldn't do that to me."

Maddy tried to put her arm around Lena's shoulder, but the other woman leaned away.

"Your reaction is normal and natural," Avril eventually said. "It's never easy news to absorb and you can take your time and ask questions. It's—"

"How do you know it was suicide? What's your proof?" Lena interrupted sharply. "How do you know it wasn't an accident or that someone pushed him?"

"You raise a very important question, and I'll walk you through the facts we have, if you want me to . . ." Avril said slowly.

Lena waited.

"Please believe me that there is always a protocol for arriving at a decision in situations like this. People are interviewed and investigators spend time at the scene. A reliable eyewitness saw Dr. Jordan approach the train crossing at an agitated pace and deliberately step around the lowered pedestrian bar and onto the tracks while the bell was clanging. From a distance, the engineer spotted him standing in the path of the train, and slammed on his brakes, but there was no time. He tried. People in the vicinity confirmed that the horn was blowing wildly, you can imagine the noise. The crossing was empty otherwise, so no one could have pushed him. Both the witness who was walking his dog and the engineer confirmed that he was alone."

"He could have fallen or not heard the bell," Lena said fiercely.

It was obvious that Avril preferred not to continue, but Lena pushed her theory, "Maybe he heard the train and wanted to hurry across, but he tripped."

Winston wanted to explain the logistics to Lena but a sharp look from Avril silenced him.

She answered. "It's unlikely—"

"What about dizziness or a brain aneurysm or heart attack?" Lena persisted.

"The coroner could not find evidence of any condition that could have caused a sudden fall or failure of judgment."

"You weren't there! The dog walker couldn't have been staring at Edward the whole time. He was probably waiting for his dog to take a shit."

"True," Avril replied and clarified her original explanation. "But, as the dog walker said, Edward paused at the sounds of the loud bell, and . . ." she added reluctantly, "Edward rushed around the gate and into its path." Avril hated to be blunt, but she knew from long experience that reality was safer and saner than fantasy. She didn't want to leave Lena imagining other scenarios if she was vague about Edward's death. Suicide was its own torment to survivors but conjuring up imagined visions of murder or accident was no better and often worse.

Maddy seemed to understand what Avril hoped to achieve and asked, "Was there any information that could explain Edward's very unusual behavior?"

Avril looked grateful. "We also know that a few minutes earlier he had left a nearby restaurant in a distressed state. He walked out leaving his coat, umbrella, and phone. The waiter ran outside to look for him when he didn't return. The accident happened minutes later.

"We are almost finished, but I do want to make you aware of two other findings from the medical examiner. He found small traces of fluoxetine, very commonly known as Prozac. It wasn't in your husband's medical record. To your knowledge, had he been taking an antidepressant?"

Lena dismissed the question. "Everybody takes some meds, but he told me he stopped a while ago."

Avril nodded and continued. "The second finding did not appear in any record, either. Edward had a serious and eventually disabling hand condition."

Winston's head snapped up.

Avril continued, "For a surgeon, this would be a career-ending disease. He had apparently been treating himself for some time but would no longer have been able to do so because the disease was advancing in his dominant right hand as well. He kept it secret from his regular medical providers. She turned and looked at Lena. "Did you know about this?"

Lena looked bleak. "It was arthritis. I knew."

"I'm afraid it was more than arthritis. It was Dupuytren's Contracture and there is no cure."

Now Maddy knew what physical problem Dr. Stanton suspected. Desperate to be useful, she rushed from the room and brought back a glass of water that she handed to Lena. "Drink this. Do it."

Then she worriedly turned to Winston, but his gaze was fixed on Avril. "Dupuytren's Contracture is a hereditary disease. Isn't it?"

Avril acknowledged his question with a slight nod.

Lena looked at him in a daze. "He had all these secrets. Your letter and the art mess and this hand thing that Avril says is not arthritis. I don't know who to believe about what. And what in the world am I supposed to do now!" She fled down the hall toward the bedrooms. They waited. She did not return.

Maddy started after her, then retraced her steps to say sternly to Winston, "Don't leave. Please. I'll be back but please wait." She turned and went to Lena.

Avril studied the pages, replaced them, and closed the folder. She passed the investigator's report to Chickie, who allowed it to drop on the coffee table. Avril watched her. "You and Maddy ought to read the results of the entire investigation. Seriously, read it. All of it; you need to go through the interviews. My card is stapled to the top sheet if Lena has more questions."

She had expected her news to be unwelcome. After a long career in medicine, Avril understood that reality is an unpopular point of view, and she was used to it. What she wasn't used to was the survivors' preference for murder. She'd seen it before, of course, the wish that evil had robbed a family of their loved one rather than a simple accident or suicide. It created an outside force, a mystery, a who-done-it. For Avril, the greater mystery would always be the internal why-done-it. But now her job was finished; favors delivered. She could depart and others would tend to Lena's and Winston's emotional needs. The pathologist said, "I'll let myself out."

When Avril reached the front door, she noticed that Chickie had followed her. "If it's agreeable, I'll walk part way with you. I need some fresh air."

Avril smiled. "You don't want to stay with Lena?"

"Maddy is skilled at picking up the pieces. I seem to be more suited to breakage."

Chapter Thirty-Two

Maddy knocked softly on Lena's bedroom door, entered, and stood quietly. Lena was curled up on top of the duvet, her face hidden. "I know you're there." Her words were rough, muffled by the pillow. "I don't think I have any tears left, Maddy. You have to help me; I don't know what to do next."

"Maybe nothing right now." Maddy walked over to the bed and sat down gingerly.

"There's no blueprint to follow. You're awash in grief and new waves keep breaking over you. This was a rough morning. After a rough night." She paused to give Lena a chance to respond. Lena turned over to gaze at the ceiling. "I want to lay here forever without moving so nothing else can happen to me, but I'm edgy and wired."

"You are entitled to lay here and stare at the ceiling."

"No. If I do that, I'm afraid I'll never get up. What else do we need to do? You're the grief expert."

Maddy winced but stayed seated with a fixed smile.

Lena continued. "I'm glad my family wasn't here to listen to the report; their judgy presence would have made it worse. They would have said terrible things about Edward, and I don't want them blaming him. It's too hard." Her color was coming back. She struggled out of the tangled duvet, got up, and wandered over to her dressing table, opening drawers and rummaging through them until she found her brush. She sat, methodically removed the clips that kept her messy bun in place, and ran the bristles through her hair, all the while staring into the mirror.

"Maddy," she whispered, watching her friend's reflection. "The body, his body. His broken body. He would hate strangers seeing him, and the coroner says we can have him back. He wanted cremation! We can do that now. You know how. You did it for Frank, right?"

Maddy feared Lena's sudden enthusiasm meant a reprise of Doughnut Day's frenetic behavior. "Chickie and I can collect his effects and make arrangements with a mortuary. Myself, I couldn't handle shopping for an urn for Frank. It was too final; my boys did that."

"Urns. An ash urn?" Lena sat up straighter and started to laugh in a giddy way that was worrisome until she explained. "God, I had an aunt in Memphis that had the most alarming set of urns on her mantle: her husband, her mother, and two pet dogs."

She was animated, but this energetic shift in conversation did not ease Maddy's mind.

Lena's mood surged when she zeroed in on a task. "Eventually Edward would want to be scattered on Lake Michigan, I know, but I'm not ready for that. I want to keep him here for a while, at home. After all, he left without my permission! I get to make some decisions now. I have some choices." She spun around and faced Maddy. "Where do you get urns?"

"The mortuary. I think the mortuary sells them. At least that's where the boys found one for Frank."

Lena dropped her brush and leaped up. "You don't have to come with me. What happened to Winston? Is he still here? He didn't leave, did he? He should come with me, shouldn't he, couldn't he? He said he wanted to help me. And now he feels terrible too. I think I want him to come. Is that crazy? Do you think he would come?"

Maddy had completely forgotten about Winston. "Uh, I told him not to leave. Chickie's probably keeping him company, and yes, I think he'd appreciate being included." Maddy went to the bedroom door, talking over her shoulder. "You're sure you want to jump into this now, today. And with him?"

"Why not? He is Edward's son! He's part of all this now!" She paced back and forth in front of the windows. "It gives us something important to do."

Maddy stopped and eyed her warily. "Okay, Chickie and I will get Edward's personal effects for you. If Winston will join you on the urn search, we'll take care of the rest."

"Go ask him, will you?" Lena wheedled. "He'd have a harder time saying no to me, and I really want it to be his decision. And, I have to get ready." She was already readjusting her hair in the mirror.

The hallway, dining room, and sun-filled living room were quiet and empty, with no sign of Chickie or Winston. Maddy worried that they'd fled, but she found Winston standing inside the library. "It's okay to go in," she said.

He swung around guiltily, embarrassed to be caught exploring the private spaces of his father's apartment.

"Of course, you're curious."

He seemed relieved.

"But I have an important question from Lena. She's afraid it's an odd request, but would you go with her today to choose an urn for Edward's ashes? She'd like to do it with you."

"Today?" Winston looked startled, then pleased. He nodded, "Yes, I'm honored to be invited. Really, today?"

"I wondered about that too, but she seems certain, even eager. Chickie and I will take care of other details. Where *is* Chickie?"

Thirty-Three

Avril and Chickie left the building and walked for several blocks in companionable silence. The temperature had risen a few degrees, and the sun was doing its best to keep the city warm. Chicagoans took advantage, jogging, walking dogs, and talking on phones. One young woman managed all three.

"Where are you going?" Chickie asked finally.

"I don't know exactly; it was the right time to leave Lena's place."

"Do you want company?"

"It's music to my ears."

Chickie turned her face to the sun and noticed migrating birds, high above the lake, leaving town in perfect formation. She envied them. They knew just what to do in early October, fly away. "In my years of accumulated losses, I've never known anyone who committed suicide. How can people do what Edward did? You must have dealt with suicide often. What are they thinking?"

"Edward wasn't thinking. Suicides aren't all identical, but in Edward's case, the evidence suggests it was impulsive."

"I've been accused of being impulsive, but I could never . . ." she trailed off and continued walking north.

"Of course you wouldn't." Avril caught up with Chickie and touched her shoulder. "You are nothing like Edward. Yes, you know the grief and rage of being a survivor. From what I've heard, Edward also had his own list of big losses early in life, but in the grip of recent events he was overwhelmed. You're better grounded, not so self-absorbed."

"Really? Can I quote you to Maddy?"

"Anytime. She knows the ingredients here. Edward dedicated his life to control and beauty. But with aging, he faced a disabling, deforming disease, compounded by a potential scandal. That's hardly where any proud man wants to be when he is faced with meeting a successful younger man who claims to be his son." They continued along Astor Street, over to Michigan Avenue and up to Chicago Avenue where Avril directed them to the left.

"But he could have avoided meeting Winston. I've always found avoidance to be a reliable tactic for managing feelings, at least temporarily. He could have suddenly required a trip to Capri!"

"He could have—but something sparked true despair. We can't possibly know everything that was going on but, in a moment of fear and dread, he decided to end his suffering."

Chickie flashed back to the impending exposure from the art scam. A reporter had tried to reach Edward. He must have known it would unravel.

Avril admitted, "These cases are the hardest for me because we know that, just as one event can set off the impulse to die, another random event can redirect the individual, just long enough for a different outcome. If the train schedule had been different, if the dog walker had fallen and needed help, he might have been diverted, if the waiter from the coffee shop had caught up with him . . ."

"But nothing like that happened."

"We'll never know what drove Edward's action that day. But I'm convinced he had not gotten up that morning planning to commit suicide."

Chickie remembered Edward's clean office and his reluctance to share a bed with his wife. She didn't agree with Avril but said nothing, just smacked the crosswalk button, and it chided her, "Wait, wait." Just for good measure, she smacked it again but remained on the curb.

"The Museum of Contemporary Art is up ahead; their collections make me happy, even when I don't understand what the artist intended.

I left my car in that direction," Avril said. The women approached the limestone block of the museum.

"This is new. Wasn't the old MCA in a crummy building somewhere else around here?"

"Your decades of avoiding Chicago are showing. This opened in 1996. Before that, the National Guard Armory was on this spot. Swords into plowshares, sort of."

Chickie was fascinated by the strength of the limestone building, powerful and rooted to place. The wide steps created a modern plaza. "Chicago's become a city I don't quite recognize. Did you know, it's my first time back since I grabbed toddler Sam, a suitcase of diapers, a dying spider plant, and drove away?"

"No, I didn't know." Avril looked pleased to learn that there weren't any other trips when Chickie had avoided her. "Do you want to go into the museum?"

Chickie didn't seem to hear. She peered into the gift shop window. "It wasn't only you that I didn't want to face. Being here, memories of Danny are everywhere—the Art Institute, the old train tracks, the hospital neighborhood. The forty-second anniversary of his death is only three days away, and when that day comes, I would like to be anywhere but here."

"He never got old, like we have."

"My life changed in a moment, and I've created a fine life, but I still have the sense there was another one back there that I was supposed to live. That one was snatched away. God, it was an awful time."

At Avril's sharp intake of breath, Chickie swung around and grabbed her arm. "Not you," she said apologetically. "You were never part of the pain, just the confusion."

"And Sam?"

"Yeah, you're right. My son was a product of this place. Okay, you and Sam are the candles. The rest is dark."

"I think you're being harsh with yourself."

"Meaning?"

"You were a young woman then and you are, pardon the expression, an old woman now. You wouldn't dream of wearing the clothes you wore in your twenties, why in the world do you refuse to update your old worn-out ideas?"

"When did you go back for a psychiatric residency?" Chickie was quickly shifting from penitent to clearly miffed.

"I don't need another residency to understand your anger at Chicago. But this city isn't good or bad. It didn't work for you or against you. It's only a place, never designed to help you or hurt you. You were a young woman who moved here with an ambitious husband, had a child, was overwhelmed trying to establish a career, be a mother and create a marriage. And then your husband did an unforgivable thing—he died. Danny took a crazy risk going to play doctor in another country and he died. And the life you expected was buried with him."

"Believe me, I blame Danny, not only Chicago. And most of all, I blame myself."

"You? You were stuck in this city with a life you didn't want, and if you were going to do more than survive, you were forced to create a new one. And you did." Avril shook her head. "I remember you so well. You tried hard."

"And messed up so much. At least I got Sam a good therapist, but I did nothing for you, except cause hurt." Chickie had never said those words out loud. With all her fears and self-recrimination, she had avoided acknowledging the damage she caused. Unintentional, but damage nonetheless; like a drunk driver. "I know I disappeared from your life without warning. I'm not proud of my behavior but believe me, I really did care."

"You cared, but you panicked. Perhaps it's time to stop pummeling that young Chickie. A terrible time changed you, but I don't think you appreciate how much the events of childhood and young adulthood inevitably shape us. I see it often, the physical and emotional legacies of unstable beginnings or trauma. Edward had all that and a war."

Their conversation was cut short by a call for Avril. She stepped away. Her call went on for a long while, so Chickie pulled out her own phone. Something Avril said about the events of childhood being formative nagged at her; it was the same thing Raph alluded to in his eulogy. Could there be something more in Edward's past? Maddy would say that present problems could be enough to drive a vulnerable man to impulsive behavior. True, but Maddy was never suspicious enough. A little paranoia wasn't terrible. Chickie reread all the notes and screenshots she had taken at the Harold Washington Library. She had been thorough and now she had an idea; it took only a few calls.

By the time Avril returned, Chickie had abandoned her plan to pretend to relax and admire contemporary art.

"Are you up for a road trip?"

Chapter Thirty-Four

Maddy lifted her buzzing phone from the library table to hear Chickie, obviously in a car talking over the sounds of traffic. "Look," she practically shouted, "I know you said we'd take care of any and all tasks, but I need to spend the afternoon with Avril, so your cooperation will earn you double loyalty points, redeemable for alcohol and other carbs. And I found a very willing substitute."

"But we have to go to the coroner's office. Who in their right mind plays backup for a visit to that place."

"Good question. Raph called to say he'd been scheduled to be in court as an expert witness and the hearing ended early." So far, Chickie was telling the complete truth; the next sentences were hyperbole for a good cause. "He asked if we needed anything, and we do. He is delighted to give you a ride to the coroner's office to get Edward's belongings, and he will call asap to set up the time."

Maddy rolled her eyes. "You are impossible!" Her phone buzzed again. She hated receiving two calls at once, and always worried that she'd somehow hang up on both. Chickie heard the familiar sound and took advantage of Maddy's dilemma. "I'll let you go."

Maddy barely contained her irritation. Did Chickie have to choose today to continue her reunion with Avril? She had waited more than forty years; what's a few more days? Maddy resented being handed off, even to Raph . He could have called her, but he hadn't. And now Chickie had hatched some plan without consulting her.

Had Chickie told Raph about the suicide verdict? It would be like her to be blunt. Maybe she should go alone to collect Edward's effects? She could. But when she heard Raph's warm voice, she admitted to herself that the coroner errand would be grim, and she much preferred company.

"Hard news this morning, I hear. How are you? How is Lena?" he asked with concern.

"I was braced for it, given the facts we've learned this week, but Lena is shocked. She desperately wanted to believe in murder, but she's coping pretty well. We're okay here."

"Chickie asked if I'd drive you to collect some personal items, like Edward's clothing and phone. I'm free and can pick you up anytime you say."

"That would be helpful. I'm at Lena's; I'll text you when I'm ready, okay? I really do appreciate this . . . and it will be good to see you," she admitted.

Ending the call, Maddy looked around and saw Winston fingering the different books on the shelves. He read titles, pulled out a volume here and there, opened it carefully and returned it. With surprise, she remembered that Raph had met Winston several days ago at the memorial service but knew nothing about his relationship to Edward. This was shaping up to be one more link on the chain of Chicago surprises yet to be revealed. Would she be handed that task too?

She went into the nearby bathroom, briskly splashed water on her face, smoothed her hair, and indulged in some of Lena's luxurious lavender-scented hand cream. Nothing like getting ready for a trip to the coroner.

Lena appeared, striding down the hall in an elegant maroon leather jacket and short boots. She invited Winston to join her in the living room while she signed the documents Maddy needed in order to collect Edward's effects. Maddy pocketed the papers and stuffed Avril's green file into her shoulder bag.

She texted Raph to meet her downstairs, glad to see that Lena was now willing to let Winston into her life, at least in small ways that were linked to Edward. This strange cemetery outing might be good for both of them.

Maddy was on the sidewalk when Raph pulled up and leaped out to open the car door for her. Just as he did, Winston and Lena emerged from the building. Raph turned to greet Lena with a tight hug. When she stepped back to introduce Winston, the men recognized each other.

"You were at the memorial service, right?" Raph asked, somewhat confused. Lena took a long breath and smiled wickedly. "What we didn't know then, but do know now, is that Winston is Edward's son. Maddy can catch you up on the details. We have an appointment." Head high, ballet dancer posture on full display, Lena, followed closely by Winston, stepped off the curb as the door attendant flagged a cab. They promptly climbed in and pulled away.

Raph looked after the taxi, his mouth open. "What the hell! Catch me up, please," he said emphatically after he slipped behind the wheel and joined the traffic on the narrow residential street.

"I hardly know where to start," Maddy said, trying to organize her thoughts.

"Start with Edward's son. That's a significant item of history missing from my eulogy prep."

Maddy shifted her cane to the other side of the seat and settled back. "Okay, it's quite a long story, and it begins in Hawaii during the Vietnam War. You drive, I'll talk."

While Maddy and Raph headed south, Lena and Winston's cab took them north on Dusable Lake Shore Drive and west to Ravenswood and the mortuary offices at Rosehill Cemetery. Winston gazed out the window at the intricate brickwork in the Lincoln Square neighborhood, knowing he would be headed back to Oxford the next day. He couldn't imagine what he'd tell his friends about this trip.

Shortly, the imposing Gothic-style Rosehill entrance came into view and Lena pointed it out. "This cemetery is actually a Chicago landmark a lot of tourists miss—hundreds of acres with a lake, deer, and amazing architectural details like Tiffany windows in the mausoleum." She shuddered slightly and added, "But we are not putting Edward in a vault ever. We are bringing him home first."

Winston smiled slightly at the use of "we."

Once they completed documentation with the solicitous dignity adviser, she led them solemnly to a softly lit room with soothing music. "There is no rush," the woman urged and left.

Lena paused at the threshold and stared at dozens of glass display shelves filled with every imaginable type of urn. For some time, she stood immobile, clutching her jacket around her although the room was uncomfortably warm. Winston hesitated before touching her shoulder. "I never imagined there would be so many choices. Let's walk outside and sort out your ideas—like size, color, material. It could narrow down the choices."

At first, she seemed aggrieved by the suggestion, but then she looked around again at the hundreds of urns and agreed. "Good idea."

They stepped out into the early afternoon sunlight and wandered down a gravel walkway lined with mature maples and elms. Winston asked, "If Edward were choosing for himself, would he prefer wood, stone, glass, metal, ceramic?"

Lena stopped and looked at a Civil War era headstone as if she hadn't heard.

"Lena?"

"Not granite, something smoother. He liked sharp, clean lines. Not ceramic, something stronger. He was tough. But metal sounds cold. Are there warm-colored metals?"

"Bronze, maybe." Winston tried another question. "Did he have a favorite color?"

Lena studied his face, moved by his sincerity. "Blue."

"That's mine too," he blurted out and sheepishly added, "I'm sorry if I'm being too personal," aware he was trying too hard.

"No," Lena said quickly. "You're helping me. Let's keep going. So, you share Edward's affinity for blue; most of his button-down shirts were shades of blue."

"I don't think we are going to find a blue button-down urn," he smiled.

They walked as far as the small lake in an open area of the park. Here, the trees were fully golden and orange. Every breeze brought down a small swirl of leaves that made the squirrels work more difficult as they frantically prepared for the weather to come. "Everybody, all the creatures, knows what to expect in a Chicago winter," Lena laughed. When they startled an urban deer grazing under a willow, she suggested they turn around.

Winston lagged behind, hands in his pockets.

"What?" Lena asked.

"There's something I need to tell you."

"No! No, I can't hear any more secrets. No!" She hurriedly began to retrace their steps.

Winston easily caught up. "Please." He reached for her arm and Lena fiercely shook him off and began to walk faster.

"Please," he hurried to explain as he kept pace with her. "I told Maddy and Chickie that I wasn't married and that's true, but unbelievably, this year I met someone in Oxford. She's wonderful and she's younger, and she wants a child. I was missing half my medical history, so that's the real reason I started searching again."

"That's your big secret? Lena asked, disbelievingly.

He hesitated.

"Oh God, is there more?"

"I'm so sorry, but when I learned about Edward a couple of months ago, I hired a private investigator. He's compiled a basic file on Edward . . . and you. So, I did know more about you than I admitted."

"You spied on us?" she said with distaste.

"Indirectly, yes. I had to know whether to announce my existence. Did I have a reason to hope? I wouldn't have arranged to speak at the conference, and I wouldn't have come if you and he were—"

"Poor?"

"No, no, I have money. The investigator provided data that made me willing to take a chance. You seemed like nice people, maybe open to meeting me."

Lena wandered ahead, carefully examining plaques and monuments along the path. "No miniature sculpture of Edward reading a book," she declared and continued to eliminate angels, flowery sayings, and heavy religious symbolism as, "Not Edward's style." This went on until they reached the building. Winston had no idea what to do, so he fell into step behind her, saying nothing.

Lena pushed against the heavily carved doors and marched through the foyer. Before she entered the cemetery office, she turned toward him, and he braced himself.

"Your father would have done exactly the same thing, being cautious, careful, protecting his heart." Lena didn't give a damn about his private investigator. In fact, it reassured her to think that Edward's son would be as careful as he was.

Winston was surprised and relieved. He took a deep breath and joined Lena as she wandered around the room. They gazed at shelves filled with a vast selection of memorial urns. She was now clear that she wanted something very simple. They found a warm-toned bronze container with a lapis inset that met all her criteria. The dignity adviser deftly handled all the details and promised to be in touch soon.

"Now, let's get out of this urnatorium," Lena said, and they hurried outside the grand limestone Rosehill gate. As the two of them waited for their Lyft ride, she suggested, "If you are interested, let's go back home for a suitable posturnatorium supper. After we are fortified with food and some alcohol, I'll show you pictures of this man you would have loved. I might cry, but there are ample tissues, and I want you to know more of who he is, was, before you leave."

Lena and Winston spent the ride home laughing about the worst possible urn choices they had seen, debating about whether the lighthouse was more outrageous than the cowboy on a bronco or the

White Sox container shaped like home plate. When Winston declared, "I vote for the Harley Davidson," the cabbie frowned at them in the rearview mirror, and they laughed harder.

Chapter Thirty-Five

During the drive to the Cook County Medical Examiner's office, Maddy gave Raph a short version of the events that had brought Winston to Chicago, including his letter to Edward. Raph listened quietly while he navigated the traffic and said nothing until he had shut the car off outside the office on Harrison Street.

He swiveled in his seat until he faced Maddy, and she could see how seriously he treated the information about his business partner. "I'm surprised, of course, but I realize everyone our age has a library of secrets," he sighed. "May I walk you in?"

Diligently, Maddy peered at the parking sign: *Visitors—thirty minutes.*

Sensing her hesitancy, Raph added, "It may be disturbing, and I admit, I'm curious. And I could help carry things."

Maddy hadn't thought of that, and for the first time, she wondered how many "effects" were left after you were hit by a train, then decided she didn't want to think about it and would wait to find out. As they walked toward the grim, angular building Raph asked, "How did Winston take the news of suicide? That's very different from a heart attack or accident—a miserable shock for him."

"I think he suspected suicide all along and feared his letter was the cause. We all tried hard to convince him otherwise. Confirming his paternity was a relief. That's something."

The ME's office receptionist was starkly efficient, and they were back in the car long before the thirty-minute parking limit expired.

Raph carried two bags of clothing and shoes. Maddy had Edward's umbrella and an authorization to pick up Edward's phone from the Chicago Police investigations office a few miles away. Raph dropped her out front; there was no parking and Maddy had to wait to sign for the phone. By two o'clock, she was climbing back into Raph's car with their errand completed.

"May I take you to lunch now?" Raph asked, pulling into traffic.

"We could get some good Cuban if you have time. Or do you need to get back to Chickie and Lena?"

Maddy wanted to go to lunch with Raph. Was it a date? Maybe. The idea of dating after seventy seemed oddly embarrassing. She actually couldn't remember having lunch alone with a man in the past year. Realizing Raph was waiting for a response, she asked quickly, "Okay. Where will you take me?"

"I want to take you to Havana." Then he laughed at the sight of Maddy's startled expression. "Havana is the name of my favorite Cuban restaurant in the Loop."

Maddy felt herself color; she hated blushing but knew there was nothing to be done. "I *am* hungry," she said, "and I don't know much about Cuba."

As they drove, Raph talked about being airlifted from Havana as a ten-year-old, one of the fourteen thousand children flown for safety in the US on "Peter Pan flights" during the Cuban Revolution. He'd spent a year with an elderly cousin in Indiana and learned to enjoy a snowy American winter before being reunited with his parents in Miami.

He hit the brakes. "A parking spot right in front! You must be my lucky charm." Raph ushered Maddy into the Havana Grill's long room. The place was quiet now that the lunchtime crowd was back at work, and they had their choice of booths. Maddy slid happily into the cushions, noticing that it was different to have a meal with Raph without Chickie's presence. She felt self-conscious. *This definitely qualifies as a date. Should I be enjoying a lunch date after a grim visit to the coroner and the police?*

When Raph recommended the Ropa Vieja sandwich with sangria, she ordered it and asked about his favorite home-cooked Cuban dishes, learned his daughter's names, ages, and temperaments, and kept him talking long enough for her to relax. He answered every question readily and when she had slowly run out of getting-to-know-you, he deftly shifted the conversation.

"What's next for you?"

Maddy looked at him, wide-eyed behind her horn-rimmed glasses. Suddenly the cozy booth seemed too small. She wanted to talk about him, not herself.

He persisted. "I've been where you are. It's more than a year since your husband died; you have obviously carried on being a good mother and friend, but what's next?"

Maddy realized that she was still bothered by Chickie's derisive "too good" comment. And there was the boys' insistence that she needed to move closer to them, and the endless reality of her diminishing physical condition. Did everyone see her as a failing Goody Two Shoes? What an awful, trite, dull image that needed revision. She definitely didn't want to talk about that to Raph over lunch.

Food arrived and Maddy welcomed the immediate excuse to avoid further conversation—at least right now. She'd been thinking about what came next but hadn't mentioned it to anyone beyond some vague talk with Chickie. She felt a deep aversion to planning for the future alone.

"I don't want to be a professional widow. Is that the way I appear to you?"

He didn't rush to reassure her. "Nooo, but are you avoiding the question?"

She bristled. "I was married for decades. That sense of myself doesn't just disappear. It's who I've been for more than half my life."

Raph didn't answer, as he was busy poking all the fixings back into the bread so he could get a good bite of his sandwich.

Maddy talked on; she described all the friends she visited, all the activities she maintained, all the Parkinson's management that absorbed portions of every day, but when he didn't answer, she stopped. "You asked me a question, and I clambered up on my soapbox to explain how busy I am and how full my life remains. Even though I've been giving you my coping speech, I did hear your question about my future. I admit, it's easier coming from you than from my adult children. I was furious with my son Rex this week when he suggested I move here."

Raph laughed good naturedly. "As I said, I've been there." Maddy studied him, recognizing Raph as a man who enjoyed engagement. *Frank would like this man.* That knowledge made it easier to admit, "Having this condition and being a widow has consumed me for more than a year. Now, you're right, there is some room in my life. This trip proves there is still more of me, unused. Chickie sees it, but the way she helps out is by poking me with a cattle prod. This aging story has only one ending. But I do need to compose a third act while I still have choices."

Raph did not offer suggestions. He spoke to the waiter in Spanish and asked for coffee and the check. Then he grinned at Maddy, "This has been a wonderful lunch."

His comment made Maddy suddenly warm. She liked the way he smiled when he pronounced the lunch to be "wonderful," so she blushed again, half expecting a teasing text from Chickie to magically appear. "I suppose I should get back to my task list and meet up with Chickie."

They finished their coffee and the *plátanos maduros* Raph had slipped into the order and headed back to his car. "I'm glad you came to Havana with me, and I am grateful to have met you. Do you have any idea when you will leave?"

"Two more days, I think," Maddy said. "Lena is regaining her equilibrium, and the vacation Chickie and I had originally planned would have ended yesterday. We both have to return home for our people and pets." Should she say that she was also grateful for having met him? Was he just being polite? *I'm also polite*, she reasoned but could manage nothing.

Ten minutes later, Raph pulled up curbside at the Palmer House. As he reached into the back seat to hand her the bags they had collected, he said, "I don't know if I'll see you again on this trip."

"I'll be back to Chicago," she volunteered quickly, not opening the car door. "My boys have started to campaign for me to return at Thanksgiving."

She was rewarded with a grin, and then it seemed like the most natural thing in the world for the two of them to lean in and hug. They smiled happily at each other, feeling bold and rather young. When Maddy walked into the hotel, she was relieved that Chickie was still reunioning with Avril. She did not plan to tell Chickie about the hug.

Chapter Thirty-Six

An hour later, after reading the documents in the green files, Maddy gently knocked on the neighboring door. "It's unlocked," Chickie called, and Maddy entered carrying two large brown bags and Edward's umbrella. She stopped abruptly. "What are you doing?"

Chickie's suitcase lay open on her bed, half full. She folded, then rolled her sweater into a tight tube and placed it against the other items of clothing before reaching for a pair of slacks and repeating the method.

"I'm trying this new technique of rolling clothes instead of folding them; I think it gives me more room."

Maddy walked closer. "No Chick. I'm not asking about technique; I'm asking, why are you packing your suitcase?"

Chickie turned wearily. "It's time to go home. We have been sturdy foot soldiers, long past retirement age for soldiering, by the way. We're done."

"What?" Maddy's head twisted like Nipper, the terrier from the old RCA Victrola ads.

She dropped the brown bags on the carpet and waited for an explanation.

Hands on hips, Chickie spoke clearly. "We've been in Chicago a week, although it's felt more like a month of digestive problems, but . . . we flew in knowing it would be rough. We visited old haunts; we did everything we could think of to help Lena. I made amends with Avril. Or I hope I did. I tried hard to be touchy feely. You bought a scarf that isn't gray. That's a lot. Not even grading on a curve, I give us a solid B-plus."

"I don't understand why you want to rush away," Maddy said with obvious irritation.

Chickie looked genuinely surprised. She took Edward's umbrella from under her friend's arm and pointed to the armchair. Maddy sat. Chickie dropped down opposite her on the bed and leaned forward earnestly. She had thought this through. "Lena has gotten her answers, and they are more awful than she bargained for. First, we learned that Edward had kept all kinds of secrets hoping to control his snow globe world, and under great strain, being more vulnerable than anyone knew, he committed suicide. Death outed his medical problems and foolish art investments and, given that death is a very permanent condition, he can't even explain himself to his wife. Second, we learned Winston really is his son and will have to live the rest of his life not knowing how Edward felt about his existence. I don't envy some of his long nights. Third, or is it thirdly, and equally surprising, we know Lena is very strong, in her own dependent way. She will crawl back to life as we all do, putting one knee in front of the other. This week is the first foray into a long grieving period for them, but it's the end of a chapter for us. And you—if you have the brains I think you do—you will flirt heavily with Raph. He and Avril are proof of enduring decency in this Windy City."

"You didn't answer my question. Why are you in such a rush to leave?"

Chickie pushed her suitcase to the foot of the bed and closed it, buying time as she tried to find words to describe her own feelings. "I'm not rushing; it's finished. Maddy, maybe you can keep this up indefinitely, knocking your head against fifty years of secrets and not developing a fractured skull, but I cannot. I was having a lovely afternoon with Avril until I did something very stupid."

"Oh no, you didn't mess up with her again!"

Chickie smiled at Maddy's concern. "Not that. I allowed my damn curiosity to escape. Avril and I visited Penny Mattingly Deutch."

"Who?"

Chickie wearily leaned forward. "Remember Edward's childhood friend? Dirk Mattingly, the soldier who died in Vietnam. Anyway, it was a hunch. I got it into my head that the past was going to answer more of our questions, so I tracked down Dirk's wife. They'd been married less than a year when he died, but she remained awfully close to his dad, Doc Mattingly. I wanted to know more about Edward's childhood. It's been bothering me. That's your fault; all the talk about being shaped by our childhood. Anyway, Penny Mattingly was the only one left. Doc Mattingly died years ago."

Maddy took a deep breath. She knew for certain that she was not going to like the story that followed.

"Remember the account of Edward's parents and their deaths? They had been visiting his grandfather's farm, and Edward had stayed behind while his parents drove back to Madison for a faculty reception. His mother, a brilliant chemist, drove and, on the way back to the farm, she smashed the car into a tree. What Lena didn't know was that Dr. Mattingly and Edward's grandfather believed she crashed the car deliberately."

Maddy covered her eyes.

"Between the two older men, they knew everyone in town and had the official results of the investigation sealed. After all, Edward was a child; no one else had a real interest in the results. The story that was circulated was that the Jordans died in an accidental crash, probably due to a deer running across the road. Both men, and the police, believed the crash was deliberate. They successfully kept the secret for more than sixty-five years. Dirk never knew about their suspicions; neither did Edward, and Penny only learned about it when Dr. Mattingly was elderly and ill. He told her. He said that Edward's mother had become increasingly erratic during the previous year. Her husband and her psychiatrist recommended hospitalization, but she refused. That was why they were spending an entire summer in the middle of nowhere. They all hoped being in the country would help. Then the worst happened."

"I wonder if that's why the families fought over Edward. His paternal grandfather wanted to keep him away from his mother's family," Maddy said.

"Wait. It gets worse. Edward's hand thing, the Dupuytren's Contractions, is hereditary and he wanted to track it down. As he got more involved, he began to remember more about his mother's behavior and his father's concern. Nothing clear but enough to make him curious. Then he got Winston's letter. The result was that he contacted Penny at the beginning of last week, days before he died. They hadn't talked since Dirk's death. He wanted to ask questions about the story of the car crash. He wanted to confirm his mother's history. He remembered overhearing conversations in his youth and thought Dirk's father might have talked about it. He was right. Penny told him everything she knew, which wasn't much. I would have pressed Penny further, but her granddaughter fell from the swing set and needed attention. Avril and I fled."

"It helps explain why he built his life so carefully; his fear of having children, his worrying about his own vulnerabilities; his need for control. And then, the surprise . . . he has a son," Maddy said.

Chickie sighed. "I'm done. I want to go home. Knowing when you've lost and admitting it is a sign of maturity, and God knows, we have plenty of maturity."

Maddy deliberated, her silence making Chickie squirm; then she rummaged through one of the brown shopping bags and pulled out a green folder. She placed it carefully on Chickie's lap. "This is the investigator's report that Avril left. I've just spent an hour reading and rereading it. I'm finished and, before you origami any more clothes, read it." She nodded to the shopping bags. "These are Edward's clothes and personal effects."

"Maddy?" Chickie asked, "Did you find the photo Winston told us he sent in the letter? The one of him with his mother?"

Maddy reached into one of the small, zippered compartments of her large shoulder bag and removed a faded photo. She held it up close enough for Chickie to see an attractive Vietnamese woman and her self-conscious preteen son. "I found this folded in Edward's wallet, a fact that Lena never needs to know. I will give her everything else tomorrow but now I need a nap. Then we can talk."

"Maddy," Chickie said gently. "It's over."

"Maybe." Maddy pointed to the folder on Chickie's lap. "Read the file before you quit." Wearily, she stood, picked up the shopping bags and limped back to her room next door.

Chapter Thirty-Seven

It was closer to an hour and a half later when Maddy, awake and worried that she hadn't heard from Chickie, tapped on the adjoining door. It was unlatched and swung open a few inches. She hesitated, afraid that Chickie had gone without even saying goodbye. Never! Maybe? Never!

She stood rooted on her side of the door because she didn't think she could bear to see an empty room. She listened but heard nothing, aware that she would have been ridiculously grateful for the sounds of Chickie tapping out her latest blog post or singing, but no, the room was quiet. Finally, she tentatively pushed the door open a few more inches and saw an empty bed, no suitcase, no Chickie.

Maddy felt tears of anger and hurt well up in her eyes and smacked the door with her hand. It flew open, slamming against the wall, and there was Chickie standing at the window. She whirled around at the loud sound of her door, but in the dimming light of early evening, she failed to notice Maddy's angry expression. "Did you have a good nap?"

Maddy took a step in, and she could see the suitcase lying on the floor at the foot of the bed in a rumpled pile of Chickie's unrolled clothes. Her anger and hurt began to ebb. She interpreted the overturned case as a positive sign and walked further into the room. "Well?"

Chickie pulled the drapes closed and said, "I did as you asked. I carefully read the investigator's report, and I see that Avril didn't provide all the details this morning. That's probably why she was so intent on handing it to us. It's just as well; Lena doesn't need details now, maybe never. The report makes it clear that Edward committed suicide, which we'd anticipated. What surprised me, and what makes me deeply angry, is learning how Charles Haskell nastily ensnared Edward in the art scheme. But there's still nothing we can do. I feel more helpless than before." As she finished speaking, she lifted her suitcase from the floor and began picking up the scattered clothing, throwing items into the case.

Maddy pointed to the suitcase, "What happened to your suitcase?"

Chickie explained, "It fell when I read about Charles in the reports."

"It fell when you got angry and shoved it off the bed?"

"Not my fault if it's flimsy. The white Naugahyde suitcase I got for my sixteenth birthday wouldn't have tumbled after just one push. And that one had my initials in gold."

"I'm sure you looked adorable lugging it around to your sleepovers."

"I could barely lift it, it was long before wheels on luggage, but we digress and I know you are itching to talk about the other interviews in the report," Chickie said.

"I am." Maddy moved the brown bags off the chair and sat down. "Did you notice the comments from the restaurant staff? They recall Edward talking loudly on the phone, leaving in an excitable state without his coat, umbrella, or phone, all of which Raph and I collected today in those bags." Maddy's temper was apparent as she gestured at the bags. "Edward, as we knew him, was never loud. Or forgetful."

Chickie was interested in the mention of Raph's name but decided not to go there. "It was Charles on the phone."

"Yes, that was clear from the report."

Chickie slipped back into thinking like a journalist. "Did you get Edward's cellphone?"

Maddy reached into one of the bags at her feet, pulled it out and waved it at Chickie. "I haven't tried to get into his phone yet; I was waiting to go through it with you."

"Is that why you were so upset about my leaving?"

"That's one reason. We can save the second for another day—if there is another day."

Chickie knew better than to talk back. "Okay. The report makes it clear that the investigators were able to check his phone."

"Yes, it led them to Charles," Maddy agreed. "So he must have been in Edward's call log as having talked with him that day. Maybe there's more from him: a text, missed calls, or voicemails. The report only said that Charles brushed off his last conversation with Edward as, 'We talked business. He needed advice; he wasn't exactly a businessman, so I gave him some information.' When pressed, Charles told them that Edward did not seem particularly upset. Lying bastard."

Chickie leaned against the desk, half sitting on it. "The Haskell brothers are a loathsome pair."

"I'm sure they have some rationalization for their behaviors," Maddy answered reflexively.

"Don't anthropomorphize those two or I'll start packing again."

"Does that mean you're staying?" Maddy asked with an edge in her voice.

"I'm staying long enough to go through Eddy's phone."

Relief flooded over Maddy. She felt sweaty and happy. She got up and went directly to the in-room bar, where she plucked a small bottle of wine from the shelf, twisted it open, and sat back in the armchair, sipping directly from the bottle.

Chickie knew that not offering to share the wine meant Maddy was still peeved or hurt or both—or some other complicated emotion that professional feeling-people have, so she trod carefully. "Maddy, what was the second reason you were upset just now?"

"I thought you had grown out of running away without saying goodbye, but your packing proved me wrong."

Sorry she asked, Chickie returned to the problem at hand. "We need to get into the phone. Do you want to call Lena for the password?"

Maddy said, "I'd rather not; it could get complicated. Let me try something. When did they get married?"

"Are you kidding? I don't always remember my son's middle name."

"It's Joshua. See if you can find their marriage date on your phone."

Chickie waited, thinking there was as much chance of finding Lena's marriage date in her phone as finding those small rose gold earrings she'd put in a safe place three years ago. But Maddy had her ways, and Chickie watched with amusement as her friend mumbled about her young sons acting as Lena's ring bearers, they were three years old, wore short pants in warm weather, and then she subtracted their present ages before triumphantly calling out, "Check the newspapers. Look up announcements in the summer of 1983, and I'll see whether I have their anniversary in my contacts' notes."

Chickie sat at the desk and called her laptop to life. It took a few minutes of sorting through wedding announcements in the *Chicago Tribune* archive, but soon she said, "June sixth."

Maddy tapped the numbers 6683 into Edward's phone.

"I still use BellaAbzug! as my password if you want money from my checking account," Chickie proffered, trying to lighten the mood.

"Bingo!" Maddy said, pointedly ignoring Chickie and squinting at the phone. "We're in and it looks like we have hundreds of emails over the past two months, and a lot of incoming and outgoing phone calls that week—twelve on Thursday, plus voicemails."

Chickie walked over and held out her hand for the phone. Suddenly, she too was all business. "Calls and emails after he died are not useful. For starters, we want incoming calls, outgoing calls, voicemails, and text messages for the day he died and a few days before. We'll work our way further backward in time if needed. You take the desk and the computer."

Maddy moved across the room and sat down. She listed the names and numbers. "We can go backward, but this is a good place to start. I'll try to identify the names of people who aren't in his contact list."

"While you do that, I'll listen to the voicemails and check whether he used anything like What'sApp. I doubt he downloaded anything fancier, but I'll go through his apps later. Let's wait on the emails because Lena said she went through them on their home computer and found nothing. He had only one personal account that they both accessed."

A few minutes later, Maddy was interrupted by a strangled sound coming from across the room. "What's wrong?"

Chickie looked stricken. "On the morning he died, one voicemail is business from the office but the other three are from Lena, each one more frightened than the last." She hurried into the bathroom.

Maddy heard water running. Being solicitous about Chickie's emotions would be unwelcome, so she went back to checking calls.

When the sounds of water stopped, Chickie appeared at the bathroom door wiping her face with a towel. "When my memory fails, I want Lena's panicked voice to be the first sound I forget."

The women worked methodically for two more hours. At some point, Maddy stopped to stretch and Chickie liberally used her eye drops. Finally, Maddy said, "I checked incoming and outgoing calls for the day he died and the three days prior. I have a dozen or so calls from his office and many calls to and from Lena." She looked at her notes again. "There is a call from his dentist and a few brief calls to other doctors. I tried the unknown numbers, doctors, pharmacies, nothing useful. Just routine."

"That's boring," Chickie said brusquely.

"You're so impatient. There is more. For the week before Edward's death, the two people who made and received repeated calls, including on the day he died, were Arden Finley, their neighbor and Charles Haskell . . ."

"Arden, the guy who bought a couple of paintings, and Charles, the slimy entrepreneur."

Maddy responded, "But we don't know what they said. These calls tally with the investigator's report, not surprisingly. Are you ready to go through his emails?"

They read Edward's emails, feeling terribly intrusive as they searched through the ordinary details of his life, but there was nothing informative. Chickie went through the browsing history on the phone and saw that Edward had looked up GenomicsX. "Maddy, Edward checked out Winston's company. He must have gotten the name from Winston's letter."

"So, for sure he read the letter and was curious. And he held on to the photo of Winston and his mother. We don't know any more than that."

Chickie nodded. "The investigators probably skipped it. They don't know about Winston, and it wouldn't have seemed strange for a doctor to look at a genetics research company. Damn, I'd love to know what Edward thought."

Maddy's voice was soft. "That's the cruelty of suicide. We're left wondering; we never get to know." When the room darkened, they turned on all the lights and brought in a lamp from Maddy's room. Just before the hotel kitchen closed, they ordered pea soup and split a roast beef sandwich. At midnight, they shared a handful of ibuprofen, then Maddy paused to walk up and down the hallway for a while, visiting the vending machine for chips. At two, they called it quits without learning anything new.

Chickie took a hot bath, vowing that future travel would include a bag of Epsom salts, and Maddy stretched her aching limbs, read one full page of the novel she had carried all week, and fell asleep.

Chickie's Blog:
Old Dogs, New Tricks
(A Writer's Reflections on Growing Old
and Growing Up)

Anthem

All day, between crises, I've been humming Leonard Cohen's song, "Anthem." I only sing out loud when I'm alone. People tell me that my voice is truly awful; I can't tell. To me, I sound fine, but even my children refused lullabies from the time they could talk. I accept the critique and sing alone. Leonard had no voice either, so I feel okay with his songs.

"Ring the bell that still can ring."

My visit to Chicago is coming to an end, and I see, no surprise, hold the applause, I was the person who gained (and lost) in unexpected ways. I half expected the past to reach up and grab me by the throat, wrestle me to the ground and pummel me with my failings. That didn't happen. Naivete and youth remained decades behind, and all week I have functioned as a grown up. In fact, I've been effective. I can still ring the bell; not as loud or as hard, but with a clarity I lacked in the past. And without apology.

"Forget your perfect offering"

I was never one of those people who wanted to be perfect. It seemed like too much work.

From a young age, I became accustomed to making mistakes and by now, I've had a lot of practice. I'm remarkably good at it. But I've never been old before, and the state of older adulthood changes things.

It's no longer about mistakes; it's about an inexorable march toward (as Petronius wrote about the dead) joining the majority. That realization is not so bad as long as I feel healthy.

When I'm dealing with the ongoing physical deterioration of aging, it's rough. I've been resentful about my marriages and even my children; some years, there was barely a moment to consider my own selfish interests, and time is running out. I need to use my time, seeking to turn back the clock provides its own punishment in self-recrimination and disappointment. Lenny knew what he was talking about.

"There is a crack in everything, that's how the light gets in."

This has to be one of Lenny's most wonderful lines.

Chapter Thirty-Eight

The enticing smells of warm bread and hot coffee reached Chickie as soon as she pushed through the revolving door to Hey Love Café on Wabash. The previous night had been grueling and provided little new information. It had only confirmed Charles Haskell as the final straw.

She ordered at the counter, picked up coffee, and joined Maddy, already seated in a booth at the window. Maddy was distracted, pretending to eat her breakfast. This was a surprise; generally, she was the most attentive and hungriest person Chickie knew. Frustrated, Chickie resorted to her normal provocations. She tried a few Girl Scout jokes and remarked on the variety of gray stripes in today's scarf with no success. Finally, she asked, "Aren't you happy that I didn't run away during the night?"

"Don't flatter yourself," was the response. "There are no midnight flights to DC." Maddy absently buttered toast that was already buttered.

Disappointed, Chickie pointed out, "I'm still here."

"For how long?"

"Hey, I'm trying. My fervent desire to get even with Charles Haskell is an excellent reason to remain in Chicago. The fifth grader in me is running through the schoolyard screaming, 'it isn't fair! Charles behaved badly! Where's the teacher?'"

"So, will you give Charles a timeout? Or take away his phone? Be realistic; what impact can we have?" Maddy asked, poking a fork into her runny egg yolks. "Don't misunderstand; I'm longing to expose him, but—"

"Stop playing with your food."

"I'm too tired to eat. I didn't get any sleep because I'm convinced we missed something critical last night. I'm exhausted from trying to remember."

"Ah, the unconscious."

"Don't be snide."

Chickie returned to her coffee, wondering if introspection was the way all shrinks started their days. She shuddered at the idea of spending so much time delving into one's inner workings. Her blog took all the introspection she could muster, and that was only safe because it remained anonymous. She tried to lighten the mood. "I dreamed about Charles last night. Do you think I could get a psychic restraining order? Or maybe there's a way to delete him from my memory."

Maddy looked confused.

"I'm kidding Maddy."

Maddy's face cleared, and she broke into a broad smile. "Delete! That's it!"

Chickie stared at the suddenly animated woman.

"Edward's phone! Where is it?" Maddy demanded.

Chickie pulled the cell phone from her backpack and entered the password as Maddy slid into the booth beside her so they could view the small screen together.

"Why didn't we think of going through the email trash on Edward's phone? He would have deleted emails that he didn't want Lena to see," Maddy said.

The excited women found a dozen deleted emails from the days right before Edward's suicide. Arden was angry, aggrieved over the paintings he'd bought, not yet ready to accept reimbursement by Edward for the purchase price and making veiled legal threats. The deleted emails from Charles Haskell were far worse. The women wondered what the investigators had thought about them; the report had referred to Charles's communication as abrasive, but it hadn't specifically mentioned these deleted emails which appeared to be legal but unrelentingly cruel.

"Edward initiated the email thread three days before his death, after a call from Arden. Edward wrote to Charles, in part, *'I'm going to return his money, and more if I need to. This is disgraceful and I'm determined to make it right, for my family and me.'*"

Charles's response, and the ones that followed, were thick with derision. He called Edward a timid old man, not cut out for business. Another referred to him as a controlling old schmuck with no balls. And a third read: *Once this blows over, no one will care. Good thing you don't have children whose fine name will be tarnished. Anyway, it's time for you to retire.*

On the day before he died, Edward insisted that Charles meet him the next day. The response was terse: *Thursday 9:00 at Shelby's in Wilmette.*

"Edward must have already been at the restaurant when he got the final email from Charles dated Thursday at 8:45 am. It read: *Can't make it. Grow up. No one will remember you in a week; hell, no one cares right now.* Shortly afterward, Edward's final call was to Charles. "That had to be the conversation that upset Edward so completely, he rushed out of the restaurant, leaving his coat and phone," Chickie said.

"We'll never know what Charles said to Edward in that call, but I see why the investigators were interested in talking to him," Maddy said.

"They were pursuing information to clarify the cause of Edward's death on the tracks; they weren't looking for criminal activity. Questions about an art scam arose later from a dissatisfied customer in the gallery world, but art fraud is hard to prove. Charles claimed he represented the art accurately. There is nothing in writing. Maybe the investigators could get a couple of customers to say Charles lied; it's his word against theirs. If they were going to indict Charles for a crime, we would have had a hint. And we never would have gotten the phone back. It's not going to happen; these emails are not obscene or even threatening. But to Edward? A man who was probably already depressed and couldn't tolerate the shame of a medical condition, an unacknowledged son, and poor judgment on art purchases? The accumulation of failure and lack of control was alarming. Edward's death was appropriately classified as a suicide. And the man who hounded Edward into rushing in front of the train will go on selling shares in the Great Wall of China." Chickie's heart beat rapidly.

"He badgered Edward; he painted him into a corner," Maddy fumed.

Chickie said nothing, rearranging her silverware in a tense and purposeful way.

"Hey . . . Chick, what are you thinking?"

Chickie said, "I'll stay. I'm not going anywhere, but I have an end-of-the-week test question for you."

"No games. I'm not in the mood."

"I'm serious."

"What's your question?" Maddy demanded.

"How far are you willing to stray from being Good?"

Maddy realized that Chickie was very serious, so she answered in kind. "After reading Charles's emails, I'm available to the dark side. Is that what you mean? Occasionally we are called to do bad things for the sake of the good. Do you have something in mind?"

"What if you have to surrender a merit badge? Maybe Transparent and Pure?"

"I could let that one go. It's become burdensome." She nodded vigorously and moved back to her seat across the table.

Chickie exhaled. "Do you remember the goddess, Nemesis?"

"Didn't she exact retribution from gods and mortals who were arrogant or prideful?"

Chickie nodded. "Charles qualifies for her wrath. And I believe we could be her modern-day protégés. I've always wanted a mentor, and we're in a position to carry on her work. You need to think psychologically, so envision revenge, tasteful and effective. What vulnerabilities do we target?" she asked, already reaching into her backpack for a notepad.

Maddy waivered. "Revenge. Targeting. Would that be ethical?"

Chickie raised one of her elegant eyebrows. "Didn't you just preach something about doing bad things for the sake of the good. What possible use is psychology if you can't make it work for us! You have a sense of Charles's personality, where is he weak? Suppose I was talking to him, God forbid, and wanted to draw him in, engage him; get him to reveal himself."

"I trust the social work ethics board won't pull my license for seeking justice," Maddy laughed.

"You already quit your day job."

"Okay, okay. Someone like Charles would be vulnerable to flattery. He'd light up at praise of his supposed business acumen, his willingness to take risks, and he would love hearing about his superiority to others. He's a narcissist that never has enough. He wants to feel special. Also, he's an angry guy who feels underappreciated. So, he longs for validation, validation, validation. His brilliance has been misunderstood, unrecognized by the inferior world he dwells in."

Chickie was worried by the last point. "Only validation? How would he respond to a challenge or confrontation?"

"A challenge he could win, bring it on. The right amount of challenge makes guys like him want to prove they're brighter than you are. Real confrontation is trickier. We want him inflated, then off balance and exposed."

"We don't want a face-to-face battle. We want his Achilles heel—"

"Squeezing one more Greek myth into revenge! Well done!" Maddy was completely energized by the idea of becoming an avenging goddess. Or at least a smart old lady. She waved at the server for a coffee refill.

"From everything I've heard over the years, there's also an ambivalent bond between him and Brian. Lena once told me that the elder Haskells had money problems so younger brother Charles got the short end of the checkbook, fewer zeros on his gifts. He's likely to be vulnerable to comparisons with his wealthier, successful older brother. Does that help?" Maddy finished her formulation and felt strangely satisfied. "I'm making room on my Girl Scout sash for the Nemesis badge."

"Absolutely." Chickie closed her notebook and outlined her plan as it occurred to her. "A journalist will interview Charles for a major magazine article and she, it has to be a she . . ."

Maddy listened intently, alternating between doubt and delight, leaning hard toward delight.

Chapter Thirty-Nine

They paid the check and walked across the street to the hotel. Maddy had one more concern. "I've transcended ethical considerations, but this plan—is it legal?"

Chickie paused; she had thought about how to avoid getting caught, but she hadn't devoted a moment to the legalities. "Let me call a lawyer friend in DC. He has an incentive. I power walk with his wife. If I'm sent to prison, he'll be out walking at six every morning."

Maddy wasn't completely reassured by Chickie's answer, but she felt certain they were on the side of justice. Was there a special cell for goddesses? What food might be served? She banished those thoughts and tapped the elevator button. "When we are ready to find your faux journalist, I'll call Gus. He minored in acting at Northwestern and has stayed in touch with many of his classmates."

"Extroverted offspring can be so useful," Chickie murmured as they returned to their rooms to prepare. She kicked off her shoes and immediately went to the desk, where she opened her laptop, sent a quick email to the DC lawyer, and began to search journalists' websites and examine photos of the writers. "Too old, too young, wrong specialty..."

Maddy knew that when her friend talked to herself, it was wise to find something else to do, so she went to her own room and called Lena. The widow was longing to talk and bombarded Maddy with details about Rosehill Cemetery and urn selection, along with a thorough description of the vessel she had chosen. Lena confessed how much she had enjoyed Winston's company and paused only when her apartment buzzer sounded. "That's Winston. We are spending the morning together before he catches a flight to London."

Between time with Winston, an appointment with her financial adviser, and a scheduled spa date later with a neighbor, Maddy was satisfied that Lena was in a half dozen good hands for the day. Fortunately, Winston's arrival forestalled any questions about their own activities, so she sent a bon voyage hug to Winston and promised that she and Chickie would be in touch about getting together with Lena the next day.

Maddy was excited. She scrambled through her exercises, texted her sons about a lunch date tomorrow, and changed into the most colorful piece of clothing she'd brought, a long-sleeved blue and gray sweater. When she entered Chickie's room, Maddy found her friend looking like the cat that had swallowed a flock of canaries. In fact, a few small feathers may have fluttered in the air as Chickie turned the computer screen toward her and pointed to the website of Alice Fay Robinson. The accompanying photograph showed an attractive woman journalist.

"We want her."

"Do you know her?"

"Not her. But we can find a lookalike. She's a real writer; we couldn't compromise her. We need an actor who can be made up to look like her and play a writer."

"Why Alice Fay Robinson?"

"She's a journalist who writes long features in top-notch magazines, so our story is believably in her wheelhouse. She's attractive, young but experienced, she doesn't live in Chicago so Charles won't drop by, and most of all, she's got distinctive features we can use to fool Charles."

Maddy stared at the laptop screen. The young journalist was very attractive, with a halo of natural curls pulled back in a colorful band that framed warm caramel skin. Her distinctive look, and the possibility of copying it, lay in her bright, thick eyeglass frames, red lipstick, and a noticeable beauty mark next to her mouth. Maddy's eyebrows rose. "How will this work?"

"People rely on shortcuts. I used to go to a writers' conference and one woman always wore elaborate hats. I can't describe one of her features to you. I depended on those hats to identify her. I think Charles will Google Alice Fay and only notice the name, hair, skin tone, eyeglasses, and mole. Anyway, everyone expects website photos to be touched, so we have some wiggle room."

"You're also counting on racism, aren't you?"

Chickie looked embarrassed. "Is it awful to think that Charles would look her up, maybe see a bunch of photos of a lovely African American writer with bold glasses, a mole, and be misled by another woman having all those features and credentials?"

Maddy shrugged. "Facial recognition drops dramatically when people identify individuals of other races; we know that from research. And Charles is self-absorbed, making him unobservant. It could work. And . . . what did your lawyer friend say?"

Chickie pursed her lips. "He spoke legalese. I caught impersonation, sting, defraud, and I think he warned us to be careful, but he also said, 'It's Chicago; you'll probably be fine.'" Maddy's heart gave a small lurch.

"Now's the time to call Gus. We need an actor who has chutzpah and who can be made up to look enough like Alice Fay Robinson to pass on Zoom with careful lighting. We can get a wig, glasses, whatever. Tell him we pay well."

"Do we?"

"I don't know the going rate for impersonations, but we will pay money, or you offer free therapy, or I give her writing lessons—whatever she wants."

Maddy got Gus on the phone and handed it to Chickie, who explained their plan and the urgent need for an actor who would work with them—preferably someone local so they could meet with her in person—but anyone who could get the job done would be gratefully accepted.

Maddy took the phone back, feeling the need to explain more. "We're gathering some evidence for leverage," she hedged.

Chickie leaned close and shouted into the phone, "Think Rudy Giuliani caught on camera in that Borat movie. But we aren't planning big-screen exposure."

"From you two, something more elegant, I'm sure." And then, not being quite as Good as his mother, Gus didn't deliberate on ethical risks and simply said, "Give me time to make a few phone calls."

Chickie texted Gus the link to Alice Fay's website.

During the next two hours, waiting for Gus to work a minor miracle, they compiled information about nearby places that sold glasses, wigs, burner phones, and most importantly, they learned how to download a program able to record Zoom conversations just in case Charles shut off the Zoom feature.

"Maybe we should try to find backup journalists; what if Gus can't find the right actress," Maddy worried.

Chickie brushed her concerns aside. "He's your son; he'll come through."

Nemesis was on their side. By noon, Gus had called Maddy with good news. "Olivia Isah may be your actor. She was a couple of years ahead of me at Northwestern. You'll love her; she also sings and dances, but maybe that's for your next crime wave. She's local, but you have to go to her house in Evanston. Her kid is sick. I gave her the outline of your scheme, but it's up to you to convince her. Having often been on the receiving end of Chickie's persuasions, I have confidence you will be able to coax her to the dark side." Secretly, he was thrilled that Saint Maddy was behaving a bit badly.

"Chick," Saint Maddy asked after they hung up, "Aren't you even a little afraid?"

Chickie was caught off guard. "You know my history. My father died when I was sixteen. My husband died and left me with a baby when I was twenty-six. Those deaths brought me to my knees. I was so scared for so long, I exhausted all my fear. It burned out like a bonfire, Maddy. I don't have any left."

Before heading to Evanston, the first suburb to the north, the two women studied online head shots of Olivia. There were a dozen or so, including character studies, on her website. Olivia did not look like the photographs. She was younger than Alice, and anyone who knew both women would laugh at the comparison, but no one can tell height or weight on Zoom and with makeup and imperfect lighting, it could work. Especially with an eager Charles.

"People see what they expect to see," Maddy said as they left the hotel. "Charles will Google her and register these outstanding features, which we can duplicate. She's a pro and he won't have her photo available to compare—"

"Unless we give him cause to suspect something."

"That's your job," Maddy reminded her friend. "Prepare her to sound like a journalist under deadline. I'll prep her to understand his psychology so she can turn on the flattery and general sucking up."

At one o'clock, the two women got off the Purple Line train at Main Street in Evanston and walked a few blocks to Oak and Oakton. Olivia's house was a quintessential Chicago bungalow built in the first half of the twentieth century. It was brick, one-and-a-half stories, with a few original leaded glass windows facing the street, and a side entry. They picked up a *Tribune* lying on the small porch and rang the bell.

Olivia came to the door carrying a little boy on her hip. At the sight of the unfamiliar women, he buried his face in his mother's neck and began whispering into her dark hair which, both visitors were delighted to see, was natural and could be easily pulled back with a headband.

After introductions, the shy boy named Zeke began to smile and the three women settled in the living room to talk. "Sorry, but he is getting over a bad cold, and no one has had much sleep for the last few nights."

Maddy smiled understandingly. "We both have children." She began to make friendly faces at the child until she had coaxed the sniffling boy into bringing out some books they could read together. Soon, they were all within view of each other. Maddy and Zeke stayed in the living room reading *I Am One* while Chickie spoke to Olivia in the dining area.

Olivia had many questions. She admitted that she would never have agreed to meet them if she hadn't known Gus for years. This was Gus's upstanding mother who he jokingly referred to as Saint Madeline, the Incorruptible. Still, Olivia wanted to hear the story firsthand before making her decision.

A sterling reputation is indeed a blessing, Chickie thought as she outlined the events surrounding Edward's death, sticking with facts. Then she explained Charles's harassment of Edward and owned up to her desire to punish the man. She answered all of Olivia's questions honestly. She also described the ways in which they would protect her identity if Charles ever got it into his head to try to find his 'interviewer.' She showed Olivia a picture of Alice Fay and offered her a hastily written contract, signed by Chickie that she had hired Olivia for an acting job, releasing the actor from all responsibility.

When Olivia agreed, Chickie and Zeke moved to the backyard swing and Maddy took over. She spent the next hour explaining narcissism and how to get Charles to talk. "He will reveal more if you go back and forth between validation and gentle challenges," she coached. After that, Chickie tackled the techniques of interviewing and described a journalistic style that would make it a believable interview. The two older women wrote down their goals and exactly the type of information they hoped Olivia would be able to elicit.

Finally, the actor was satisfied, and the child was ready for a nap. When Olivia returned to the living room, she offered some excellent ideas about staging and acting. Chickie appreciated her professionalism, particularly in such an unprofessional endeavor. After they laid out the plan step-by-step, they composed an email, "bait" Chickie called it. They would email Charles now, follow up with a phone call in a couple of hours, and schedule an interview for this evening, if at all possible. Chickie wanted it wrapped up while Charles was feeling flattered, before he could question the unlikelihood of this opportunity landing in his lap. Their success depended heavily on Charles's greed and narcissism as much, and maybe more, than Olivia's portrayal of a journalist.

The actor studied Alice Fay's photograph and decided she needed the glasses, but she could manage everything else. "Actors, especially struggling actors, know makeup; you will be surprised."

The email would go out from Chickie's computer, and it would be written from the newly opened account of AFRob71818@gmail.com. They gave Olivia the password and agreed that the journalist Alice Fay Robinson might have several accounts; this seemed plausible.

Chickie and Olivia composed the first draft, then Maddy changed some wording to make the query psychologically more compelling. The final draft read:

Dear Mr. Haskell,

My 10,000-word feature for Vanity Fair's holiday issue is in jeopardy. The article is about the risks and benefits of investing in emerging artists, and the piece depends heavily on interviews. Unfortunately, and as you are probably aware, Frink Hofstader, the famous art critic, died last month. He was one of the piece's five subjects, and his family has decided to withdraw permission to use his quotes. I don't want to force the issue. I have a very short time to find and interview another strong voice in the art market or lose the spot indefinitely. I want you to be that voice. I heard that you have intimate knowledge of the China market. That's fantastic! Exactly what I need. I will follow up this email with a phone call shortly, but I wanted to give you an opportunity to think about it. I will explain more when I call.

Regards,
Alice Fay Robinson

Maddy whispered a nondenominational prayer, they pressed send, and the email zipped away. Maddy and Chickie left. They planned to reconvene in two hours after securing eyeglasses, a phone, and installing specific recording software on Chickie's laptop. "We can't use Olivia's computer; we don't want to get her in trouble."

Within the hour, they had visited an optometrist on Main Street and overpaid for eyeglasses, purchased a phone at the local Target, and changed Chickie's laptop to read Alice Fay Robinson on her Zoom account.

"How do you know how to do this?" Maddy asked, sitting across from her in a diner near the train platform. "You have never been a tech wizard. I see you count on your fingers."

Chickie pretended to be insulted. "I spent two years holed up at home during the pandemic and was on Zoom every day. If I hadn't learned how to manage some tech, my career would have ended."

They returned early to Olivia's home, but she was ready. When the door opened, the two older women blinked at the appearance of Olivia/Alice Fay.

"Wow, you look amazing," Chickie marveled. Olivia had combed out her hair, bound it with a bright band and worked wonders with makeup to look like the computer headshots.

"I wanted to be in character for the phone call."

Both women agreed that was a marvelous way of thinking, but they would have been on board if she'd confessed to multiple personalities or channeling Alice Fay. They handed her the eyeglasses and phone.

Olivia explained nervously that, in the intervening hours, she had received a return email from Charles in the AFRob71818@gmail.com account. It was short and arrogant. *Please call between four and six; I may be available.*

"Good," Maddy said. "Ignore the tone. This changes nothing. We planned to call then anyway; he is simply asserting control."

Relieved, Olivia told them that Zeke was watching TV, and her husband would be able to take charge of him later so they could work undisturbed. Meanwhile, she had set up the call from her desk in the study, "where I write my Alice Fay articles," she beamed. They entered the room. Notes were strewn all over the desk.

"Chick, this looks like your home office," Maddy laughed. Olivia had gotten into character and seemed remarkably confident for a woman who had been a journalist for only three hours.

Chickie checked her watch. "Show time."

Olivia sat at the desk and tapped numbers into the phone. Chickie and Maddy did not want to distract the actor, so they hovered quietly out of sight while Olivia/Alice Fay made the call. Charles had enjoyed receiving the email; he was agreeable and flattered, even willing to discuss the pitfalls of collecting art. He had obviously looked up the original Alice Fay and made a few references to previous articles. Olivia was prepared and also dropped a few celebrity names. Interviewer and interviewee agreed on the parameters of the interview, and Charles proposed it for the next afternoon.

Then, with well-rehearsed spontaneity, Olivia pouted, "Oh, no that won't work. Given the urgency of the revisions, you will have my eternal gratitude if we can go ahead this evening."

When Charles balked, Olivia sounded disappointed but said that the ceramicist Hei Chen was willing to step in and be interviewed instead. Charles suddenly discovered an opening in his schedule. Olivia expressed her pleasure; she meant it.

"I'll send you a Zoom link shortly before eight p.m., Detroit time," Olivia said, now beginning to sweat and intent on wrapping up the initial contact.

"I'm vacationing in the Cayman Islands; that's the same as Detroit. This will work after all."

Olivia, now picturing herself as Alice Fay in Detroit, nodded and purred into the phone, "After this, we'll meet in person; maybe there will be a book on the topic."

"I would be great in a book. I have more stories than you can imagine."

Maddy looked disgusted.

Olivia wrapped it up. "Talk later. I'll send you a Zoom link." She pressed the button, the small screen went dark, the call ended, and her shoulders sank.

Maddy rushed over and the three of them began to talk at once. The relief felt like a drop in temperature. "Thank god for Second City improv training," Olivia laughed when they complimented her lavishly. Worn out, the older women refused Olivia's offer of wine and took an Uber to Avril's home, a few miles south. Avril was unaware of exactly what they were up to, but Chickie had explained that they would be in the neighborhood and that was enough to get them an invitation to meet her wife Chrissie and have an early dinner.

By 7:30, they were back in Olivia's bungalow chatting with her husband, a lanky engineer she'd met in college. He was intrigued by his wife's adventure and amused to have the job of keeping Zeke occupied and quiet. The three women went back into the study and scoured it for telltale signs of Olivia's residence rather than Alice Fay's. Maddy scooped up photos and toys and got them out of sight.

Their anxiety inched upward; all three women felt the pressure. Chickie set up her laptop, now equipped with a program, VideoSolo Screen Recorder, which would capture the interchange without Charles's knowledge. She explained it to Olivia so that the actor could feel free to shut down the Zoom recording whenever Charles wanted, knowing the conversation would continue to be recorded. Olivia sat in front of the screen so they could get a look at her on the platform. They turned it on. The Zoom program read *Alice Fay Robbinson*, and she looked the part.

"Let's go over your goals in this interview and how best to accomplish them," Chickie said.

Soon they were ready. Shortly before the interview time, Olivia turned on Zoom and sent the link. Maddy watched over her shoulder. "Ahhhh!"

"What?" the others asked in unison.

Maddy pointed at the screen. "You misspelled Alice Fay's last name!"

Chickie shoved Olivia aside and made the correction. They still had five minutes when Olivia ordered them out of the room.

"We can sit in the corner, out of view," Chickie protested.

"No."

"I'm your director."

"You're too much like my mother—twice over! Trust me; I've trusted you."

They left unhappily and Chickie leaned against the closed door, straining to listen. Maddy knew better and found a comfortable chair and an old copy of *Variety*. About thirty minutes later, she was jolted out of a story about the Cannes Film festival.

"Maddy," Chickie hissed. "Did you hear that?"

"Of course not. I'm not pressed up against the door like a lunatic."

"Charles just hinted at a partnership with Brian!" She explained exactly what snippet she'd overheard.

Maddy snapped to attention. "We have to find out more. We want Olivia to provoke him into more impulsive revelations." She thought for a quick moment, then grabbed a pen, scribbled a sentence in the margin of the magazine, ripped the page out and handed it to Chickie who silently opened the door, bent low, crawled over to Olivia on her hands and knees, and slipped the challenging comment on to the desk.

They waited, both of them now pressed against the closed door. In a few moments, they heard Charles erupt but could not make out his words. It was impossible to know how the interview progressed.

Ten minutes later, Olivia opened the study door and joined them. She carried Chickie's laptop and appeared calm, but the sweat stains on her shirt suggested otherwise. Chickie and Maddy waited, pretending to be patient while Olivia handed Chickie the computer and doubled over, nauseated, and shaking. Deep breaths later, she was seated and more relaxed, even buoyant. She eagerly assured them that Charles had offered a lot of information. They asked if he had questioned her identity. "He was so busy promoting himself, I was a prop, like a piece of furniture in an actor's monologue."

In forty-seven grueling minutes, Olivia had learned to dislike the man and hoped there were enough incriminating comments now on record to complete Project Nemesis. Gratitude flowed, all sincere, and by the time the two older women left, everyone was teary from fatigue and tension. Chickie and Maddy praised their favorite actor, promised to be in touch very soon, and swore to follow her career, predicting a collection of Oscars. At the door, they gratefully hugged Olivia, who was sorry to see them go. "My role as mom gets kind of boring," she whispered to Maddy.

They both dozed in the taxi, although they would have sworn they were too hyped up to ever sleep again. When they reached the Palmer House, they climbed out wearily, Chickie clutching the laptop to her chest. People strolled past, walking off dinners, browsing in shop windows, and, as always in Chicago, commenting on the weather regardless of the season. But tonight, they looked like alien creatures, these people who had probably spent the evening discussing Cubs vs. Sox rather than attempting their own sting operation.

Maddy optimistically insisted on walking a few doors down to get a celebratory bottle of Veuve Clicquot while Chickie went inside to set up the video. The lobby was noisy; guests perched on bar stools and chatted in small groups. In the elevator, Chickie was joined by a family of four who argued the merits of deep-dish pizza versus thin crust. At another time, she might have entered the dispute, but she was exhausted and single-minded. In her room, Chickie set up the laptop right next to her bed, pulled the armchair around, and waited. Shortly, Maddy returned and poured the champagne into bathroom glasses. She stretched out on the bed and Chickie sat stiffly in the armchair, braced to replay the interview.

Chapter Forty

Now they would see and hear what Charles had to say. Chickie was relieved that the VideoSolo Screen Recorder actually did its job, even though she had tested it several times earlier in the day. Quickly, Charles's screenshot materialized. A man, presumably him, was posing on the deck of a large sailing boat.

The recording was good quality. Olivia did not appear on the screen; they would see and hear the conversation from her vantage point. The still photo of Charles remained as Olivia's voice broke the quiet. She sounded clear, if a bit unsettled, as she recited the date and added, "This is an interview with Charles Haskell. Mr. Haskell, may I record you?"

Charles's unctuous response was barely audible. "Yes of course, doll," he said, low and garbled. Background noise on his end threatened the sound quality. The women held their breath, but at that moment, Charles Haskell's live smiling face came into view, filling the screen. They gasped, startled as if he had entered their hotel room. He sat in a straight desk chair and leaned toward the screen. Behind him, they could see a portion of the room, an ordinary Caribbean vacation rental painted a sunny yellow. Against the far wall, wooden bookcases held paperbacks, magazines, a couple of conch shells, and blue bottles.

Chickie and Maddy stretched forward and scoured the screen with their eyes. Charles had obviously been outdoors during his Cayman Islands escape. His face and arms were red, apparently sunburned from the strong Caribbean rays on pale Midwestern skin. He wore a printed blue shirt that was open at the neck. Small gray hairs curled over the top button.

"Are those dolphins on his shirt?" Chickie mocked. "Should be cockroaches."

For the first time, it dawned on the women that pushing the interview to the same night, forcing the Zoom meeting to happen quickly, had worked to their advantage more than they had anticipated. They knew he hadn't time to carefully check out Olivia/Alice Fay or recognize the absurdity of him being the subject of a *Vanity Fair* article, but they hadn't counted on him being less prepared, less rehearsed, and as Maddy noticed when she studied his face, "less sober." Charles was younger than Brian, probably in his mid-sixties, and was a puffier version with small veins around his nose. If you didn't overlay knowledge of his personality, he was conventionally attractive. Would Maddy have bought art from him? She hoped not.

"Thank you," Olivia said, "Mr. Haskell, I—"

"Please call me Charles." The sound quality had improved.

"Charles, it's a pleasure. As we discussed on the phone earlier, I sought to interview you because I want insights into the edgier aspects of buying and selling art—how to locate and promote artists that other people haven't discovered yet—emerging talent, riskier finds. I was told that you are a man who is not afraid to take risks and make discoveries."

Maddy winced. That was hackneyed flattery, but to her surprise, Charles didn't seem to think so. He laughed in appreciation. "You got me! Buckle your seatbelt; you may need a cocktail. I have one." He held up a tumbler with ice and an amber liquid.

Olivia held up a white coffee mug. "Boring," she apologized, "but I hope you feel free."

"I'm a free spirit, always have been. You're too young to remember free spirits, but we're still here," he chuckled.

From the armchair, Chickie lifted her glass of champagne, "To free spirits everywhere!" The quality of the sound continued to improve, and the women settled in, giving themselves over to the onscreen drama they had produced and directed.

"Do you think Spielberg feels this nervous watching his films?" Maddy asked. Chickie reached over and patted her friend's leg. "We'll ask his mother. She's probably on Facebook."

The interview formally began. "I'll dive in," Olivia said. "How long have you been collecting art? I didn't find a history—"

Charles interrupted, "I haven't been in the art game long; my investments are extensive, but I use the same strategy in art that I do with all my businesses."

"And that is . . ."

"My ideas are constantly evolving. I'm always ahead of the curve. I can sense trends, and I am always ready to make my move. I think on my feet. Now, it's art. Why art? That market is perfect for a decarbonized economy and it's an anywhere operation: China, US, Greenland, who cares. I find a niche that hasn't been exploited sufficiently and I bring it to market. It's a winner!"

Chickie strained to keep up. "Is he speaking English?"

"Shh."

"I understand that the Chinese art market is big and growing," Olivia said.

"The Chinese art market is huge, second only to our own US of A." Charles waved his hand and liquor sloshed out of the glass. He licked his wrist.

"Not his first drink of the day," Maddy said in an unnecessarily soft whisper before Olivia's voice returned.

"I see. That's where emerging Chinese artists come in."

"You're catching on, honey. The US market has gone through the roof. Most people can't afford high class original art, but they do have money, and they want paintings with a story. That's significant—they want paintings with a story. You might want to write that down." He paused and from the movement of his arm, it looked like he was pouring more liquid into his glass. He lifted the tumbler, and they could see that it was full. He took a swallow, grinned, and resumed his lecture. "Chinese art has a great story."

"Especially art from artists who painted in secret during the Cultural Revolution," Olivia coaxed.

"Yes . . ." His voice was changing; his presentation slipped as he warmed to his audience, aided by heat and abetted by alcohol. "The Orientals want to do business with us, and new buyers here want the, the . . . exotic crap they can show their friends. Wait, let me say that for publication: Okay, the Chinese Art market is thriving, and Americans are looking for artists they will not be able to afford in a few years. My ability . . . I'm not saying I'm the only one—Buffet and Jobs had the vision—my ability is seeing around the corner."

Olivia softened. "Charles, I'm impressed. So, you had the brilliant idea of finding artists from the Cultural Revolution who painted while in hiding and were now willing to show their work. Is that correct?"

"Not quite."

"Oh, sorry." Olivia reversed herself and sounded genuinely upset.

"Don't be sorry. You're making the same mistake everyone else makes."

"I don't want my article to be like everyone else's," she confided.

Charles grew serious. "Then listen. I'll tell you something, but we have to stop the recording. This is off the record."

She pressed the pause record button so Zoom recording ended, but VideoSolo kept right on documenting sound and images.

He leaned close and his face again filled the screen. His nostrils expanded as he inhaled, ready to expound. "I got taken for a ride once, only once. Now *I'm* in the saddle." He laughed, spraying the screen with spittle. "Get it?"

They heard throaty laughter coming from Olivia.

"A couple of years ago, I was in China scouting for opportunities. It's an amazing place. Ever been there?"

"Unfortunately, no."

"Get your husband to take you, or better yet, you can come with me."

"So, you were in China."

"Yeah. A group of good-looking young Chinese spotted me touring the Dafen Oil Painting Village. You never know where the opportunities arise. They followed me and wanted to pick my brain. I don't know how many Americans they meet. They wanted to sell art in the US. They told me they were art students who studied with some has-been artist who painted in secret during the Cultural Revolution. I was curious so I bought a piece and investigated their claim."

Maddy leaned over and pressed pause. "That's not quite the same story we heard from your sources, Chickie."

"This is the Haskellized version. Charles is like Brian; they turn ugly versions of themselves into more attractive models. This interview is verbal collagen." Maddy sighed and pressed play.

"I assume the painting you purchased was not created by the has-been artist from the Resistance," Olivia said. "The students took you for a ride."

"A small ride, a pony ride. I never believed them. Anyway they gave me an idea of turning their amateur scheme into a real business, a legit business. I decided what's good for the Peking duck is good for the Midwestern gander. I hired them to find paintings that I would import and promote."

"Very bold. Spinning straw into gold. You investigated the market and obviously have talent for promoting art," Olivia sighed with seeming admiration. "I'm turning the recording back on."

The two friends cringed at her simpering. "I could never be an actress," Maddy declared, as if she had to choose.

"Maybe when they remake *The Flying Nun*."

Maddy's foot shot out and poked her.

Olivia followed up, "I'm not entirely clear. Were the paintings made by artists during the Cultural Revolution or not?"

Charles smiled at the camera but did not answer directly. Instead, he expounded on the provenance of the art, sounding like a high schooler bragging to his friends that he'd copied his term paper.

"He's proud of himself. He loves the idea of getting away with it." Chickie snorted.

Olivia listened patiently before she moved on. "Now, changing directions a bit, I want to ask you about this recent uproar and tragedy in Chicago with your associate Dr. Jordan? Was he also supporting artists from the Resistance?"

"Ha!"

Maddy jumped at Charles's loud bark, but relaxed again when Olivia giggled, "Well, I guess not."

"Let me tell you something," Charles said, literally pointing his finger at the screen, slurring his words. "I know you're a journalist, and I looked you up so I know you can write, but I got a tip for you. If you want big shots to talk to you when your clothes are on, remember this—doctors all think they're clever, but they're book-smart, life-stupid. Because they could memorize body parts, they think they're gods. Once they have degrees and money, they are cocksure they know everything."

Olivia cut him short. "Was Dr. Jordan like that? Did he think he was clever?"

To everyone's amazement, Charles shut up and gave the question some serious thought.

"No," he finally said. "Edward was an old man who didn't want to be an old man. He was rigid and self-satisfied, raking in money on nose jobs or whatever he cut and pasted. No, Edward wasn't being clever. I think he was close to retirement—he knew he would become irrelevant, and he couldn't stand that idea. I've known Edward for years. He liked to think of himself as a risk-taker. Yeah, his idea of a risk was to try a new fancy restaurant instead of his old fancy restaurant. My brother used to do impersonations of him strutting around, pleased with himself." He raised his voice. "Brian, my brother, knows that real money doesn't happen from one chin implant at a time; it comes from investments. I was the one who taught him to look around corners."

Maddy hit pause. "This is where he mentions Brian! Do you think Olivia followed our advice?"

"We're going to find out."

Contempt crept into Charles's voice. "All I did was mention the struggling artists and the Resistance and my willingness to take big chances and import paintings from China. Edward drank it all in; imagined himself jetting off to China with his pretty wife and discovering hidden talent."

Olivia smoothly cut him off. "I don't want to offend you, but the art business you describe sounds like privileged White men indulging in a new hobby."

Charles exploded. "You don't know shit about me. My father lost all his money shortly after he set my brother up in his Michigan Avenue medical practice. I had to leave school. But these days I'm an entrepreneur and my brother is my junior partner. That's how he assuages his guilt about getting Dad's financing. Now it's become the most exciting thing in his life. Brian said Edward was freaking out because his neighbor accused him of fraud. Edward had delusions of helping out aging artists, promoting the cause. He was losing his grip. Edward babbled to me about the shame to his wife and son. But he doesn't have a son. That's delusional, right?"

Maddy and Chickie stared at each other, not saying a word. The voices continued to come from the screen until Chickie stopped the recording.

"Rewind it," Maddy said. "I have to hear that section again."

Chickie replayed the last few minutes. They listened once more before letting the recording continue.

Olivia only laughed. "Delusions are not my field. I have a few more questions before I let you go."

Charles rushed in. "I don't want you to think I'm heartless. I was sympathetic at first and let him talk, but finally I called him out. I told him exactly who he was—a frightened over-the-hill hack who depended on a wall of diplomas to reassure him that he was worth something. You have to be brave and tough to be in the art market."

"So, you're a tough guy, I guess," Olivia interrupted.

Charles finished his drink. "Yep, you've got that right."

"So, is it legal to sell art as having been created by Resistance artists when the canvases were painted by current young artists?"

"They are also part of the Resistance. The Resistance lives on."

"You know what I mean," Olivia pursued. "Is it legal?"

"Slavery was legal in more than a dozen states."

"Charles . . ."

"Listen honey, you can record this; get straight about your facts. It's legal to sell art. I did not assert attribution on any paintings. I never guaranteed the work was painted by hidden old guys from the Cultural Revolution. Buyers may have thought that was the case, but I never told them; I never wrote it down, nothing."

Olivia tried some gentle confrontation. "But I called you as an expert. I read your statement that 'marvelous art was created during the years of the Cultural Revolution 1966–1976 and there is little left. Luckily, some of it has been smuggled out by young people in an attempt to get money for their old professors who can no longer paint.'"

"So?"

"Doesn't that imply you have access to those pieces?" Olivia asked.

"No. I import art; I create opportunities. If Edward, or anyone else, made assumptions, they were confused. Hey, why are you asking about the legal issues? I thought you wanted to know about collecting emerging artists."

"I do. My focus is on the emerging market going forward. You have been marvelously helpful, and I am grateful that you indulged all my questions. I'll let you go. Thank you so much."

"Wait!" Charles called urgently. "When will the article come out? Don't I get to read it first?"

Olivia hit the *End for All* button and the screen went blank.

For several minutes, the hotel room was quiet—a cautious silence in which the two women prudently put their thoughts in order.

"So, Brian was complicit. He knew more than he admitted." Chickie wasn't surprised. She rose and stared out the window, scanning the nearby buildings. She looked into the windows of vacant, dimly lit offices thinking about greed and cruelty and missing her dog and her own home.

Maddy replayed portions of the interview in her mind. Charles had answered their questions with remarkable candor, having no idea how appalling his admissions sounded. As a result, she had trouble sorting out her anger from satisfaction. Yes, Brian was involved, and yes, Charles had hounded Edward, but Maddy felt a surge of relief that Edward was a dupe, not a criminal. His suicide made more sense now.

They would never know Edward's thoughts in those final hours; that was the nature of suicide, but clearly shame had driven his desperation. Edward's carefully controlled world was crumbling. In his own eyes, he had failed as a man. Suicide was his impulsive, tragically permanent solution.

To Maddy, the startling revelation, even more shocking than learning Brian was duplicitous, was Edward's reference to having a son. She could comfort Winston with that recognition. And now that she understood the relentless badgering of Edward, she would be able to honestly reassure Lena that Edward had fled the torment of shame, not their marriage. The interview had worked—it provided knowledge that wouldn't remove the pain but could reduce Lena's suffering. She knew how to weave the story but wondered whether to explain how they'd acquired the information. Olivia and Alice Fay? The call? The promise of a *Vanity Fair* profile? Chickie would figure out how truthful to be. She seemed to have developed remarkably varied talents during her years in DC.

Maddy broke the silence with a rising sense of glee. "Chick, I think we got what we wanted." She examined the bottle of Veuve Clicquot, pleased that several inches of champagne remained.

Chickie spun around. "Yes. Charles never asked her a damn question. His self-aggrandizement was all that mattered to him." She wasn't as gleeful as her friend.

"I don't want to say I told you so. But I told you so! It's all about him." Maddy glowed smugly, oblivious to Chickie's somber mood. "Thank God. Olivia was brilliant. On tape, she never said the piece was for *Vanity Fair* or even that she was Alice Fay. Does that bit of honesty make it legal?"

"Who do you think is going to complain? Certainly not Charles: he can't afford to go public with the information we have," Chickie told her.

"But you don't seem happy. You should be; your crazy idea worked. This will help Winston and Lena deal with Edward's death. We can help them understand Edward's actions," Maddy said, holding the bottle in the air and offering more bubbly to her friend.

Chickie refused. The success of the interview hadn't altered her disposition. "I'm not happy. I'm not used to being up close and personal with other people's tragedies. Yes, we can reassure them, but we can't make it right. I guess it's another reminder that life is short, bad things happen to good people, this life is not a rehearsal, make hay while the sun shines . . ."

Maddy sobered immediately. "What would make you happy?"

Chickie knew the answer. "Punishment."

Chickie's Blog:

Old Dogs, New Tricks
(A Writer's Reflections on Growing Old
and Growing Up)

Regret

Dear patient readers, if you've kept up with my blog this week, you know I've returned to Chicago because of the death of an old friend. Not surprisingly, several posts have been about friendship and loss. Now, my activities have led me to a topic I rarely contemplate, but today's the day—Regret.

Years ago, research by Thomas Gilovich and Victoria Medvec found that people's biggest regrets tend to involve things they have failed to do in their lives—actions NOT taken rather than actions taken. This makes a great deal of sense; I wish I'd thought of it. Actions that we take (think romantic break ups or confrontations) cause more pain in the short-term, but inactions (think unfinished projects, opportunities missed because of fear, or words unspoken) are regretted more in the long run. Interesting, yes?

Stay with me . . . it gets better. When we act, brilliantly or foolishly, we see results pretty quickly. When we don't act, regrets are different and may emerge slowly. Earlier in the week, I wrote about deeply hurting a dear friend. I bolted out of a relationship with no explanation. During the years that followed (many years), I had two thousand imagined conversations, at least. The possibilities were infinite! There was no end to the regret that resulted from my inaction. Had I stayed for a discussion decades ago, I would have saved myself all the imaginings. That's the key.

When we act, we may have regrets, but the regrets are finite because we know the results. When we don't act, the regrets spread without limit because our minds have no reality to rope us in. And to quote the famous sage, Lucille Ball, "I'd rather regret the things I've done than regret the things I haven't done."

So, my conclusion this evening is that I ought to act in ways that leave me satisfied, no regrets, starting today. It so happens that I have a situation that calls for action or no action. I found out that a man I barely know was terribly cruel to people I care about. He admitted his behavior and saw the harm he caused but considered his actions to be "just business." I don't agree. He has no regrets, Readers, but if I want to have no regrets, I think I have to act—call it The Final Act of Project Nemesis.

Chapter Forty-One

Friday morning was filled with activity. Both women had been able to book last-minute flights home: Chickie back to DC in the late afternoon and Maddy to Minneapolis in the evening, so the day was destined to be an anthology of goodbyes.

Maddy had awakened early, stiff and uncomfortable. Even so, she hadn't felt this alive in a long time. Her mind tumbled with ideas, and when Chickie didn't appear by eight, or even start singing in the shower, God forbid, Maddy took a quick walk to Millennium Park to stretch her tight muscles and savor the skyline. Admiring Cloudgate in the bright October light, she could see that returning to Chicago had been an automatic response because Lena needed help. But the week had renewed her love for the city. She had special memories of Chicago as a child and selected it carefully when she applied to college. Her career began here, and it had been good luck to meet Frank and start their family. It was her first grown-up home. Yes, she had a safe and settled life in Minneapolis, but safe and settled had become stale and stuffy. Her rejection of the twins' suggestion that she move to Chicago was pure stubbornness. *I'm the mom, don't tell me what to do.* Well, if she wasn't going to listen to them, she damn well better think for herself while she still had choices. She laughed and walked quickly through the Lurie Garden and back to the Palmer house to call Oxford, England.

Half an hour later, Maddy balanced two coffees and rapped on Chickie's door. Rumpled and groggy, Chickie explained her appearance as a result of staying awake "to write the blog post; it wasn't easy."

Maddy dropped into the armchair and recounted her phone call to Winston in Oxford. "I wanted to tell him what we learned from Charles, but the plain facts were terribly raw. So, I provided a different way to think about Edward's death. I explained that we could never reveal how we received the material, but we knew, without a doubt, that Edward was foolish, not criminal, and Charles had hounded him right up until a few minutes before he died. I wanted Winston to understand the intensity of Edward's stress and feel less guilty. I also told him that Edward had confided to someone that he had a son and seemed shocked but pleased."

"You what?" Chickie came close to spitting out her coffee. "You told him Edward said he had a son and was pleased? What Zoom interview did you watch?"

Maddy looked sheepish but not apologetic. "Hyperbole?"

"Complete fabrication." Chickie started laughing and fell back against the pillows, holding on to her cup.

"I went for compassion and justice rather than pure facts," Maddy insisted with a touch of defensiveness.

Chickie laughed harder.

Maddy put her hands up like a traffic cop. "Stop it. Now that I've swapped my badge sash for a cape, or whatever avenging goddesses wear, I like the fit."

Chickie stared. "Nemesis wore wings in lovely shades of gray. Cape, sash, scarf: I'd never want to interfere with your sartorial decisions. I'm impressed. Maddy my dear friend, you are no longer Good, capital G. You are Great, but I'm exhausted. We're not quite finished, and Lena is waiting. Let's get organized so we can depart Chicago. I look forward to a quiet flight back to DC and picking up my dog, who has probably forgotten me. Even the pile of political junk mail collecting in my hall sounds dreamy."

"Food will help," Maddy said. "And trust me, when we can finish our work, you'll feel righteous joy!" Chickie doubted that she knew what righteous joy would feel like, but sluggishly began to crawl out of bed.

The evening before, they had kept the adjoining door open while they packed their suitcases and debated exactly what to tell Winston and Lena. Finally, they agreed on enough information to provide consolation, but no details that mentioned Gus, Olivia, or Alice Fay.

What to do about Brian and Charles Haskell evoked different possible solutions. If they went after Brian, Lena and Raph would suffer, so their hands were tied. But Charles? Predictably, Chickie started off with extreme and illegal ideas. Maddy wondered if Chickie was serious or strategic, imagining that if she horrified Maddy initially, then her lesser ideas might find favor. They compromised; less dire than Chickie wished for and harsher than Maddy would have accepted several days earlier. Now they would put that plan into action.

Maddy hummed and pushed her suitcase toward the elevator. It was a little lighter; she had left two gray scarves in the drawer with a note for the housekeeper, hoping she would wear them. Chickie was amused by her friend's enthusiasm. The women left the room keys and suitcases with the lobby bellman so, except for a bulging bag filled with Edward's effects, they would be unencumbered until their departure. Their jobs almost complete, they headed back to Lena's penthouse for the final visit of the trip.

In the cab, Maddy grew impatient. She was unable to wait for Chickie's coffee to take effect. "Wake up, Chick, we've got more to do in the time we're here. Pay attention. Punishing Charles is not enough. Brian is okay with his brother's behavior; he is unbearable and self-absorbed, and he tried to assault Lena! There must be consequences."

"Come on Maddy. We settled this last night. Lena will continue to receive money from the Tabernacle of Beauty for some time, and the surgery practice is Raph's livelihood. Don't you care about Raph's ability to buy you lunches?"

Maddy brushed her arguments away. "Of course, we would consult the two of them, but remember Lena's threat to Brian? She said she knew enough to keep Sean Mulvaney and his reputation defenders in business. She might be ready to challenge him." Chickie made a face, so Maddy pressed her point. "I feel very strongly about serving consequences to Brian."

She's waited seventy-two years to express strong feelings, Chickie thought. *Why today when I'm exhausted?* Luckily, they reached Astor Street. "Don't forget your wings," she murmured as they exited the cab.

An agitated Lena met them at the door in baggy pants and without makeup. She had been battered mercilessly for a week and it showed, but she didn't waste a moment. "Raph called me about an hour ago. Felice, you remember their receptionist, the pretty young woman? She waylaid Raph at the end of yesterday and said terrible things about me! She said I was disloyal and unfaithful. Horrible. How could she!"

Maddy and Chickie stood in the foyer and stared at her. They became more confused when Raph came from the living room and put his hand gently on Lena's shoulder. "Let's all sit down, and I'll try to explain."

Chickie slipped Edward's effects into the hall closet, with a reminder to herself to tell Lena about the bags later on and followed the others into the library. She closed the door, although no one else was in the apartment.

Raph began. "First of all, you ought to know that Felice always had great admiration for Edward and has been mildly jealous of Lena. Haven't you noticed how she copies Lena's style? Anyway, she managed to wait until after hours yesterday, after my patients had gone, before she showed up at my door crying and making little sense. I had no idea what was going on, but I have three daughters who have provided an education in talking with women, so I kept quiet and listened. Eventually. Felice's story was this: as Brian was getting ready to leave for the day, Felice asked about his swollen nose, and Brian being Brian wove an outrageous tale about Lena coming on to him." Raph looked at the three women, embarrassed.

Chickie peeked at Maddy in time to receive a look that said, "You ought to listen to me more often." She returned her attention to Raph.

"Brian cautioned Felice to avoid contact with Lena because she was out of her mind with grief. When Felice replied that Lena appeared calm at the memorial service, Brian claimed that the next night, when they were at the penthouse, Lena declared she'd always had a crush on him and wanted him to become her lover. When Brian reminded Lena that he was married, she exploded and smacked him in the face with a book. He attempted to calm her, but she was hysterical and ordered him out of the apartment. Felice was incensed; how could Lena disgrace Edward's memory? On and on. The only course of action was to tell her the truth, so I did."

"Thanks for setting Felice straight." Maddy shot him a thumbs up. "How did she respond?"

"At first, she was skeptical. Then, I have a feeling she remembered some behaviors at the office, or in phone calls, that called Brian's sainthood into question. It didn't take long. She was stunned that he would behave badly toward Lena and lie about her. That was the biggest shock. By the time I sent her home, she was what my daughters would call a hot mess. And I'm pretty fed up myself. I no longer want to be in a partnership with him, not with Edward gone. I've turned down other offers because the three of us made a great team, but I'm tempted."

He looked at Lena, who laughed bitterly and said, "Don't worry about the income from the practice. I told you; I've always managed our money and even my financial guy says 'we' are fine even though Edward did spend a significant amount on the paintings. You all forget I had rich parents—neglectful but rich. Last year, when my mother died, I inherited more money than Edward and I saved, so don't suffer Brian on my account."

"Well, my reputation is all I have."

"What will you do?" Maddy asked.

"The University of Chicago hospital has been after me for years and I've always turned them down. I think they are still willing to offer me a half-time hospital, half-time teaching position and I'm ready to negotiate a contract."

"What about Felice?" asked Maddy.

"You couldn't remember her name and now you want to be her career counselor?" Chickie asked. But Raph also had spent time coming up with ideas for the receptionist.

"She might want to stay with Brian, but I doubt it. There's a chance I could bring Felice to UChicago—"

"Better still," Lena interrupted, "The Before and After Surgery Center might find a spot for her; they're expanding, and they might let her do some marketing. I'd love to see her at Brian's competitor if you leave, but she will certainly need a job if she wants to finish her courses at City College. We can figure it out. Brian deserves to lose all the people who made him successful."

"Well done." Maddy sighed deeply with satisfaction and turned to Chickie. "I told you Brian needed corrective measures."

"You did, and justice has been successfully outsourced. Nemesis has more acolytes than I ever imagined," Chickie agreed with pleasure. "Raph, do you know whether Brian and his brother Charles have been business partners?"

"I've often wondered because of vague comments he's made over the years; he's oddly supportive of Charles's strange schemes, but I don't know. Why?"

Maddy answered, "We think Brian is more involved than he lets on, but that's not your problem. You've been a great help."

Relieved, Raph said, "I do have a very full afternoon with patients, and my granddaughter's seventh birthday party is later today." He kissed them each goodbye and lingered for a moment to whisper, "I'll call you" to Maddy. The other two women grinned at each other as if they had done something clever.

Lena walked him out and returned to her friends. "Raph said that I ought to be the one to call Felice. I agree that it works better if I present options and encourage her . . . no pressure."

Maddy nodded approvingly and Chickie tried to hum a few bars of "Turn! Turn! Turn!" but the sounds she produced were unrecognizable to her friends.

"Onward!" Maddy tapped her cane on the carpeting. "Before you call Felice and sink Brian, let's discuss the other member of the duplicitous duo, Charles."

Chickie had always known that her old friend had grit, but she hadn't observed it in action in a long time. What a week. It was as if the patterns for each of their lives had been unpinned, torn, and tossed high into the air. And now, the pieces were floating down to earth, familiar but reassembled.

Maddy and Lena sat down together on the couch. Maddy kept her voice steady and explained Chickie's invention of the fake *Vanity Fair* interview. Lena looked at Chickie knowingly. "Like I said, you've tried to be the round peg in the square hole. I guess our little round peg is on a roll."

Chickie pretended she hadn't heard and insisted that Maddy summarize the interview with Charles. Lena listened intently. She asked very few questions and didn't care how they'd extracted the information from Charles; she only cared that Edward loved her.

When Chickie took over and cautiously described Charles's callous attitude toward Edward, Lena's reflective mood vanished, replaced by rage. Much to the relief of Maddy and Chickie, she insisted on helping out when Chickie explained Project Nemesis, Part B.

Chapter Forty-Two

Done well, revenge takes time and finesse. The friends had some finesse, little time, and no experience, but possessed unquestionably high levels of motivation and distinctly different talents. Maddy probed Lena's memory for knowledge of Charles's social activities and desires. Lena delivered, and Chickie used the information to compose emails and scripts for phone calls. They spent the next hour putting their plan together.

Lena's first call went to the wife of the vice commodore from the Chicago Yacht club to thank her and her husband for coming to Edward's service and for his elegant speech. Before hanging up, she mentioned "for your ears only" that Charles Haskell was not an appropriate nominee for a desirable, vacant seat on the board. Lena then called an acquaintance who could be relied on to spread the word to people who "mattered" that Charles's name on programs at the hospital fundraisers would be suspect. The word *toxic* was mentioned, along with a few other code words that translated into *untouchable*. *Lena has a deft touch*, thought Chickie. *I could take lessons.*

Lena made several more calls and sent emails to set up lunches with people of influence. The three women envisioned Charles's precious social position dissolving over the next months like wet cotton candy. If the consequences reverberated and tarnished Brian, all the more delicious.

"Is that all? If we are satisfied that Project Nemesis has been launched and is in orbit, it's time to call Felice," Lena said and phoned the young woman. She empathized with Felice's disappointment in Brian and explained the possibilities of a new position with the competition or with Raph, spontaneously threw in an offer of continued help with school tuition, and in a burst of energy, invited Felice to join the marketing committee for the hospital gala.

"Get her off the phone before she adopts Felice," Chickie hissed to Maddy.

"Shh, if you ever criticize Lena again, I will hide your favorite pieces of jewelry."

If the pitch of Felice's voice was any indication, she was thrilled at hearing so many options and talked on for quite some time. Lena listened and encouraged her. When the call ended, Lena's face glowed. "She's working on a degree in marketing and the practice has helped with tuition money. Felice has marketing and computer skills. At her age, I could only stand on my toes in satin shoes for long periods. What happens next?"

"Will you trust us?" Maddy asked. "Chickie and I are confident that during the next couple of weeks, Charles's pervasive arrogance and braggadocio will do the rest of the work for us. You don't have to do another thing except enjoy the gossip and keep us posted."

With Part B underway, Maddy and Chickie left to meet the twins for a goodbye lunch. Maddy pointed her cane due south. "I've spent my social security check on cabs this week. Let's walk." She was in an expansive mood and admitted that she enjoyed swapping Always Good for Occasionally Vengeful. "Will that make me Interesting?"

"Raph finds you interesting," Chickie said.

"If I'm Good and you're Interesting, what's Raph?"

"Reliable, I think."

"That's fine," she admitted, looking pensive. "I had this thought that Frank would like Raph." She paused when she realized that Chickie was watching her intently, speechless.

"Stop looking at me like that. Raph asked me some pointed questions the other day at lunch. It made me realize I've been stalled in a holding pattern, a holding-on pattern. It didn't start with Frank's death; it probably began years ago, after my brother died. To me, change has always meant loss. I believed that if I could avoid change, I could avoid loss, so I kept to a pretty narrow path."

Chickie was amazed. Maddy had always been so private, reluctant to divulge her darker moments, always cheerfully coping, staying positive and strong. "Has your strategy stopped working?" she asked tentatively.

"Yes," Maddy said. "I have choices, and I've avoided them. Being in Chicago with you made my modus operandi painfully clear. I'm seventy-two and less mobile, but I can be freer of other people's needs and opinions than I've ever been. I've done Good well. Especially on this trip," she grinned. "Now I can wear my wings and become Interesting before I die. Don't panic—you don't have to become Good," she laughed. "I intend to focus my choices on when to do what and what not to do."

"What are you going to do with all those whens and whats?"

"I have this idea, but don't say a word to the boys yet. I'm not deserting Minneapolis, but I might find a small condo in Chicago. It would make them happy. You know I've always loved Chicago."

Chickie kept a straight face. As they arrived at The Original Pancake House, she relented. "I think it's a marvelous idea to get a place here, and when I return, which I will, I can stay with you instead of the Tante Lulu Suite at the Palmer House."

Outside the restaurant, the twins greeted the women with hugs. "Grab Yin and Yang and let's get in line," Gus instructed his brother. They joined the long queue of locals waiting to order the famous apple pancake or Dutch Baby. Chickie whispered with Gus while Rex showed Maddy the latest photos of his partner and pets, and Maddy silently wished that one day there might be a human grandchild in the picture.

Finally, they were seated at one of the wobbly wooden tables and the women caught Rex and Gus up with an edited version of Project Nemesis. The twins roared with laughter.

Eventually, it was time for Chickie to return to the hotel for her bag and head for O'Hare airport. Gus grabbed her arm. "What's next, Aunt Chickie?"

Chickie smirked at Maddy, always delighted to startle her. "I was about to tell your mother when we arrived at the restaurant. Once I'm through teaching this semester, I've decided to go ahead with the novel I always longed to write. My grandmother Chickie was friends with Gertrude Stein in Paris when they were both young, before Alice B., when Gertrude wrote in secret and hid her stories. In addition to my grandmother's name—"

Gus interrupted. "There was an earlier Chickie? It's hard to believe."

"Her name was Ruth, like mine, but her brothers called her Chickie. Back then, if you were a lookout when your pals were committing a crime, you yelled, 'chickie, chickie' when you spotted a cop. I'm sure her brothers thought the nickname was hilarious—mine did. In addition to her name, I inherited a suitcase filled with journals."

Maddy looked at her closely, refusing to show surprise. "Going to Paris for historical research? And perhaps see more of your daughter?"

The boys pleaded for invitations, but Maddy raised her hand. "Me first! I've never been to Paris!"

Chickie's Blog:
Old Dogs, New Tricks
(A Writer's Reflections on Growing Old and Growing Up)

Letting Go

I'm on the plane headed home. I came to Chicago with such reluctance, it seems hypocritical to depart awash in sentiment. Returning brought back difficult memories; I expected that. The surprise is the collection of wonderful memories that have also reemerged in my mind. Here is one—learning to let go.

Years ago, when we were in our twenties and all in Chicago, my friend Maddy was leaving town to attend a wedding and mentioned that she didn't have jewelry to wear. Without thinking twice, I offered my pearls (in those days, women wore pearls). She accepted. After she left Chicago that Friday, my pearls in her suitcase, I panicked. What if she lost them, broke them, mistreated them? I had received those pearls from my parents, and they mattered to me—a lot. I berated myself for letting them go and worried all evening.

The next day, Sam developed a bad earache, and I took him to the pediatrician. While we were gone, our apartment was burglarized. I had very little of value, except my jewelry. The thieves took it all. Gifts from my parents and my late husband, my wedding ring, my great aunt's watch, and the silly odds and ends I'd purchased as a teenager were all gone. Nothing was left except my engagement ring hidden in my pantyhose and the pearls that Maddy returned safe and sound to me on Monday.

I've let go over and over since then—people, clutter, ideas, old habits. Letting go is different as I age; the future doesn't stretch out so far anymore. There are inevitable, ordinary losses. Time plagues me. But letting go happened again this week, for me and for Maddy, too. We watched our friend brought to her knees by the death of her husband, and we each had to decide again, in our own way, do we freeze in place trying to hold on, or do we let go and look ahead?

Chapter Forty-Three

One month later, Lena Zoomed with Maddy and Chickie. "I kept busy and followed your instructions," she reported. "I recommended Gus's friend Olivia to perform at the hospital gala and the producer loved her. You never explained exactly why I am indebted to her, but I'm happy to remain in the dark.

"More importantly, my mani-pedi appointment, always informative, was outstanding yesterday. Charles's sister-in-law was getting highlights, so she was at Massimo's on Oak for hours. I lingered and listened; you would have been proud. To stay close, I examined and purchased more hair products than I can use in this lifetime, and that's saying something.

"Anyway, she's worried about her brother-in-law's mental health. Since Charles returned to Chicago a couple of weeks ago, he bragged incessantly about his important interview with *Vanity Fair*.

"Evidently, he posted 'It's coming!' on his company website, tried to solicit TV and podcast interviews, and had a catered party planned to celebrate the *VF* holiday issue. But two days ago, Charles waited outside his local CVS pharmacy until the delivery van pulled up. He had prepaid for dozens of magazines at several stores. The issue arrived and it featured a holiday scandal involving Italian nobility, recipes from celebrities, and two hundred other pages, none of which mentioned him. He was enraged. This is where I joined the conversation and asked what went wrong. She said Charles was put on hold when he called the magazine to get information. When he attempted to call the journalist who interviewed him, her outgoing message said she was on assignment elsewhere. He emailed her; nothing. He found a different phone number, her home, and called but she told him he was crazy. He called again and was rewarded by a call back from the journalist's father, who seems to be a well-known attorney in Michigan."

Watching the delighted, smug expressions on the faces of her two friends, she asked sweetly, "Could this be the fruits of your labor?"

The following week, Chickie and Maddy celebrated Thanksgiving apart, but tapped texts and emails back and forth throughout the day as they peeled potatoes, disputed the best stuffing recipe, and gathered with friends and relatives.

Maddy texted Chickie:

The boys are over the moon that I am in Chicago for the holiday. Lena arrived late to Gus's apartment but was forgiven when we saw the dishes prepared by her housekeeper. And she brought me an apron emblazoned with NEVERTHELESS, SHE PERSISTED. Yours is in the mail.

Lena texted Chickie:

I still desperately miss Edward and know I always will. As they say—a day at a time, but I am going to the UK to attend a Youth in the Arts conference and will visit Winston. I can't think of him as my st—— son yet, but maybe soon.

Chickie texted Lena and Maddy:

> I'm feeding a crowd. It's marvelous to have Steph home, even for two weeks. She came to visit and, believe it or not, to attend my ex-husband's engagement party. He plans to marry the woman who helped him decorate his apartment. They have doves in preparation for the big day, but they refuse to leave the cage. Maddy, don't interpret.

Lena texted Chickie and Maddy:

Hang on to the doves. Maddy is trying to hide her delight that Raph is stopping by later, after dinner with his daughters. The twins are singing that tacky tune from the Brady Bunch. I have a lot to be thankful for: you two broads pulled me through a rough time.

Chickie texted back:

> A hundred years ago, most women were dead by sixty-five, so I figure everything after that is a second chance.

Carol and Linda, 1985

Acknowledgments

It's fitting that a novel featuring long friendships was nudged along by a lot of old friends. First, to the people who read early drafts of the manuscript and provided feedback and encouragement, thank you, thank you: Anita Adams, Sherry Astmann, Hedda Leonard, Margit Kir-Stimon, Elisa Spain, Jennifer Dubowsky who later dragged us through the world of online marketing, Karen Drill, Janice Prochaska, Ginnie Job, Kiki Bolender, Elizabeth Uncovic, Nick Uncovic, Marilyn Englander, and Lia Rudnick. Rewrites later, Kat Braeman, Alex Kerr, Sophie Thompson, and Ailie Kerr read the manuscript and kept us going. Special thanks to Doug Kerr and Ken Adams, who read more than one draft of the manuscript: that's above and beyond. Your kindness and support meant the world to us, then and now.

Goldie Goldbloom was our developmental editor way back, and it took time to implement many of her suggestions, but we got there. Keira Dubowsky helped with creative ideas, the blog, and a million computer questions. At Koehler Books we have been most lucky to have Becky Hilliker as our kind and talented editor, John Koehler as our guide in all things marketing, and Suzanne Bradshaw, who beautifully translated our ideas into a book cover. You have all been patient, enthusiastic, and remarkably skilled.

Thank you. L & C

www.ingramcontent.com/pod-product-compliance
Lightning Source LLC
LaVergne TN
LVHW041750060526
838201LV00046B/961